Newman Hall

Newman Hall

An Autobiography

Newman Hall

Newman Hall
An Autobiography

ISBN/EAN: 9783337014803

Printed in Europe, USA, Canada, Australia, Japan

Cover: Foto ©Raphael Reischuk / pixelio.de

More available books at **www.hansebooks.com**

NEWMAN HALL

An Autobiography

WITH A PORTRAIT AND VIEW OF CHRIST CHURCH
WESTMINSTER BRIDGE ROAD

CASSELL AND COMPANY, LIMITED

LONDON, PARIS, NEW YORK & MELBOURNE

1898

In Memory

OF

MY MOTHER

CONTENTS

CONTENTS.

ILLUSTRATIONS.

NEWMAN HALL

CHAPTER I.

CHILDHOOD: 1816–1830.

THE first use of my pen on this morning of my eighty-first birthday (May 22, 1897) is to commence a narration which has often been solicited by personal friends, and which may interest and possibly benefit others to whom my name is more or less familiar.

On this day what more natural than reference to the parents to whom I owe my birth, and whose character has influenced my whole life? Even a stream, small and insignificant, with no place in history or atlas, may irrigate some meadow where sheep and cattle quietly pasture and where daisies smile—a silent stream, fringed here and there with forget-me-nots, helping to swell the river in which it seems to be lost on its way to the ocean. The character of the parents influences that of the children.

My father, John Vine Hall, was born in a cottage home at Diss, in 1774, and at eleven years of age was sent as an apprentice to Mr. Blake, bookseller and printer at Maidstone, and proprietor of the *Maidstone Journal*, the oldest Tory paper in Kent. How he became chief assistant there, took a business in Worcester, won for his wife Miss Mary Teverill, and in 1814 returned to Maidstone, where I was born, as proprietor where he had begun life as junior servant—all this has been described in his autobiography. This remarkable history, edited by myself, and published at

B

his special injunction, and entitled "Conflict and Victory,"* is so graphic a narration of his own deliverance as to be regarded by many as scarcely second in interest to Bunyan's "Grace Abounding to the Chief of Sinners."

Eleanor Pickard was grand-daughter of a City merchant of the time of George II. She married James Teverill, of the Ivy House, Worcester, whose daughter became my mother. Lovers of ancient genealogies have discovered the name of Picard among the Conqueror's followers, in Domesday. After a long gap the name occurs in City records as a Lord Mayor, Sir Henry Picard, feasting King Edward III. and John, King of France; but what is the missing link between the Mayor and the Marauder this deponent careth nothing. After another similar gap the name comes into evidence in the form of an old engraving hanging up in my study, representing the "Reverend Edward Pickard," habited in full, powdered wig, black gown and long bands. I now hold in my hand two of his manuscript sermons in very small quarto, three inches by four inches, dated June 7, 1741. He was one of the founders of the Orphan Working School, now at Haverstock Hill. Arthur Pickard, of Hackney, cherished a father's love for little Mary, who used to call him "Uncle Arthur." More than all genealogies, fanciful or true, I value this Puritan picture and record of unsectarian philanthropy, and the certainty of being a child of "parents passed into the skies."

My earliest memory is of sitting on my mother's knee, learning from her to repeat these precious words: "God so loved the world, that He gave His only begotten Son, that whosoever believeth in Him should not perish, but have everlasting life." Of course, I did not understand them. Who does? Is not the knowledge of the wisest merely superficial, compared with what will be known? Is it not the knowledge of the child?

I did know this, that out of sight was One to whom my mother prayed—whom she loved very much and tried to

---

* "Conflict and Victory": Autobiography of the Author of "The Sinner's Friend." Edited by Newman Hall, D.D. 2s. 6d. Nisbet; Snow.

please. She wanted me to please Him too. I knew what love meant by the love of my mother, and I wished to love my mother's Friend who also loved me so much. This was my infantine "system of theology"! In after years these words seemed to me to embody the essence of Christianity—that God loves all men; that His love is seen chiefly in the gift of His Son; that His Son died to save sinners, and therefore to save me. These words were the text of my earliest sermon, which, after preaching a hundred times, I expanded and published under the title of "Christ for Every Man." It is an example of the great influence in all after years of little lessons during childhood.

My mother's old diary, recently brought to my knowledge, contains the following entry, made just after my birth :—

"July 7, 1816.—Once more God permits me to raise my Ebenezer. On the 22nd of May a fine healthy boy was born, and was this day baptised. O that the Lord may indeed baptise him 'with the Holy Ghost and with fire'! I trust I have been enabled to offer him to the Lord, and ardently desire that he may be a child of God. I feel very anxious for grace to bring him and my other children up for the Lord. O that my feeble cries may be heard and answered!"

Then under date December 31, 1816 :—

"O Thou that hearest prayer, receive my unworthy sacrifice of praise. . . . Thou hast fulfilled Thy promises, granted my desires, restored my peace. Should my dear children ever read this, may they learn to trust God at all times. I have *experienced* it. Bless the Lord, O my soul !—MARY HALL."

My likeness was taken in a water-colour miniature when I was a year or two old, and hangs now in my library. My mother, in a light-blue dress and white cap, her dark hair parted on her forehead, is seated at a table on which is a workbox, which I well remember. I am on her knee, in white frock and white lace cap, with very blue eyes and light-coloured hair. Standing by his mother's side is a bright little boy of about four or five, in a short yellow frock. How little she supposed that this one would command the largest ship ever afloat, and the younger become a successor of her friend Rowland Hill.

In 1819, when a mere baby, I was exposed with the other

children to some peril. I have often heard my father relate how on the occasion of a political party illumination he refused to conform. In vain his friends besought him simply to show a few lighted candles and so avoid injury. A vast crowd gathered round a bonfire near the house. Loud calls to illuminate rose from an excited multitude, who began to throw stones and firebrands through the windows. We children were shut up in an upper back room. My father wrote a note to the commandant of the cavalry depot— a personal friend—asking help (as the police were powerless), so that, without use of force, the mere presence of some troops might save life. The cook went out by a back door and delivered it. When the crowd seemed about to gain their end, the tramp of horses and then the sudden appearance of a squadron of lancers turned the attention of the rioters, who at the word "Halt!" scampered off. The street emptied, and the house and family were saved. This occurrence illustrated my father's strength of will, daring to be alone and incur peril in obedience to conviction of duty.

In my father's diary I find the following memorandum, dated—

"September 30, 1820.—On Sunday morning, 24th September, as I sat playing a hymn upon the organ, my little boy Newman interrupted me by saying, 'Papa! will you hear about Jesus?' and then turning to his mother, who was reading the Bible, he said, 'Mamma, will you read about Jesus?' I was so delighted with the request that I could but praise God who had so mercifully taught my children to lisp His blessed Name. This may appear a trifling anecdote, but it may hereafter become very interesting."

I well remember, on occasion of my mother being away recruiting from illness, how I used to creep into my father's bed in the early morning and ask him to tell me a story. He narrated the history of Joseph with great emotion. Next morning I said, "Please, Pa! tell me again about Joseph." He repeated it, and this happened morning by morning; he being never tired of telling, nor I of listening. His mother had been for several years dependent on his care, and sometimes addressed him as "My Joseph in Egypt, the corn is nearly gone." It was his sacred joy to nourish her during her long famine, and this intensified his emotion when repeating one of the most touching narratives ever written. The effect on myself has been so lasting that I seldom venture to read this lesson in church; and when I do I have to resort to the stratagem of violently pinching my flesh to prevent a failure of my voice.

In the room of my birth it was my delight, when my mother was ill, to sit and read to her. A most accomplished reader herself, it must have been some trial to listen to my stammering efforts, but a mother's love was stronger than criticism, and she always made me feel that I was giving her the greatest possible delight, which I still believe. I remember once, when I had been reading many hymns, the nurse sent me away, saying, "Master Newman, you'll kill your mamma—that you will."

My birthplace was a house two centuries old. It has been supplanted by a handsome banking office; but I possess a curious mantelpiece which adorned the back room. It represents four female figures dancing among graves and a man sitting on a tombstone playing a pipe. Round this mantel we used to sit in the evening, and after dinner. I can see my father sipping his hot milk and water flavoured with sugar and ginger, and a peach leaf, and he called it his "nectar." I can feel myself sitting between his legs, which he would cross and I would call it my arm-chair, and sometimes I would sit on one foot and he would give me a ride.

Sunday was religiously and happily observed. The evening before, toys and work were laid aside, but pious picture-books and Noah's ark took their place. Bible stories told by our mother became vivid realities. At breakfast each of us took pride and pleasure in repeating a text. After breakfast we amused ourselves till ten o'clock, when we prepared for chapel. I can see the family procession as we turned out two and two: my elder brothers and myself, and two younger sisters. We were always in good time, occupying a square pew which had a table in the middle. After tea we sat in a circle to repeat hymns, and my father used to lead off with "O for a heart to praise my God," or "Guide me, O Thou great Jehovah," or "How sweet the Name of Jesus sounds," and then, beginning at his left hand, each of us in turn followed. It was always an interest to learn some new hymn. The youngest was encouraged to repeat something; it was never regarded as a task, but always as one of the great delights of the week. Each listened to the hymns of the others, and noticed any new ones. My mother knew about one hundred, and my father fifty. I knew perhaps at one time forty or fifty, and could repeat them accurately.

On Sunday evening my mother generally remained at home to conduct her "infant class." Our great delight was to hear her read and explain "The Pilgrim's Progress." The very copy is before me as I write, with the date of its publication—MDCCLX. On the fly-leaf is written, "Elnor Pickard, 1774—E. Teverill," in old-fashioned hand; then, in clear, steady writing—

"To dearest Newman, in memory of years gone by, in which this book was his delight, and *he* was, and still is, the delight of his
    "May 31, 1862."   "MOTHER.

It is full of both grotesque and terrific pictures—Apollyon "straddling over the whole breadth of the way," and the Valley of the Shadow of Death, with its monsters. I am told that when our mother had a special wish to go with our father, I used to say, "Ma! don't go chapel to-night, but read to us 'Piggy Pogey.'" We had but dim notions of the spiritual meaning; but Christian and Faithful, Evangelist and Interpreter, were realities, as also the Slough of Despond, the Wicket Gate, the House Beautiful, and the Dungeon of Giant Despair. The Delectable Mountains made me long to ramble there, and perhaps helped to nurture that mountain-passion which increases with years. My mother's favourite Passage of the River to the Celestial City divested death even then of much of its terror. Oh, how I loved to listen as she read that wonderful dream, and how I longed to be a pilgrim to that city of splendour, guided thither by our Christiana!

Religion was not limited to Sundays. Every morning, as the clock struck eight, the bell rang, and to servants and children, with mother at the head, our father read a short passage from the "big ha' Bible." This I possess as one of my treasures, the margins bearing names of ministers who had been guests, and had read the adjoining passage, including those of R. Hill, R. Knill, Leifchild, Moffat, and others. His prayer was no mere routine, but the utterance of a fervent heart, which frequently was a repetition of his constant belief and desire. I remember the following:—"O blessed, blessed Jesus, the One among ten thousand! come, and take full possession of what Thy blood has purchased; reign within us without a rival and with uncontrolled sway, that wherever we may be, however circumstanced or placed, we may always feel Thee within us as the Spring of Life: and if opportunity occurs this day of speaking in Thy Name, O help us to speak as taught of Thee."

On weekdays we had our rompings like other children; but our greatest pleasure was to go rambling with our mother, or, in the evening, to listen as she read to us children's tales and rhymes, and, as we grew older, history, biography, and poetry. I have often felt what an addition to social pleasures it would be if some young ladies who have no natural taste for music, instead of spending tedious hours daily in strumming the piano, or screaming scales, would acquire the high art of good reading, for which the vast wealth of literature would furnish endless variety.

At my mother's bedroom door I often lingered, wondering to hear her speaking so earnestly to an invisible Being. She would pray for her children by name, and I often longed to be converted—whatever might be meant by it—so as to give her pleasure, because I was sure nothing else would make her so happy.

I have been told that I took great interest in looking from the front sitting-room window, especially on market-days, when sheep and cattle, farmers and fruit vendors, crowded the street, and that I used to say, "It's boofly all, ebery man and ebery beast." At a certain election, when rival partisans waved their purple or light-blue banners, I am told that I sometimes shouted, "Hooray for eberyone!" It was an unconscious premonition. Members of opposite parties too often condemn as if morally bad the advocates of differing opinions, when both may be equally sincere in promoting truth and humanity, though adopting different methods. Without losing sympathy for our own side, we might often cheer the other as true patriots and Christians— sincerity causing party earnestness. Through life I have increasingly been disposed with real consistency to shout, "Hooray for eberyone!"

Great was the delight of us children when our mother took us into the fields and woods to pluck flowers, or play hide-and-seek among the bushes, or sit with her on some mossy bank while she read to us. An intense lover of nature herself, she nourished the same love in us. How we loved to bring home nosegays of buttercups, anemones, daisies, and cowslips! The Boxley Hills, near the town, yielded as much delight with their five hundred feet of elevation as the Alps in after years. For this excursion, a donkey-chaise was necessary for our mother, and I am told I sometimes said, "Whenever I'm Lord Mayor of London, Ma shall have a donkey-chaise once every week."

I remember that when whooping-cough broke out in the family I was sent away to board with a respectable family at Faversham, and that the children after every meal went round the table, bowing to their parents, and saying, "Thank you, father, for my good dinner; thank you, mother, for my good dinner." And I am told by one who has visited a noble family in Norway that something like this is said by every guest of all ranks at the close of meals. In the case of children of the present day perhaps, there is excess in the contrary direction.

When a mere boy, I was fond of narratives of battles and heroes, and interpreted "battalion" as a sort of *lion* employed in *battle*. With my brothers I played at soldiering, with buckram uniform, wooden sword, and a shilling drum. My father had been a "yeomanry cavalry" volunteer, when invasion was threatened by Bonaparte, and a strong camp was established at Coxheath, near Maidstone. At a review in Lord Romney's park my father was selected to perform the sword exercise at full gallop in front of the regiment. His sword is among the many cherished relics of our family. I was eager to see the champion who had so triumphantly checkmated the great foe. Occasion came when Wellington reviewed some troops near Maidstone. I forget how I pushed through the crowds, and with boyish impertinence got close to the Duke's horse, but I do not forget how my heart thrilled when he took kindly notice of his child-worshipper, and extended to me his hand.

My father was for some time greatly interested in cures apparently resulting from the use of "Perkin's Metallic Tractors." When King George IV. was suffering from some ailment of the eyes, my father wrote to the Duke, then Prime Minister, suggesting a trial of this small magnetic instrument, and received the following characteristic reply, in the Duke's own handwriting, which now lies before me :—

"The Duke of Wellington presents his compliments to Mr. Hall, and has received his letter. The Duke is responsible for a great deal, but that for which he cannot make himself responsible is the care of His Majesty's health, and most particularly of His Majesty's eyes. The Duke therefore begs leave to recommend to Mr. Hall to make his suggestion to His Majesty's physicians.
"London, Sept. 28, 1829."

My early passion for war changed to a more ardent and better-based passion for peace. I witnessed the grand funeral of the hero, in November, 1852, and preached at Hull a funeral sermon, in which I said :—

"It is because Wellington hated war that I chiefly honour him. He said, with reference to Waterloo, ' I know nothing more terrible than a victory—except a defeat.' When he thought of the slaughter of so many thousands, 'full of lusty life,' swept away by the iron tempest of artillery, the wild tornado of cavalry, or the fierce thrust of bayonet, and the bleeding hearts in desolated homes, what men call glory was eclipsed by the dark figure of distress which brooded over that sanguinary plain. It is not that at Waterloo, when the devastator of Europe, whose intellect was great as his ambition, roused to fury, sought to stamp his iron heel on all his foes at once, but chiefly to trample out England from among the nations : it is not that there the cool intrepidity of Wellington hurled back in headlong rout the massive columns of the vaunted Imperial Guard—no! but because, amid the roar of war, he strained his ear to catch the gentle tones of peace— because he would rather wave the olive-branch than brandish the sword —therefore is it we say of him, as David did of Abner, ' Know ye not that a prince and a great man is fallen this day in Israel ? "

My mother refers in her diary to a very dangerous illness, which for a fortnight threatened her life, the doctors giving up all hope. This was, perhaps, the occasion to which I have often heard my father refer with deep emotion. The children were taken to the bedside for the mother's parting kiss. The husband also with breaking heart commended her to God. He retired to another room and thought, " There is yet a promise I have not pleaded. O Lord, Thou didst say, ' If ye ask anything in My Name, I will do it ! ' Now, Lord, fulfil this to me. O God, for the honour of Thy beloved Son, grant me the life of my wife." He could say no more ! When he re-entered the chamber, the nurse said, " She seems reviving, and has taken some milk." From that moment she began to recover, and was spared above half a century, to comfort the last years of her devoted husband and to counsel and bless her children and children's children, by whom her body was laid to rest in the same grave as his.

At the early age of eight (1824) I was sent to a juvenile boarding-school at Rochester. It was one of the bitterest trials of my life. Children differ much in temperament, needing difference of treatment, so that what may be good for one may be ruinous for another. My very life seemed bound up with my mother. Perhaps it was thought wise, on this very account, that I should be thus prepared for the necessary separation of future life. I know that whatever was done was with the best motives of the most tender love ; but this was an agony I have never forgotten.

The hills seemed to be the boundary of " the happy valley "— all beyond was another world. Now I was taken across these hills, and I felt eight long miles so far away ! All day I concealed my sorrow, but when bed-time came my tears used to find vent, unperceived beneath the clothes, and night after night I lay awake counting the weeks before returning.

Some readers may think this affection was inordinate, and that the confession of it is foolish. But I wish these pages to be true, whether praised or blamed. Reverencing the memory of my parents as I do, I yet think their sending me away at that age, with a breaking heart, was unwise. Some children are too soon willing to leave home; but when love for parents is a passion, it may be quenched by lack of consideration, and love be exchanged for indifference or even dislike.

There were curious punishments at that school, in addition to birch and cane and fool's-cap—a log of wood fastened by a chain to the ankle, for going out of bounds, or a pair of stocks to confine both feet.

At nine years old I began to smoke. At nine years old I left off "for good." In my ninth decade I do not desire to recommence. On a certain Saturday during our weekly walk, my schoolfellows found some dried cane branches (perhaps "traveller's joy"), and cut them into cigarettes. I smoked with the rest, but, becoming very sick, I threw my "weed" away. During seventy years I have pursued my life-travels so pleasantly as not to need this "traveller's joy."

Oh, the delight of coming home for the holidays—the deep, wild, absorbing joy! I wonder my little heart did not break with very gladness, as I wonder it had not broken for grief. With what rapture I looked forth from the top of Blue Bell Hill over the beautiful valley, in the centre of which was my native town, the centre of which, and of the whole world, was my mother, who, I knew, was expecting me with as much earnestness as I was longing to see her; and then when the coach drove round into the High Street, and I saw her at the window looking out for me, the delight was such that after years have not surpassed. How swiftly the hours flew! The chief charm of them was my mother; to be with her in rambles into the lovely country round, or to sit leaning against her knee while she read

Rolando's "Travels," or Belzoni, or, in after years, the tales and poetry of Scott.

I remember going with her on benevolent visitations, carrying the immense muff which was then in fashion, and which was often filled with packets of tea, sugar, and sometimes more solid food. I knew what delight such work gave her. She often visited, I remember, a very poor old woman, grievously oppressed by a drinking husband, but whose great comfort was in being taught to read the New Testament. I felt greatly honoured by being employed by my mother to help in teaching her simple texts. I remember this poor woman saying, "With this dear book and Jesus, I'm as happy as a queen." I early learnt that Christ has " chosen the poor, rich in faith, and heirs of the Kingdom."

At the age of ten I was sent with my brother Vine to a higher school. My first introduction to the boys was unfortunate. A stand-up fight was commencing between two of them, one much bigger than the other. The cry was raised that this new-comer should join the lesser boy. So without my consent I was at once made an ally, whereupon the bigger combatant in a moment disabled poor me by a blow on my cheek, in some slight degree putting out of place my lower jawbone, which for several years reminded me, by a slight click, of my first campaign, and perhaps this illustration of the folly and injustice that often also characterise the wars of nations helped to make me ever after an advocate of peace.

The master was a very strict disciplinarian. Any slight neglect of laws was punished as a crime. My brother of twelve years and I often slept together, and one night broke the rule by whispering our brotherly sympathies. This offence was visited by severe strokes of the cane on the hand. Mistakes at lessons were treated in the same way. The cane was gifted with perpetual motion : its bruises were to concentrate attention on the book, memory of them to deepen the records of history and the rules of grammar ; the stiffening of the fingers to improve the handwriting ; the sense of injury to increase respect for religion !

I remember a severe punishment for the trifling offence of disobeying a junior usher, who on a Saturday afternoon ordered some of us, who were specially eager to get ready for Monday classes, to close our books and turn out for military exercise. This crime was followed by punishment which should be reserved for immorality. The effect of indiscriminate discipline must be very injurious, whether on children or on soldiers and sailors, as at that time was very common. I protest against confounding an accidental breach of discipline with deliberate disregard of eternal obligations.

Another trouble was of a religious nature. The school was strictly "Church of England." Our parents made no objection to our "attending church" with the other boys; but we, although piously trained by our real parents from infancy, had not the privilege of godfathers and godmothers, and could not truthfully have declared we had received our names from them in baptism, having thus become "members of Christ." It was, therefore, arranged that we might remain seated while all the other boys stood up to repeat the prescribed form. This was intended as a generous consideration of diversity of opinion; but it operated on us as the modern conscience clause has often done on others. We were laughed at and insulted by the other boys as heretical and "vulgar."

My next school was Nonconformist, conducted very religiously, and so had special attraction for my parents, though the terms were high. Each morning and evening we assembled for the reading of Scripture, extempore prayer, and a hymn. Some of us cultivated part-singing, among whom was Andrew Reed, son of the Dr. Reed famous as pastor and author, and especially as the founder of philanthropic institutions such as the Reedham Asylum for orphans. My schoolfellow has been an honoured author and pastor till recently, and, conversing on school-days, he has just reminded me that he established a weekly prayer-meeting among the boys, and that in it we encouraged one another, as we have done ever since.

Another religious difficulty met me in connection with

catechism, but on the opposite side to the former one. The boys had actually to repeat, every Sunday afternoon, no less than twenty questions of the " Assembly's Shorter Catechism," with all the proofs. The few Church boys were excused. How I envied them! One boy in turn answered the question, and then each in order had to give the illustrating text with the chapter and verse. I never was able to remember figures, though I knew every answer and every text. The boy who sat next me knew all the figures, and often helped me by whispering the numbers of chapter and verse.

It is a great mistake to turn God's word, pious truths, and sacred hymns into an implement of torture! It was enough to create dislike to religion itself. The earlier religion of the home—cheerful, voluntary, loving—was to me a counteraction to this forced, formal, detested toil, in relation to a formulary which has been so honoured by a great historic Church on both sides the ocean, and which in riper years I have admired as a comprehensive, though in some instances questionable, summary of theological dogma, but which was certainly un-suitable as a forced task for children whose parents themselves failed fully to understand it.

On Sundays we marched to a small Independent chapel at Whetstone, built of wood, very like a barn. Several good families came there to worship, such as Sir John and Lady Easthorpe with their fashionable daughters. Lady Easthorpe had been at school with my mother at Kidderminster. Her husband had become proprietor of the *Morning Chronicle* and an M.P. of some importance. They lived at Barnet, and once in each half-year I was invited to spend a day there. My school-fellows rather envied my going to the great house on a pony in company with a groom.

It was supposed that we went to sleep after the lights were put out in our room, but we often kept awake for recitations and stories. I remember three nights running giving a narration of Cooper's " Last of the Mohicans," which our mother had read to us during the holidays.

I think it was a great defect in the curriculum that the teaching was almost entirely confined to classics and mathematics. History, science, poetry, logic, even the critical and grammatical study of our own language, were neglected. We knew nothing of the structure and functions of our own bodies. It was supposed we might obtain such knowledge ourselves. My mother appealed to the head master, who replied : " Our object is, not to send out shining boys, but thinking men." As if such ignorance aided thoughtfulness !

I recall a frolic which might have brought on me a severe and merited chastisement. The boys in our room resolved to startle those in the room exactly below, by dressing up a "ghost" and lowering it before their window. They saw the white figure dangling there, and tried to capture it, while we tried to draw it back. The string broke, and the guy fell into the garden. Discovery was certain in the morning unless one of us would rescue it. This I volunteered to do. I remember stealthily going downstairs at midnight, opening the inner door of the un-known kitchen, groping through the scullery, unbolting the garden door, discovering the "ghost," fastening the cord, giving the signal, and seeing it hoisted up. Then I crept backward as noiselessly as possible, till, without misadventure, I was greeted by my grateful comrades.

. Some boys in a lower bedroom were to have a magic lantern entertainment. It was a great secret. When the lights were put out and all the masters were at supper the invited guests came down to the magic chamber. My delight was the more intense because of the danger, for we knew what a row there would be if we were discovered. Conscience made us cowards. A door was heard to slam at the bottom of the stairs. Fear made us noisy in our retreat, and so really caused the danger of discovery. Our monitor continued to seem un-conscious. Presently the head master entered and demanded who were the wicked boys who had been out of their room. We all remained asleep. Presently he resorted to his usual method of appealing to our sense of honour. " Am I to understand that no boy in this room has been downstairs ? " Silence. " Then every boy here denies that he has been out

of the room?" Silence. "If any boy has been out of the
room and does not at once say so, I take it that every boy
denies it." Silence. "Any boy who has been out of the
room, and who does not confess it, will be telling a lie." I
could not bear this, so I said, "Please, sir, I only just went
down to No. 2 for a minute and came back." Then said he:
"I will give you a little assistance," which was his favourite
euphemism for a caning. He disappeared. I had my wits
about me, so I hastily put on my jacket and my nightshirt
over it. Presently I heard avenging steps, and was called out
of bed to receive the caning, which was given with due consideration of thin clothing, although there were a few needless
contortions. I should not have cared for the thrashing,
however severe; but I did care for what was said next day.
There was a solemn assembly of the boys, and a long harangue
on the wickedness of what was only a boyish joke, for which
I was denounced as if one of the worst boys in the school.
I worked hard at lessons, and won a prize every half-year. I
did not object to the caning or the 500 lines of Virgil I
had to repeat (twenty lines daily), or the lecture on the
breach of law; but I did (and do) condemn the judgment
passed in anger by a misconception of a frolic. This has
impressed me with the sensitiveness of children to praise
and blame, and their capacity rightly to judge of the
difference between a breach of man's regulations and God's
moral laws.

Though fond of study, I was also fond of play, and was
most enthusiastic at football, whether leading the attack,
guarding the base, or floored in the *mêlée*. In the evening
I was sometimes encouraged by the other boys in spouting
a pretended epic in the style of Pope's translation of Homer's
"Iliad," introducing the exploits of some of our heroes, whose
names are still known, or those of their sons—Gregory,
Strachey, Bompas, and others. This I wrote out, and possess
the original manuscript. It seems dreadful rubbish now, but
my schoolfellows thought much of it.

I quote from my mother's diary when I was thirteen,
away at school, so that I did not then see the venerable

preacher whose unworthy successor I was to become twenty-five years afterwards.

"April 28, 1829.—The Rev. Rowland Hill preached at our chapel last night. Our domestic afflictions prevented our entertaining him at our house as heretofore, but he kindly called to sympathise this morning. He is now eighty-four years of age, has preached the Gospel sixty years, and still maintains his great popularity, being attended wherever he preaches by overflowing congregations. In the pulpit he is still vigorous and lively; out of it, he is quite the old man; still in conversation he makes occasional remarks which are pleasing and edifying, and occasionally a little of his native humour displays itself. Speaking of some who profess an experience which forbids all fear, my husband observed that he was not there yet; he had got no farther than when they met last. 'What! No farther?' 'No,' said my husband, 'I rejoice with trembling.' 'Don't wish to get any farther—remember, "Blessed is the man that feareth always." I am not afraid of the faithfulness of Christ, but I am afraid of the deceitfulness of my own heart.' Speaking of reading the Scriptures, Mr. Hill said: 'Some people read their Bibles in a hurry; they seem to try to get through and through without thinking of what they read, or applying it to themselves; they do not "mark, learn, and inwardly digest it." Ah, these are the best words of all that prayer! That is what we want.'"

From my mother's diary when I was thirteen:—

"September 11, 1829.—If my children recollect circumstances in their mother's temper and conduct which ever made them doubt the sincerity of her religious profession, let them here see that she hated herself for sin; she did not *allow* it, she wept over it, strove against it, and cast herself on the atonement of Christ; and O my children! let not my inconsistence deter you from pursuing the path I have so often directed you to. There is no peace in any other; and though from nerves shaken by continued indisposition I have made such low attainments in the Christian life, I am persuaded of the beauty of religion. I would not give up my hope for a thousand worlds. Christ is mine, and when this life closes, then with renewed powers, with holy raptures and unmixed delight, I shall mingle with the joyful throng around the throne! My children, I charge you to meet me there!—MARY HALL."

At length drew near the happy time when I was to leave school! Away we boys drove in several coaches through Whetstone and under Highgate Archway, to the Old Bell, Holborn, and thence to our various homes. Again I came in sight of my beloved Boxley Hills, and the old house, where I was to live for seven whole years with my father and mother.

c

CHAPTER II.

My fourteenth birthday. It had been determined I was to leave school at the end of the half-year, and go into business. It was a crisis of life. Mr. Cox, the mathematical master, strongly urged me to remain two years longer, and then go to college. I was getting on decently with Virgil, Horace, and Homer; reading Greek plays, and playing at making Greek verses. I was familiar with six books of Euclid; algebra was a passion, and architectural drawing a recreation; but this was only the alphabet of the language, the preface to the book. Why throw away the opportunity of securing the treasure, the first step toward which had alone been taken? Had study become distasteful? Was I enraptured by the thought of commerce, or the hope of wealth? The passionate love of mother solved the problem. By becoming apprenticed to my father I should secure seven years of residence with her under the same roof, guided by her counsels, and cherished by her love. To human judgment this decision was a mistake; but in the light of love it was a joy beyond words, and a blessing for all my future life.

It was well for me to acquire business habits—to gain some knowledge of the world—to be at the college of which my mother was Principal, and eventually to be better fitted for that special mode of serving God and man which, on looking back, I would not have exchanged for any other vocation, whatever its worldly and social advantages.

My happiness was now complete. I was "at home," and "for good." No going away to school or college. Business, of whatever kind, would become a delight, if it kept me near my mother. Reverence for my father made me determine to be "diligent in business," when it was *his*.

I desired thoroughly to qualify myself in the printing business, and soon was able to set up type, and occasionally, as printers call it, to make "pie." I can still fancy myself "locking up" the "forme," rolling the inking cylinder, laying on the sheets, arranging the "tympanum," and pulling down the press upon the type. It was a maxim with me to do thoroughly whatever I undertook to do at all. So I did not scorn the lowest kind of work, beginning at the very beginning, as, I suppose, all cadets do. I was regularly at business by half-past seven, continuing on duty (with short intervals for meals) till nine at night, with no regular half-holiday or an evening to myself, except three hours once a week for a country ramble. But though the work was sometimes distasteful, it was for my father. His approving eye was upon me, and I was often enjoying the smile and conversation of my mother.

After awhile I was raised to the dignity of a reader of copy, and afterwards a corrector of proofs. Having taught myself Odell's shorthand, I took reports at the assizes, both in the Crown Court and at Nisi Prius, greatly enjoying the speeches of counsel, with some desire for the Bar. I attended public meetings, and gathered "tit-bits" as though I were a penny-a-liner; wrote letters to the editor and sometimes answered them, and reviewed books, which I treasured as my fee. Now and then I was allowed to try my "'prentice-hand" on a short leader. Thus there was no department of a newspaper of which I had not some practical knowledge, including afterwards the keeping of the accounts. The Government stamp on each sheet was fourpence, and the price of the paper sevenpence. The tax on each advertisement was 3s. 6d., and the lowest charge 6s.

In former years my father was led into danger by his love of the theatre, and occasional acting, and now, as proprietor of the county paper, he refused, at great pecuniary sacrifice, to advertise or report any theatrical performances. Some may consider this to have been a mistake, but it showed his resolute obedience to conscience. For the same reason he rejected all advertisements of questionable remedies, or of immoral books.

About this time the venerable philanthropist William Wilberforce was residing with his son Robert, the Vicar of Farleigh, near Maidstone. Chiefly by his labours and eloquence had the Bill for emancipation become law, but limited by a period of "apprenticeship." Slavery died hard. It was said by its votaries that riot and murder would result from such a horde of slaves suddenly obtaining a freedom to which they were unaccustomed. Therefore the process was to be made gradual, the masters still retaining a limited control for three years. But if the slaves were unaccustomed to freedom, so were the masters unaccustomed to treat their servants as human beings under protection of equal laws. Outrageous cruelties were still practised. The people at large denounced the wrong. The nation claimed perfect liberation for the £20,000,000 of compensation. Public meetings were held all over the land, demanding instant liberation. One of these took place in the Town Hall, Maidstone, adjoining my father's house. There I heard the aged orator deliver his very last speech. As editor's assistant I had the privilege of being sent over to Farleigh with the proof of the speech. How clearly I remember that interview! Wilberforce was seated askew in an arm-chair, exactly in the attitude represented in the admirable sculpture in Westminster Abbey. It is true to the very life. When I look upon it I am carried back sixty years. All I remember of the interview is the earnest attention with which he revised the proof, and with what emphasis he said, "Upon! upon! why *up?* Don't say *upon*, but *on*"—an interesting illustration of the orator's careful attention to trifles in speech.

In the same capacity of reporter I went over Boxley Hill to Rochester, where the great Repealer O'Connell was to speak at an open-air demonstration. I remember his stately form, his massive head, his expressive countenance and changing features. I see the listening crowds, with eyes intent and gaping mouths, now with tears starting at his pathetic tales of misery, now roaring with laughter at his wit, now making the welkin ring with shouts of applause, especially when he demonstrated his argument by saying of some noble lord, "He wasn't born in breeches and you without." I much enjoyed my assize work and the pleadings of barristers, and I remember, among others, the silvery eloquence of Thesiger, and the raciness and fun of Sergeant Spankie.

Elections were times of great interest. At one of these I first saw Benjamin Disraeli ; youthful, elaborately dressed, florid in speech, exciting great interest. He had hitherto been on the Liberal side, but now he came forward as a Conservative, with Wyndham Lewis as colleague, and was diligent in canvassing with Mr. and Mrs. Lewis. The wealthy and elderly M.P. died soon afterwards, and his widow became the devoted wife of the junior member, who, as Prime Minister, obtained for her the title of Countess of Beaconsfield.

In connection with my sub-editorial experiences I remember the poet Campbell taking tea with us in our office. How I felt thrilled by conversing with the very man who wrote the verses on Hohenlinden which I was so fond of spouting !

An amusing incident was the delivery in our office before the editor and myself of a flowery oration prepared for a public dinner by a great county baronet, but not delivered because the chattering feasters were unable to listen to any other speaking than their own. So our great orator, disappointed in his expectation of fame, asked us to hear his address, so that it might be circulated as a " speech delivered at Maidstone by Sir John ——." It was in the style of the following phrase, which his enthusiastic manner printed on my youthful memory: " These revolutionists would batter down the throne with the ruins of the altar."

Owing to the multifarious labours of business, I had little leisure for study, but " where there's a will there's a way," and I often secured an hour for my Homer or Euclid, concealed under my ledger, though never to the neglect of duty. The books were always posted up to date.

My conscience accuses me to this day of one deliberate violation of duty. Our parents very wisely forbade our playing with gunpowder. On our brother Vine returning from one of his long voyages, we resolved to give him a royal salute from a sham fort in the garden. By accident a powder train fired, and the next minute a bottle of powder would have exploded had not Vine deliberately taken it up and thrown it out of the window. But the next moment a smaller bottle did explode, a fragment of glass cutting a small blood-vessel on my wrist, the mark of which I still carry. The flame scorched my face, causing great pain. When the flow of blood was staunched, my father applied his " tractors " to my face, and within half an hour the pain was gone. His forbearance in withholding a reprimand when I was suffering the natural penalty which he was endeavouring to mitigate was a lesson never forgotten. No need again to forbid fireworks.

Our mother in various ways encouraged me and my sisters in our studies. She secured for me two hours weekly for lessons from a French teacher, with whom we conversed in his own language ; and were rude enough to smile, when, practising English, with a bad cold, he informed us he had " horse in de trote." She also secured for me occasional lessons in Greek. She was fond of reading to us Milton, Thomson, Cowper, Scott, Byron, and could recite favourite passages from them, especially Scott. Sometimes we were treated to an historical novel — " Kenilworth," " Ivanhoe." As a grand treat, we sometimes got an hour or two for drawing and listening to her. She had no ear for music, and very wisely did not waste time at the piano ; but she had a most refined and musical voice for reading. Excepting Fanny Kemble and Brandram, I never heard such reading. Her whole soul was in the subject, and though she so disapproved of the theatre that she would have been shocked to think her reading was dramatic, yet she made her characters live and speak, so that I felt no need of costumes to add to the effect, or any wish to visit a theatre. Her reading was successful in enchaining our young minds because it was so natural.

In the summer-time it was a great delight to go with our mother for a country walk ; my sisters were a little younger than myself, and we were congenial companions, and often, with "little Arthur," we used to gather flowers, or sit on haycocks while she read to us. She loved nature in all its forms of beauty—the wide landscape; the swelling wolds; the glories of the clouds; the beauty of flowers, not the grand products of the greenhouse alone, but every primrose and daisy; and, for music, the songs of thrush, blackbird, lark, and nightingale. Her joy in such charms made us love them the more for her sake, and gave me that intense delight in nature which grows with growing years, and which I often feel too intense for words or even tears to express.

Thus it was that, though I was not at school or college, I was under an educating influence of the most powerful kind during these seven years of business. How many fatal mistakes are made by young clergymen who go at once from college into a large congregation or parish, and are apt to speak and act as if they were oracles of wisdom, treating with indifference the opinion of men much wiser and often better than themselves. I sometimes think it would be well if all who have to "preach the Word" were first to learn something of the business ways of the world.

I little thought that my mother was secretly cherishing the hope which possessed her at my birth, that some day I might be a preacher of the Gospel; but she felt that I had far better never enter the ministry than do so without a distinct "call" from God. She therefore would take no step in it. God in His own way would make the path plain.

But all this time she never ceased to promote my spiritual good. For two or three years after leaving school, she used, after breakfast, to take me into her bedroom, when, after reading a few verses from Proverbs, she would kneel with me at the side of her bed, and earnestly implore God to keep me from the snares of youth and give me His Holy Spirit. Her constant and supreme desire for my spiritual good impressed me more than any formal admonitions would have done. The conversation of some parents impresses their children with the idea that admiration, success, money and fashion, are their chief aim. Most people get what they

supremely seek. "Verily they *have* their reward." My
mother's piety was a balmy atmosphere pervading the house
—it was herself.

All who came to preach were hospitably entertained.
I remember Mr. Knill coming to preach for missions. I
went with him one Sunday afternoon to address the hop-
pickers. Arthur, then quite a little boy, went also. Mr.
Knill at family worship that evening prayed that little
Arthur, who had begun his missionary work that afternoon,
might become a preacher or missionary some day.

Village pastors of humble culture were treated with
honour for their Master's sake. My parents in this were
so different from some who are willing to entertain bishops,
deans, and celebrated preachers, but who care not to receive
the poor and unknown for the Master's sake. But my
parents always manifested and inculcated honour for the
office and the work itself, and never criticised the humblest
or sanctioned our doing so. Parents often prejudice their
children against religion by criticising, ridiculing, and even
censuring, preachers in the presence of those children,
who are not likely to profit by these preachers. My parents
little thought how their hospitality to preachers would
in after years be more than repaid to their two evangelist
sons, in their frequent journeyings to preach the Gospel.

My father was in practice a Nonconformist, but in politics he was an old-fashioned Tory and was opposed to
the separation of Church and State. He was a Nonconformist because he preferred the mode of worship, social
spirituality and Gospel-preaching. For many years no
real "Gospel" was preached in the Church of England in
Maidstone. We knew of only two or three pious Church
families. They used to lament the state of the parish, and
said how they prayed God to send them the Gospel and how
they waited for better times. Yet all the while the true
Gospel was being preached in at least three Dissenting
chapels. This is all changed now: God be praised for
faithful Episcopal clergy, Gospel sermons, and diligence in
visiting the poor and the sick! Our pastor, Mr. Jenkings,

was of blameless life, and had never taken any part in attacks against the Church of England; yet these good people continued to go to listen to what they themselves condemned as calculated neither to convert sinners nor edify believers. I fully believe that if at that time St. Paul had come to preach in one of the Dissenting chapels at Maidstone they would have refused to listen, saying that the place disproved the apostleship. When I think of such exclusiveness, I am not surprised that the Jews rejected Christ, saying, "Have any of the rulers or the Pharisees believed on Him?"

I never heard my father find fault with any other Church. He often said: "Show me a man who loves Christ and hates sin, and that man is my brother, whatever his denomination." My father's intense religious fervour—not for system, but for Christ—made it impossible for him to breathe the atmosphere of sect. At the same time, he was faithful to his own opportunities, was the chief supporter of the church of Christ in Week Street, and treasurer of its funds.

My father now spent much of his time in bringing out improved editions of his "Sinner's Friend," which at length attained a circulation of several millions, in some seventy languages. He gave away many thousands annually, and always had his pockets stored, putting them into hedges and slipping them under doors and dropping them on the road— as he said, "every copy with a prayer." He was very enthusiastic in his manner, and when speaking of religion was in a glow of rapture which rendered him an object of great interest to religious people far and wide, who came to converse with him.

I have often seen him in the midst of business lay down his pen, close his account-books, and for five or ten minutes engage in most fervent discourse with Christian people, kneel down and pray with them, and then return to business with all the eagerness he had manifested before the interruption. I could never doubt the reality of religion when I thought of him: it possessed him. The very Name of Jesus seemed to set him ablaze. I never saw anything in his conduct contrary to the religion he professed. Though religion in him did not impress my young heart, yet it convinced my reason, and in great degree contributed to aid the influence of my mother.

Under a transitory ambition to play on the piano or organ, great was my delight when allowed at the afternoon service to play the tune " Job " or " Bradley Church "; but, as I wanted all my spare time for reading, I was not able to cultivate music also.

I do not remember ever going away for any holiday during these six or seven years, except once for three days to Calais, but I was quite satisfied with home enjoyments.   We had boatings on the Medway and bathing from the meadow banks, rambles with dear mother and sisters in the fields, and now and then—the greatest treat of all—an excursion to Boxley Hills. How vast the view!   How lovely the flowers, the shady walks in the woods, and the excitement of seeing, far, far away towards Sheerness, the real sea! "There go the ships!"

CHAPTER III.

WHAT I consider my conversion to God took place in connection with a circumstance thus recorded in my mother's diary :—

"December 31, 1832.—On April 2nd, while playing with my infant boy, a sudden fit carried him from me. I made it a season of peculiar intercession for my surviving children, especially for my eldest, dear Edward. At the close of the fourth day, while on my knees pleading for him, the words 'Go thy way, thy son liveth,' were presented to me with such power that I could ask no more, but rose, blessing God. . . . On the day of the funeral of the child I was ill, and Edward came, and while he was bathing my temples I spoke to him of the uncertainty of life, and urged him to seek Christ. What was my joy to hear him sob out, with many tears, 'I have been praying that I may.' O the joy and gratitude that filled my heart ! I could scarcely keep in bed. I thought I could have gone into the street to proclaim the goodness of God. I add—to His glory, and the encouragement of my children—that He who awakened this feeling in the heart of my dear Edward, raised to a flame the smoking flax, and on his twenty-fourth birthday he publicly, with dear Newman, aged sixteen, professed himself a follower of Christ, was received as a member of the Church, and my dear husband, now a deacon, and myself, had the delight of partaking with two of our sons of the Supper of the Lord. May salvation-work go on in our house till every child is brought into the fold, and may we all meet around His throne.—M. H."

I well remember witnessing the bereavement thus recorded. Great awe came on me when I felt that Death had entered our home, that life was uncertain, and the eternal world quite near.

That day, April 2nd, was the fourteenth birthday of my sister Nora, two years my junior. She wrote from school telling her mother that she had that day resolved to set out on pilgrimage to the Celestial City. My mother gave the letter to me ; she was full of emotion, but she said not a word. How eloquent was that silence ! It said : "Shall your younger sister set out for heaven and her brother linger behind ?" I took the letter into a small room, and there, feeling quite alone, I spread it on a chair, and as I knelt beside it, and my tears fell on it, I prayed God to enable me also to set forth on this pilgrimage. Then and there I accepted Jesus as my Saviour, sought through His Sacrifice the forgiveness of sin, and the aid of the Holy Ghost to consecrate my life to His service.

I then began in reality to be a Pilgrim to that City of which, as little children, we had so often heard our mother speak. I am deeply conscious that my " Progress " has, alas ! been sometimes hindered by drowsiness, by my longing for wayside weeds, beguiled by distant sights or sounds of Vanity Fair, haunted by evil ones in the dark valley ; but—all praise to God !—never have I been caught by Giant Despair, and I have sometimes climbed the Delectable Mountains, and seen the City from afar. Though sometimes wounded, slumbering, losing my " Roll " of full assurance, I thank God I have never turned back, but with face " Zionward " have been, " though faint, yet pursuing."

Now I understood why my parents prayed so fervently for us. The Bible became as a new book, even the Will of my Father. I not only believed that Christ died for sinners, but I could say, " He loved *me*, and gave Himself for *me* "; not only that He had died, but that He was still living and present. I now always secured time early in the morning for prayer and Bible-reading, making an old greenhouse my oratory. With alacrity, in the depth of winter, I hastened to the early Sunday meeting in the tomb-like, cold vestry, to meet about a dozen poor friends of Jesus, and I remember with what trembling I first ventured to open my lips before others in prayer.

What is the meaning of conversion to participants of Christian Sacraments ? In the words of the Great High Priest: " Except a man be born again, he cannot enter the Kingdom of Heaven." What, then, is this new birth ? Not merely intellectual assent to doctrines, but sorrow for sins, reliance on Christ, surrender to His authority, yielding heart and life for Him to dwell and rule there for ever.

"Conversion" is turning round, "from darkness to light, from the power of Satan to God." But it does not always demand a visible change of conduct. To confess repentance of offences against my fellow-men would have been hypocritical humility. I do not remember a disrespectful, unkind word to my parents, but I bitterly repented of disobedience to the first and great commandment: "Thou shalt love the Lord thy God with all thy heart."

But now, what had been only objective Truth became subjective Life. I had seen the Divine landscape only in twilight shadow, now it was illumined by the sun. "Old things passed away, and all things became new." "Pilgrim's Progress," instead of a beautiful tale, was now an intense personal reality. I was myself "Pilgrim," though with unequal steps. I did not fall into any Slough of Despond, but, bending under the burden of sin, I went up at once to the Wicket Gate, and found rest at the Cross. Yet afterwards I fought with Apollyon, and trembled in the Valley of the Shadow of Death.

The religious ways of the family, which I had always reverenced from love to my parents, I now loved for the sake of my heavenly Father—Saviour—Comforter.

Without delay I felt it right to "confess" Christ. So I did this, first to my father and mother, then to our pastor, who might have said, as the Apostle said to Timothy, "Being mindful of thy tears, that I may be filled with joy when I call to remembrance the unfeigned faith which dwelt in thy mother"—and father—" and I am persuaded that in thee also." Then I was advised, as a follower of Christ, to come to His Table, and "shew forth His death."

Having been welcomed by the congregation as a fellow-disciple, and been confirmed, as I trust, by the grace of God and the prayers of the church and of our godly pastor and my parents, I felt increasingly resolved, in the language of the Liturgy, to "try and always follow the leading of the Holy Spirit in the knowledge and obedience of God's Word, that in the end I might obtain everlasting life." Christ is the One, the only Door, by which I had entered the one household of faith—the Catholic Church. I rejoiced in that holy fellowship, and I earnestly prayed that, by the grace of Christ, the Bread and Water of Life being received by faith into my soul, I might "walk worthy of the vocation wherewith I was called."

I never had a doubt as to the truth of religion; but now that it was my chief object I began to think—"Suppose it is a delusion?" I thought it must be the devil himself who whispered, "Your God is but the creation of your own brain." This assault of unbelief continued for months. I feared to tell my parents, lest it should break their hearts. I would not give up my outward profession, because I still kept on fighting. I thought, "Surely the existence of such a God as the Bible reveals is *possible*, and to desire to know, love, and obey cannot be absurd. In such continued prayer may not God be revealed? Some doubts may linger in the intellect, but will they not at length disappear in ' the light of God?' "

While the foe was holding me fast he lulled with narcotics, but now that I was escaping, he used all his subtlety to retain me in his grasp. Now, verily, Apollyon "straddled over the whole breadth of the way" to resist any further "progress." My sword nearly fell from my hand. Then I thought of the multitudes who had lived and died saying, "I believe in God the Father Almighty." I thought of my own parents, whose faith was their life. "If there be a God, and I pray to Him to help me, surely He will not leave me in ignorance? The Bible tells me that when we pray according to His will He heareth us. That I may believe in Him must be His will." So I resolved to test the promise. "O God, if Thou art indeed my Father, reveal Thyself to my soul!" And thus I went on praying, day by day, till the clouds dispersed and the Sun of Righteousness arose "with healing in his wings."

I have never doubted since. I employ various arguments with unbelievers; and I thank God for the numerous learned and thoughtful minds He has endowed capable of combating their objections. But for my own assurance I rejoice in a fact no logic can destroy, shared by each one of countless believers, learned and unlearned—" I know whom I have believed." I know more than the mere fact that I have trusted in Christ : I know the Christ Himself in whom I trust—" I know *Him*." I have experienced His loving power ; I enjoy intercourse with Him ; I know His inward presence. How? As I know my own existence—by my inner consciousness. I feel I exist—*I am.* So I know there is a God, for He lives in me—as said the Apostle, "I live, yet not I, but Christ liveth in me." Experience generates hope, and "hope maketh not ashamed, because the love of God is shed abroad in our hearts by the Holy Spirit given unto us." Fiery trials have tested faith. I have often prayed seemingly in vain, but I have proved that in the end God is " a rewarder of them that diligently seek Him." I might not now enjoy this full assurance of hope but for this former doubt. " Thanks be to God who giveth us the victory !"

I remember a clever atheist assailing my father's faith, saying he had never heard an argument for religion which he could not demolish. My father replied, " I have an argument I never found anyone able to meet. Jesus Christ dwells here in my heart, where the devil once reigned, and helps me to conquer sin and rejoice in hope. You cannot overthrow that ! "

Trials grievous at the time "afterwards yield the peaceable fruits of righteousness." One fruit has been compassion for others similarly assailed. There may be more religion when struggling against infidelity than in slumberous orthodoxy, free from doubt but devoid of life. It is reasonable to become anxious about that in which we have begun to feel a personal interest, as it is natural to sleep over that which we do not value. When Christ was curing the demoniac "the demon tare him." I have learned to listen with pleased hopefulness to objections urged against truths I valued more than life, the sincerity of the doubter leading to assurance of the truths themselves. Earnest faith stirs up many a lurking foe and

provokes many a fierce assault. Few have reached the
higher peaks and been able to guide others who have not
struggled with steep rocks in the climb. Many who eventually have doubted least have at some time doubted most.

As instrumental in my conversion I must not forget the
influence of my father. When by unceasing industry
he had discharged the whole of his financial responsibilities, and the business with all its stock was absolutely
his own, his general manner became far more cheerful, he
had increased leisure for domestic enjoyments, took a small
residence—" Heath Cottage "—close to Penenden Heath,
Boxley, and presented to the children a religion less awful
in its solemn earnestness, but more cheerful and alluring.
His occasional exhortations were enlivened by his habitual
joyfulness of faith and hope.

The quarryman breaking a big stone gave it eight heavy
blows seemingly in vain. At the ninth it broke in two. By
which blow? The last? No; all the nine. All helped to
put the stone into vibration, preparing it to yield at the last.
Parents, preachers, teachers, and others may be partners in
the work, the success of which is unduly ascribed to one.
Thus in my own case. It was not merely my sister's letter
that aided me, but the life-long influence of my father and
mother.

Having thus experienced the peace and joy of believing, I
felt desirous of imparting the knowledge of Christ to others.
To do this in a way least observed, I obtained a supply of
Gospel tracts, and in my weekly walk I left these at remote,
scattered cottages. After some time I was asked to help in a
Sunday school at Coxheath, a wild district three miles from
Maidstone, where a small wooden room had been built for
a scattered and neglected peasantry. Here I exercised myself
with little children, on the wild heath where my father
had often " exercised " with the " yeomanry cavalry " volunteers
when Bonaparte was threatening to invade England by the
Kentish coast not far off. My first address was from the
words of my own first lesson—" God so loved the world."

Observing the large numbers of " hoppers " assembled to

pick the hops, I felt constrained to speak to them of Jesus. I waited for no committee, and took no companion to witness my failure. I began by reading a passage of Scripture, and this soon attracted a crowd. I selected a long text, because I had so little I could say of my own—the parable of the prodigal son. At the end of five minutes I had exhausted my preparations and concluded—wiser than some of my elders, who go on after they have finished.

I was then about eighteen, and now, at eighty-one, I look back, thanking God that, up to last summer, when I preached on Hampstead Heath with the Salvation Army, I have been enabled to address multitudes, chiefly of the working classes, in streets and market-places, on village greens and the seashore, never but twice encountering any incivility, and never suffering either from cold or hoarseness. Oh that, whether ordained by men or not, all who have common sense, audible voice, and love to Christ, would thus exercise whatever talent God has given them, as ordained by Him!

My small efforts to teach the Gospel gave me such increasing delight that the thought of consecrating life to such service took possession of my heart. I searched the Scriptures for guidance, read books on the Christian ministry, and earnestly prayed for Divine direction. My great fear was lest I might be influenced by self-pleasing motives. I had no real taste for business, though I was considered to possess some capacity for it. But I never seriously thought of any substitute for business, except the ministry. I wanted to use whatever power I had for some object of greater importance. There was one vocation in which every power might be fully employed with adequate result. One soul saved was more worthy of effort than any mere earthly object.

If anyone with similar thoughts were to consult me now, I should say: " You are wrong if you think you can serve God in the ministry alone. If you spend all your life in diligent labour to obtain an honest livelihood, you are not living for a mean end, but to do the will of God. Any work may become a service of lofty devotion ; therefore as lawyer, doctor, merchant, tradesman, or day-labourer, you may be truly serving

D

God. But if my inquirer said, "Yes; but for myself I feel I can never settle to any other work than teaching the truth of God to save the souls of men," I should then begin to think it might be a Divine call.

I had very exalted ideas of the ministry being a vocation and not a profession; that no one could be a true minister of God unless he was *called* of God; that I might choose a profession simply because I liked it or considered I might succeed, and that it would yield me status, wealth, ease, or pleasure; but I felt that I must not on such grounds choose the ministry. I felt it would be better to do anything else, however distasteful, than enter the ministry unless called of God. Then arose the anxious inquiry: "Have I received such a call?"

I often communed with myself: "If everything connected with the ministry, except the work itself, were alien to my tastes, I should have a clearer conviction that my motives were pure."

Then I told my mother, not knowing that at my birth she had consecrated me to the service of God; but she felt that this must come by the prompting of the Divine Spirit, and not by any effort on her part. It was abhorrent to her mind to train up a boy for the ministry. So, telling to God her desire, she had never given me a hint in this direction. Now she urged the solemnity of the office and the danger of entering it from unworthy motives. She gave me Bridges "On the Christian Ministry," which I read with great attention.

Afterwards I wrote to Mr. Bridges and told him my difficulty. He said in reply that if I had no taste for study and no capacity for it, but a much greater relish for *business*, this would be a sign I was not called to the ministry, and that the question should be *not* whether the ministry was pleasant, but whether I was seeking it to glorify God by doing good. This cleared away much of my difficulty.

I asked myself again and again, "Am I willing to enter the ministry for the ministry's sake alone, rather than be in some other position with fame and wealth? 'Search me, O God, and try my heart!'" During more than a year this mental conflict had lasted. I spent long and frequent seasons in prayer. In my walks into the country I loved to seek out lonely spots, and under some shady tree pour out my heart to God. There are two ancient yews on Boxley Hill which are enshrined in my memory, and which I still reverently revisit, beneath which I often knelt on the moss-covered roots, and with many tears implored guidance, again and again pleading the words, "If Thy presence go not with me, carry me not up hence." At length my doubts were removed, and I seemed to hear the words, "Go forward!" My father, to whom I had become valuable in business, gladly surrendered me; my mother felt that the prayers she had offered from my birth were being answered. Then I consulted my pastor or bishop, and he consulted his elders, and then the body of communicants. After preaching before them, they unanimously sanctioned my call, and recommended me to the Ministerial College at Highbury. In her diary, dated December 31st, 1836, my mother records:—

"At our Church meeting my daughter Mary was received as a member of Christ, and my fourth son, Newman, gave an address as an introductory step to the high and holy office of a minister."

Having answered some written inquiries, I was invited to meet the committee and professors of the college, and to deliver a short address. Seeking a quiet spot for meditation, I strolled into St. Paul's Cathedral. In those days very few people visited it, even at service-time. I had the grand cathedral to myself, and quietly paced the south aisle, repeating in a low voice my prepared address on " God so loved the world." I felt it strange that a candidate for the Dissenting ministry should choose St. Paul's Cathedral for such an exercise. I now rejoice that it was an appropriate illustration of true Catholic unity. When entertained by Archdeacon Sinclair some time ago at the Chapter-house, to meet a party of New England Puritans, I informed him, to his surprise and satisfaction, that I had thus preached in his grand National Cathedral without appointment or censure from men.

I met the committee, and was asked a number of questions.

An elderly gentleman said, "What is your opinion about an Established Church?" I knew that almost all Dissenters were strongly opposed to the establishment of religion, and that a plain reply might frustrate my desire. But having been accustomed to say what I meant at all cost, I replied, "I think that Government should give official support to religion, and I do not approve of the opinions and conduct of the political Dissenters." The response came with warm haste, "Political Dissenters, young man? Political Dissenters? We don't like to sit under you, young man!" I made no reply, but Dr. Halley, the Principal, calmed the indignation by saying, "He's only young; he does not understand the question. He'll improve when he has come to us." And so the committee, though strong in their own political bias, unanimously admitted me as a student for the ministry.

In September, 1837, on the evening before leaving home for college, I sat with my mother and sisters on "grandmother's seat" at the foot of a spreading oak at Boxley. I have always felt a strong attachment to places, linking them with whatever of love and happiness I have known in connection with them. On this occasion I scribbled a few rhymes and read them to my mother, and though I feel constrained to record them, I advise all but my younger readers to pass them by:—

Scenes of my childhood! fare ye well!
Oh, who the bitterness can tell
Of that heart-thrilling word—Farewell!
How can I leave without a tear
A spot to memory so dear?
Farewell the wood so calmly cool;
The sheepwash, clear translucent pool;
The murmuring stream, now lost to sight,
Now bursting forth with sparkling light,
Meandering now o'er the meadowy plain,
Now rippling over the rustic lane,
O'er the mimic cascades now joyfully leaping,
'Neath the green bank's dark shades now silently sleeping;
Oh, where is the bard all thy praises can tell,
Thou dearest of streamlets! farewell, farewell!

August, 1837.

It may be thought that I have occupied too many pages in narrating the insignificant incidents of my earlier years; but a true autobiography does not commence with public actions, and I plead excuse in the words of Milton :

> "The childhood shows the man,
> As morning shows the day";

and this is one essential to an autobiography. I kept no diary till middle age, and rely only on memory, which recalls facts and feelings of seventy years ago more vividly than those of yesterday.

> " Dear native regions, I foretell,
> From what I feel at this farewell,
> That, wheresoe'er my steps may tend,
> And whensoe'er my course shall end,
> If in that hour a single tie
> Survive of local sympathy,
> My soul will cast the backward view,
> The longing look, alone on you.
>
> "Thus from the precincts of the west,
> The sun, while sinking down to rest,
> Though his departing radiance fail
> To illuminate the hollow vale,
> A lingering lustre fondly throws
> On the dear mountain-tops where first he rose."
>
> — *Wordsworth.*

CHAPTER IV.

COLLEGE: 1837–1841.

At Highbury College, besides tuition, board and lodging were free. I had £20 yearly of my own, and resolved to make this suffice for personal expenses. Some students engaged a servitor to light their fire, black their boots, and sweep their room. I thought it no degradation to perform these offices for myself rather than be dependent on others. So I rose a few minutes earlier, and at 6 a.m. was generally ready for devotion and study.

The number of students, all training for the Congregational ministry, was forty, for four years, ten leaving and as many entering every year. Some of these had scarcely any other qualification than piety and a natural fitness for preaching. All of the same year were placed together in a class, and thus I found myself sitting with men who were beginning the Greek grammar, and stumbling over the *pons asinorum*. I think that some young men of between twenty and thirty years of age lose their time in a vain struggle with dead languages as a preparation for preaching. Better trust to the Revised Version, and employ their time in studying the Bible, theology, science, and English literature.

Professor Henry Rogers I remember with gratitude for his faithful comment on one of my early essays. He looked up with twinkling, merry eye, and asked quietly, "What do you call that? Is it fustian, or prose run mad?" The critique was rather severe, and drew on me the laugh of my less ambitious companions; but it did me good; it was a wholesome check to vanity and bad taste. Yet it might have been well to encourage the imaginative faculty, while correcting its expression. The vine with no redundant branchlets needing the pruning-knife is not likely to be very prolific. We much enjoyed his lectures and conversation—the

logical force, the critical skill, the genial humour, the kindness
of heart. He is best known by works which the Church
will not let die, such as " The Eclipse of Faith " and " The
Superhuman Origin of the Bible."

Dr. Halley was Principal, and, after two years, Professor
Godwin succeeded. His class on the Greek Testament I
thought invaluable—so much so that on my coming to reside
near " New College," in London, I partially renewed my
student-life by regularly attending his weekly Greek Testament class. Dr. Henderson, the learned Hebraist, held
the Theological Chair.

Though I needed little time to prepare for lectures, ten
hours a day were spent in diligent study. I am not sure I
was wise in my selection of subjects. I read poetry, a little
fiction, Gibbon, Rollin, and Hume, writing long abstracts. I
was enamoured of mental philosophy, reading Brown, Stewart,
Reid and Locke. I also enjoyed books on natural science.
I have several thick quarto manuscript volumes full of
condensed epitomes. I have scarcely ever read a line of
any of them. No doubt, writing them did me good; but
they have been dry bones—very, very dry—ever since.

At the end of three years the charter of the London
University was extended to Highbury and other colleges, and
to meet the case of students who were in their last year the
matriculation or " Little-Go " examination was dispensed with.
I wished to secure this opportunity of taking my degree. So
did the occupant of the adjoining study. He was worthy
of his imposing name, Bernard Bolingbroke Woodward, a
relative of the eminent scientist. He was a good German
scholar, and seemed to have a vocation rather for the literary
path of usefulness than the pastoral. We agreed to " coach "
each other, and so, after reading during the week the same
subject, we spent Saturday evenings in a mutual written examination, each supplying to the other a list of questions,
omitting none we thought might possibly be asked. At the
close of the anxious days at Somerset House, we were
rewarded by finding our names in the First Class of the B.A.
candidates.

After a few years' pastorate, Woodward answered an
advertisement for Librarian at Windsor Castle, and was
honoured by a long interview with the Prince Consort.
Out of a multitude of applicants the Nonconformist
minister was chosen. I had the pleasure of seeing him
in the Royal Library. He told me of frequent visits of
the Prince, who thoroughly unbent in converse on all topics—
political, social, sacred. Woodward spoke enthusiastically of
the Prince's genuine goodness and broad catholicity.

He told me how the Princess Royal, in one of her visits,
asked to inspect the large collection of miniatures, and as the
face of Cromwell came into view she said, " Oh, Mr. Woodward,
you cannot like *that* man." He replied, " Your Royal Highness must know that my admiration and loyalty towards your
Royal Highness's mother are such that I cannot but reverence
the memory of the man to whose struggles for liberty we owe
the unspeakable blessedness of possessing such a monarch on
a constitutional throne."

Letter from B. B. Woodward.

" The Prince commanded the Baron Triqueti (who is the head of the
Protestant movement in France) to execute a statue, rather less than
life size, of Edward VI, and it now stands on the landing at the head
of the Queen's private staircase, looking into the grand corridor at
Windsor. It represents the young king standing with a Bible in his
left hand and his sceptre in his right, seeming to mark the passage he is
reading, and on the pages you can see these words—from 2 Kings
xxii. 1, 2—'Josiah was eight years old when he began to reign, and he
did that which was right in the sight of the Lord.' This was done for
the express purpose of keeping this example always before the eyes of
the heir to the throne.

" You refer to the inscription in front of the Royal Exchange : 'The
earth is the Lord's, and the fulness thereof.' The face of the square
block which now bears those words was blank, and the Prince inquired
if it was intended to use it for an inscription. Tite said it had not
occurred to them to use it, and then the Prince suggested the putting
on it of that most appropriate motto for the Exchange in London.

" Do you know the Psalm tunes composed by the Prince, published
by Nisbet? My *impression* was always that he was, in the truest
sense of the words, 'a religious man,' and it was from the truthfulness and general scope of his well-balanced life, and his gentle and
gracious demeanour—from a certain ground-level to all I saw—that
I received it."

Among other friends at college was Baldwin Brown, nephew of Dr. Raffles. He relinquished good prospects at the bar for the higher call to the ministry. I greatly valued his friendship to the close of his useful life. He was eloquent both by pulpit and press, and the author of well-known books such as "The Divine Life in Man" and "Pilgrimage of the Soul." He was always in the forefront of every battle for truth and freedom, and closed a too brief pastorate at Brixton, where he had gathered a large and influential congregation. Because entertaining hope that for those ignorant of Christ on earth there may be, in the exercise of the love of God, some influence of the Holy Spirit to lead them to repentance, some feared he had departed from the fundamental truth of the Atonement. I always felt sure that he never ceased to preach "Jesus Christ, and Him crucified," as the sinner's only hope.

Near to my study was that of Dr. Legge. It was his last year at college, and, as he had just been appointed to China by the London Missionary Society, he resolved as far as possible to master the language before going out. His study walls were covered with sheets of paper inscribed with Chinese characters. He allowed himself only four or five hours' sleep, and I feared his health would break down through his indefatigable labour. After many years of translation and missionary work in China, he had well earned the repose and dignity of an Oxford professorial chair, from which he was recently promoted to the eternal rest.

Another friend was De Kewer Williams, faithful as pastor, and well known and amusing as lecturer, overflowing with innocent humour, teaching that godliness does not mean gloom. Mr. Thomas Wilson, the founder and treasurer of the college, took a deep interest in all his students. "He yet speaketh" from the pulpits of churches he built and the pages of authors he was the means of training.

The Rev. James Sherman, of Surrey Chapel, and his cultured and godly wife, were dear friends to me. Earnest total abstainers, they frequently urged me to "take the pledge." I was fond of argumentation and tried to prove that my moderation was more influential than abstinence. Since then, during more than half a century, I have endeavoured to prove, not that taking a little, but that taking none, is the best example to persons whose moderation is the road to intemperance. One day, after a long discussion, my friend with "sweet reasonableness" said: "Do drop your logic. My dear wife has been praying for you that you may at least make trial of abstinence." I replied : "Who can resist a lady's prayers ? I'll try it for one month." I have been trying it ever since, with daily reason to bless God for constant capacity for service, and above all as the most effectual ally to the Gospel in doing good to the bodies and souls of men. This was in 1840, and now, in 1898, after nearly sixty years, I am increasingly convinced of the privilege—and in my case, as a preacher to the multitude, the duty—of personal abstinence from the greatest curse of our land and chief hindrance to the Gospel.

Edward Gilbert Cecil was my most precious acquisition in friendship while at college. He was related to the Cecil of the "Remains," and connected with Isaac Taylor, and the sisters Ann and Jane Taylor, authors of "Hymns for Infant Minds." Well versed in classical and English literature, I am grateful to him for revising many of my publications. I had the privilege of his company in visits to Switzerland and Italy. I called him my "walking encyclopædia." Like myself, one of the "older school," he appreciated the labours of modern critics. He usefully laboured as assistant to pastors Conder, Cousins, M'All, Samuel Martin, and myself, his memory being cherished with grateful honour. His preaching was scriptural and earnest, but he had not the gift called "popularity," which may exist without culture, learning, and eminent godliness. He was not invited to vacant pulpits as likely to "draw," but he never uttered a syllable of complaint, as if overlooked. The only harm he ever did me was to make me doubt the orthodox dogma of universal depravity. I often felt ashamed of my own popularity compared with his superiority in qualities recognised in a higher court, and I applied to him the words: "Many that are first shall be last, and the last first." Tried by this standard, I would gladly exchange with him.

His earthly end was like his life. When a telegram told me of his sudden illness, I hastened to his bedside. He grasped my hand, but he seemed gazing at what was beyond my vision. Until all vocal utterance ceased, he repeated favourite texts and the Benediction as if in a religious assembly; he sang snatches of favourite hymns, in which I joined, and often addressed favourite writers—"John Angell James, come near me; John Bunyan, come to me! come nearer!" and, calling on Jesus, he verified his favourite hymn—

> "And may the music of Thy Name
> Refresh my soul in death."

He responded once to me, when I repeated the text, "Fear not, for I am with thee——." He followed with, " I will hold thee by the right hand——." l sang the first verse of the hymn "There is a fountain filled with blood," and he joined in with, " The dying thief," with earnest but quavering voice for a few bars. He recognised no one after this. I sat on the bed holding his hand, but his spirit was "going on before." He peacefully passed away in sleep. On returning from his funeral I wrote the following :—

HALLELUJAH AT THE GRAVE.

> Although with mournful memories
>> We gather round the bier,
> The hope Thy word enkindles
>> Illumes the falling tear.
> They are not dead or distant,
>> But loving, serving more ;
> Such friends are never parted,
>> But only gone before.

> With dear ones reunited
>> They bend before the throne ;
> With angel-choirs their voices
>> The Lord of Glory own ;
> In holiness made perfect,
>> In rapturous tones they sing,
> With angel-choirs in chorus,
>> The praises of their King.

We join in adoration,
  Though gathered round the grave,
To Christ the Resurrection,
  Who life eternal gave;
We glorify, we bless Thee,
  Their Saviour Lord and ours,
With angels and archangels,
  And all the heavenly powers.

Some readers may think I have dwelt too long on my friend. Yes; if for his sake alone. But I have purposely given this sketch as representing thousands of others little known, saintly servants of Christ, both Nonconformists and curates and vicars in the Established Church, who during many years have lived in obscure villages or city slums, with inadequate incomes, with none of the encouragement of crowds, newspaper praise, and hopes of preferment, but satisfied with simply doing their duty in the service, not of men, but of the great High Priest and Bishop of the Church. There may be some, alas! whose great aim is position, advancement, emolument, laudation. "They (may) *have* their reward"; but the highest honour of all is to merit and receive the approval, "Well done, good and faithful servant!" Thanks be to God, not alone for celebrated servants, but still more for the vastly greater number of the unknown but equally faithful ones, with little earthly recompense, of whom it may be said, "Great is their reward in heaven."

During my four years at college I had the opportunity of hearing many famous London preachers of the day. I often walked to Camberwell, glad of a standing place in the aisle, to listen to Henry Melvill, whose elaborate rhetoric fascinated me for awhile. His delivery was so intensely earnest, and his voice so varied in its inflexions, that the preaching combined extemporaneous force with the correctness and beauty of careful composition. At the end of each climax his hearers broke silence by a chorus of coughs. I never witnessed such an effect by a written and read discourse. But it was *such* reading! the whole mind and heart finding utterance.

Other preachers were Baptist Noel, simple, graceful,

evangelical; Binney, an original thinker, a clever defender of the faith, addressing a very intellectual audience, chiefly of young men, in the old "Weigh House," giant champion of the old Gospel; James Parsons, when he "supplied" at Surrey Chapel, thronged by crowds intent on catching every sentence leading up to his carefully prepared climaxes, which used to be followed by a universal coughing and shifting of posture, all ready for the next "head"; and though at the time I shared in the delighted excitement, I do not think that his style would prove so attractive in these days. Sometimes I heard James Sherman discourse at Surrey Chapel to a vast congregation, of all classes of people, with unsurpassed tenderness, seldom without tears. Once when he had preached, with Dr. Winter Hamilton as a hearer, the latter asked if Mr. S. was suffering any ailment of the eyes. No! it was a natural weakness, and might be cured. "Do no such thing, brother; you'll lose half your popularity!" Mr. Sherman's aim was conversion and consolation, and in this "verily he had his reward." I also occasionally, on their visits to London, heard Jay of Bath, Raffles of Liverpool, and Winter Hamilton of Leeds.

"Billy Dawson," a Yorkshire farmer and Methodist local preacher, attracted vast crowds by his graphic illustrations. I remember hearing him discourse on "Weighed in the balances." He pictured the weighing of a variety of sinners in such a vivid manner that some of the people stood up to gaze as if they actually witnessed the weighing and heard the sentence. On another occasion he described a culprit in the condemned cell being visited by a succession of friends, one of whom brought him a new coat, another a dainty feast, a third a purse of gold, the poor man expostulating with each, asking what good these things could be to one who was to be hanged next day? Afterwards another visitor came announcing a free pardon! After examining the document, the prisoner exclaimed, "God bless the King!"—the preacher actually waving his own hat in the air as he shouted his joy and gratitude. Then he applied the parable, saying that some eagerly accepted the things that perish, perishing with

them, while indifferent to the eternal life procured for them
by King Jesus!

I frequently heard Dr. Leifchild when Craven Chapel used
to be thronged with thriving merchants and mechanics.
Though for the first half-hour scarcely audible, he gathered
force till at the end of the second half-hour he closed with a
thunderclap of voice that well-nigh shook the windows and
electrified the audience. Howard Hinton was a combination
of stern logic and tender emotion. I well remember once
hearing him for half an hour speak in a condensed, argumentative, critical style, without a trace of feeling, on the
Resurrection, and then, suddenly dilating on the blessedness
of possessing a risen, living Saviour, every eye was moistened
as he said, with deep emotion : " We have known what it is to
say, 'I had a son, a brother, a husband'; but we shall never
say, ' I *had* a Saviour.'"

I remember hearing Mr. Aitkin, father of the eminent
evangelistic preacher of to-day, in a Methodist chapel in the
East of London. He was so heated that he took off his coat
while preaching, and afterwards went among the crowd with
personal appeals. He spoke to myself, asking if I was saved.
To my reply that I hoped so, he said, " Don't be content with
hoping ; make *sure* of salvation."

We students used to compare notes at the supper-table on
Sunday evenings. I noticed how to each famous preacher
some special characteristic was assigned, either argumentative,
or exegetical, or rhetorical, or consolatory, and we knew what
sort of a sermon to expect from each. I thought whether,
instead of the same congregation going to various preachers,
each preacher should not try to give variety to his own people.
Thus it has been my endeavour, instead of cultivating one
style alone, to preach in various ways to my one congregation, always endeavouring to have a distinct aim with a
varied method in each service of the same day.

It is a fact that more than a hundred of my first
addresses at college had only one hearer, and that was
myself. I had a very painful sense of inability to speak
extemporaneously. I knew that frequently a minister is

called upon suddenly for an address when unable to respond with credit to himself or benefit to others. I resolved to fight this inaptitude. Directly after breakfast I locked myself in my study, placed my Bible on the mantelshelf, opened it at random, read out the first verse that caught my eye, and at once began to discourse on it as a text, keeping on during ten minutes without pausing. Of course, what I said was frequently far away from the text, with plenty of words and little thought, yet sometimes a train of meditation would be evolved, which I entered in a book. But this confession is not an apology for want of preparation or for empty verbosity. I never have preached or spoken by arrangement without careful forethought. This private exercise was merely to give facility when there was no time for preparation.

Students often preached at Union Chapel, Islington, on Sunday afternoon, in good old Mr. Lewis's time. I remember preaching there to domestic servants, and lamenting that we never heard of good resulting. About twenty years afterwards, when in America, preaching in some far-off city in the West, I had scarcely taken up my quarters when I was told a lady had brought me a basket of roses, and wished to speak to me. She said: "I remember hearing you preach to the young at Union Chapel; it was the means of my conversion, and I have brought these flowers as a tribute of gratitude!" I was deeply affected. She was a poor sempstress; the flowers must have cost her several shillings at that time of year. I have often told the story as an encouragement to preachers and teachers not to think God has failed to bless their work because they have not heard of any result. "Cast thy bread upon the waters: for thou shalt find it after many days." It may not be well for us to know all that God does by us; we might become vain, as if it were our own work, whereas it is God's, and every instance of good done should make us humble by the contrast between the great result and the poor performance.

Though "only a student," I was everywhere kindly received. The following slight exception proves the rule. I was appointed to take an afternoon service in the New Road, and, as I entered the vestry, a deacon encouraged me with : "This is too bad! Mr. A. was to have come, and they have again sent a student." I expressed my regret and explained I had only come because so ordered by the college. Not much encouraged by this greeting, I very likely made a poor deliverance. After service, the deacon kindly offered me a glass of wine, which I declined, saying I should be much obliged by a cup of tea, as I had to walk several miles to take an evening service in Lambeth. But this he was unable to give me as he must go home for his usual afternoon rest. So I marched on four miles to the immediate neighbourhood where I was to spend thirty-eight years of pastoral life.

Since my first attempt at outdoor preaching to hoppickers at Maidstone, I had not ventured again; but a request came from the deacons of Craven Chapel for a student to conduct an afternoon service on the site of the future Great Western railway station. I went in my turn, and remember the preceding sleepless night. After dinner at Mr. Cutting's, in Oxford Street, I was marched along with a friend holding each arm. On reaching the place of "execution," I found a small pulpit from which to hold forth to a small but increasing company. These open-air services soon became a great delight.

One of my first regular sermons as a student was at my native town, Maidstone, in the Town Hall, on occasion of the Queen's Coronation in 1837. My text was : "King of kings and Lord of lords." From the same text I preached on the occasion of the Diamond Jubilee, June 20th, 1897, and I have been spared to proclaim the reign of Christ till now [June, 1898]. On a very cold Saturday I had to go to Colchester outside the stage coach. After several hours I arrived almost frozen, and was introduced into a room full of good people invited to look at the young preacher. They wanted a pastor, but I was in no mood to make myself agreeable. I sat close to the fire and was long getting thawed. I received for my two sermons just enough to pay for my outside fare. I hope that students are better paid now. Recognition of service is much needed by students, who often find it very difficult to meet their personal expenses. When I had to preach at Welling there were only about twenty people at the morning service. I resolved not to preach to empty pews in the evening, so I spent all the afternoon in calling from door to door, saying I had come from London to preach to them, and hoped they would come and hear me. The chapel was crammed at the evening service.

On one of the college vacations I was sent to preach several Sundays at Dover. I told some of the people that I intended to preach on the pier to sailors and fishermen. Some of the officials hoped I would not do it, because some of their congregation considered it not at all reputable. I asked, "Who thinks so ?" There was some difficulty in giving any names, but at length they said : "The Misses So-and-So," fashionable young ladies. I called on them and asked why they thought so. They said : " Oh, we do not ourselves object, we only fear others may." Though they declined to give me names, they consented to join me on the pier and lead the singing. Soon after I was invited to preach at Paddington Chapel, then regarded as one of the most "aristocratic" of the Independents. A lady said to a friend : "We had Newman Hall to preach. All well enough for Dover Pier, but it won't do for Paddington Chapel ! " I have never preached to please either rich or poor, but to be "understanded" of all the people, and to invite all alike to the Gospel feast.

Bathing one day at Dover, I was in some danger. A friend agreed to go with me when there was a rough sea. The breakers rolled in upon the pebbly beach with great force. We dived through the body of the water and enjoyed our swim outside the surf. My companion, who had landed and was dressing, shouted a warning, and I saw an immense wave just curling beyond me. Too late for the safety dive, I was whirled about in the surf utterly helpless, till I was violently dashed face downwards on the pebbles. Though almost stunned, I was sufficiently sensible to remember

E

that the return rush of water might carry me back into the
angry cauldron, and so I plunged my fingers amongst the
pebbles for an anchor, and then scrambled up into safety.

I was very fond of a boat when the weather was too rough
for other people. One Saturday, when my boatmen were
watching a chance to push through the waves, a deacon of
the church begged me not to risk my life, or, at least, to
postpone my venture *till after Sunday,* when I was expected
to preach.

At Plymouth my ministry was again in danger of abrupt
termination. I was announced to preach on Good Friday
evening at Devonport for Mr. Pyne. With his son and
another young man (Derry) I walked over Dartmoor, and
took boat on the Tamar, where it is very narrow. We pulled
easily down stream till encountered by a strong tide and contrary wind. During an hour or more we made scarcely any
progress, and evening was coming on. When we reached a
wider channel we hoisted sail, which our boatman managed,
my companions pulling and I steering. Under the lee of a
great man-of-war we avoided the gale, which, as we emerged
from the bows, filled our sail and put our gunwale almost
under water. The boatman's " Down with the helm ! " was
misunderstood ; he tried to let go the "sheet," but it had been
made fast ; he struggled to get out his knife, when the boat
righted just in time. Many were on the quay anxiously watching us. The pastor was there, of whom I inquired where the
crowd were going so fast. " To hear you preach." I begged
him to commence at once—with a long hymn, long lesson,
and long prayer ; for I was soaked, weary, and hungry, but
would be at church very soon. I preached under the solemn
but thankful feeling that, though an hour before I might have
been in eternity, I was still spared to proclaim eternal life.

Sir Culling Smith, Bart., was interested in an association
for the purpose of promoting Evangelical preaching on a
catholic basis, apart from any distinct denomination. He
designated it " The Evangelical Voluntary Church Association." He practically seceded from the Established Church,
and erected a preaching tent in his own grounds, Bedwell

Park. At Highbury College anniversary he was interested in an essay I read on "Sensation and Perception," and invited me to his house and to occupy his pulpit on two Sundays. Here I first met the Hon. W. Cowper, with whom I recently renewed my acquaintance as Lord Mount Temple at a religious conference. When Sir Culling Smith left Bedwell Park for Belvedere, Erith, he, now as Sir C. Eardley, erected a beautiful little church on the same principles, which Mr. Binney opened, and at which Established and Free Church clergymen for some time ministered in turns; but the movement halted, and after his death an Episcopal church, limited to one order, took its place, and is well used and attended.

When I had yet two more years for college, I visited Oxford, where I preached several Sundays in the Congregational Church, and was asked to become the pastor; but I declined to leave college till my term expired. For the same reason I declined a very tempting offer to be assistant to Mr. Sortain at Brighton, taking the afternoon service, and enjoying the privilege of the friendship and assistance in study of this eminent and popular clergyman of the Countess of Huntingdon's Connexion. Although offered £200 to begin with (very much for a student), I reluctantly declined it, that my studies might not suffer.

Some of our students went on several occasions to meetings of atheists and secularists. One very prominent leader proclaimed man's non-responsibility, asserting that every person's "will" was governed by circumstances, so that no one merited either praise or blame. One of us—it may have been myself —retorted that a murderer was therefore not to be punished or even censured. "In fact, you put the dagger into his hand and applaud him for using it as he pleases." At this a great clamour of indignation arose—hissing and groaning. After a short interval one of our number said, "Gentlemen, you are converted to our opinion; for you have just punished us for what your advocate says we could not help." This was at once appreciated, and followed by hearty applause.

Sometimes we students happened to hear one another, and I regret that we sometimes gave way to criticism and even to smiles. I remember my own failure in this respect. The youthful orator was drawing a terrible picture of sin, which he said would hereafter rise up as a mountain to overwhelm the sinner—" as high as heaven and as black as—as black as" —(he evidently felt afraid to utter his climax, " hell," so he paused to find some gentler word)—" as black as—as black as —as it possibly can be."

My college life closed with a knapsack tour in the Highlands with my old friend and schoolfellow at Totteridge, Nathaniel Jennings. We first visited Melrose Abbey. I had frequently heard my mother read " Marmion," and had been deeply impressed by the narrative of Michael Scott, the magician—how he was buried in the chancel under a big stone, and how, when the clock struck one, he appeared—to all who saw him ! I had never seen a ghost, and resolved to give myself the chance. My friend preferred a good night's sleep. So I went alone, furnished with a club, and locked myself within the abbey. The long, lingering twilight deepened the shadows and intensified the beauty. I paced the moss-carpeted aisles and wandered among the foliated columns. The fateful hour approached. I seated myself on the tombstone. Minute after minute slowly crept along. Then solemnly the clock tolled ONE ! The stone did not move—not the slightest vibration ! Michael Scott came not to threaten or to laugh. I unlocked the gate, and was soon in bed and asleep. At this distance of time I could imagine it a dream ; but it was a reality for which I deserve the laugh which this narration evokes.

We did the customary clambers or walks up Lomond, Ledi, Venue, and other "Bens," according to guide-books. On Schiehallion we lost our bearings, wandered about the uninhabited wilderness, and were glad to appease hunger by devouring some grouse-eggs. Late in the evening we stretched ourselves for rest on the floor of a solitary hut. In the Trossachs we were shown the identical spot where the "gallant grey" of FitzJames fell dead, and on Loch Katrine the silver strand of the Lady of the Lake, whose footprints on the shore had unfortunately disappeared.

On Ben Nevis our boy-guide only knew the way we climbed up. As we wanted to descend in the contrary direction, I undertook the guidance of the party by following the first stream in that direction, and thus scrambling, wading, sliding on our backs, we quickly reached the bottom. In later years I have exulted in wandering on Goat Fell in Arran and among the crags of Skye.

I include here some memories of a subsequent visit to Edinburgh. During my college sojourn in London I heard Dr. Chalmers deliver a lecture in Hanover Square in defence of Church Establishment, in the presence of several bishops, when prelatical priests applauded to the echo a Presbyterian pastor advocating a principle from which he soon after found himself practically in revolt. The Free Church secession had just begun when I breakfasted at his house in company with an elder learned in the law. All through the meal the great divine and the clever lawyer discussed Church temporalities, the sum already subscribed, and persons who might hopefully be solicited. I was astounded at the particular knowledge of items displayed by this master of philosophy. The combination of diligence in business with fervour of spirit was strikingly exhibited at the close of family prayer. He had been very fervent, foot and hand helping in the emphasis of his tongue. I remember a single clause: "May every morning that dawns and every evening that darkens remind us of our frailty!" When he came to the doxology he began to rise, and before he was on his feet, and with the same breath as that with which he had said, "For ever and ever, Amen," he exclaimed, "Mary! did ye put that letter in the post?"

I once witnessed another phase of prompt evolution of practical out of devotional religion in Scotch sheep-dogs on a Communion Sabbath among the mountains. The churchyard was crowded with shepherds accompanied by their dogs, which lay quietly asleep at the feet of their masters. The sermon was finished, the psalm had been sung, the final prayer was being offered, and there was no sign of impatience; but at the moment the benediction commenced the devotional doggies all roused themselves, and before the " Amen " they were in marching order.

My friend Dr. Guthrie told me with great humour the following incident : "A clergyman neighbour to Dr. Chalmers at Morningside once asked him to be so good, if ever he purposed to honour him by visiting his church, to inform him beforehand that he might not feel discomposed by seeing him enter without having made due preparation. The warning was in due course given. The preacher prepared his sermon with special care, and committed it to memory ; but in course of delivery memory suddenly failed ! After a few seconds the thread of discourse was recovered, and the preacher went on to the end with unhesitating fervour. Not long afterwards, meeting him in the street, Chalmers accosted him with, ' Cultivate the pause, brother ! Cultivate the pause ! ' Great was the preacher's chagrin, thinking that the Doctor meant to ridicule him. Again they met, and again the same advice was given. The preacher could bear it no longer, and besought the Doctor to spare his feelings, already too much wounded. The Doctor then assured him he meant praise and not censure. ' I thought it a fine piece of oratory ; and I say, again : Cultivate the pause ! ' " Some preaching is such an impetuous tide of words, or such a dreary, continuous monotone, that a pause here and there would be an immense relief to preacher and hearer, and add to the impressiveness of the discourse.

I remember hearing Dr. Guthrie humorously refer to the objection to his zeal in raising the " Sustentation Fund " for the Free Church clergy. In the early Church holy men of God went about clothed in " sheepskins and goatskins," and why should they not do so still ? " Just fancy Dr. Candlish and myself walking along Princes Street, Edinburgh, I in a sheepskin and *he in a goatskin !* "

In reference to his very illustrative method of preaching, he told me that in his first country parish, when he gathered the young people round him in a class, and questioned them about the sermon, they always remembered the truth that he had illustrated. " Therefore," said he, " I determined that whenever I specially wished some lesson to be well remembered and stick, I would 'wing it.'" He says of illustration: "By gratifying the imagination, the truth finds its way more readily to the heart, and makes a deeper impression on the memory. The story, like a float, keeps it from sinking; like a nail, fastens it in the mind; like the feathers of an arrow, makes it strike; and, like the barb, makes it stick." He used illustrations on his death-bed at Hastings. He asked for a small mirror to look at himself, to see, by his wasted features, how much nearer his vessel was getting towards port, as a sailor looks through his telescope at the harbour he is approaching.

On a Sunday afternoon I walked to Calton Hill, and, being impressed with the multitude of people sauntering about, was sorry that none of the clergy of the city were there to take advantage of the concourse. I felt an inward impulse to do it myself; but I had no one with me to help. Still I could not disobey the call, so I mounted a stone and gave an address on my old text, " God so loved the world," to a multitude who had soon gathered. When I had finished, some man said to me, " Young man, it will take you a long time to persuade Edinburgh people that Christ died for everyone." That was all the encouragement I received. Five-and-twenty years had passed away, when I was taking part in jubilee services of Sunday schools at Glasgow. As the speakers were passing into the great hall, a clergyman whispered to me: " Do you · remember, years ago, preaching on Calton Hill one Sunday afternoon? I was one of your hearers. It led me to Christ. I am now labouring in a poor and populous parish in Glasgow, trying to induce sinners to come to Jesus." He disappeared in the crowd; but here was another illustration of the promise, " *after many days.*"

Brothers and sisters are within the range of personal remembrances. Before entering on the record of my public life I may here recall the companions of my childhood's home.

My eldest brother, Edward Pickard, for several years was

editor of my father's paper, the *Maidstone Journal,* a strong advocate of " Church and State." His taste for liturgical worship and intimacy with the three Wilberforces at Farleigh, Robert, Samuel, and Henry, led him into full communion with the Church of England. By invitation of the governors of the Oxford University Press, he became one of the managing partners, and devoted his brief leisure to the mental and religious improvement of the boys and workmen. The University conferred on him the honorary degree of M.A., and, recalling his youthful drilling of his younger brothers, in full uniform he led a company of Oxford volunteers as captain. So I beheld him at the grand volunteer review at Brighton.

He bequeathed his example to his children. Of his sons, one was for twelve years Precentor and Sacrist of Worcester Cathedral, and is now Rector of Bromsgrove; another achieved a high position as magistrate in the Indian Civil Service, and after twenty years has retired on a pension; another won a scholarship at Merton College, and took a " double first "; another took honours at Oxford, and is Fellow and Tutor of his college. One daughter was for several years head-mistress of the High School, Exeter, and is now doing mission work as a Sister among poor women in South London; another daughter died at her post as nurse at St. Mary's Hospital, Paddington, the medical staff placing a window to her memory in the chapel.

My second brother, Stephen, after being for several years a merchant captain in the East, devoted time and income in benevolent zeal as member of a Congregational church. When one day summoned to dinner, he was found kneeling in the summer-house, lifeless, in the attitude of prayer.

My third brother, John Vine, had an early passion for the sea. I remember how our father took me with him to go on board his first ship, the *Inglis* (East India Company), and how I admired his uniform with the dirk in his belt, the exciting climb up the mountainous side of a ship of 1,800 tons, and dining with Captain Dudman, who was surprised that so

young a boy could take "observations" correctly. His next
voyage was as a junior officer on the *Lord Amherst,* which,
during a heavy gale and tide, was cast high and dry, with
broken back, on the Hoogly, when he aided the captain in
cutting away the masts. At the merging of the "Company"
in the Empire, he became commander of a small vessel, in
which my younger brother Arthur was a "middy," who has
related to me how one day, in the Mediterranean, the captain,
having observed a sudden fall in the barometer, ordered all
sails to be reefed. The crew were astonished, because
they felt no wind and saw no ripple. Another vessel was
in sight under full sail. Soon a little cloud arose, "like a
man's hand," and overcast the sky. A white mist of foam
covered the distant sea. Presently the tempest burst, the
bare masts bent as reeds, lightning ran along the deck, the
sea was laid level by the blast, for as soon as a wave tried to
rise, the crest was carried off in spray. It was, indeed,
the "white squall." When it passed, the other vessel had
disappeared.

There was a worse storm, for a mutiny was brewing, owing
to hatred of the chief mate. Arthur was sweeping the
quarter-deck. An ominous group of sailors was approaching.
The captain knew what it meant, but with deepening frown
kept pacing to and fro. The leader now touched the
quarter-deck, one step across which meant mutiny. In a
moment the captain snatched the broom-handle from the
midshipman and with one blow levelled the leader. All the
rest, cowed by his bravery, submitted. The ship and lives
of the officers were thus saved.

The following occurrence I have heard him minutely
describe. He was captain of the large ship *Crœsus,* carrying
the first detachment of Italian troops to the Crimea. A day
or two after leaving Genoa it was ascertained that by spontaneous combustion the coal-store was on fire. The captain
searched the distant coast with his telescope, and discovered a
spot where there appeared to be an opening in the cliff. To
this he steered. It was a race with time. Troops and passen-
gers were stationed forward, so that the smoke and scorching

fumes were carried astern. Just before it became impossible to work the engines, the ship grounded in the snug cove. Then in good order boat after boat landed the soldiers safely; then the crew. The captain was, of course, the last; the only property he carried away being his favourite canary bird. He had scarcely reached shore when the great ship burst forth into flame from stem to stern. He received much commendation for his conduct in thus saving the lives of crew and soldiers.

After a short interval he was invited to take command of the *Great Eastern* on her first voyage across the Atlantic. He had a grand reception at New York, multitudes of vessels going out to convoy to harbour the biggest vessel ever yet afloat. A few years were now spent in quiet retirement. For some time he attended a church near him, but the Athanasian Creed drove him some distance to the Presbyterian Church, where he greatly profited by the ministry and friendship of my beloved and widely-honoured friend, Dr. Monro Gibson. He was a great reader, and spoke four languages. He played the flute and concertina with much taste, and has left many portfolios of sketches both in pencil and water-colours. Towards the end, he read nothing but the Bible, "Pilgrim's Progress," and his father's autobiography. He closed his long voyage in the calm of faith and hope.

My brother Arthur has written a graphic sketch of part of his earlier life under the title of "*I Will;* or, The Boy who Would Go to Sea." At one time he was greatly in danger from bad companionship, but says that the mere thought of his parents, and his certainty of the truth of religion, as seen in their consistent lives, often held him back when near the precipice. I have elsewhere related how his adoption of total abstinence was the beginning of a religious life. He left a profitable business to preach the Gospel. After toiling successfully in raising up to prosperity several struggling congregations at Luddenden Foot, Edmonton, Tolmers Square, and Craven Chapel, he is now pastor of a Congregational church in Hastings. His eldest son is minister of a church in Cape Town, and was recently Chairman of the South African Union. He lately published a poem on "Table Mountain," which at once obtained a large circulation.

My younger brother, Warren, was for some years an active deacon of his intimate friend, the venerable and beloved Joshua Harrison, and is a zealous promoter of the London City Mission. His "Caxton Press" is a small Tract Society in itself, having sent forth half a million copies of my works and of others. His son, William Newman, is pastor of the Congregational church, Dublin, of which Dr. Urwick used to be the minister.

My sisters married two brothers of the name of Allnutt. One of these is rector of a small village in Suffolk, and one of their children is a minister of the Episcopal Church in Australia. My other sister, Mary, lived several years at Chilworth, a small village in Surrey, where she opened her house every Sunday evening as a Sunday school, and after teaching the children she held a devotional service for the villagers, to whom she habitually ministered both in body and mind. She also has a son rector of a parish in Australia. I mention these particulars to show how the prayers my parents offered daily for years that their children might be truly "converted" and be servants of Christ have been answered to children and to "children's children." It is my confidence that those parents in glory rejoice that all have chosen the "narrow way that leadeth unto life."

Two years before my birth the following letter was sent by the Rev. Rowland Hill to the town where I commenced my ministry, and from which I went to occupy his pulpit at Surrey Chapel:—

"*To William Bowden, Esq., Hull.*

"My dear Sir,—I should certainly have accepted your very friendly and affectionate invitation to Hull had Providence directed me further towards the North. But our Northern brethren conceive that the ground is so fully occupied, and so much has already been done on behalf of the Missionary Society, that an additional visit just at present would be deemed an unpleasant intrusion on the generosity they have already displayed.

"It is well to be enabled to follow the cloud of Divine Providence wherever it moves ; it is a cloud that leads well and drops fatness as it moves.

"I am somewhat the less anxious to visit Hull as perhaps there is not a town in the kingdom more highly favoured with the privileges of the Gospel than that favoured spot.　Still, it is pleasant to visit those places where the Divine Presence seems to be vouchsafed.　O for the time when all that is designed in that great prayer may be more fully answered!—'Thy Kingdom come'—when the kingdoms of the earth shall become the kingdoms of the Lord and His Christ.

"I am, dear Sir,

"Yours very affectionately,

"R. HILL.

"Surrey Ch., Ap. 21, 1814."

CHAPTER V.

In 1842 I preached on several Sundays at Sheffield, with
some view to the pastorate. I was boarded in a small house,
the entrance to which was direct from the street into
my sitting-room, which, on a Saturday evening, was suddenly entered by two deacons, who respectfully asked me to
preach a sermon on "doctrine," as this was much desired by
some of the people. I told them I had been doing nothing
else—the doctrines of repentance, faith, prayer, and good
works. They still asked for "doctrine," by which they meant
" election."

Next morning I took for my text, " Elect according to the
foreknowledge of God the Father, through sanctification of
the Spirit, unto obedience " (1 Peter i. 2). I pointed out that
Christians are elected to obedience by the help of the Spirit,
which we are commanded to pray for, and therefore God thus
invites everyone to become elect. Two prominent members
rose, and, shutting their pew-door sharply, marched out of
church. That congregation in a few days invited me to be
their pastor.

An urgent request came from the deacons of the new
"Albion Church " at Hull to help at the opening services
on the next Sunday, in place of my friend, Mr. Sherman, who
was unwell. The other two preachers were Thomas Binney
and Winter Hamilton. I felt appalled at the idea of preaching
in their presence, and was tempted to write a sermon fit for
their special approval rather than thinking of the 1,500 people
who needed plain, practical Gospel. I retired early, and laboured
hard to prepare my grand sermon. But in vain. Thoughts
would not come; pen refused ornate expression; I could not
ask God's blessing. Hour after hour struck, and I said, " No,
it won't do. I can't prepare it, and if I did, I could not preach

it." So I cast my unfinished manuscript aside, and selected the notes of one of my very simplest sermons—"Enter ye in at the strait gate."

There was a densely-packed church to see the new building and hear the young preacher. In the desire to be useful I forgot the two great divines. Three members of a family who became afterwards most useful supporters of my ministry were, by means of that sermon, induced to "strive." I preached twice more during the week, and on the following Sunday. On the departure platform next day the deacons met me with a unanimous and cordial invitation to become their first pastor. This step may appear too hasty; but the deacons had made careful inquiry of the authorities of the College and of others. On reaching Sheffield, the deacons of the church there were waiting to welcome me with a similar invitation; and when I reached London, a third came to me from Craven Chapel. As I had been visiting the churches during a whole year, everywhere welcomed but nowhere "called," other students who have waited long for a settlement may be encouraged.

I had often said to myself that I could not live away from hills, and during my few first days in Hull felt that I could not be happy in a smoky, damp town, built on a marsh, on the flat shore of a broad, muddy estuary.

The building, resembling a Doric temple, was somewhat imposing in appearance, with sittings for 1,600 people. There was a building debt of £8,000 and a membership of only forty-two. This was a formidable difficulty for a young man fresh from college. But the opportunities of usefulness in the midst of a great population, a first pastor's freedom in moving on his own lines, and the fact that this was my first actual call, induced me, after prayer and counsel, to accept the invitation.

My ordination was on July 13th. Albion Church was crowded. After suitable prayers and hymns, an address was given on the nature of a Christian church and of the pastoral office. Then, standing near my parents in the body of the church, I answered questions put to me from the pulpit on my creed, conversion, and motives. Then one of the deacons declared the full accord of all the members in the invitation, and the concurrent approval of the ordaining presbyters. I knelt in front of the pulpit surrounded by them, while special prayer was offered "with the laying on of the hands of the presbytery." Among these ordaining elders were Dr. L. Alexander, of Edinburgh; Dr. Winter Hamilton, Thomas James, my pastor, E. Jenkings; Thomas Stratten, pastor of the old Congregational church; and James Sibree, of Hull, and other neighbouring pastors. After the prayer of consecration, they gave me the right hand of fellowship. Then a solemn "charge" was addressed to me on the duties, responsibilities, and encouragements of the ministry. The doxology closed a very solemn service of three hours.

I do not question the validity of other modes of introduction to the ministry—whether Episcopal, Methodist, or Presbyterian—but when for any other method is claimed *exclusive* validity, I ask whether such a procedure as this does not also demand recognition.

It is not claimed that every part of the ceremonial should correspond with this example, or that any other should be condemned as invalid; but we do claim that those whose conviction of a Divine call is assented to by a congregation of believers, and confirmed by Divine co-operation in the conversion of sinners and the edification of saints, need have no qualms of conscience as to the validity of their ordination. In my own case, having had frequent opportunities of accepting other ordination, offering worldly advantages, I have felt I should dishonour God and my own conscience by appearing to disown what I had received from the Great Head of the Church, even as I would not wish to induce any brother in the ministry of any Church thus to stultify his own position. It must be a great help to any minister in his arduous work to be convinced that he has been duly called, and has become associated in the brotherhood of all ministers of the Universal Church. How can the real unity of the Churches be demonstrated if any one section denies the orders of all the rest?

The sermon preached to the congregation by Dr. Winter Hamilton deserves record. His text was, "He shall receive of you his standing," in which he showed that while there is truth in the saying, " Like priest, like people," so the reverse is true, for the spirituality, prayerfulness, zeal, and catholicity of the people are sure to encourage similar virtues in the pastor.

Having been then ordained, I commenced my regular pastoral work the following Sunday, preaching from the words, " Brethren, pray for us ! " and " For I determined not to know anything among you, save Jesus Christ, and Him crucified." This has been my determination ever since. I have endeavoured to teach " the whole counsel of God," but the dominant note has been the atoning and ruling Saviour. I have sought and found in the Word of God an inexhaustible variety ; but I have felt that there is no phase of Gospel truth which does not shine in the light of the Cross, and I have during these sixty years never consciously omitted from the discourse such reference to Christ as might by the Divine blessing direct to Himself a soul ignorant or careless of salvation.

It is said of the celebrated Puritan divine, Andrew Fuller, that a young preacher, having preached an eloquent sermon, asked his opinion of it, to which the faithful veteran said, "Very grand, but no Gospel." " But, sir, it was not in the text ! " He responded, " There is no lane in the land which does not lead into the King's highway ! " I was one day thanked for a sermon on " The Cross " by an American gentleman, who said, " As a lawyer, my opinion is that the Gospel without atonement is illogical. It is like telling a man to lift himself from the ground by pulling at his own boot-tags ! "

In America they call the congregation of " communicants " the parish. Mine was a very small one, only forty-two. At first the novelty attracted all sorts of people, aisles and pulpit stairs being crowded ; but when novelty ceased the church continued to be crowded at the evening service throughout twelve years, and increased in the morning from 500 to 1,000. The membership rapidly multiplied. Many divided their favours. A certain " professor " of haircutting boasted that in the morning he " patronised High Church and in the evening Newman Hall." Several eminent citizens came regularly, with sundry " Jews, Turks, infidels," and some Roman Catholics. But I studiously avoided controversy, always preaching the positive truths of the Gospel.

The "King's Town," on the little river Hull, flowing into the Humber, was built below highest tide level, when the surrounding region was a marsh. The old walls, whose gates were closed by Sir John Hotham, by command of the Parliament, against the King, exist only in the docks and quays which occupy their site. Within their small compass are some handsome old mansions on the bank of the river, which was the ancient port, once occupied by thriving merchants, one of them by the parents of William Wilberforce—his birthplace—in memory of whom an imposing monument fronts the entrance to the old town from the populous and ever-spreading suburbs towards the west and north. One of the old streets bears its ancient name, " The Land of Green Ginger." In the centre is the grand old parish church, of which Andrew Marvel's father was rector, near which is Fish Street Independent Church, the oldest of that denomination, of which the Rev. Thomas Stratten was the honoured pastor during my twelve years' ministry at Hull. From this church, and with his benediction, went forth the small colony to found the new church where I preached on the day of its consecration.

The prime mover of this effort of Church extension outside the walls was Sir William Lowthrop, a former mayor, a chief magistrate, and my senior deacon, wise in counsel and distinguished by devotional zeal and generosity. Three others, likeminded merchants and shipowners, supported him by their influence and contributions. Persons in humbler condition made up the forty-two, who were brave enough to build a large church with 1,500 sittings at a cost of some £12,000.

Soon after my ordination Dr. Candlish and other Scottish clergy came to seek English sympathy in their great struggle for Church freedom. They had not objected to " Establishment," but they contended for the ancient rights of congregations to appoint their own pastors. This claim was rejected, and the majority of the clergy and their congregations, under

F

the leadership of their most eminent preachers—Chalmers, Candlish, Guthrie, and others—seceded, advocating "the Crown Rights of the Redeemer," by which they meant the liberty and duty of the Church of Christ, a spiritual kingdom, to appoint its own ceremonial, and ordain its own pastors and elders.

This secession demanded no less a sacrifice than the surrender of all their churches, manses, and colleges, thus necessitating voluntary contributions for rebuilding and maintenance. They thus were led to see that State control was inseparable from State support. The response of the nation was immediate. The "Free Church" has covered the whole of Scotland with places of worship and supplied with a learned, evangelical, and devoted ministry, not only towns and cities, but small villages and highland glens. It was a great privilege, so early in my ministry, to open our pulpit for their deputation.

I had been only a few weeks pastor of Albion Church when I was preserved from sudden death in it. My vestry was lighted by a very massive brass chandelier, suspended from the ceiling. In the centre of its four branches was a ponderous, sharp-pointed pendant. One evening I was writing beneath this, when the whole machinery suddenly fell on the table, the head of the battering-ram just grazing my nose, instead of splitting my skull. I thank God for a protecting Providence which prevented such sudden termination of my ministry; and I also thank God for hundreds of other providences, protecting me, not only from accidents, but from alarm. A man once expressed to me his wondering gratitude at Divine intervention, in that, though thrown down that morning by a cab, the wheel of which nearly passed over his head, he was still alive and well. I replied, " You are rightly grateful; and I also am grateful, because this day I have not only escaped being run over, but escaped the shock you have experienced."

Not long after the building was opened I observed some ominous cracks in the wide ceiling of sixty feet span. Then I observed a downward curve, and measured day by day an increasing depression. One Saturday morning a large piece of cement fell into the middle aisle. I at once secured the largest hall in the town and sent out notices that services would be held there next day. Surveyors found that in order to conform to Greek architecture the roof was too flat, and failed to achieve structural safety. Too little downward pressure was thrown on the walls; too much was demanded of the queen-posts, the heads of which were being crushed, and in a short time the whole roof would have fallen in, possibly during service, with the destruction of hundreds of people.

The cost of restoration was formidable. There was a building debt of £6,000, the interest on which was £300. The incidental expenses were upwards of £250. The stipend assured to me was £300. Without consultation I announced that I would take no more salary from the funds, but trust to my people. This at once made us solvent, with a little margin, after paying interest and all expenses. We also established a weekly offering at the doors after every service towards debt extinction. No one was pressed to subscribe, but in the most generous way, by the poorest as well as others, my personal income at once amounted to as much as previously. There was soon no further need of the extra pastoral fund, and the stipend rose gradually to about £600.

The first use I made of this was to repay to my college the cost of my board for four years. I do not regard this as any generosity, but simple payment of debt. If this were generally done in after-years by students at colleges and scholars at orphanages, there would not be so much need of the help of outsiders.

I did not postpone Open-air Preaching, but there were such long deliberations of committee, arranging times and places, and so on, that the season for such services was quickly passing; so I one day said to my verger, " Come with me, and let us hold a service in the slums near." So without prearranged method we went into an obscure street, and began a hymn-duet. A fashionable young surgeon of my acquaintance drove past in his gig, and was amused at seeing me performing to a small group of children. He smiled good-humouredly, driving on, and we two, parson and clerk, smiled also and sang on. This little one became a thousand as the commencement of regular open-air services, which continued throughout the whole of my pastorate. Vast numbers of artisans and others, who seldom entered any place of worship, thus heard the Gospel, and many became attendants at various churches.

A neighbouring Evangelical Rector wished to do the same, and wrote for sanction to his Bishop, who replied that he was sorry the question had been asked, for he would not have objected, but, his sanction being asked, he felt obliged to withhold it.

To one of such open-air services may be ascribed instrumentally my little book entitled "Come to Jesus," the origin of which I have often been asked to explain. After our annual missionary meetings a dinner was given by a wealthy merchant to the "deputation" and local clergy. After dinner clay pipes were brought in and whisky toddy. My next neighbour at table, a Presbyterian clergyman, was, like myself, an abstainer both from alcohol and tobacco ; so after politely remaining an hour, we thought that we might quietly escape from uncongenial smoke and savour. I do not suggest that there was any approach to intemperance. All present were godly men, and their mode of enjoyment was not considered inconsistent with the clerical office. On walking away, we went through a very poor district, and we proposed that, as we had been at a missionary dinner, it would be suitable to have a missionary dessert. So I borrowed a wooden chair, and we began a hymn, which attracted a number of children, whose attention was soon won by the story of Jesus. Women who had been listening from their windows now gathered, curious to know what we were saying to their little ones. Some men now joined the group, and I proposed to sing a sacred ditty, well known to the Primitive Methodists, the chief workers among the poor— "Come to Jesus, just now! Come to Jesus, He is willing. Come to Jesus—Hallelujah," and so on. My address was suggested by the hymn. "Come to Jesus. Who is He?" God! Man! "Where is Jesus?" In heaven; here! "How come?" By prayer

"Why?" To be forgiven—made good, made happy, and get to heaven hereafter. "Who should come?" The rich, the poor, the old, the young. "When?" Now!

The people listened intently. As I came away I said, "That shall be my subject next Sunday evening—'Come unto Me.'" I had never heard of such a sermon, with above twenty heads and divisions for a large and intelligent congregation. But it was received with attention, and was instructive to the preacher in cultivating condensation.

Soon after this I suffered from the only serious disease of my life. When convalescent, I said to myself that had I died I should have left in print tracts on temperance and Christian union alone. I ought to write a Gospel tract of invitation to the Saviour, after the method of my father's "Sinner's Friend." It should be of the same size, sixty-four—twice thirty-two pages; on every double page one complete chapter, each consisting of just so many lines. I resolved that I would write one of these daily. On counting up the words, I often found twice too many. Then there was the amusing recreation of abbreviating sentences, substituting short words for long, Saxon for Latin, and banishing repetitions, till the page was reduced to its proper size.

I used to read the result of the day's work to my delighted parents each evening, and then committed my booklet to the printers, venturing to order 2,000 copies at threepence, half of which I would give away, and the other half my congregation would purchase. The tract was neither advertised nor commended in the press. To my astonishment, within a month, an order came from Mr. Snow, the London publisher, for 10,000 copies, and before long there were issues of 100,000 to supply a demand by wealthy Evangelical people, who said it was just what they needed for general distribution. Thus the circulation extended till the tract became known abroad and was translated into all the languages of the Continent without any act of mine. Then foreign missionaries translated it, saying the style was so simple that its transference was comparatively easy, and the mode of presenting the Gospel plain. The reproduction is free to all countries, also to the Religious Tract

Society and the Stirling Tract Society in leaflets, and it is now in use in most of the lands where the Bible is circulated in native languages. It has been printed in vast numbers in the United States of America. As far as I can ascertain, I believe the circulation has reached four millions, in about forty languages, including English, Welsh, French, German, Spanish, Dutch, Russian, Italian, Polish, Greek, Arabic, Tamil, Telugu, Hindi, Turkish, Chinese, Norwegian, Kalabar, and Malagasy.

When at Hull I was informed, soon after its publication, that " Come to Jesus" was read in the Royal nursery by the special desire of the Queen. My informant, who had lately married a Lutheran clergyman in Hull, had been German governess to the Royal children, and was treated as a personal friend by her Majesty. Rich and poor thus meet together. No credit is due to the writer. It needed no research, it cost very little trouble, it was merely the utterance of the simplest truths, the spontaneous expression of the writer's own experience, and the substance of his constant ministry. But in this, as in multitudes of modern as well as ancient instances, God chooses the " weak things of this world" to accomplish His gracious purposes, apart from any merit in the instrument, and despite a multitude of imperfections.

I once kept a record of instances of usefulness, but the collecting and writing became too onerous, and I discontinued what might tempt me to think too much of the instrument, whereas I did (and do still) desire to say with my whole heart, " *Non nobis Domine.*" But I venture to record a few recent instances rather of God's blessing on the distribution of tracts than on the writers of them.

To an invalid daughter of an Episcopal clergyman a lady gave a copy bound in emerald green. Her cousin, a young surgeon, also at Torquay for his health, saw it on her table, and said, "What gay little book is that you have there?" Though very unwilling to part with it, she felt she must ask him to accept it, on condition that he would read it. He said : " It is not the kind of book I ever read, but for your sake I will take it." A few weeks afterwards he wrote to her that he had found the Saviour of whom it spoke, and had renounced his infidel opinions, and asked her to tell the author that he hoped to meet both the writer and the giver of the book in heaven. He was then dying in consumption, and very near his end.

Lately, one dusky evening, I was met by a gentleman on Hampstead Heath, who asked my name, and said, "I have a message for you. A year ago I went, as a Methodist minister, to preach at a Yorkshire village, where I visited a poor man very ill. I spoke to him of Christ, and gave him your book. A year afterwards I went there again, when his widow gave me the copy I had given him, now soiled by constant use, and which was clasped in his hand to his heart at death. He said, 'If ever you see the giver of this book, let him have it. It has opened my heart to receive my Saviour.'" I was so deeply impressed that my informant passed out of my sight in the darkness, leaving me "blinded by excess of light."

I have been told that during the American War between North and South, this book was carried in the breast-pocket by a hundred thousand young men, who often perused it in the pauses of battle or by their watch-fires. Very lately I met a Polish gentleman, who told me that ten thousand were printed every year in Warsaw and sold to Roman Catholics, who loved to read about salvation, and were not forbidden by their priests, because there was nothing in it assailing their Church. In order to teach the foundation facts and doctrines of Christianity, is it essential to begin by condemning the errors of Popery, and thus to repel our hearers and readers from the "Common Salvation"?

This day [May 13th, 1898], while correcting the proof of this sheet, the following letter has come to me :—

"To-night at the Mission House (L.M.S.) the Rev. J. Hacker, of Neyoor, told of an incident which he said you would be glad to know of, and I promised to write and tell you. A Brahmin told Mr. Hacker that he was a Christian, but could not confess it because he was delicate and knew he could not live long, and to confess Christ meant to leave his wife and children to beggary. In the course of time the man died, and when his cold fingers were unclenched, they were enclosing a copy of your 'Come to Jesus,' from which he had found comfort in his dying hours.—H. C. RICHARDS."

A very short experience in Hull proved to me more vividly than before that beer- and spirit-drinking chiefly caused poverty, vice, crime, and irreligion. Temptations abounded on every hand, and although the middle and upper classes did not set an example of drunkenness, they did set an example of the drinking which was the temptation to the sin—the dangerous slope down which multitudes slide to ruin.

Working-men themselves were the first to teach that the only effectual remedy was voluntary total abstinence. It is said that a man who stammered, being asked whether he totally abstained, replied, " Yes! tee-tee-tee-totally," and that this was the origin of the inelegant word "Teetotal." At its commencement this new advocacy was carried on, with few exceptions, by working-people alone. They met together delivered addresses in the open air; out of their small earnings met the expenses of lecture-halls, and by personal exertions persuaded multitudes to accept the pledge: " I promise, by the help of God, to abstain from all intoxicating drinks as beverages."

Very few of the upper classes gave their sanction—very few of the clergy of any Church, very few people of culture. " The drink " was on every private table, and honoured in all public entertainments. The medical profession, with rare exceptions, condemned total abstinence. We were made the objects of innocent joking in private and public.

" Poor simple teetotallers ! The only vegetables they eat are water-cresses ; their only fruit, water-melons ; their only song, 'The Jolly Young Waterman'; the only soldiers they look at, the 'Coldstream Guards'; the only pictures they admire, water-colours ; and when in London, the only bridge they cross, 'Waterloo '!"

But the minority knew they were right, and God blessed

the labours of the poor. Multitudes, by the adoption of this principle, have been themselves rescued and the means of rescuing others. This is compensation a thousandfold for all the opposition and all the ridicule. I have sometimes applied to this subject the reply of a soldier in a coloured regiment during the great American War. When recognised in Washington, on the eve of a great battle, by "What! you here, Sambo?" "Yes, I've got leave!" "There is to be a great battle soon!" "Yes, I calculate so." "But many of your people will die covered with glory, while you will be called a coward as long as you live!" "That's so; but I'd rather be a coward all my life than a corpse one ten minutes!" That was shunning duty which is life, for sinful safety which is death. We say, "I'd rather be a poor simple teetotaller all my life than a drunkard one ten minutes!"

I felt urged to speak and write for the purpose of persuading Christians to abstain for the sake of others. My argument was briefly this: Drunkenness is so destructive and prevalent as to demand the especial efforts of all Christians to repress it. The drunkard is only secure by totally abstaining from what has been the occasion of his sin. Those who would successfully persuade others must themselves abstain. St. Paul teaches: "It is good neither to eat flesh, nor to drink wine, nor anything whereby thy brother stumbleth, or is offended, or is made weak."

This argument I expanded into a small tractate, " The Scriptural Claims of Teetotalism," published in my penny series. I wrote to Dr. Guthrie for permission to dedicate it to himself, and received the following reply :—

"MY DEAR MR. HALL,—I will consider it an honour to have your Tract dedicated to me. I have just finished reading it, and a more calm, kind, telling appeal on behalf of Total Abstinence I have never read. I hope that it will be scattered over England thick as snowflakes. The cause is one in which I not only feel a deep but a deepening interest, and I am astonished that so many ministers of the Gospel and good Christian people, can turn aside from the light as they do.—Ever believe me, yours, with much esteem,

"THOMAS GUTHRIE."

Dr. Guthrie appended an introduction, of which the original lies now before me.

"Salisbury Road, Edinburgh.

"When as one of the parochial ministers of this city I laboured among the lower, and indeed lowest, classes of society, I was met at every corner by the Demon of Drink. I found it utterly useless to attempt to evangelise the heathen and raise the lapsed masses without the aid of total abstinence. With all my trust in the promises of God and blessings of the Holy Spirit, I felt that I must be able, as a worthy leader, to say to the people, not '*Forward*,' but '*Follow*.' This first induced me to become a total abstainer, and I am convinced that it is the duty of every man who would do his utmost for the glory of God and the good of his fellow-creatures to discountenance by his example the use of intoxicating stimulants. They are the cause of almost all our poverty and crime, the great fountain of domestic discord and misery, and the lives they destroy and the souls they ruin year by year in our country are to be numbered, not by thousands, but by tens of thousands."

Some years afterwards, when Dr. Guthrie had recently recovered from severe illness, he said to me: "The doctors recommended wine, saying I should die if I did not take it. I am not dead. I find total abstinence makes me better in health, lighter in heart, heavier in pocket, and better all over."

Now after fifty-seven years' practice of total abstinence I can confirm the testimony of Dr. Guthrie, and, still vigorous at the age of eighty-two (1898), urge with increased earnestness what I taught when twenty-seven (1843).

John Jackson, a sailor of drunken habits, was invited by a member of my church to attend a grand solid tea, arranged by friends of sailors. She left with his pious wife her card for him : " Lady B. presents her compliments to Mr. J.," etc. I remember arriving at the " Sailors' Institute," at which a number of sailors were waiting to enter. I addressed them kindly, and said I would try to find room for them, and this I did.

When Jackson returned, he astonished his wife by saying, " Hulloa, missis ! what do ye think ? I've been and signed teetotal, and mean to keep it ! How did this happen ? Why, I showed my ticket, but there was no room for me and a lot more. But a gentleman kindly told us he would get us seats. A jolly good tea we had. Then the meeting began, and after some speeches, the chairman said the Rev. Newman Hall would address us. Says I to myself, ' Why! that's my wife's parson ! She has often asked me to go with her to his church, and I never would. Why! it's the very same man that spoke to us so kind and jolly at the door and got us seats. I'll hear what he's got to say. When he spoke of the evil of the drink to sailors, I felt it was all true. And then he told us he had taken the pledge to help us to do the same, and begged us to sign teetotal and weigh anchor and steer for heaven. And I said to myself, ' I'll sign to-night,' and I've done it, missis ! and, what's more, I'll go with you and hear him preach next Sunday."

It was the first time he had been at church since his marriage. He found work on shore. He began to pray with his wife, and with her was regular and attentive at church. One day he came to me and said, " I'm like a ship becalmed. City of Destruction is astarn o' me and the heavenly Jerusalem ahead, but far away ; and I'm thinking I ought to be a member of the Church and come to the Sacrament with my wife." When I visited Hull year by year afterwards, I saw the happy couple seated together. This illustrates how those who receive present advantage by renouncing the drink are inclined to seek the companionship or ministry of those by whom they were persuaded. My experience of above sixty years has proved abundantly that while temperance is not religion in its highest sense, it constantly leads to it. In hundreds of cases, associated with myself, of drunkards becoming true Christians, there was only one in which the first step was not total abstinence.

Another case is nearer my own heart. A great temperance convention was announced to be held in London. I went up to it, and, meeting my brother Arthur, gave him a ticket for a reserved seat. To please me he went, thinking to amuse himself by humorous sketches of some of the "fanatics." But the speeches were too rational for caricature, and after listening to the physiological argument he resolved, in prospect of a swimming match, to test the question. His companions jeered him with the certainty of defeat. But he won the prize in a race of three miles in fresh water. He then resolved to sign, and at the very temperance office at Maidstone where he was known as a ringleader of the opponents. Then he reported himself to his parents, who with grateful exultation said how that very day they had specially prayed that he might be delivered from the dangers of London. He remained unchanged in his sceptical doubts and love of worldly pleasures, and consorted with his old companions; but while they took their alcoholic drinks he took coffee or soda-water, and could no longer laugh at and applaud songs and gestures which required some physical stimulant to render them amusing.

Former comrades no longer cared for an uncongenial companion. Left to himself on Sunday, he went one day to hear a sermon from a working papermaker he had formerly known, who said, " If you had a ripe plum you wished to give to your father, would you leave it till the bloom was off and the flies and wasps had half eaten it ? Don't thus leave your life to decay, but give it to God at once with the bloom on." This went to my brother's heart, especially as he was then watching a tree, the firstfruits of which he designed for his father, and then and there he consecrated his life to God. Soon after he relinquished a very promising business, went to college, instituted a Band of Hope, superintended a Sunday school, was ordained, and during thirty years has been labouring chiefly amongst the poor in the work of the Gospel, heroically struggling with difficulties, and greatly blessed by God with usefulness. One such case is a reason more than adequate for me to persevere in this advocacy.

These facts are narrated as a very few illustrations of many of a similar kind occurring constantly and illustrating in a concrete form my chief reasons for the advocacy and practice of total abstinence, a cause which has gained so much attention during my life that it claims special mention in my Autobiography.

CHAPTER VI.

I HERE place together without classification a variety of incidents of my many recollections of Hull.

It was always my custom to do as all doctors do—*i.e.* visit every sick person desiring to see me, whatever the ailment—cholera, small-pox, fever—observing a few obvious rules : not to go with an empty stomach, not to stoop over the patient so as to inhale his breath, to take my place between him and the door, and not between him and the fireplace, and so to keep to leeward, and not to stay long at a time. One Saturday evening, feeling very well and buoyant, I visited a young man suffering from rheumatic fever. On my way home, I walked lame. On Sunday I hobbled up into my pulpit before the congregation assembled, and came down sitting on each stair, but never preached with greater freedom. That night was a terrible one. Next morning I was in acute rheumatic fever.

My friend, Dr. G., had recently been studying the new treatment of hydropathy. Each joint, as it in turn became affected, was wrapped in towels soaked in cold water and carefully packed. Within five minutes of the application all pain ceased. After three or four hours the pain returned. The towels were removed, smelling strongly like sour vinegar, and on renewal of the application the pain again ceased. I lost only three Sundays before I was in my pulpit again, unwise zeal overcoming prudence and advice. But all was not over. In consequence of imprudence other symptoms developed, and during recovery I wrote my tract, " Come to Jesus "—two pages a day. This was when being nursed at my old home, under care of my parents. Not a drop of wine or spirits was administered.

I remember, and record as a warning, that during the severity of the fever I was mentally incapable of exertion. I asked neither for religious reading, conversation, nor prayer. I was apathetic, and friends wondered at my apparent callousness: but I felt a placid assurance that I had long before committed my soul to my Saviour. It was an emphatic lesson that sickness may be the worst time for seeking salvation. The intellectual and moral nature may be incapable of any exertion, especially the most important.

Cholera was very destructive at Hull in 1849, several thousands being carried off within a few weeks. From an average weekly mortality of forty the deaths in one week mounted to 700. Funeral processions were passing my windows all day and far into the night. Husbands were ordering graves for wives in which their own bodies were buried three days after. All whom necessity or duty did not detain fled from the plague. Fires were burning in some of the streets. Often our open-air sermons were interrupted by passing funerals. The clergy of all Churches were constantly visiting the dying without injury and without fear. Services were held in all places of worship every evening, in which the Gospel of repentance and faith was proclaimed.

A week was by common consent set apart for fasting and prayer in all the churches, and repentance was urged for sins which might have caused such judgments. Some emphasised sabbath-breaking, infidelity, Popery, or drunkenness. I advised that we should consider what the relation might be between the sin and the punishment. The town was pre-eminent for small houses crowded together to produce as much rent as possible, and without proper regard to sanitary conditions. Some new streets had become watercourses or muddy sloughs. Many tenements were crowded beyond all possibility of health or decency. Such sins against God's natural laws were followed by natural retribution. For these sins we should repent, not merely by prayer and preaching, but by such reformation as was in our power. This was soon done by Boards of Health—draining, ventilation, good water, and so on. After a few years, on comparing the bills of mortality, it was found that, including the ravages of cholera, there had been fewer deaths than preceding the plague. The cholera had thus been not so much punitive as corrective a scourge not to torture the victims, but to drive off the assassin.

Ideas of disease and the mode of treatment were illustrated by a poor woman from a village in Holderness, who asked advice of a medical friend of mine; and while holding her hands on the lower part of her stomach said, " I'm very bad here with the lungs." Another, from a village where some fever was making great ravages, being asked how the sufferers were treated, said, " They bleeds 'em and blisters 'em, and gives 'em wine; then they bleeds 'em and blisters 'em again and gives 'em wine; and then they bleeds 'em and blisters 'em again, and then 'em dies."

On certain days some of the medical men gave advice gratis to poor people. Many came every market day from the country. Thus a certain well-to-do farmer came and gave a fee of half a sovereign. A few hours after he returned and claimed it, because advice was free that day. The physician, indignant, replied, " It's a hard job to get back a pat of butter out of a dog's throat !" Alas for the covetous selfishness which often steals the benefit of institutions intended for the poor, instead of supporting them—too often the case with schools, asylums, hospitals, and, alas! with churches.

From medical friends in Hull I obtained simple hints about treatment which may be worth recording. I asked one why, when poorly, he said he took scarcely any but the very simplest remedies and yet gave physic to his patients ? " Because they would not believe you were doing anything to cure them if you did not give them something in pills or in coloured water. The great healer is Nature, and the doctor's chief business is, not to supersede it, but to remove obstacles. The chief medicine is rest. Is the stomach disordered ?— starve it. Is the brain upset ?—do not bother it. Are the eyes out of order ?—shut the lids. Are the limbs overworked ? —rest them; the voice ?—hold your tongue. This advice has reservations, but, as a general principle, acting on it would lessen the toils of the profession."

I may record here some simple rules and remedies, tested by many years' experience. Secure seven hours out of the twenty-four for sleep, and more after seventy years; avoid late dinners and heavy suppers; take a cold bath every morning. When preaching away from home, a grand supper is often provided, but my rule is to avoid animal food and pastry, tea and coffee, and mental toil, within two hours of bed. Bread soaked in hot water may always be had, and prove a wholesome repast. In case of indigestion, a tumbler of cold water is effectual. When a cold is caught, at once take a few camphor globules, inhale Dunbar's alkaram, but especially, on going to bed, involve the whole head and shoulders in a woollen shawl, widely woven, so as to breathe through it easily. It acts as a Turkish bath, and almost invariably the bad cold of the evening departs before morning. In walking, fear not rain, if you keep in exercise, but never rest in wet clothes ; especially guard against dampness from perspiration—more colds are caught from within than from without. If possible, walk, cycle, or ride an hour every day. Finally, avoid all intoxicants.

When I began my pastorate I resolved that nothing should interfere with my regular evening devotions, or by late hours hinder my resolve to rise early for study. So I declined to accept engagements which would keep me after nine o'clock. Thus wherever I went I suggested family worship early, and came away before supper. Of course, this was much regretted, as it broke up many a pleasant gathering when my presence might have been useful. It might also appear like a parade of piety, which I hated.

Another mistake was a resolve to keep up my college reading; so I went on with several courses—classics, mathematics, philosophy. I was up early; and after devotional study of the Scriptures had a long forenoon for books. But invitations to preach poured in from all quarters, which I felt bound, as far as possible, to accept.

I reasoned thus. While at college, such study was my duty to fit myself to preach. Should I not do now what God seems to bid me do now ? " Whatsoever thy hand findeth to do, do it with thy might." So I tried to do it; and this is one of the causes of my not having approached that intellectual ability which I so much honour in many of my contemporaries, and which often increases their usefulness.

Let me confess another mistake. At the time of the French interference with our missions in Madagascar, Dr. Winter Hamilton suggested that a British gun-boat should be sent to our station to overcome the intruders. Just then a comic paper depicted him as a missionary holding a pistol, while a tract with the word " Peace " was protruding from his pocket. I was sent as a representative of the London Missionary Society to take part at the annual meeting at Leeds, in the large church of Dr. Hamilton, who presided. I was then, as ever since, an earnest advocate of peace, especially in connection with efforts to spread the Gospel. With no thought of offending, I gave utterance to the condemnation of all force in connection with missions. I feel I did right according to my convictions, as often on the slavery and drink questions, but my method was indiscreet.

The audience burst out in applause. The chairman called me to order by " Question." I quickly said I considered I was within the question and sat down. The people shouted for me to go on, but I kept my seat. I very soon felt that my zeal had betrayed me into apparent disrespect to a highly honoured and much older friend of missions. I might have been faithful to my convictions, but guarded my utterance so as to avoid any personal application. A neighbouring pastor, eminent for his brotherly spirit, the Rev. John Ely, told me that evening how very deeply Dr. Hamilton felt it. Early next morning I sought him out to express my regret and honour of himself, and our friendship was strengthened for life. I was somewhat relieved a few days afterwards by receiving from one of his deacons a letter highly commending my conduct, and saying that all his brother-deacons, and those of the Rev. John Ely whom he had seen, felt in a similar manner. Though this vindicated my purpose, it did not excuse my indiscretion.

G

Whenever I visited London to preach, as I occasionally did, at Spa Field's (Lady Huntingdon's), Craven Chapel, Whitfield's Tabernacle (Moorfields), and Surrey Chapel, I never failed to visit my parents in their pretty cottage on Penenden Heath, Boxley, accompanying them in drives and rambles in old and beloved haunts, and listening as they spoke of the Saviour they so loved and of the heaven towards which they were pursuing their pilgrimage with ever-brightening prospects. They took a deep interest in all my work, aiding me by their sympathy and prayers. I used to write to my mother every Sunday after evening service, and she never forgot to send me at least a weekly letter, and never ceased to be my "ministering spirit." It may be appropriate to introduce a few remaining extracts from her diary and correspondence, 1837–1854.

Soon before my leaving college, my mother wrote the following lines, the last in her diary :—

"October 10. This day I am fifty years old. How innumerable the mercies of these years !—the only and cherished child of a tender mother, then a beloved wife, cared for by a most indulgent husband, still happy in each other, and surrounded by loving children ; pleasure in the society of Christian people; permitted to receive His dear ministers into our house ; delight in contributing to the comfort or soothe the sorrows of His afflicted ones. How many gracious answers to prayer ! My few remaining years may be attended with infirmities, but His everlasting arms will still surround me. May I ever trust His faithfulness to preserve what I have committed to Him !"

July 20, 1839. From my mother's diary :—

"This day, my dear Arthur has left the parental roof for a sailor's life. O the agony I have endured in parting, but I am now able to commit him to the care of my prayer-hearing God. My heart sinks when I feel that my care over this dear child ceases. He must now be in the world, far from his mother's eye and restraint. My God ! be his protector !"

Written on the margin of this entry, many years after, is this memorandum :—

"Arthur, referred to above, brought by Divine Grace to be a Christian and a Christian minister ; and in July, 1859, twenty years after the above was written, was chosen pastor of the Independent Church, Luddenden-Foot, Halifax. Bless the Lord, O my soul !"

I have kept no copies of my ordinary correspondence, but have found the following letter to my mother among her papers:—

"Harrogate, 1844.

"In my journey from Hull I had some agreeable companions. An old friend, a philosopher, much beloved, somewhat mystical, very congenial. His name? Coleridge. Next a Scotch metaphysician, a clever old gentleman, who deals most famous knocks at Hume, and makes dry subjects fascinating—his name is Reid. More than these I've a companion grave, solemn, soaring, divine, harrowing, soothing, bewildering, rhapsodising, whom I intend to follow as my Guide, through Hell, Purgatory, Paradise; one Carey acting as interpreter. Besides these, I have, superior to all, 'the goodly fellowship of the prophets' and 'the glorious company of the apostles'—a mine inexhaustible, a banquet that never satiates, an anthem which never tires, a sun that's never dim, a philosophy that never misleads, a wisdom which God imparts, and, better still, the Great Teacher Himself. I wish my dear mother were with me, helping me to learn of Him!"

It was a great joy to me when my parents came to Hull and joined me in my work. My dear father took a very enthusiastic part in our prayer-meetings, visited and addressed the inmates of our penitentiary, and preached to sailors in the "floating chapel." Wherever he went about he distributed his "Sinner's Friend," with a few words of advice to each recipient. At Hull I presented to him the following hymn as expressing his own feelings in his little book. The hymn has been introduced into several hymnals.

Friend of sinners, Lord of glory!
    Lowly, Mighty!—Brother, King!
Musing o'er Thy wondrous story,
    Grateful we Thy praises sing:
Friend to help us, comfort, save us,
    In Whom power and pity blend—
Praise we must the grace which gave us
    Jesus Christ, the sinner's Friend.

Friend who never fails nor grieves us;
    Faithful, tender, constant, kind!—
Friend who at all times receives us,
    Friend who came the lost to find:
Sorrow soothing, joys enhancing,
    Loving until life shall end,
Then conferring bliss entrancing,
    Still, in Heaven, the sinner's Friend.

O to love and serve Thee better!
From all evil set us free;
Break, Lord, every sinful fetter;
Be each thought conformed to Thee :
Looking for Thy bright appearing,
May our spirits upward tend,
Till, no longer doubting, fearing,
We behold the sinner's Friend.

Extract from a letter on return to Hull duties :—

"On Sunday I preached on the Penitent Thief and warned against misuse of his late repentance by putting off salvation to a dying hour. Wednesday I met inquirers and proposed new members. Typhus prevalent, visited several by whom religion was quite neglected. One woman in despair could only say, 'I've lost my soul.' Another, quite a heathen; her friends sent anxiously for me, but she was delirious. Another had been four months in Hull, but to no place of worship—sent for me—hope she knows a little of the Gospel : hope—but with trembling—in these late apparent 'conversions.'"

From my mother :—

"No other incidents with which to fill my sheet. I could fill a volume with my love for you, my darling N., and with my hopes and fears and good wishes, but they have often been expressed, and if not constantly repeated are constantly felt. I can no longer be to you what I was for so many years, but you will be to *me*, as long as life and memory remain, the cherished object of my fond affection and tender anxiety. I am thankful you have around you so many who love and respect you, and may you by prayer and example promote their spiritual interests."

After preaching one evening to a crowded Primitive Methodist congregation, I went away without observing any special result. A few days afterwards the pastor congratulated me on my sermon, saying that about fifty had been " converted," and explained that they held a special prayer-meeting after the public sermon, and that these had come forward to the penitent seats and were prayed for. He said, " You Congregationalists have better nets than we Primitives, but you don't 'draw them' as we do and gather our chief result from these after-meetings."

I took the hint, with similar results, and now in my eighty-second year, after every evening sermon I carry on the service by a prayer-meeting, to which the majority of the congregation remain. After a few words on intercessory prayer for the undecided, I invite the brethren, any brother or sister, to lead us briefly in prayer. Generally six respond about three minutes each, when any who desire special prayer are invited to raise their hand, and prayers of confirmation follow. These very solemn occasions are seldom without several responses.

There was a young man, son of a widowed member of the church, a cripple from childhood, his mother's darling, and the care of him her daily delight. She would sit by him at the fire in winter, or take him out into the sunshine of their tiny garden in summer. At length, when about twenty years of age, his Heavenly Father was calling him home. The mother sat by him, weeping bitterly. He said to her, "Don't fret, mother, you can gang into kitchen! I can die alone! Jesus is wi' me!" What a Gospel for the poorest as well as the rich! Alas! that any, by undermining the authority of the Bible, should try to rob the poor and the sick of their supreme, their only blessedness!

A little boy of our infant school, sick unto death and somewhat delirious, asked his father to pray, but he had never prayed. He asked his mother in vain. Then he said, "Loose me, and let me kneel up." He put his little hands together and said :

> "Gentle Jesus, meek and mild,
> Look upon a little child,
> In the kingdom of Thy grace,
> Grant a little child a place."

There, that'll do." Yes, verily! and so his spirit went to Jesus. The result was the conversion of the mother, who gave me this account.

I have always given opportunities of meeting me privately to those troubled with doubt. Many inquiries were beyond my capacity, and in such cases, instead of attempting weak explanations, I confessed my ignorance, stating that in all science there were difficulties none could explain, but which did not contradict facts otherwise established.

I was often asked about the eternal future of those who die without evidence of repentance; and when belief in unending punishment was a hindrance to acceptance of the Gospel, I have replied that it was by belief in salvation through Christ we are saved, and not by belief in damnation, and that I knew many eminent Christians whose faith in Christ could not be doubted, but who were doubtful on this question. A plain but shrewd member of my church, told me that, after listening to a long argument with an unbeliever who urged the objections of Bishop Colenso to the accuracy of the Old Testament, my friend looked at him keenly and asked, "Does this prove that Jesus Christ did not rise from the dead?"

I was often consulted by persons in deep affliction, who had prayed earnestly for the removal of sorrows which they nevertheless continued to suffer. I tried to relieve my own difficulties in replying to those of others, by the following rhymes to show that no "strange thing" happens to us when God blesses us by disappointing us.

> "Come quickly, Lord, and heal this wounded heart : "
> *Still more He made it smart.*
> "At length from trouble bid my soul repose : "
> *Yet thicker came the blows.*
> "At least give peace in triumph over sin : "
> *More loud grew battle's din.*
> "O let me rest with thee in pastures green : "
> *Only steep crags are seen.*
> "Why with keen knife, dear Lord, dost prune me so?"
> *Grace will more quickly grow.*
> "Why in my portion mix such bitter leaven?"
> *To fit thee more for Heaven.*
> "Lord, take Thy way with me—Thy way, not mine : "
> *My child, all things are thine!*
> *All in the end, though grievous, shall prove best,*
> *And then—Eternal Rest!*

The town council and civic officers were men of good repute, intelligent, righteous, and benevolent, but of various degrees of culture. The clerk to the magistrates told me that on one occasion a claimant, breaking down in his evidence, provoked the mayor to say, " Get down ; you've no *locum standum.*" The clerk whispered to him, " *Locus standi*, your worship." Whereon the magistrate at once corrected himself, saying, " *Locus standi ;* it's all the same; I never learned *French.*" I heard this very popular and worthy mayor, at the beginning of the war with Russia, denounce that great "*Democrat* of the North"; and at a public meeting at the beginning of his mayoralty say, " Fellow-citizens, I mean to follow in the steps of my successor, and do all in my power for the detriment of my native town." He himself heartily joined in the appreciative laughter which followed. He was a diligent and righteous magistrate ; he also possessed a renowned cellar, and gave very hospitable entertainments.

Third-class carriages from Hull to Selby were simply open cattle-trucks with wooden seats, and no shelter from the weather. I obtained a huge thick great-coat, down to the feet, buttoning well round the neck, with a deep cape and hood. Thus encased, I could keep dry in heavy rain two or three hours when I went to preach in surrounding villages — Snodland, Welton, Ferriby, Cottingham, Beverley, and Hornsey.

With perhaps less luxurious comfort, third-class carriages have a great advantage for those who desire to make travelling an opportunity of usefulness. Fellow-passengers here are less likely to take offence if you address them, and with very rare exception they receive tracts and booklets with gratitude. I may not have always *done* good to others by such intercourse, but I have *received* much good myself. Amongst a multitude of other illustrations I mention this one. Passing through a long dark tunnel, a baby child cried with fear, and was thus calmed by its mother : " Don't cry, dearie ; look at the lamp, and we shall soon be out of the dark into the sun, and mother is with you and takes care of you." " Mother " did not know how her gospel entered the heart of the preacher, and would thus reach many other hearts.

In a family of my church was a devoutly-behaved dog, which regularly occupied its accustomed seat at family prayers, and remained motionless till the " Amen " at the close. One

day when I was conducting the service, I read the fifth chapter
of the Revelation, and when I came to the fourteenth verse,
"And the four beasts said Amen !" the dog jumped from his
chair and began barking as usual, as if all was over. This
was too much for the assembly's gravity; host and hostess,
servants and friends, could not prevent laughter blending with
barking, and the service ended with the dog's "Amen."

My verger's dog was a very intelligent spaniel, always
glad to see me. I took a great fancy to it, and proposed to
purchase it, but the dog, as if fully understanding, manifested
great disapproval. This was repeated whenever I called to
speak about the purchase. The dog's evident objection to
leave its home was such that I relinquished my purpose, and
we were good friends ever afterwards. A critic suggests this
is too trivial. But it helps in the study of the mental capacity
of animals. The only expression of the dog's displeasure was
when I spoke of buying it.

For recreation I learned to play the cornet, and mastered
a few tunes. To avoid annoying neighbours, I sometimes
took my instrument into the fields, and, behind a gate, pretended to be a disciple of Orpheus. If human beings did not
appreciate my performance the cows did, and crowded around
on the other side. Someone asked Mr. Spurgeon if he thought
cornopean players would get to heaven. He replied that he
had less hope of their next-door neighbours. So, not to hinder
mine, I gave away my instrument of torture. Ought I not to
have smashed it ? No ! in other hands it might have soothed
pain, roused courage, kindled hope, inspired devotion. Do not
let us deprecate what may be valuable in other hands because
we have not faculty to perceive and employ it.

The following note was sent to me for thanksgiving in
church :—

"Mary Ann H. wishes to retearn Thank to all Mighty God for
save driveler N.S. of Childbearin."

I was told of a young preacher who had recently been
pleading earnestly for a good collection towards an important
mission, using the following mathematical argument: "If the
benighted Jews, who did not know the Gospel, gave to God

one-tenth, we, on whom the light has shined, ought at least to double it, and give one-twentieth!"

People sometimes put a simple meaning on what is obscure. Two girls were returning from hearing a sermon of which one complained as having something in it she could not make out. "What was it?" "Oh, it was about money being a *sine quâ non.*" "That's plain enough. What he said was *money's a sign of getting on.* Isn't that true?"

I was preaching at the anniversary of a Primitive Methodist Sunday school when a part of the service was a recitation by a very little girl. She stood on the central table and repeated St. Paul's description of "charity," with the following emendation: "When I was a child, I spake as a child . . . . but *when I became a woman*, I put away childish things." She was about eight years old.

By religious cant I mean words and phrases perverted from their usual meaning—very current when I went to Hull. A regular hearer of a preacher "sat under" So-and-So, and sometimes complained of his being "heavy." Attendance at Holy Communion was spoken of as "sitting down," confounding the sacrament with the attitude. "Chapel begins at half-past ten," though it began with the foundation, and is "over at twelve"—so much the worse for those inside. "Travelling preachers" were residents for three years. Ordination for the ministry was "entering the Church," though, according to those who used the expression, this took place at baptism. And surely those fit for ministry in the Church are already members of it, by entering through faith in Him who said, "I am the door." There were old-fashioned ways of reading the Scripture, not only by unnatural tones, but by added syllables, as "touch-ed" for "touch'd," "sail-ed" for "sail'd," and "call-ed" for "call'd." Fancy asking that a cup might be fill-ed, or being told of a family being distress-ed! Why should not words expressing religious thought be used as in good English on other matters?

At the beginning of my pastorate an elderly Methodist lady took sittings. After the first quarter she resigned them, saying, "I only left my own chapel to encourage the young man in his difficult work. But now he has got such a large congregation he does not need me any longer, so I go back to my own people. God bless him and you!"

A very godly lady, a regular communicant and diligent visitor among the poor, was constantly groaning under the fear that she should finally be lost. No arguments of mine, either in sermons or in frequent conversation, seemed to relieve her. One day she was nearly killed in the street, and during some months of slow recovery all those fears vanished, and she rejoiced in the love of God and full assurance of eternal life. When her physical ailments were cured, her mental anguish returned in full force. Were not those fears simply physical? And though her last moments were overclouded, was not her whole life a plain testimony? Jesus said of a certain woman who had a spirit of infirmity, and could in no wise lift up herself, " This woman, being a daughter of Abraham, whom Satan hath bound, lo, these eighteen years."

Mysterious knockings were currently reported as being heard in a workman's dwelling—knockings which magistrates, police, and the Philosophical Society endeavoured to verify, explain, or expose. Always curious to explore the unknown, I visited the house with a clever young surgeon. Testimony of facts witnessed is not opinion as to their cause.

The building was of ordinary brick, in a row of similar construction, with six small rooms. We went about dusk. The husband had not returned from work. The wife was busy washing, but courteously allowed us to sit with her in the kitchen. She told us the rappings came at various times, by day as well as by night ; on some days not at all. She was not afraid, but disliked being disturbed and so many people coming to ask about it. After waiting an hour, we suddenly heard an emphatic knocking apparently on the inside wall, as if someone struck it with the flat of the hand, giving five distinct blows, each louder than the one preceding, and ending with one very emphatic. To us both the knocking seemed like that of a messenger endeavouring to summon the inmates in a case of emergency. We rushed into the passage, to which the knocks seemed to retreat.

I took a seat on the stair, my friend in the passage, and waited in silence. After about half an hour another knock, exactly similar, seemed to come downstairs from the front room. This we entered, certain that we had secured the agent. We searched a wardrobe, and looked under a table, the only furniture, but nothing was discovered. Suddenly another knock was heard, now coming from below, but as if retreating, and we rushed down in pursuit, but saw nothing. The woman was quite collected, and said the sounds were always like that.

We were convinced that the raps were produced by some intelligent agency, but what that could be was a mystery. Police had surrounded the house, and the garden had been dug up. Scientific people had explored again and again, but the mystery was never solved. After a few months the sounds ceased, but nothing was found to explain them. In reply to inquiry, I received the following :—

"Brigg, 12th May, 1882.

Rev. Sir,—I am in receipt of yours inquiring how the rappings were produced in a house I occupied in Hull. In reply, I beg to say that the mystery is as great as ever, and that the slightest trace of the cause was never discovered.—With compliments, etc.,   " W. H. Reed."

I do not say that such phenomena must be supernatural. May they not be developments of some natural law not yet discovered, just as other facts of nature hitherto unknown are being now revealed, the statement of which half a century ago would have been attributed to ignorance, delusion, or insanity ? Would not professed scientists be more scientific if they examined with utmost care such facts of the universe, to discover the law of their existence, rather than deny the reality of those facts because not in accordance with laws already known ? In reference to the whole region of spiritualistic phenomena it may be true that " There are more things in heaven and earth, ... than are dreamt of in *our* philosophy."

I have taken pains to investigate the subject of "Spiritualism," and am disposed to think that some of the phenomena cannot be regarded as the result of deception or delusion, but resemble what in the Old Testament are denounced as dealing with demons, and in the New Testament are described as actual calamities caused by evil spirits and cured by Christ. If so, here is confirmation of Scripture. At college I was taught that allusions in the Bible to visions of angels, and possessions by demons, were made only in compliance with popular ignorance, and were not actual facts. Is it not more reverential to interpret them as facts, for which some modern phenomena may be illustrations?

I knew a young preacher of small stature, but no small confidence, who came to preach on some public occasion. Before a large audience, he mounted a stand that he might avoid appearing "in form contemptible." With considerable emphasis he announced his text, "Now then we are ambassadors for Christ," and by his energetic action the stand upset, and he fell prostrate in the pulpit—not hurt, but perhaps healed.

At a missionary anniversary, a deputation of ministers went to a village meeting at Ferriby. Walking from the railway, we stopped to admire the prospect. A boy who carried the bag was asked if he did not admire it?—the broad Humber, "sweet fields beyond the swelling flood," this village church amid the trees? He stared and was silent. "Tell us if you ever saw anything more beautiful and I'll give you a shilling." After some pondering, he burst forth confidently, "Yeas, a cheesecak!" Cheesecakes were essential features of the village festivals.

In a neighbouring village churchyard I read this :—

> "Here lyes I—old Jeremi—
> Ah who nine times marry-ed been,
> Now in my old age, I lyes in my cage,
> Under the grass so green."

It was here that the old parish clerk one Sunday surprised the congregation by announcing, in his usual monotone, "Let us sing to the praise and glory of God, a psalm of my own composing—a psalm of my own composing!"

It has been my misfortune, or my privilege, on several occasions of public controversy to be in a small minority of my brethren, a minority which soon became large and, as events have proved, lasting majorities. The first related to National Education. A Bill was brought into the House of Commons by my friend, W. E. Forster, for universal rudimentary instruction, including the Bible, which was to be read without comment. This was strongly opposed by many Dissenters, led by another eminent friend, Edward (subsequently Sir Edward) Baines, a veteran Sunday-school teacher of Leeds. The argument was this : No true education without religion—for this the State is incompetent—therefore it must be left to the Churches. My reply was, that Christian Churches, consisting chiefly of poor people, and a minority, are incapable of supplying education for the whole nation. Therefore the whole nation should benefit the whole. Dr. Vaughan, one of the chief lights of Dissent, took this ground, and advocated undenominational teaching, including Scripture without comment, and fundamental morality. I was one of a very small minority in Hull, and was subjected to severe criticism. At the present day Dissenters are the strongest supporters of Board schools—that is, of Government schools, as opposed to those called voluntary, which are exclusively denominational.

Another instance of hostile criticism was connected with the Papal Bull in 1850, which gave local titles to Catholic dioceses. Dissenters were in the van of the forces against what they regarded as a peril to British Protestantism. An honoured Canon said "he would be glad if, when his so-called Eminence landed in England in proud and arrogant assumption, he found a couple of policemen to walk him off." This was matched by an Independent clergyman, who in the *British Banner* prayed that the " long indolent patriotism of Dissent might rise into a fury till its work is done." Though I saw in large letters on the walls, " Would-be Pope, Newman Hall," and so on, they excited not " fury," but pity.

My argument was briefly this. We have always been advocates of civil and religious liberty. With no civil rights does the Papal movement interfere. The Cardinal and his bishops have a right to call one another by such titles as they please, to adopt any ceremonies and wear any dresses, so long as they do not interfere with our own similar liberty. If we assert the right to interfere with them, so may they with us. We are in danger of the advance of Popery by the spread of its errors and the zeal of its members. This should be resisted by greater efforts in spreading Bible truth. Any semblance of unfairness will act as persecution—rousing anger and prompting retaliation.

If we are lukewarm in opposing Popish errors by scriptural truth, while busy with political weapons, Popery will progress more rapidly, and so an unreal aggression will become a sad spiritual reality. Has not this been verified? All that was done by legislation to stop the "aggression" was soon repealed by Queen, Lords, and Commons; while the people have more and more been made familiar with Romanist teaching and preachers, multitudes have been attracted to their services, some Protestant ministers have become Roman priests avowedly, and many more are secretly endeavouring to make our Protestant Establishment appear as Romanist as the laxity of the law or its guardians will permit.

I appealed to our Radical M.P. against his support of the Ecclesiastical Titles Bill, as contrary to the religious liberty which Liberals championed. He, laughing, replied that the popular excitement demanded this repression Act to appease it, but that within two years the measure would be withdrawn. This came to pass; the measure was futile, the "titles" remain in common use, the Papal bishops exercise authority over their own flocks, and over these alone; and the Cardinal is recognised on State occasions, and receives invitations from which Protestant Nonconformists are excluded.

Another example was the great struggle between the Northern and Southern States of America, resulting in the emancipation of millions of slaves; and afterwards another question, still pending, which for a time has divided the Liberal party.

"Christian Union" is the title of my first publication, during the first year of my pastorate, 1843. The occasion was a sermon preached by the Rev. Andrew Jukes. On his conversion, he had resigned his commission in the army to become a soldier of Christ, and was now curate of St. John's, of which the venerable Thomas Dykes was the Evangelical incumbent. In this sermon he maintained that true unity was to be looked for in the common faith of all Christians, and not in ecclesiastical uniformity. Archdeacon Wilberforce ordered him to withdraw it on pain of losing his license. Mr. Jukes, to the grief of his congregation, thus forbidden to minister in the Church of England, conducted services in a small iron room at the back of Albion, my church. I knew and revered him for his devout piety and his conscientious self-sacrifice. Since then he has become widely known by his thoughtful works on Exodus, Leviticus, etc. In defence of this soldier of Christ, commencing his ministry in the same town, I published a discourse to show that there might be essential harmony along with circumstantial diversity.

The Great High Priest just before offering Himself as the One Universal Sacrifice, prayed for His followers, that " they all may be one, that the world may believe." During nearly two thousand years the prayer of the Head of the Church remains, on this theory of uniformity, unanswered. It was answered at once at Pentecost. The Acts and Epistles indicate varieties, but breathe the same promises and precepts, building up the saints everywhere into one Holy Church, endued with the same Holy Spirit, and revealing the same life of holiness and martyr zeal.

So it is in our own day. By worship and by work are not all real Christians more united than by conformity to ritual ? There is scarcely any collection of hymns which is not enriched by every age and every Church. Alas, that some Christians should have obscured essential resemblances by parading small differences ; taking greater pains to piece together irreconcilable systems than to demonstrate inseparable realities. There is already a Divine unity which will abide when all separating systems shall have been buried with universal To Deums and Hallelujahs. My object in Hull was and ever since has been to promote this manifested unity by marked respect for conscience in difference, and thus for loyalty to the same Divine Head. "Grace be with all them that love our Lord Jesus Christ in sincerity." If angels minister to "heirs of salvation" *as such*, let this be a sufficient warrant for our own brotherly service. Mr. Jukes said, "Intolerance is dignified by the name of 'Catholic Unity,' Christ's Body is rent, God is grieved and Satan laughs." Archbishop Tillotson said, "Ought not the great matters on which we are agreed to be of greater force to unite us than differences or circumstances of worship to divide us?" To me it has always been a delight occasionally to worship and work with fellow-believers who in minor matters dissent from me, as I from them. At Hull I used, from my pulpit, to announce the Church Missionary meetings, and suspend my own services for the same day. The final Judge makes brotherhood with Himself the great test of conduct: "Inasmuch as ye have done it unto one of the least of these *My brethren*, ye have done it unto Me."

A tract was published by me which has helped in some small degree to diminish obtrusive distinctions between "church" and "chapel." The word "church" is derived from "kuriakos" (*belonging to the Lord*), contracted to "Kirk." The word "ecclesia" (*assembly*) meant those who worshipped in the kuriakos. Webster says that "In war, St. Martin's hat was carried as a precious relic, kept in a tent called 'capella,' *little hat*, and the priest who had charge of it was 'capellanus,' *chaplain*. Hence 'chapel' came to signify a private oratory." Church is for *public assembly;* chapel for private use—recess in a church dedicated to some particular saint, implying subordination to a larger building or higher authority. "Chapel," in primitive usage, was always identified with Popery; "church" is universally employed by Presbyterians: *kirk*. The general use of the word "church" would avoid some absurdities, as "The church will take tea in the chapel"; or, "Chapel begins at eleven," though it was begun when the foundation was laid; or "Chapel is over"—so much the worse for the worshippers. Why should Christians when they meet, at once parade their differences? "I'm going to church"—"And I'm going to chapel." A great change has taken place, and at present nearly all places for Christian worship are designated churches, and all worshippers are " church-goers."

This dissertation is strictly autobiographical. It sets forth the principles and conduct of every year of my life, and what I taught at twenty-five is the habit of my life at eighty-two, illustrated in the following sonnet, written on occasion of an Evangelical Convention at Lydney Park, 1870 :—

THE CHURCH, ONE GARDEN.

The garden of the Lord spreads far and wide ;
But not in one huge bed, unvaried, grow
The trees which He has planted ; fruits and flowers,
The lily, rose and jasmine—fragrant bowers,
In differing borders the same beauty show.
Such varying forms true oneness cannot hide ;
They beautify the garden, not divide.
We hedge and fence our favourite bed—but lo !
Beyond the barrier, to reprove our pride,
Are flowers as sweet and fair ; the heaven-taught bees,
Seeking the honey, scorn the fence ; the breeze
Incense from all alike to God doth blow ;
On all the beds He pours His showers Divine,
On all the garden makes His sun to shine.

CHAPTER VII.

THE first to welcome me were Sir William and Lady Lowthrop. His political and ecclesiastical views were united with such breadth of sympathy that leading people of various opinions gathered at his house. Here I met the chief Noncon-formist clergy of Yorkshire, such as Ely, Hamilton, Parsons, Mellor, Raffles of Liverpool, with Episcopal clergy, Deck, Dykes, Scott, grandson of the commentator, and other minis-ters of various denominations. I cannot enumerate all the pastors and missionaries whose friendship I enjoyed at Hull; but I must again mention the name of the Rev. Thomas Stratten, the venerable pastor of the mother church in Fish Street, and of my friend James Sibree, many years pastor of Salem Congregational Church, who greeted me as a brother when I first arrived at Hull, remained such till I came to London, and met me occasionally at the house of his cousins, Mr. and Mrs. Williams and daughters, highly honoured members of Surrey Chapel. He went to heaven after attaining fourscore, preach-ing to the last. He "still speaketh" by an accomplished literary daughter, and by a son, architect, translator, and mis-sionary in Madagascar, the Rev. James Sibree.

Here I gained the friendship of John Angell James, of Birmingham, who invited me to preach in his "Carr's Lane" chapel. He was known all over the land as an eloquent and faithful preacher, honoured and loved by all denominations. He prepared his sermons with great care, and delivered them without aid from notes. Among other useful publications he is chiefly remembered by "The Anxious Inquirer." Once, on a visit to Windsor Castle, I was conducted through the Queen's sitting-room, which she had just left for her usual drive, and I was much interested in seeing a copy of "The Anxious Inquirer" open on her reading-desk. A few days before his decease a friend told me he had just seen Mr. James, who said he felt he had preached his last sermon to his church. On the following Saturday he suddenly "entered into rest," and his desire was granted, as he used to say that he never feared death. but only the pain of dying.

Professor Sedgwick's society was a treat. He told us how on a certain Sunday morning he strolled before service to Salisbury Crags, and, seated on a rock, took out his pocket-hammer, and, after his habit, was reading God's book in Nature, when a pious Scotch-woman, hymn-book in hand, looked at him solemnly and said, "Ye think ye're breaking stanes, but ye're breaking Sabbath!" He was one day sitting on a heap of stones on the roadside near Scarborough, and examining them with his hammer, when a fashionable horse-woman stopped at a gate closing a horse-track, evidently wishing to pass through; whereupon the stonebreaker at once arose and unlatched the gate. The lady, mistaking the philosopher's profession, thanked him, while offering a penny, which he, like a gentleman, accepted with thanks, and returned to his work. Next day he found himself seated beside the lady at the Crown Hotel dinner, with mutual recognition.

Richard Cobden visited Hull during the Corn Law agitation. He was regarded by many as a dangerous demagogue, and his principles as likely to ruin the country; all the land would go out of cultivation and the fields and farms lie waste if the poor man's loaf was not taxed in keeping out the food which was plentiful across the narrow strait, while many of our own population were starving. Sitting beside him at dinner, I told him how pleased I was to see that he drank only water, and that his example helped to fortify me in my total abstinence. He said, in reply, that he took a little wine when at home and not campaigning; but when in full work, speaking night after night, he could not afford to take alcoholic liquors, as he needed all his strength of body and brain to do such work—a strong practical testimony to the physical advantage of total abstinence. I heard him on several

occasions, and admired his style of oratory—so simple, yet so
effective; effective because simple; no words used beyond the
comprehension of people of ordinary understanding; sentences
clear as crystal; the logic of facts; figures arithmetical, more
forceful than rhetorical; and a delivery impressive because
evidently sincere.   Opinions once considered dangerous have
been for years the statute law which all parties in the
State agree to uphold as essential to our national prosperity and promotion of peace among the nations. I was
invited to his funeral, and went in the same carriage with
my friend Charles Gilpin, who then held office in the Government, Milner Gibson, and Mr. Gladstone. Elihu Burritt,
the "learned blacksmith," who could speak in some dozen
languages, sat opposite to me, and, not aware that the great
statesman was so near him, spoke enthusiastically of his desire
to see him. What surprise and delight overspread his features
when I at once said, "Mr. Gladstone, Elihu Burritt wishes the
honour of taking your hand." The pleasure was mutual, and
deeply interesting the conversation that followed. In the procession to the grave I walked by the side of the celebrated
Dr. Hook, of Leeds, whom I had recently heard preach from
the words, "Hear the Church," in defence of Episcopal
authority. I preached a memorial sermon at Surrey Chapel
and at St. James's Hall, and published it as a small booklet,
which, at the time, had a large circulation. I desired in a
very humble way to help in perpetuating the memory of a
great benefactor of the people of England.

Henry Vincent often visited Hull, where his lectures on
Cromwell were very stirring, inculcating temperance, patriotism, freedom, and religion. Because he advocated the cause
of the working-people, he was unjustly charged with being a
Chartist in the evil sense of lawlessness, whereas, while condemning injustice, he was a constant advocate of loyalty
and peace. He was made responsible for some rioting which
he had striven to prevent, and was sentenced to two years'
imprisonment, but long before the expiration of the term
he was discharged by special vote of the House of Commons.

A few days before his death (December 29, 1878), he said to me that amid the false philosophies of the time he felt increasingly the universal need of humanity of the universal provision made in the Gospel. I spoke at his funeral.

Samuel Warren, as Recorder of Hull, was a periodical visitor to the town, and used to introduce the business of the court by a carefully prepared oration to the grand jury, not merely on the cases to be tried, but on the state of public affairs; discourses which were generally reported at length, not only in the local, but in the London papers. He occasionally favoured me with his company, and amused my friends with his fluent and anecdotal talk. The barristers on circuit seemed to get much amusement from him. I heard from one of them an illustration. At the York assizes he felt that a brother-barrister had attributed to him some action which he deemed discreditable. He privately remonstrated with his learned brother somewhat thus : "Of course you could not suppose that I really could have acted in such a way. What! I, Samuel Warren, Doctor of Civil Law, author of 'Ten Thousand a Year,' of European reputation, etc., etc.; that I could have acted so! Impossible! Surely you will rectify this when the court opens to-morrow?" "Certainly, certainly," was the response. So at the opening of the court, the offender craved indulgence, while he apologised in the very words of his aggrieved brother, saying : "My lord, it is impossible that I could have intended to impute such conduct to my learned friend. What! Samuel Warren! Doctor of Civil Law, etc., etc.," repeating all his titles, and so exactly in the tone and manner of the "aggrieved brother," that the barristers around, and even the judge, were scarcely able to restrain their laughter. When the facetious orator sat down, Samuel Warren shook him warmly by the hand, saying: "Thank you, thank you, brother! I was sure you would do the generous thing!"

I remember my interest in Cowden Clarke's lectures on the minor characters of Shakespeare; but especially the fascination of Mrs. Fanny Kemble when she read at the Literary Institute. Her sweet voice and expressive features, varying with the different characters, brought them in turn before us more vividly than perhaps any acting could have done. Shakespeare's page may be more vivid to some minds than any performance. I cannot forget a well-merited rebuke from Mrs. Kemble at my house. Our conversation turned on the subject of the theatre, and I was explaining that Christian ministers did not visit theatres, because many were objectionable by reason of the representations and the company, and because some theatres of the highest character occasionally had performances unfavourable to religion, and even modesty, and calculated to injure the minds of young people, and that Christians should be willing to abstain from what might injure others if not themselves. Therefore, I said, the clergy should patronise such readings as hers, presenting the beauties of Shakespeare harmlessly. With courteous but impressive emphasis she said, "I suppose you mean *recognise*," a correction I acknowledged as just.

Dr. Winter Hamilton, of Leeds, held a distinguished position for character and learning. His eloquence was rather ponderous and magniloquent, but in him it had become natural. He had a generous and devout heart. He assisted at my ordination, and when in the prayer of dedication solemn confession was made of the shortcomings of ministers, tears were seen flowing down his cheeks. Once at a dinner party he took notice in a humorous but rather satirical way of something I said, but he sought me out in the grounds soon after, and in a very touching way asked me to pardon what was likely, but was not meant, to grieve me. I was deeply impressed with this illustration of Christian humility in one so much older and so widely honoured, thus speaking to one just out of college and unknown.

As often happens, solemnity was linked with fun. When chairman of the Congregational Union, his eloquent oration was interrupted by the loud cheers which greeted the entrance of John Angell James. He looked up from his paper, and, seeing who it was, said, "Honour to whom honour is due." Another interruption followed on the entrance of a brother of totally different style, about whom there was an excited controversy, but who had some devoted partisans who always loudly cheered him. Again looking up, Hamilton quietly said, "And custom to whom custom."

I must not be forgetful of the many zealous men and women who helped me in my work, and ever treated me, not only with respect as their pastor, but with affection as a friend. Among others, I recall the memories of Kidd, Squire, Bowden, Burril, Darling, Towers, Gibson, Tarbolton, Oldham, Westerdale, Cross, Ostler, and others—brothers and sisters in Christ, "whose names are in the book of life."

I was invited to preach at most of the Yorkshire Free Churches—Beverley, Selby, Leeds, Huddersfield, Filey, Harrogate, York, Ripon,—but can only allude further to two.

Halifax was the town I first visited from Hull. I was the guest of Sir Francis Crossley, then occupying a house small in comparison with the palatial residence he afterwards built. He took me to see his mother, dwelling in the original family house attached to the mill. He seemed proud of telling me how his father had risen from being a hand-worker at the loom, and how his mother had been a domestic servant with a ten-pound wage. Unlike some small-minded people who, having risen to great things, are ashamed of their little origin, he never deprived himself of this honour. He would have placed his mother in the best apartment of his big house, but she preferred to dwell in the home of her husband and earlier domestic life. I so well remember her fervent responses of "Amen!" as we knelt together. A true "mother in Israel."

When he was Mayor of Halifax, he stood beside me on the top of an old terrace-wall, holding my hat as I preached to a crowd of working-people, shod with "clogs," the women with shawls over their heads instead of "hanging gardens."

I remember at a great meeting, while he was making a speech, hearing an admiring workman shout, "Spak oot, Frank, lad!" I still more remember his occupying the chair when I delivered a lecture on "Teetotalism," because at the close, as his practical approval of the "vote of thanks," he took a pen, and before his own people and fellow-citizens, signed the pledge. He inherited parental religion, and was elected to Parliament as Member for one of the largest constituencies—the West Riding ; and was subsequently honoured by the Queen, by advice of Mr. Gladstone, with a baronetcy.

He and his brothers did not in their prosperity forget the poor. One of other memorials is the vast Orphanage School on the rocky heights near his former residence; another is the row of comfortable almshouses just behind it. I was visiting one of the residents, an old, worn-out, decrepit workman, rich in grace. We prayed together, and at my request, leaning back in his easy-chair, he prayed for me in terms I have never forgotten: "God bless him ! make him like the candlestick— beaten gold! Help him to say as the sailor when he rounds a dangerous point, ' All is well !' If Thou make him useful, Thou wilt give him trials ; but it's grand cross-bearin' when it's tied on wi' love !"

Another of his benefactions was the "People's Park." It commands extensive views, and is adorned with sculpture. As I was inspecting a large statue of himself, I said to a boy, who also was looking at it, "Who's that ? " Boy : "It's Frank Crossley !" N. H. : " He'll be cold out there all night ? " Boy : " He ain't wick ! it's nobbot shaape on 'im !"

The first wedding at which I officiated after the Dissenting Marriages Act was at Halifax. The bride and bridegroom were very youthful and uncultured. It was before the age of Board schools. I had to instruct them in the ritual. Prior to the declaration, "I take thee to be my lawful wedded wife," I said to the youth, "You are to repeat after me," and then, as he did not know what to do, I whispered, " Take her right hand," on which, in a loud voice, he shouted, " Tak' 'er roight aand !" much to the amusement of the bridesmaids. Then came a difficulty in placing the ring on the finger of the bride, who suggested as a remedy, " Wat it !" and, acting on this affectionate counsel, he put her finger into his mouth, and, after lubrication, succeeded. Again followed the unavoidable laugh, which the officiating clergyman only avoided by a very severe pinching of his thigh.

On occasion of the opening of a new church, erected on his great manufacturing estate near Halifax, by Sir Titus Salt, I was one of a large company who spent several days together at "Crow Nest." Among the officiating clergy were Thomas Binney, Enoch Mellor, and Dr. Guthrie. The sermons were of the highest character, and the conversation at dinner was natural, intellectual, devout, and sometimes humorous. Mr. Binney had a natural aversion to caper-sauce. This was being handed to him, when he started up with sudden revulsion. Someone asked what was the matter. Guthrie at once replied, "It's only Binney *cutting his capers!*" A lady observed, "What a *saucy* remark!"

One of my chief ministerial friends was Enoch Mellor, D.D., a great reader, a profound thinker, a prince of preachers. Uniting as he did great forcefulness of argument with brilliant imagination and beauty of language, I used to compare him to an iron column wreathed with flowers. Many a walk we had together on the hills and through the dells of the West Riding, especially Todmorden Valley. Preaching was his passion. I could seldom be in his company without his telling me of some recent sermon—text and treatment—and making similar inquiries of me. Thus we have passed many a happy hour, climbing and sermonising. One would suggest a text or topic, the other would propose first head, and so on, illustrations being thrown in by the way. Then we agreed to preach on the same subject on some fixed day, each according to his own natural style. Thus we passed a very happy day together in Switzerland, on a mountain excursion, suggesting to each other analogies illustrating the text, "Thy righteousness is like the great mountains."

He told me of some peculiar though very sincere petitions at his prayer-meetings by some of his members from the mills. During the American War there was a great dearth of cotton, and a quantity of inferior short fibre came from Surat in India. One good man prayed, "O Lord, send us cotton! send us cotton! but not Surat, Lord!"

Dr. Mellor was continually invited to preach special sermons in distant places; but he was chiefly appreciated

at home, by rich and poor, his condensed, pungent style
being thoroughly understood by an audience very varied in
worldly position, but very much alike in shrewd intelligence
and Bible knowledge. The only objection to him was his
popularity elsewhere. In praying for him one day, a good
man said, "O Lord, bless our Enoch! we love him, Lord!
but, O Lord, tie him by the leg; tie him by the leg!"

Dr. Mellor preached many years at the large and beautiful
"Square Church" erected chiefly by the Crossleys. Then for
a few years he took the church at Liverpool vacated by the
decease of Dr. Raffles; but the enduring affection of his former
flock prevailed on him to return to them, and there he closed
his earthly ministry.

Some little time ago the following incident was narrated
to me by his daughter :—

"Travelling to Halifax, my father felt concerned for a
young girl in the same carriage, who seemed very unhappy.
On sympathetic inquiry, he was told that she was leaving
home to be a housemaid in a family at Halifax. He tried to
comfort her, and gave her suitable advice. As she said she
had been brought up to the Church of England, he begged
her to go to the nearest church, and join the Sunday school.
She had no idea who he was, but she followed his advice.
On occasion of a public election there was a great open-air
meeting, and she saw a gentleman announced as Dr. Mellor,
step on the platform, welcomed with loud cheers. She
recognised him as her kind adviser, and in grateful memory
she cheered the loudest. Years passed, she married, and
had joined a mothers' meeting conducted by Dr. Mellor's
daughter, to whom this young woman gave this history, saying
that the kindness of the gentleman and his good advice had
been her salvation."

I was much interested in the building of the "Bar Church,"
Scarborough—so called because near to the old Gate House
or "Bar." It was erected in Gothic style, with tower and
transepts. My dear friend, Robert Balgarnie, was the first
pastor, and preached to crowded congregations every Sunday,
and in the afternoons on the sands to large multitudes of

seamen, fishermen, and visitors. This work, during many years, resulted in the salvation of many people. It was my privilege on several occasions to take part with him in these preachings and the subsequent distribution of tracts. As I write this (June, 1898), I am reminded of a week of sermons there, and of the good impressions received, forty years ago, by my informant, when a child.

The "Bar Church" became too small for the increasing congregation. The "West Cliff Church" was erected chiefly by the zeal of Sir Titus Salt. I preached at the opening, and Mr. Balgarnie removed to it as its first pastor.

On a ten-days' voyage across the Atlantic, I was witness to his zeal and tact in reaching the hearts of the seamen, whom we met on the forecastle at the dog-watch. My friend had a treasury of pleasant stories, and the men urged us to visit them again. Afterwards a passage of Scripture was explained, with prayer, the men joining lustily in a hymn. Had we attempted to get up a regular service we might have failed. But "where there's a will there's a way." Alas, how many opportunities of usefulness are missed because we are slaves to formalities!

Mr. Balgarnie was much sought by the sick and dying, residents and visitors, of all denominations and of none. He took a lively interest in all philanthropies, especially caring for policemen and carriage-drivers. He also visited cottages in the country. One day I accompanied him in a long ramble on the Downs, and called to see an aged parishioner of his, a very small farmer. The cattle disease was prevalent, and the poor man had lost two or three out of his dozen. In reply to our sympathy, he said, "The Bible tells us that the cattle on a thousand hills are His: so when He wants any He knows where to find 'em." I cannot forget his unconventional response to my friend's prayer—"That's capital!"

I am reminded of an unconscious benefit rendered by my friend Balgarnie—one of many hundreds of a similar character. A lady wrote saying she owed him more gratitude than she could express. She had a son who was struggling against the evil habit of drinking. She dreaded his going to Scarborough lest the customs of society might lead him away. She dreaded the example, not of the worldly, but of Christian professors, who took wine. Her son had written to say he was at an evening party where wine was handed round, and he was about to take it, enticed by the example of some very respectable and good people. But he saw you refused it, and this fortified him in resisting the temptation, which with *him* might have led to ruin. By simple, silent abstinence Mr. Balgarnie had saved her boy.

After many years devoted and useful work at Scarborough, Mr. Balgarnie resigned the pastoral office for evangelistic work, and has since been continually engaged in holding " missions " in all parts of the land.

CHAPTER VIII.

I CANNOT omit the long struggle of the Chartists. Except by
their own class, they were generally shunned as dangerous. I
was among a minority who expressed any sympathy with
them, and who went among them to advise and counsel them.

I remember the great Chartist Day, when tens of thousands
carried the monster petition over Blackfriars Bridge to Kennington Common. The Bank was fortified, sand-bags were
on the walls, guns were in position at the bridges, special
constables were sworn in—Louis Napoleon was one of them.
The Government contrived to frighten the country with fear
of a revolution. The Chartists asked for what is now the law
of the land. They carried no weapons and intended no violence, but the preparations to resist them might have led to
bloodshed. I was in Blackfriars Road, near Surrey Chapel,
looking at the crowds who were allowed to go out to Kennington Common; but the police blocked the bridges on their
return, so that the crowds pushed from behind but could not
get across, causing a terrible squeezing and great danger of
collision.

Rather than identify myself with any political party, I
have always regarded the New Testament as the Bible of social
law and public policy. It was with peculiar interest that I
read the weekly numbers of the *Christian Socialist*, conducted
by Charles Kingsley, Frederick Maurice, and "Tom Hughes."

I preached several times on the subject, and condensed the
matter into a small pamphlet, entitled, "Divine Socialism; or,
The Man Christ Jesus." The title was appropriate to theme
and purpose, but not conducive to a large circulation; for
the word "Divine" repelled some Socialists and the word
"Socialism" alarmed some Christians. But I trust it may

still be of use to render more scriptural the notions of those who regard Christ as solely proclaiming a Kingdom of Heaven hereafter, instead of also a heavenly kingdom here.

Men have always been following other men with all their imperfections, instead of accepting the headship of Christ, ordained to be "the leader and commander of the people" of every region: Christ the man—poor, sorrowing, toiling; champion of justice, freedom, and love; a martyr—the sacrifice for the world, conquering the grave by dying, by living for ever, to bless by ruling, to come again to "reign in righteousness and break in pieces the oppressor." Whatever part I ever took in politics, this has been the motive, the object, the rule —Christ Himself: the fulfilment of His prayer, "Thy Kingdom come." I continually tried to impress on the multitude that the only true universal brotherhood and practicable socialistic equality was in loyalty to the people's Divine Friend, the King of kings. I used to quote the grand words of Milton:— "To be free is the same thing as to be pious, wise, temperate, abstinent; and to be the opposite to all these is the same as to be a slave, and it usually happens that those who cannot govern themselves, but crouch under the slavery of their lusts, should be delivered to the sway of those whom they abhor, and made to submit to an involuntary servitude."

Men are truly free when, serving God supremely, they are delivered from all other fear. Christ, the elder Brother, is the head of all true fraternity. Love thy neighbour as thyself. Honour all men. This is the only true brotherhood, attainable not by impossible levelism, not by destructive revolutionism, but by love, to begin at once with every believer in Christ, and to go on advancing till all are one family.

Christ crucified is the banner of brotherhood. The Church may have failed to wield aright the "sword of the Spirit," but it has lost none of its heavenly temper. The restless tide that sweeps to and fro the shifting sands of theory leaves no trace on the granite cliff. When philosophy asks for doctrine suited to the age, and moralists a system to promote virtue, and reformers a check to selfish greed and pride, Christian teachers should proclaim, not mere dogma, however correct, but a personal, living, present Christ; not chiefly churches, creeds, sacraments ; not the mere doctrines, but the Christ of the Gospel.

Never let it be supposed that men who think lightly of Christianity are more concerned than ourselves to promote the present welfare of mankind. The Christian Church, as tribunes of the people, should be ever ready to plead the people's cause. As at the battle of Hastings, Kent claimed its ancient privilege of fighting in the front, so Christians—not by arrogant assumption, but by more ardent zeal—should be in the forefront of the battle of philanthropy. Oh, for the time when the sublime hymn of the ancient Church shall be manifested in fact—" The holy Church throughout all the world doth acknowledge Thee. . . . Thou art the King of glory, O Christ !" * I sent a copy of my tractate to Charles Kingsley, with thanks for his writings, and received the following reply :—

"Eversley, June 1, 1851.

"MY DEAR SIR,—I cannot sufficiently express the pleasure with which I have read the sermon, ' Divine Socialism,' which you have been kind enough to send me. It is most delightful to find the same ideas springing up, as if by a general moving of the Spirit, which ' bloweth where it will,' in independent and isolated quarters. It is a sign that God is with us—that *this* is the word which He will have spoken just now, *this* the side of Christianity which is to give power and life to the New Reformation which is surely coming. Pray let me have the honour of hearing from you again, and believe me, yours most faithfully and obliged, " C. KINGSLEY."

At Sir W. L.'s I first met his brother-in-law, William Gordon, M.D., who devoted all his leisure to the welfare of the working classes. There were demagogues whose evil counsels, tending to violence, he laboured successfully to controvert, so that in Hull no danger was apprehended. His Chartism was the upholding of law in constitutional efforts to improve it. Instead of holding aloof, and from a distance censuring the masses, he went among them and expressed sympathy with their troubles, while exhorting them to refrain from violence, and better themselves by temperance, industry, and patient advocacy of their just claims. Thus he was maligned as a Chartist in the sense of violence.

* See my tractate, "The Man Christ Jesus," in my penny series of tracts. (Nisbet).

His temperance labours were misconstrued, to his pro-
fessional injury. Because teetotalism was opposed to the then
prevalent medical practice, he lost most of his paying patients,
but his gratuitous advice to the poor filled his consulting-
room, and enlarged the circle of his poor friends. He grieved
at the "idolatry of Drink," as impoverishing homes, causing
crime, engendering disease, counteracting all religious and
educating influences. By medical science he disproved prevalent fallacies about alcohol being necessary for health and
strength. He was one of the very first of the medical advocates of abstinence, now, happily, so numerous. He addressed
crowds of eager auditors, with a clearness of argument, a
beauty of diction, and a force of eloquence, little known then
on the temperance platform. Many were our journeys together for the delivery of addresses on this great question.
It was always a delight to listen to him and to witness the
enthusiasm evoked.

He had been a diligent student in science, and, like many
medical men in those days, was supposed to be a materialist.
I often had pleasant arguments with him, encouraging him to
tell me all his doubts. He came regularly to my evening
sermons with his relatives, and was impressed by the sincerity
of their religious profession and with the Christian fervour of
my parents on their visits to his house. While his creed
seemed doubtful, he was an earnest seeker after truth; but
was sometimes hindered by the reproaches of some who illustrated Milton's words: "A man may be a heretic in the
Truth; and if he believes things only because his pastor says
so, or the Assembly so determines, without knowing other
reason, though his belief be true, yet the very truth he holds
becomes his heresy." I often feared that intellectual difficulties might hinder his reception of the Gospel, and that his
beneficent life might interfere with his being conscious of his
need of a Saviour. But gradually, and unknown to me, the
Holy Spirit and the truth of the Gospel had been influencing
his heart, and this great change was eventually expressed in
terms which delighted those who for years had been praying that
the good physician might become the happy, penitent believer.

The following collection of some of his own actual words at different times and in broken sentences during a long and painful illness must be pardoned because illustrating what was then, and has continued to be, my desire to experience and to teach.

"When I look back on my own life, I see that imperfection or mixture of selfish motive was in my most benevolent efforts. . . . If consciousness of my own unworthiness and reliance on Christ alone be a proper ground of peace, I have it, and have long had it. I have long been feeling my way after the truth . . . . The New Testament is the Book. We can only obtain peace by casting ourselves on Jesus."

"Almighty God, unto whom all hearts be open, all desires known, and from whom no secrets are hid ; Cleanse the thoughts of our hearts by the inspiration of thy Holy Spirit, that we may perfectly love thee, and worthily magnify thy Holy Name ; through Christ our Lord."

To a nephew :—

"Good-bye, dear boy. Let me tell you what Adrian said to his soul in prospect of death :

> ' Animula, vagula, blandula ;
> Hospes, comesque corporis,
> Quæ nunc abibis in loca
> Pallidula, rigida, nudula ?
> Nec ut soles, dabis jocos.'

I will translate it for you : ' Kind little wandering soul, companion, and guest of my body, into what places art thou now about to depart ?' O my dear boy, remember what a much better hope the Gospel gives your uncle. . . ."

He received nearly three hundred visits during the last three weeks of his life from persons of all ranks, and delighted in bearing witness of the hope within him, making that sick-room, as one of his visitors said at the grave, "not at all the chamber of death, but the robing-room of heaven." To my father, the author of " The Sinner's Friend," he sent this message :—

"Tell him that I'm the sinner, and that I've found the Friend. Though I've not made a profession, it was not because I was *ashamed* of Christ, but I was so often shocked at the conduct of some professors. . . ."

He said to me :—

"Preach earnestly and simply, so as to be understood. Men think more of sincerity and consistency than anything. I think little of preaching about evidences. Scripture is its own witness—its great truths. The facts of Christianity are granted. I always acknowledged its historic truth. I did more ; I loved and honoured it, and always

I

felt the religious man the happiest, though I did not feel as now the
need of Christ for myself. . . ."

"My chief hindrances were professors who could approve methods
and actions from which I revolted—injudiciousness of some Christians
in their mode of talking piety, also intolerance. Anxiety about religion
made me ask questions which were put down as infidelity. Often I have
not dared to make free inquiries. This looked to me as if they distrusted
their own religion. I remember giving lectures on physical education
to which someone replied on behalf of Christianity, as if the science and
the religion could not both be true. . . ."

He was much interested in listening to the following
letter of Oliver Cromwell:—

"'Love says, 'What a Christ have I! What a Father in and through
Him! What a covenant! I'll do away their sins ; I'll write My law in
their hearts. What God hath done, and is to us in Christ, is the root of
our comfort. Acts of obedience are not perfect, and yield not perfect
peace. Faith, as an act, yields it not, but only as it carries us unto Him
who is our perfect peace. This is our high calling. Rest we here.'"

Another letter addressed by the Protector to his daughter,
Bridget Ireton, specially interested him :—

"'Your sister seeks after what will satisfy. Thus to be a seeker is to
be of the best sect next to a finder, and such an one shall every faithful,
humble seeker be at the end. Happy seeker! happy finder! Whoever
found that the Lord is gracious without some sense of badness? Dear
heart, press on. Let not husband nor anything cool thy affections after
Christ. That which is best worthy of love in thy husband is the image
of Christ he bears. . . ."*

To an elderly non-believer, who told him he had always
lived a good life, he replied:—

"All my reasoning brings me to this—I must rest on Christ."

His infidel friend said :—

"I would give worlds to be in the same state of mind. He would be
a vile man who would try to shake your confidence."

Referring to this conversation, Dr. G. said :—

"Some object to Christianity because against reason, but all things
are incomprehensible. We know not what an infinitesimal atom is. We
conceive of its infinite division, and yet every particle must have its
upper and its under side. We know not the end of space or time. We
must come to the Bible and trust as little children. God seemed determined to save me, and has been, so to speak, running after me. He is

* Carlyle's "Oliver Cromwell's Letters and Speeches." "The Protector,"
by Merle d'Aubigné.

always asking us to join Him, yet we refuse. The great evidence for the Gospel is its adaptation to our wants. With this inward evidence I could laugh to scorn the sophistry that calls in question the truth of Christianity. But many are anxious for truth who are unable to find it, and deserve pity. Intolerance is a curse to society. As for Mr. X., I believe he will die a Christian."

This hope was verified. I knew him well. He never forgot this interview. After years of professed unbelief he became an earnest Christian, and died in peaceful hope.

" I see where Christians are wrong. We do not make a companion of God. We should treat Him much as a friend, always near, so that we are continually in His company. Ordinary duties of life may be solemn acts of worship. It is this having God with me as my companion makes me so happy. I dislike to sleep because I lose the enjoyment. I have often been surprised that Christians seemed to be made so little happy by their religion. They have looked for happiness in themselves instead of to what is in Christ. And this is the best source of holy living. His salvation is offered to all—the very worst, to everyone ; and so there is no room for doubt. Some dread death because they must go alone. But I shall not be alone. Christ will not only receive me at the end, He accompanies me on my journey."

Asked if we had done right in not urging religion on him more personally, he said :—

" You did right. You knew my disposition. You have preached to me in the best way."

To a nephew :—

" Seek Christ early. . . . I love my rich friends, but the poor are my flock. Be great and seek little things; don't be little and seek great things."

Asked whether by renouncing controversy he meant his former political efforts, he said :—

" Certainly not. Were I to recover, I should do as I have done in these respects, only more enthusiastically than ever, as the cause of truth and human happiness.

" All the analysis I can make of my own mind proves the truth of Christianity—it so provides for all the wants of the soul. How reliance on Christ's works would purify my own works, were I going to live ! Faith in Him would prevent my doing anything against the will of God. I am a mass of corruption, but I revel in the atonement. To know it in the head is not to know it. . . . I feel at home already. No more dying in the heavenly Jerusalem. There is none here."

Again at his request the Lord's Supper was observed, at

the close of which we sang "Rock of Ages." During the next twenty-four hours his strength rapidly declined. After a pause, during which he seemed gazing on unseen glories, he said, "Repeat that about the great multitude in white robes." Then the passage was recited, "These are they which came out of great tribulation, and have washed their robes, and made them white in the blood of the Lamb" (Rev. vii. 9–17). Then he seemed no longer conscious of what was visible here, but he gazed upward as in rapt vision. Features which had become motionless suddenly yielded to a smile of ecstasy no pencil could depict, and when it passed, still the face continued to beam and brighten as if reflecting the glory on which the soul was gazing. It appeared to those around, about twenty in number, as if, in fact, luminous. Did he not, like Stephen, behold "the Son of Man standing at the right hand of God"? It is not too much to say that as far as the expression of holy rapture could contribute to it, "his face was as if it had been the face of an angel."

Ten thousand people, chiefly artisans, thronged the road to the grave, over which was raised by public subscription a marble obelisk with the inscription:

WILLIAM GORDON,
THE PEOPLE'S FRIEND.

In memoriam I wrote the following sonnet:—

"DEATH IS SWALLOWED UP IN VICTORY."

Are death's dark emblems suited for the grave
Of those who dwell in Heaven's unclouded light?
For souls arrayed in robes of dazzling white
Shall blackest palls and plumes funereal wave?
Shall lilies drooping with untimely blight,
Torches reversed whose flame is quenched in night,
And columns shattered, our compassion crave
For those whom Christ, by death, did fully save—
Who now, made perfect, serve, and in His sight
Drink of the fountain of supreme delight?
Rear high the shaft! "NEW LIFE" thereon engrave!
Turn up the torch! it never burnt so bright;
A richer beauty to the lily give!
The Christian dies that he may fully live.

In apology for this lengthy narrative I plead that it is really autobiography, because it is a summary of my teaching during sixty years. The Gospel in its power to meet the chief necessities of the human heart is its own best witness ; the universal need of the atoning sacrifice and the results of accepting it in producing righteousness and peace ; and eternal life, the present possession of all who really trust in Him who said, " He that believeth in Me shall never die." He who had been the teacher felt himself to be a humble learner in that sick room, and has been instructed by it ever since.

The loss of my dear friend and other sorrows weighed heavily on me, but I found great consolation in contemplating the presence of Jesus in the storm, and His voice saying, " It is I ; be not afraid ! " This formed the subject of several sermons, afterwards condensed in a tractlet, the third of my publications at Hull. This has had a circulation of 150,000, and has been translated into several languages. Some years since I casually read in a newspaper report of a Tract Society meeting the following instance of the usefulness of tracts. A tourist in the north of Italy saw an invalid Italian soldier sitting in a garden reading a small book, in the French language, entitled " It is I ! " He stated that it was given him by a French comrade, who used to read it constantly by the watch-fires at night. They promised that if either of them were killed, his little belongings should be the property of the survivor. This comrade said that this little book had been a great comfort to him, and he hoped, if his friend survived, he would take this from his pocket as a dying keepsake and find from it the same peace. This French friend was killed at Solferino. The wounded survivor was now, from his comrade's book, enjoying the same peace. In connection with this tractate I may here recall a Sunday spent in the Ormonds valley near the Diablerets. I attended the village Protestant church in the afternoon, and at the close of the service spoke to the pastor, who asked my name. Then with a loud voice he summoned his departing congregation to tell them I was the author of " Come to Jesus." A country-woman came to thank me, and said, as she pointed to a châlet high on the mountain slope, that she had left open on her table my book, "It is I!" which she was reading with profit. I thanked God that in a very humble measure I was not only a Swiss tourist, but a Swiss pastor.

Albion Church was strictly Congregational, as its name imports. All officers were appointed, all members admitted, and all arrangements, financial and other, made with the concurrence of the congregation. All the accounts of the church and all its societies were annually audited, passed, and published.

A few days before leaving Hull I wrote in the Church book a summary of my work in Hull, and a statement of my proposed methods on entering an enlarged sphere. The general principles are applicable to my whole pastorate of fifty years, and need no formal repetition. This memorandum has been kindly copied from the Albion Church book by the honorary secretary:—

MEMORANDUM BY NEWMAN HALL, B.A., FIRST PASTOR.

"On Sunday, June 25th, 1854, I resigned the pastorate, having held it for twelve years. I did so with very great pain, having enjoyed uninterrupted harmony during my connection with a loving and zealous flock. But as I obeyed a conviction of duty when I came, so also I go, as I believe, at the call of my Master, after long deliberation and earnest prayer.

"When I came the members were 42 ; 647 have since been added. A branch chapel, with all the sittings free, and school have been opened. In our Sunday-schools there are 768 children and 72 teachers. Other institutions include a young men's Bible-class of 60 members ; Christian Instruction Society, visiting 1,000 families in thirty districts ; a town missionary, who, besides paying 4,000 visits yearly, has preached 200 times in cottages and the open air ; clothing society ; inquirers' class, admirably presided over by Mr. Kidd, in preparation for membership ; class meetings, etc. etc.

"The congregation have laboured with me in prayer and works of faith. The deacons have preserved peace by their courtesy and encouragement in all holy service. In the ministry I have made no pretension to learning or eloquence, but I have preached the Gospel with simplicity and fervour. A personal Christ, and not a dead theology, has been my subject, and my endeavour has always been to reach the hearts of my hearers, and by all means to save some. I may also mention that taking an interest in the general welfare of mankind— mingling with the poor, attending meetings of the working classes—

efforts in the temperance cause, preaching frequently in the open air
delivering lectures on secular topics, interwoven with Christian truth—
may have tended to create sympathy in the hearts of the great masses
of the people.

"Our Temperance Society and Band of Hope has 1,200 members.
The experience of twelve years confirms my conviction that the full
efficacy of the ministry cannot be proved, under the existing circumstances of our country, except in connection with the practice and
advocacy of total abstinence from intoxicating beverages.

"I leave this book to my successor, whoever he may be. I pray
that the blessing of the Great Head of the Church may most abundantly be with him, and that he may be far more successful than God
has rendered my poor labours. For the work which God has done I
rejoice. For my own work, before the Searcher of Hearts, I have to
humble myself in repentance, my consolation being that Christ bears
the sin of our holy things. And for my beloved people, I pray that
grace, mercy, and peace may be with them from God our Father and
the Lord Jesus Christ.

"In hope of eternal life. Amen.

"NEWMAN HALL,

"First Pastor of the Albion Congregational Church, Hull.

"Albion Church, Hull,
"June 30th, 1854."

At a farewell meeting of the congregation various
addresses were presented from the church, the schools, and the
mission, expressing affection and gratitude for my twelve
years of pastorate, together with a handsome gift of plate.

CHAPTER IX.

ROWLAND HILL was born at the ancestral seat of his family, Hawkstone Hall, Shropshire, and was educated at St. John's College, Cambridge. His ministry commenced in the Established Church, but his fervent zeal would not be restrained by ecclesiastical order, and he preached the Gospel to listening crowds wherever the opportunity was presented, and laboured fraternally with all Christians. He was ordained deacon, but because of his disorderly catholicity he could not be ordained "priest," and so he said he went about preaching "the common salvation" with only one ecclesiastical boot on. In order to be unfettered in a ministry thus unsectarian, he, with the aid of sympathising friends, erected Surrey Chapel, the foundation being laid on June 24th, 1782.

It was opened by him on June 8th, 1783. His text was, "We preach Christ crucified." It was designed to be, and has continued to be, a Free Church. Clergymen, both Established and Nonconforming, preached in it; among the former, Berridge, Venn, and Scott the commentator; among the latter, Bull, Jay, and James frequently occupied the pulpit. The worship included both liturgical and free prayer. Christians of all ecclesiastical opinions were welcome to its communion, and preachers of all Evangelical Churches to its pulpit, on the common ground of faith in Christ and practical benevolence.

By no act of his own, he was excluded from the Church of his fathers, which he still loved while lamenting its imperfections. The question of "Establishment" was not then discussed. He did not object to the theory of Episcopacy, but only to its defective working. He used the liturgical service with a few verbal alterations. He opposed the parochial system because of its restrictions, as in his own case, and in that of

Wesley, who claimed " all the world as his parish." He declined to ally himself exclusively with any particular " denomination," regarding all believers as the one true Catholic Church.

During a ministry of sixty-six years he preached at least
23,000 sermons, of which many were in streets and fields. He
spent very little time in studying them, but was a constant
student of the Bible, and used human character and daily life
for illustration. In the vestry there is a set of volumes
containing reports of his sermons, transcribed from shorthand
notes. I have several times looked to see what he had said
on a particular text, but seldom found any direct reference to
it in the way of interpretation or exposition, though a rich-
ness in pious thoughts.

It is said that on one occasion when he had to preach in
Edinburgh, the elders suggested that as the Scotch were
accustomed to orderly discourses, Mr. Hill might indulge them
with a few heads and divisions. He thanked them for their
counsel, and thus began his sermon, " I ask you first to go
round the text." After quoting the context, he said, "Secondly,
we will go up to the text"; then he read the verse preceding
it ; " Thirdly, we will go through the text," and the words were
emphasised. Then, within five minutes of the first announcement, " Now, fourthly, *we will go away from the text;* and
now I find myself quite at home."

He was eminently gifted with wit, but this very seldom
appeared in the pulpit, and then not by any effort to show it
off, but because unable to restrain it. The following instance
is I think new to print, and only traditional. There was some
disturbance in the crowded gallery while he was in the
fervour of preaching. He stopped, and then said, " Whenever good is being done, the devil gets into the gallery and
makes a disturbance." A man rose and said, " Please, Mr.
Hill, it's only a lady fainting." To which the preacher
responded, " Oh, I beg the lady's pardon and the devil's
too ! " Some will think this was carrying too far his gentlemanly politeness. He was falsely reported to have said in the
pulpit, " Here comes Mrs. Hill with a chest on her head."
When told of this, he remarked with indignation, " Sir, I hope

that the Minister, if not the Gentleman, always prevented me from making my wife a laughing-stock for the amusement of the vulgar."

Mr. Hill spent the summer in evangelising throughout the country, having his central home at Wotton in Gloucestershire, but he occupied his London manse and pulpit at Surrey Chapel during six or eight months of winter, where he continued pastor fifty years. His last sermon was delivered, within a fortnight of his decease, to Sunday school teachers on words to which his nearness to eternity gave peculiar emphasis—" Therefore, my beloved brethren, be ye stedfast, unmoveable, always abounding in the work of the Lord, forasmuch as ye know that your labour is not in vain in the Lord." His last few days were spent on his bed in the Surrey parsonage, looking upon the chapel. A London friend came to see him and told him how deeply the city felt for him. His wit was not yet asleep. " Indeed ! have the funds gone down ? " The faithful workman entered into the rest of his Lord on April 11th, 1833, at the age of eighty-eight.

After a short interval, the Rev. James Sherman, of Reading, was called to the pastorate in 1836. Under his faithful and affectionate ministry of twenty years the membership doubled, fresh societies were formed, and five schoolrooms were opened or enlarged.

Owing to increasing toils, with diminished strength, Mr. Sherman removed to Blackheath, where he continued his useful ministry for several years. On the first Sunday of July, 1854, he bade farewell to his sorrowing flock, and on the following Sunday he entered the pulpit with his successor, commending me to their sympathy and prayers. Thus there was no interval of ministry, no vacant pulpit.

I carried forward his various methods of work, so that the congregation might not lament that the old order had changed. At the outset I recognised that the various claims of the church—intellectual, pastoral, evangelistic—were too much for one man to meet, and that he should have an assistant. This was at once agreed to, and was continued with satisfaction to all. First I had the joy of my dear friend

Edward Cecil's help and companionship during several years. Afterwards came Dr. R. Thomas, now of Boston, U.S.A. He had been Scripture-reader in the parish, and on one Sunday read prayers for us. For this he was rebuked by his vicar, and required to promise not to repeat the offence. As he had read only his own liturgy, he declined, and was thereupon dismissed from his office, and accepted the post of curate with us. After some years of growing efficiency, was during several years pastor of the church in Mile End Road, formerly occupied by the celebrated Dr. Reed, which became crowded with working-men to listen on Monday evenings to instructive lectures. By such means the church was soon filled on Sunday. Dr. R. Thomas has now for many years been pastor in one of the handsomest structures and of one of the highest-class Congregational churches in America. The Rev. Henry Grainger has since won, and retained during twenty years, the respect and affection of pastor and people. It was by such coadjutors that I was enabled to give increased attention to pulpit preparation, and also, after the example of my predecessors, to respond to many invitations from the wider sphere of the country at large. As at Hull, my morning sermons were generally expository. My evening subjects were very varied—evangelistic, didactic, illustrative, argumentative, hortative, consolatory, and lessons from passing events.

Instead of detailing my work during thirty-eight years, I will simply, once for all, give a general idea of it. To avoid interruption and secure mental rest, I slept at a distance to enable me to work properly at the centre. But the assistant-minister lived at the parsonage, where Rowland Hill had resided, and attended to visitation of the sick, and to classes, marriages, burials, and so on.

I spent Sundays at the church, preaching morning and evening, visiting the schools and the sick in the afternoon, except during the ten years when I preached at St. James's Hall in the afternoon. After evening service I either held an "after" prayer-meeting in the church or preached outside. At the St. James's Hall services in the afternoon, inaugurated

by my zealous friend Mr. Miller, I read the Litany, with a
short lesson and brief extempore prayer and three hymns, the
sermon occupying half an hour. The hall was generally full,
sometimes even the upper gallery. People of all conditions
assembled. The seats were all open and free. As the service
was not identified with any one section of the Church, many
came who otherwise would have held aloof. I have heard of
and from people of high as well as of humble rank receiving
benefit.

I may add that, although on weekdays I was very
often preaching elsewhere, I sacredly reserved Sunday for
home work, and between October and July was scarcely ever
absent from my own people. Monday forenoon was occupied
with correspondence, mostly in connection with church work.
In the afternoon I visited the sick and poor in South London;
met my elders at five, and conferred in reference to relief of the
poor and admission of members ; weekly prayer-meeting and
address at seven ; after which, committees, "inquirers," and,
during summer, open-air services, week-night service and
sermon on Wednesday, and frequently some important meeting of societies during the week. Wednesdays and Thursdays were frequently occupied in preaching for other churches,
or speaking at temperance and other philanthropic meetings.
Friday and Saturday were reserved for pulpit preparation.
More or less this was habitual, and needs no repetition.
The following records relate to what was occasional and
supplementary.

As a relief to readers weary of church facts, I may be
excused for introducing a rhyme of church fancies by an
old friend of Mr. Sherman and myself, who united forensic
solemnity with platform fun. He was greatly esteemed in
Exeter Hall as an enlivener of dull meetings, as well as in
the City as an able judge in criminal cases at Guildhall.
Judge Payne was an earnest pleader for evangelical truth,
for temperance, and benevolence, and was well known by
his habit of closing his addresses with rhymes which
lightened learning with laughter. These were expected and
welcomed as Judge Payne's "tail-pieces." At a tea-meeting

soon after my introduction to Surrey Chapel, he thus finished
his speech :—

> " Old Man Sherman away has fled,
> And New Man Hall has come in his stead ;
> Our sun has gone down, and yet no night
> Has followed its setting, but all's still bright !

> " Old Man Sherman has got good looks,
> And Old Man Sherman has written good books ;
> And New Man Hall, as the Public says,
> Is very well off in the self-same ways.

> " Old Man Sherman possesses great power
> To please the young in devotion's hour ;
> And New Man Hall, as I've heard tell,
> Can do it almost, if not quite as well.

> " Long may it be ere the Lord shall call
> Either Old Man Sherman or New Man Hall ;
> And may they both live to be seen as lights
> Which never burn dim either days or nights.

> " And may we all, when our course is run,
> And our work for God upon earth is done,
> Before the throne of His glory fall,
> With Old Man Sherman and New Man Hall."

A clerical critic writes, " Too poor ! Pray omit ! One of
my deacons could do better." I beg to differ. If the rhymes
were better poetry, they would be worse for my purpose—to
illustrate mental culture and superior position, recreating
itself and amusing others of lowly degree. Of course these
lines could be improved by the critic, but, when polished up,
would not be so expressive of the varied capacity and kind-
heartedness shown by a learned judge for a philanthropic
purpose.

Soon after beginning work in London, I was invited
to join a fellowship of Free Church ministers, who met,
at each other's houses once a month for breakfast, followed by two hours' devotional intercourse in the study of
the Word of God. Of this, Thomas Binney, Joshua Harrison,
Baldwin Brown, James Fleming, and, with others, Thomas

Lynch, were members. The latter published a volume of
hymns entitled "The Rivulet," which was at once fiercely
assailed by Dr. Campbell in his weekly journal, the *British
Banner*, as teaching and introducing into public worship a
"negative theology" which ignored the atoning sacrifice and
was silent on justifying faith. I have seldom taken notice of
censures on myself, but have often indignantly condemned injustice to my brethren. On this occasion, at my first perusal
of the book, I deeply felt the falseness of the attack, and, as one
of the fraternity implicated, made a speech at some public
meeting held in the City that day, quoting from the book
with warm approval. Then the attack was turned on myself,
and our whole fraternity drew up a protest, which was published, with the names of the fourteen who, in a pamphlet
circulated by the hundred thousand, were condemned for
negative theology and Unitarian tendencies. Hymns from
the maligned "Rivulet" are now found in most of the Church
hymnals—an enduring testimonial.

Being appointed to preach the annual sermon for the
London Missionary Society, I took for my text, "We preach
Christ crucified"—a practical refutation of the calumny. The
sermon occupied an hour and a half in the delivery, but a
hymn in the middle gave opportunity of leaving to those
unable to remain.

"Sacrifice; or, Pardon and Purity by the Cross," was the
title of a small volume in which the argument was expanded
and illustrated. Its object was to show emphatically that
it is by the Atonement that forgiveness is bestowed, and
that also obedience and holiness result necessarily from the
faith that justifies. Some appear to teach that by the Cross
we become righteous by a purifying influence on the heart,
and this alone. Others appear to teach that the object and
result of the death of Christ are deliverance from guilt and
punishment, and that this alone is salvation. Pardon and
purity together are salvation by the Cross. During several
years I heard of no good resulting from this publication.
About thirty-five years afterwards I received the following
letter :—

"South Molton, Devon.

". . . Some twenty-eight years ago I was led to Christ, and prayed earnestly that I might lead some others. Close to our house lived a drunken man professing to be an infidel. He fell ill. In great fear, I knocked at his door ; but fear was banished by his saying, 'Glad to see you. Hear you've turned Christian. Wish I could be ! You know how great a blackguard I've been ? Well, a few days ago somebody left a book written by some minister in Blackfriars Road, and this is it—"Sacrifice."* Oh ! this book has broken my heart ! It has taken all the infidel ideas out of me.' That man I saw again and again, and am quite confident of the work of grace. He died full of joy. Later, the Lord called me into His service. As a village pastor, let me express the deepest joy in your firm adherence to the blessed truth of salvation by Christ alone. It is happiness unspeakable that in the present day of change so many keep true. "T. Breewood."

In 1855, a year after leaving Hull, I sent to every member of the congregation a copy of my new booklet, " Follow Jesus," and received a letter of thanks, saying :—

"We shall value it not less as a proof of your abiding interest in our spiritual prosperity than for the affectionate counsels it contains. We entreat your prayers that we may so 'follow Jesus' that it may be manifest to all around that we are truly His disciples, increasingly imbibe His spirit, and follow His example. We do not cease to pray, both in private and in our public meetings, that the blessing of the great Head of the Church may prosper all your efforts for His glory. Pray for us that, as a church, we may be united and devoted, and that the blessing of God may rest on him to whom we have been directed as our future pastor."

* This book is now published by the Religious Tract Society, entitled "The Atonement."

CHAPTER X.

As without a single week's interval I left my work at Hull for more onerous duties in London, I felt that I needed a few weeks for recreation on my favourite playground, Switzerland. So, prior to recording remembrances of my new sphere, I will endeavour to refresh my readers and myself by changing the scene from Southwark and the New Cut, to the land of lakes, passes, peaks, and glaciers. I have no continuous record, but put together memories of various visits. Without reference to guide-books I shall simply narrate personal incidents, which make no pretension to Alpine Club exploits, but may interest more readers because shared by a larger number of ordinary tourists.

On my first visit to Mount Blanc, when inexperienced, I had outstripped my guide, and was standing at the foot of the great Mer de Glace ice-cliff, overhanging the birthplace of the torrent river, when I heard cries from my guide, who was earnestly gesticulating; I at once moved away, just in time to escape a big boulder which fell from the glacier down upon the spot I had left.

The first time I spent a Sunday at Chamounix, as there was no English church, I endeavoured, as always, to supply the gap. The landlord could not grant the use of a room in the hotel, because it would cost him his tenancy, under the law of a Roman Catholic Government. So I proposed to hold evening worship under the trees, using the liturgy with free prayer and hymns. I was afterwards informed that some who were present petitioned, through our Government, that English visitors should be allowed freedom of worship. Permission was then given to build an English church.

A few years after, I had the great pleasure of worshipping in the beautiful little church erected outside the village, and I thank God for allowing me, in however small a degree, to have been instrumental in its erection. On this occasion I wanted a companion on a stroll, and, as the congregation dispersed, selected the owner of an intellectual and genial face. A kind word elicited a sympathetic response. We enjoyed a long walk together, and on Monday night I found myself a fellow passenger with him on a long journey which his interesting conversation made too short. I have since had occasional correspondence with him, he has given me the pleasure of his company at my manse, and I once met him at the Bishops' banquet in the Guildhall, where he was representing the Presbyterian Established Church of Scotland, as Moderator.

I intended to have passed the night in sleep; but little did I either get or desire, so full of interest was my companion's talk. He seemed to know most of the literary men of the day, and had anecdotes of them without end. I heard so much about Archbishop Whately that I since seem to have known him personally. My companion was talking with him about popular superstition when the dread of dining in a party of thirteen was referred to as a laughable absurdity. Whately surprised him by saying solemnly, "I for one should not like to do so." "You astonish me; I could not have conceived you sharing this objection." "No. I assure you I should object to dine thirteen—if there was only dinner for twelve." Some friends after dining with the Archbishop asked him to show them a specimen of Irish wit. Taking a stroll in the street he asked a crossing-sweeper to tell him which of the two the devil would take if he was obliged to secure one of them. "Plase your riverence, ask Father Malony yonder." "No; I want your own opinion." "Och, your riverence, I'm sorry to say he'd take me!" "Why so, Pat?" "Och, because he's sure of your riverence any time!"

As he referred to one author after another, I playfully asked if he happened to know A. B. C. D., etc. He confessed to being "A. K. H. B." So I did not wonder at the interest of

J

the conversation of one whose "Recreations of a Country Parson" were being read with so much enjoyment. We got upon the subject of Establishment. He thought that Christian governments should care for the religion of the people. I contended that the authority of the Church was higher than that of the State, which had no right or capacity as such to interfere with the doctrines and worship of a spiritual body deriving its authority from Christ Himself. This subject was prolific of talk. We separated in Paris. A few days after I received a letter from him, saying, that in a shop window in London he recognised my photograph, and learned my name, and expressed his regret that he had not known it before, that we might have conversed more on the work on which we were both engaged. Dr. Boyd has had much influence in introducing more of the liturgical element into Presbyterian worship.

The letter is as follows :—

"I was vexing myself by thinking I should never know who you were ; but in a photograph shop I suddenly recognised your face, and was much disappointed to have missed an opportunity I should greatly have prized. Your name and work are well known to me, and I say sincerely there are very few men I should so value an opportunity of talking with on many things. Somehow I had set you down for a barrister of the Tom Hughes school. Had I known, I should have wished to speak with you about many things of greater importance, and especially I should have liked to learn a great deal about the details of the work of our common profession, and find comfort and help in speaking to one who is labouring with your great success in the good cause. Whenever you come to Edinburgh I hope you will make our house your home."

Dr. Boyd afterwards told me why he thought I was a High Churchman. He had said that the religion established by the State had a prior claim on loyal citizens, unless conscience absolutely blocked the way. I had contended that the Church had authority within itself superior to all political claims, and that the civil power must not invade the prerogative of the Divine Head of the Church. The true Church is spiritual, and magistrates as such have no place in it, and therefore no power over it, except members by faith in the Lord Jesus, and by His laws and ordinances. In this senso alone, the sole authority of Christ as supreme, I am, together with all Free Churchmen, a High Churchman.

This letter contains a deserved rebuke—not that I reserved my name, which was of no importance, but that, knowing his, I did not allude more to the work in which we both were engaged, and to the great theme we both preached. I have often felt self-reproach for not embracing opportunities of conversation on the most important of all truths and common interests, from fear of seeming impertinent. Why should Christians be slaves to a society-law which forbids any reference to religion in conversation? How many opportunities of presenting truth to the ignorant or careless are lost, and how many of obtaining help to our own faith by communion with those who share it, but are equally averse to speaking of it!

1878, DIARY.—A delightful week round Mount Blanc with my dear friend Charles Edward Reed, Co-Secretary to the Bible Society. From Chamounix we walked over several "cols" to Martigny by way of Courmayeur. At this place, at the foot of the majestic southern precipices of the mountain, we spent with God a memorable Sunday afternoon on the great Brenva glacier. While Reed rambled amongst the ice-cliffs, I bowed under the shadow of "a great rock," in homage to Him who "setteth fast the mountains," and then with special earnestness sought help under a special burden. I suddenly felt my prayer was heard, and, looking up, beheld a marvellous vision on the summit of Mount Blanc, surpassing all the possibilities of pen or pencil, beyond anything I ever saw before, and the like to which I never expect to see on this side the veil. I interpreted a natural phenomenon as an assuring emblem, and so it proved. I know what may be said of refraction and reflection, and coincidences, and I do not presume to suppose that there was any special interposition on my account, but I thanked God and took courage, and from that hour went on my way rejoicing.

I copy from a memorandum made the following day :—

"It seemed as if the glory of God appeared on that mountain, as it did to Moses, but though awful, not terrible. The sky had been cloudless, but now there arose from the summit of the mountain a succession of fleecy domes—translucent, one above another, all radiant with rainbow splendour, blending together. Then the appearance of a majestic form bending over the mountain with extended wings iridescent —wrapped in a mantle, with arms stretched out as in benediction— radiant with amber and azure and gold, burning with glory. I could not restrain myself. No one was present to see or hear me. I wept ; cried out in ecstasy. From prayer I broke out in praise to Him who seemed responding to His child's appeal. Then the vision faded, and vast volumes of thick vapour rose on the other side as from a great volcano, 2,000 feet above the dome. Sinai was not more 'altogether in a smoke.' Then all faded away, and the sky was cloudless as before. All Turner's pictures are tame compared with what God gave me to see. I know what may be said in scientific explanation of phenomena frequent among mountains ; but in all my many rambles I never saw the like of this ; and at the risk of being set down as a visionary, I narrate this as an actual picture which can never fade from memory, especially as the typical became realised. May not the supreme Lord of Nature, without any miracle, have permitted me to see that special vision at that particular time, and in answer to the prayer of faith? How wonderful, how beautiful God must be, and what possibilities of glory heaven may contain ! I felt in a far inferior degree that I had heard 'unspeakable words,' and beheld indescribable glories."

During this excursion my companion sometimes diverged with a guide to explore some strange peak or gully, and I shouted after him, " Remember Ailie and Violet," his wife and child. A few years afterwards he was advised by his doctor to take a short visit to the mountains. As there were now several little ones needing a mother's care, and as he was to return within three weeks, Mrs. Reed remained at home. At Pontresina he took an easy stroll up a safe glacier, and was returning along a well-traversed and safe path near the edge of the rocks. Stopping for a farewell look at the mountains, he showed the guide a photograph of his wife and children ; then, turning to resume his journey, his foot slipped on the smooth grass, he slid on his back over the crag, and striking his head on a projecting rock, fell lifeless on the moraine. " Absent from the body, present with the Lord."

I visited the spot shortly afterwards, with the same guide, who narrated the circumstances, as I stood on the very spot whence he fell. On my walk back I wrote the following sonnet :—

AT THE CRAG OVER THE MORTERATSCH GLACIER FROM WHICH
MY DEAR FRIEND CHARLES EDWARD REED
FELL AND SOARED, JULY 29, 1884.

A stone was gate of Heaven when Jacob slept,
And saw the glistening causeway to the skies :
Thus every spot on which a Christian dies,
O'er whose long sleep heart-broken friends have wept,
Becomes Heaven's portal, whence a soul has leapt
To glory, waking up with glad surprise :
The chamber, hallowed home of love and prayer,
The couch, the empty cot, the old arm-chair,
The sea, the ship, the crag, *the mountain side,*
The darkest mine—where'er 'tis said " He died "—
Has witnessed angels ministering there,
Is rendered noble, holy, glorified !
Each Christian's death-place bears the title given,
" This is the house of God, the gate of Heaven."

His body rests in the English Church cemetery.

On a Saturday forenoon I set out from Chamounix simply to walk up to the Pierre Pointu. There I was accosted by two guides, who prevailed on me to cross over to the Grands Mulets. I had no axe or rope, but entrusted myself to their care, and had a most exhilarating passage over the frozen sea. My men, having taken note of my walking capacities, urged me to try the summit. Though it was already noon, they said I could easily get to the top and return before dark to sleep at the cabin, and on the next morning get back to my hotel. This was very tempting, but there was the Sunday difficulty. I knew I could be back long before church-time, and before some of the congregation were awake ; and that all the way I should be adoring the Lord of the mountains, and perhaps thinking of the sermon on the Mount, or the ascension from Olivet ; but my return would perhaps, as usual on such occasions, be signalised by firing a gun, and the fact would surely be misrepresented and cause surprise if not stumbling to friends, and so, though an intense disappointment to be " so near yet so far," I resolved to act on the counsel of St. Paul to " abstain " from a gratification, though to my own conscience "lawful," yet for the sake of others " not expedient."

On recrossing the glacier, a crevasse which my guides wanted me to visit preached me a useful lesson. The chasm was about ten feet broad, the bottom invisible, the walls blue, smooth, solid ice. I stood on the extreme edge looking over the abyss to the valley beyond. The view was ravishing, the excitement intense—beauty, sublimity, awfulness combined. Dangerous? Not to me with glacier nails, a spiked alpenstock, a stout cord round my chest held by two strong men in my rear. Imagination produced a transformation scene. A street-thoroughfare close by, with many pedestrians. Suppose by my safety and evident enjoyment I practically encourage them to join me on the sloping edge? Relying on my experience and evident enjoyment, many approach and some fall over—now an old man, now a happy girl, now a child, now an eager youth, now a strong man—but I remained there saying, " I am not responsible; I invited them to stand where I stand, not to fall into the gulf I avoided." Should I not be condemned as instrumental in their ruin? I have often used this as an illustration in addresses on total abstinence. " And through thy knowledge shall the weak brother perish, for whom Christ died?" " But take heed lest by any means this liberty of yours become a stumbling-block to them that are weak."*

My first visit to the Riffel was when its rough mountain-house was the only hotel. The Riffelberg is about 8,000 feet high. When I arrived late in the day, somewhat weary, I was told that all the beds were engaged. The Hon. Arthur Kinnaird, M.P., hospitably offered to make room for me in the garret where he and three others had a resting-place of hay spread on the floor. This was the beginning of a long friendship and frequent co-operation in religious and philanthropic work.

The Riffel Alp Hotel, with 200 beds, is on the edge of an ancient forest of stone-pines, of grand and sometimes grotesque forms, which I took great interest in sketching. The

*See 1 Cor. viii. 9-13; and Romans xiv. 20, 21.

roots of one of the pines had surrounded and embedded a great rock; two others were embracing with their gigantic arms; three were growing perpendicularly out of an old trunk lying prostrate; in many cases, from a branch shooting out horizontally, another branch grew perpendicularly to a great height; the roots of many were so twisted about among the rocks, and showed such signs of contrivance and perseverance to secure a strong hold, as to illustrate human struggles against difficulties and to teach that "nothing is impossible to him who wills."

And what a view! The Matterhorn towering just across the deep valley of the Gorner glacier, the glittering Dent Blanche, the Gabelhorn, the summit of the Weisshorn beyond a group of other peaks; then, fifty miles off, the Oberland group with the Jungfrau just visible, the glorious Dom or Mischabel, and the long valley of the Visp, with its villages and church towers and winding river! A short stroll from the hotel brings into view the Riffelhorn, the Theodule glacier, the Breithorn, the Twins, Lyskam, and Monte Rosa. I was one of a large luncheon party gathered on a grass slope near the Riffelhorn overlooking the Gorner glacier, when a fierce thunderstorm came on. A dozen of us were crouching under an overhanging cliff, our parlour. Several ice-axes were piled in front of us, and lightnings flashed threateningly. Dean Lefroy of Norwich quietly rose, gathered them in his arms, and carried them to a safe distance.

The eye, when weary with gazing upwards at these stupendous mountains, looks down on velvet verdure and flowers of every form and hue—mosses, ferns, gentians, mountain-pinks, edelweiss—and on meadows where the varied grasses are hidden by such multitudes of flowers that it would seem as if the field were a garden solely for their growth. Here we have often met Dean Lefroy, whose instructive and amusing conversation, valuable guidance amid peaks and glaciers, and, above all, whose eloquent and profitable Sunday discourses, together with his daily brief morning prayer in the neat little church built chiefly by his exertions, are a peculiar attraction of this deservedly famous mountain-home.

He told me of his new order of worship in Norwich Cathedral on Sunday evening. Instead of the whole service, he now had a selection of collects, a reading of Scripture, some familiar hymns, and a free popular address suited alike to poor and rich. He was gratified by the large attendance of worshippers, including as many Nonconformists as Church folk. He recommended those who objected to changes to " go to sleep and wake up after twenty years and they would quite approve."

I have enjoyed many rambles with him. He took me more than once across the glacier to the hut on Monte Rosa, also to the lovely Findelen Valley and its picturesque glacier, on which he told me that one day he lay down for a brief repose on a huge boulder, basking in the sun. He left this couch for another ramble, and afterwards sought the rock in vain where he had left it, eventually finding it far down on the glacier—no doubt truly grateful it had not taken this Alpine tour bearing him on its back.

One Saturday night I reached the Eggischorn Hotel, knapsack laden and drenched with rain. Next morning I saw an announcement that there would be English service in the *salon* at ten o'clock. I met there a dozen Alpine men waiting for the clergyman, who did not arrive. I went to make inquiries. The landlord said, " You are the chaplain." I undeceived him and asked why he had announced a service. He replied that I looked like a parson, and he made sure, therefore, there would be service. So I explained the matter to the expectant congregation, and said if anyone would read the morning service of the Church of England, I would endeavour to preach. This was done, and I spoke from the words, " Thy righteousness is like the great mountains "—in steadfastness, majesty, beauty, utility, the righteousness of God Himself, revealed in Christ, and provided for man. Among the congregation was W. H. Gladstone, M.P.

Rambling with my brother Arthur on the Aletsch glacier, and, attracted by the beautiful tint of the lake in the ice, the Merjelensee, we plunged into the freezing water, but were out again almost before we got in !

One of the easiest and most delightful walks is from the Eggischorn to the Bel-Alp. You stroll along almost level pastures with a majestic range of snow-mountains in front, to the Rieder Alp Hotel. Thence you descend through a pine forest to the Aletsch glacier, which you cross easily (as do also cattle and mules) to the foot of the opposite mountain precipice, up which a very steep but safe winding path takes you to the Bel-Alp Hotel. Here I have often met, among other friends, Dr. Ellicott, Bishop of Gloucester, with whom I have enjoyed many pleasant rambles on the ice. One day he conducted C. E. Reed and myself to an ice-cave. On a steep slope above it rested an immense granite boulder. I remarked that at any time it might become dislodged, roll down to the cave, and overwhelm the Bishop and his friends. I suggested that as he and Reed had ice-axes, they should anticipate the avalanche, while I, standing aside, would sketch them. So the Nonconformist with vigorous blows cut away the ice foundation, and the Bishop cleared the way for the rock, which then by their combined efforts rolled harmlessly down into the cave. I asked the performers to inscribe their names opposite my sketch, to which the Bishop appended, " Disestablishing a big stone." This is a parable.

I first met Professor Tyndall coming down from Zermatt (1863), carrying his ice-axe and a big coil of rope. He was looking sad. He had been spending several days searching for the bodies of those mountaineers who had just perished by the breaking of their rope, when near the summit of the Matterhorn. He told me that the mother of Lord Douglas had a morbid idea that her son was still alive on the rocks. He knew this to be impossible, but to calm her mind he had gone to Geneva and purchased 3,000 feet of rope, by which to be suspended so that he could with his eye sweep the precipice. He had risked his own life for the comfort of the survivors. He supposed the bodies had fallen into some crevasse or been covered by an avalanche, and that in about thirty years they would probably reappear at the bottom of the glacier. Some years afterwards we met on the Bel-Alp. A few hundred

yards above the hotel is the picturesque cottage which
Professor Tyndall built for his wife and himself, and where
they resided during a few months every year. Here I was
frequently privileged to be a guest. On Sunday afternoon
Mrs. Tyndall invited a few friends from the hotel, including
alpine climbers, authors, scientists, professors, bishops and
clergy of various schools, and ladies. The conversation was
varied and unrestrained. If any of the guests were on distant
terms outside, all were as one in the presence of the genial
host and hostess.

When I was in my room—No. 28—at the hotel, one window
commanding a view of the Mischabel and Weisshorn, and
the other the Aletsch glacier, there was a rap at the door and
an inquiry, " Will you admit a heretic ? " It was Tyndall,
who said, " How odd such heresy and orthodoxy should meet !
This was my room for several seasons—the best in the house."
He had come to ask us to afternoon tea to meet Bishop Ellicott
and others. He took me to the terrace of his sitting-room,
commanding grand views of the Matterhorn and Weisshorn,
and said, " Some people give me little credit for religious
feeling. I assure you that when I walk here and gaze at
these mountains, I am filled with adoration."

I have met him walking with Mrs. Tyndall, carrying a
basket containing medicines and food for invalid peasants to
whom they ministered, she as a sister of charity, and he as
the only resident physician, whose refusal to take any fee
greatly surprised the patients to whom he acted as the good
Samaritan.

I have often listened with transport to the music of the
cattle-bells. Each cow carries a bell suspended to its neck.
Sizes and tones so vary that when very near we fancy no two
are in accord, but when at a distance the discords all blend
into delicious harmonies. After conversing one day on the
unkind censure often passed on mere differences of opinion
or of methods, when, in the ear of God, there may be true
harmony, I presented him, on the mountain he loved, with
the following lines, which he asked me to dedicate to his
wife :—

ALPINE CATTLE-BELLS.

How soft the music of the bells,
Borne by the breeze from sheltered dells,
Where herds of mountain-cattle feed,
In friendly groups, on flowery mead.

Those bells send forth, not one alone,
But vibrate notes of every tone ;
This chorus of the Alps is sung,
With one accord, by old and young.

Such artless music of the hills,
The soul, with a strange rapture, fills ;
So many sounds, so varied, meet
In such sweet harmony complete.

The distant blending with the near,
The tenor, bass, and treble clear,
The bell sonorous slowly swung,
With the small heifer's sharply rung.

Help us, O Lord, to raise to Thee
Music, each one in his degree ;
Despising none because their note
In varying tone may heavenward float.

For though to listeners, standing near,
Some notes discordant may appear,
Yet unto Him who hears above,
All blend in harmony of love.

Tyndall's Châlet, Bel Alp, August, 1887.

He was always ready to converse with those from whom he differed. I lamented his supposed ignorance of truths dearer than life to myself. But I always thought that he believed more than he professed, and hope that, having been a sincere seeker after truth, he may have made attainments in the higher school of God to which the infant school was leading.

I never heard from him any antichristian sentiment, or any word of disrespect towards any church or clergy, but he was indignant when he learned that by the chaplain in charge I had been requested not to come to the Communion. The chaplain of the S.P.G. was a young man, born after I had been some years in the ministry. In reply to his inquiry I said it was my habit, whenever from home, to join my fellow-Christians at the table of our common Lord. On the ground of my not having been confirmed, he said it was his duty to ask me to abstain. I said I thought he contradicted his own Church, which invited to approach all those who were "in charity with their neighbours and desired to lead a new life." I told a clerical friend, who much condemned the chaplain's conduct, but regretted he had no authority to interfere. But he kindly comforted me by saying that he could assure me that the Lord would accept my purpose equally as if it had been performed. Several other clergy of the Church of England warmly expressed to me their regret.

Though forbidden Communion, I checked resentment by attending prayers and sermon, and then in the great temple of Nature worshipped the one God, and composed the following verses :—

There is music on the mountains,
  As amid their wilds I roam ;
In the avalanche's thunder,
  Bursting from yon stainless dome ;
In the carol of the peasant,
  As she leads the cattle home.

There is music on the ice-fall,
  As its glittering crags I climb ;
Music in the storm-cloud, sweeping
  Round the granite peaks sublime ;
In the roaring of the torrent ;
  In the cow-bell's soothing chime :

Music in the honeyed flowers,
  Where the bee its task fulfils ;
Music in the swaying branches ;
  Music from the infant-rills ;
There is music in the silence
  Of the reverent listening hills.

Music in the words of Jesus,
  Fuller, sweeter, all Divine ;
In His matchless life and actions,
  Life where God and man combine
In His wondrous cross and passion,
  When that life He did resign.

Grant me, Lord, a soul responsive,
Music breathing aye to Thee;
Motives, conduct, thought, emotions,
Linked in sweetest melody,
With the voice of grace and nature
Blending in true harmony.

At Zermatt I conversed with Dr. Campbell, Principal of the College for the Blind. Though himself totally blind, he had climbed the Matterhorn with safety and delight. I asked him to explain the causes of his pleasure. "The bodily exercise, the mental excitement, the sense of difficulty overcome and danger escaped, the mental vision of what I knew was present. Besides, I saw more than my companions. A thick cloud concealed everything from them; but I had impressed it all on my brain in preparation, and I saw everything I expected to see."

The Cima di Jazzi has no special difficulty, but is linked with the memory of a special Providential deliverance. My brother Arthur and myself started from the Riffel with a young Cambridge student, who ridiculed our teetotalism as a hindrance to our climb. As we ascended the long slope of the Gorner glacier, whenever a somewhat steeper gradient or a wider crevasse appeared in advance, my brother was there first, quietly disproving the opinion of our companion. At length we left the ice and were plunging ankle-deep up the snow-field. Alas! a thick fog came on and concealed all view. Our three guides suddenly halted, right about face, and grounded axes. We had reached the solid summit, but beyond it was only the overhanging cornice of snow, beneath which was a precipice of several thousand feet. My brother, supposing we had not yet reached the summit and determined to be first, rushed up between the guides. I was somewhat in the rear, but knew what their excited shout meant. In a moment the thought flashed on me: "It will take me three days before I can find his body. How tell his wife, his mother, his church?" I saw him begin to sink through the snow, nearly up to the hips! The youngest guide, at great risk, rushed up the slope and seized his coat, which began to tear away, but the wearer was dragged back into safety. I was overwhelmed with the fright, and for the first time in my life had a fit of hysterics, weeping and laughing by turns.

On his return to Edmonton he visited two godly invalid sisters, who told him how anxiously they had prayed for his safety, especially on one particular day at a certain hour. The time corresponded. Many will say, "Remarkable coincidence." We continue to say, "Merciful deliverance by Him who promises to give His angels charge concerning his children."

Crossing the Simplon Pass, my old cab-driver told me that as a boy he led the mule of Napoleon when the road was on the opposite side of the gorge. The great General said, "Boy! did you ever see a carriage go along that side?" The boy said, "Never! it can't!" On that side, a rocky spur of the mountain descends perpendicularly to the river, while a great torrent falls over it forbidding all passage. Napoleon said, "One day you shall see a carriage and four horses go along there." It is now made easy, the rock tunnelled, the torrent bridged. The old track was in constant peril from avalanches, which still fall, but harmlessly, because no one goes that way.

In childhood my favourite hero was Hofer. When in the Tyrol I took a long walk from Botsen to the head of the Passeyr Valley, where he had kept a small hotel on his farm. To this I went, full of interest, to the very house, and when I learned that the landlady who waited on me was his grand-daughter, I gratified my admiration by treating her as I would Royalty, making my homage and respectfully kissing her hand, to her great amusement.

One rather difficult ascent I made was of the Diablerets. With a fellow-tourist and two guides, we left the hotel before daylight, carrying lamps. After several miles up the valley we began to ascend the mountain, skirting it by a narrow rocky ledge. On our left an almost perpendicular precipice rose abruptly, and on our right was a gulf increasing in depth at every step. After two hours we stopped for hurried breakfast, squatting on a narrow ledge, looking over our

knees at the abyss below without any intervening fore-
ground. No rope was used, because the fall of one
would involve that of the other three. Sometimes the
ledge sloped sideways as well as backwards. I began to
feel it advisable to look only to the feet of the man close
before me; and I asked myself, "Is this pleasure?" At
length we rejoiced to stand on the level glacier, where we
were rewarded by a marvellous view of mountains, including
Mont Blanc. Here we roped, and went "quick march" till we
came to a very steep bank of snow sloping down to a lower
plane. I felt it difficult to go down it face forward, fixing my
alpenstock behind, and kicking my heels into the snow. We
were soon off again over the ice, till we reached a wide *bergschrund*, a crevice between a rocky precipice and a glacier,
which was several yards below us. We had to scramble like
goats down this rock, the irregularities of which furnished
good hand and foot holds. When on a level with the ice, the
foremost guide jumped over the abyss and held the rope.
Then followed my companion. I resolved to make sure of
clearing the gap, and exerted all my strength, with the effect
of breaking away the opposite ledge, which fell off into the
invisible, while I, by force of my projection, fell full length on
the sloping ice, and began a rapid slide towards another
crevasse. But far quicker than the motion of my pen in
describing, the guide in front sprang below me, supported by
his axe, and the guide behind me, firmly fixed on the rock,
tightened the rope, which held me back. The words suddenly
seemed to sound in my ears—" Hold Thou me up, and I shall
be safe." After this we were soon on the summit. We
clambered along the very narrow crest to the highest peak, on
which there was only just room for us to stand.

We soon recrossed the *bergschrund*, and after scaling the
rock I stood a moment or two on the edge to survey the scene
and exult in our victory, when my guide, indignant at my
loitering there to indulge in scenery, lugged me into safety
with strong reproofs. At the edge of the glacier the guides
debated whether to return by the narrow track, or clamber
down direct into the cirque. They said that this was the

shorter, and as to danger, there was nothing to choose. So we went single file down a narrow gorge, called a *cheminée*, then across a small glacier bending over the precipice, and so to another narrow gorge, when the guides warned us to lean back while an avalanche of rocks leapt over us. Thus we went down what seemed an impossible route—steep rocks and narrow ice and snow slopes. I felt that any moment we might fall into the profound depths below, till after an hour of this we came to a small tuft of grass and a daisy! Now, thought I, we are safe! What joy that daisy gave me! Now our guides advised rest and food. So we reclined among crags and glaciers, but with a possible and pleasant route below us, although requiring caution and courage. It was about three p.m. when we regained the hotel, thankful for safety, for visions of grandeur long to remain, and for perilous places delightful to have visited, but—shall I say it to the disgust of Alpine-men?—"never again!" Yet "the works of the Lord are great, sought out of all them that have pleasure therein."

Omitting other mountain-memories, I will merely enumerate climbing at the age of seventy-eight, the central ice-fall of the Gorner with Dr. and Mrs. G. Adam Smith; the Aletsch glacier, on which I met Professor Agassiz; and rambles on the Morteratsch, Diavolezza, Upper Grindelwald, and the "Jardin" on the Mer de Glace, and the ordinary Alpine routes.

I am thankful that I have suffered from no accident; that I have enjoyed seasons of ravishment which no words could describe, and which needed tears to express. I have come away thinking of the child's hymn, "I have been there and still would go"; only now, with increasing years—in my eighty-second—I am doubtful about the latter.

CHAPTER XI.

Soon after the publication of my book, "The Forum and the Vatican; or, An Easter Pilgrimage to Rome" (1853), two priests with whom I had been on terms of ordinary courtesy "cut me dead," and in explanation said they could not recognise the author of "a bad book." I have reason to think my book had a little influence in modifying some of the ceremonies described. It has passed through several editions, and on my last visit I saw it in a public library in Rome.

This is truly part of my autobiography, since what is recorded I myself saw or heard, and made notes of at the time. This record of what the rulers of the Roman Church then sanctioned may help us to judge of their infallibility.

Near the entrance of St. Peter's is a very ugly bronze image, supposed to be an ancient statue of Jupiter, seated, with outstretched foot. I saw many, of all conditions, who knelt as they approached, kissing the toes, and placing their forehead against them. The toes were half worn away by this homage of many generations. Thus Romanists paid reverence to Peter, their tutelary apostle. The famous Bambino in the church of Ara Cœli, is a little wooden doll, one mass of jewels. I have not myself witnessed the annual *festa*, but the fact is admitted that once a year, on the summit of the lofty flight of steps, priests hold up this figure amid the blaze of torches, before the thousands below, uncovered and kneeling in adoration. It is carried to the sick, and is generally believed to ensure a safe delivery in confinement.

I thought of the words of the Hebrew prophet, "One cutteth a tree out of the forest, the work of the hands of the workman, with the axe. They deck it with silver and with

K

gold . . . they must needs be borne, because they cannot
go. Be not afraid of them; for they cannot do evil, neither
also is it in them to do good";* and I asked if a Church
can truly claim infallibility when it sanctions what so much
resembles idolatry in the face of the law written by God:
" Thou shalt not make unto thyself any graven image . . .
thou shalt not bow down thyself to them."

In the church of S. Praxede I copied from the official
list of relics — " Bones of John the Baptist, tooth of St.
Peter, piece of *camicia Beatæ Mariæ Virginis*, part of the
swaddling clothes in which the Lord Jesus was wrapped at
His nativity, three thorns of the crown, one of the stones
which killed Stephen, and Moses' rod." In the church of
S. Maria Maggiore, " The cradle of Christ, some of the hay that
was in the manger," and so on. From a public list of relics on
the wall of S. Croce in Jerusalem, I copied: "The title placed by
Pilate on the cross, a finger of S. Thomas, a tooth of S. Peter,
part of the veil and hair of the Virgin, a bottle of Christ's
blood, a bottle of the most blessed Virgin's milk (*Un altra
piena di latte dell' B^{ma} Vergine*)."

On Good Friday I saw a grand procession of Pope,
Cardinals, and other dignitaries, with priests bearing torches,
move up the nave of St. Peter's, and stop before one of the
massive piers, high up on which was a small gallery where
some priests were exhibiting the relics. Pope and Cardinals
prostrated themselves on the pavement, after which they
left the church, having set an example to the Roman
Catholic world of how the relics of the Church should be
venerated. If the rulers of the Church do not believe these
relics to be genuine—what insincerity! If they do—what
insanity !

In front of many churches I saw a notice of plenary and
perpetual indulgence both to the living and the dead. In
the church of S. Croce, " on the second Sunday in Advent,
may be obtained ELEVEN THOUSAND YEARS OF INDULGENCE,
and the remission of all sins." In the centre of the arena of
the Coliseum was then a cross with this inscription, " By

* Jer. x. 3–5.

kissing the holy cross two hundred days of indulgence are obtained." On the wall an inserted cross was still more potent, promising, for one kiss, one year and forty days' indulgence.

In the church of S. Pietro in Vinculo, visitors are informed that they may obtain "the remission of a *third part* of all sins, together with 1,040 years and as many *quadragenœ*" (altogether 1,153 years, 355 days). The Scala Santa, or holy stairs, are supposed to have been trodden by Christ on His way to crucifixion and carried through the air to Rome. One hundred days of indulgence are promised to anyone who, climbing these stairs on his knees without help of hand or foot, recites the prayer, "Angel of God, my guardian, this day enlighten, defend me, entrusted to thy care." I saw as many as fifty men and women clambering up together. Up these stairs Luther began to climb, but seemed to hear the voice of God, "The just shall live by faith," and, starting to his feet, rushed down the steps, and preached forgiveness by faith in Christ. Is Rome scriptural in implying that the sacrifice of Christ is of itself insufficient? If "Purgatory" is necessary to fit some souls for Paradise, how is it that the same result can be secured by kissing a cross, by repeating a sentence, by paying a small sum of money? If 11,000 years of release can be secured in three minutes, where is the need or utility of 11,000 years of discipline? If in such matters Roman authority is in error, what becomes of the claim to infallibility?

It is denied that adoration to the Virgin and saints is of the same kind as that paid to the Divine Being. In the church of Jesus and Mary I copied: "Mary, Mother of Grace, protect us from the enemy and receive us at the hour of death." On the church of S. Maria Liberatrice in the Forum (Holy Mary the Deliverer): "Sancta Maria libera nos a pœnis inferni." She is invoked to deliver from hell! Is not this prayer of the same kind as used to be offered on the same site to a heathen goddess? In the church of Ara Cœli I copied a prayer printed in Italian: "O Mary, sweet refuge of miserable sinners, when my soul must depart, by the grief you felt at the death of your Son, come to take to yourself my soul and present it to the eternal Judge." In the same church I copied : " By reciting the three following ejaculations, three hundred days of indulgence are obtained : Jesus, Joseph and Mary, with all my heart I give you my soul ! Jesus, Joseph and Mary, assist me in the last agony ! Jesus, Joseph and Mary, may my soul depart in peace with you ! " With this identical prayer to Joseph and Mary as to Jesus, what becomes of the plea that the prayers to the Virgin are not of the same kind as those to God ? On the front of the church of S. Maria in Gratia, within a few yards of the Vatican, in large letters, the very words in which the Bible directs us to offer prayer to God were applied to the Virgin : " Adeamus cum fiducia ad thronum virginis Mariæ, ut gratiam inveniamus in auxilii opportuno " (*" Let us come boldly to the throne of the Virgin Mary, that we may find grace to help in time of need "*). When in Rome in 1896 I was unable to find this inscription, but it was there, and I copied it, in 1853.

To test the question personally, I visited various book-sellers' shops and asked whether the sale of the Bible was forbidden. The answer was given with a start of alarm, as if I had asked a dangerous question, " Tutto prohibito ! " I heard of English Bibles being taken from travellers' luggage at the Custom House. Passing through Florence, I gazed, with sympathy for the sufferers and indignation at the persecutors, on the old prison tower where the Madiai husband and wife were in captivity for reading the Word of God !

At Hull I was acquainted with a Roman priest who had a most compassionate heart, and would not needlessly set foot upon a worm. I asked him how he could defend the cruel persecutions of his Church. His reply was this : " The soul is far more precious than the body. If a tiger were loose in your streets, would you not shoot him ? How much more should we put to death those who try to destroy the soul by heresy ? It was love to the souls of men which induced the Church to punish propagators of falsehood."

Cardinal Manning, spending an evening with me in

London, denied the fact of religious persecution. When the Inquisition pronounced prisoners of the State to be heretics, the State inferred their disloyalty and punished them for this. Thus he disavowed all complicity in the persecution of heretics, all incitements to it, all commendation of it. The fact remains so glaringly opposed to the spirit and teaching of Christ that a Church so fallible in this matter cannot be trusted as infallible in all else.

Romanists retort that Protestants have persecuted. If so, they have violated their own principles, and renounce their own evil practices, while Rome admits and defends its persecuting acts. Its Church, if infallible, has nothing to retract, and is, therefore, responsible at this day for all its persecutions in the past.

My first visit to the Holy Land, under medical orders, was hurried. Among the thirty strangers with whom I made the tour I was glad to find my honoured poet-preacher friend, Dr. John Pulsford. My brother Arthur devoted himself to me in a time of need.

My second visit was in 1886, accompanied by my beloved wife, whose acquaintance I had providentially made on my former visit to Jerusalem. We had the privilege of travelling with a company of devout Bible scholars of the Presbyterian Church, among whom were Dr. Monro Gibson, the Rev. R. J. Taylor, Dr. Thain Davidson, the Rev. J. Fraser, and others, with whom we had most delightful fellowship, intellectual and spiritual. Memories of both journeys are here combined.

With my brother, in 1870 I crossed Mont Cenis deep in snow. We slept at a rough shelter on the summit of the pass, hair and whiskers frozen by Zero. Steaming from Trieste, we encountered a severe gale in the Adriatic, and afterwards I preached on deck from "Tossed to and fro in Adria." On the quay of Alexandria we seemed to see Joseph's brethren loading their asses with sacks of the corn of Egypt.

At Cairo some of us were invited to an Oriental dinner, and sat around a table with a soup-tureen in the centre;

into this each dipped his own spoon. A well-cooked turkey
followed, and the hostess with her fingers plucked from the
breast a goodly portion, which she handed to me as senior
guest. My companions similarly helped themselves, and then
servants came round pouring water on our hands and wiping
them with towels. I remembered the words, " He that
dippeth with Me in the dish."

In the museum we were presented to the mummied
monarchs; penetrated the tombs of the sacred bulls; saw at
Memphis the gigantic monolith statue sprawling face downwards in the mud and seeming to say, " I am Pharaoh."
We climbed the Great Pyramid, and on the summit held
a short service, which was disturbed by the disputing of our
guides respecting " baksheesh," when I suddenly in my
prayer changed the name of Deity, saying, "O Allah! Allah!"
At once and to the end there was reverential silence. Visiting
the remarkable schools of Miss Whateley, it was very interesting to find the Egyptian children using as a class-book the
author's " Come to Jesus."

At Joppa we visited the ancient house near the beach
reputed to be Peter's lodging. What seemed heavy mist at
sea was sand blown some hundreds of miles from the desert.
Here we were interested in visiting the hospital and the
schools, where Miss Arnott, and nursing sisters from Mildmay,
have done and are doing such good work.

On Arab horses we trotted over the Plain of Sharon, all
radiant with anemones (rose of Sharon ?). We approached
the Holy City in the evening, singing " Jerusalem, my happy
home," till we reached our camp at the north-east angle in
silence. Early the next morning, a few of us walked across
the Valley of the Kedron, and sat on the slope of Olivet, just
above Gethsemane. The sun rising behind us cast its rays
on the city in front, illuminating its roofs and mosques, the
old wall immediately before us, and the Mosque of Omar,
where once the Temple stood. Lovely flowers were blooming
near, and we heard the Voice that was still saying, " Consider
the lilies," and watched little birds sipping at the small
puddles on the rocks, and thought of the " birds of the air "

whom "the Lord feedeth." Beholding the supposed scene of the crucifixion, we tried to sing "When I survey the wondrous Cross," and prayer was offered till the voice failed, and tears alone spoke the heartfelt worship of each one. In the afternoon, by invitation of Bishop Gobat, I preached in the Mission Chapel on Mount Zion, from the words, "He led them out as far as to Bethany." Why was this route thus specified?—past Calvary and Gethsemane, up Olivet, in view of Jerusalem, and of the Jordan Valley, and near to Bethany, in token of His grateful memory of the reverential love of Lazarus and his sisters, who doubtless were in the little company; and then, the disciples being reminded of the facts and lessons linked with those places, He ascended to His Father, His last words and actions those of blessing; His Church being reminded of the continued life of love, and promised return of "this same Jesus." The Bishop closed with the benediction. A certain Ritualistic newspaper thus noticed the occurrence :—

"We hear that Mr. Newman Hall, a Dissenting teacher, when at Jerusalem, was invited by the Bishop to preach at the English Chapel. We do not know if he accepted the invitation, but whether or not, the scandal is all the same."

Which of the three was the greatest schismatic—the Bishop, the Preacher, or the Editor?

The weather being bad, with rain deluging our camp, the Bishop kindly opened his house to the ladies, who were glad to escape from the thick mud of the interior of the tents. He also entertained at tea those of our party who were willing to make a pilgrimage in the dark to his small but comfortable "palace," where we communed together in prayer, with "psalms and hymns and spiritual songs."

I was rather amused at the hotel *table d'hôte* by seeing some zealous teetotalers pouring a few drops of spirit into their water. I asked an English physician if this was necessary. He was not an "abstainer," but said that, though the water was bad, the brandy made it worse. He recommended simply to boil the water and filter it, which with me has always sufficed.

During ten days at Jerusalem we quietly visited the most interesting spots, greatly aided by the kind attentions of Dr. Merrill, the American Consul, whose house was a museum of antiquities and natural objects. We came to the conviction that the rock opposite the Damascus Gate in the North Wall is, as General Gordon after careful surveys considered it, the true Calvary. At the foot of the rock is an ancient garden, with an old watercourse, and an excavated tomb, which was revealed by removal of long-accumulated rubbish. " Nigh to the sepulchre was a garden." On the summit we held a prayer-meeting on two Sunday afternoons, Dr. Gibson speaking with much devotion, and clergymen of various Churches offering prayer.

On Saturday night I was the guest of the learned and godly Dr. Barclay. I rose early to enjoy a devout solitary ramble before any travellers or beggars would be about. So I strolled along the Via Dolorosa, supposed to be the way of Christ to the cross, and under the arch of the " Ecce Homo," where Pilate exhibited Him to the populace, and out at the (as then called) " St. Stephen's Gate," and through Gethsemane, where I knelt on the contorted roots of an ancient olive; and then sat on the side of Olivet, surveying Jerusalem in the glowing light of the rising sun, picturing to my mind the scenes of our Lord's last days. But I deferred lengthened meditation till I should return by the old road, from which Jerusalem bursts on the view of the approaching traveller. I resolved to kneel and pray there as on holy ground.

At the summit, pausing to gaze with solemn interest at the prospect, two rough-looking Bedouins disturbed my reverie by solicitations which developed into demands to buy some rubbish which they described as "antikitees." When their manner became hostile, I took from my pocket all that was in it—a penknife and a small pencil-case, presenting one to each with an amiable bow. While they were eagerly examining these spoils, I rose and walked quietly away. But I heard a small company of Bethany Arabs running after me, shouting " Baksheesh !" and my two friends were in pursuit

also, so I changed the dignified pace which I had assumed as
an Englishman, and set off in a run. I thought that in one
respect they had no advantage, for though their teetotalism
helped them in running, I was equal to them in this respect.
How I did race them, as their approximate roar suggested
wild beasts! Now I am nearing the historic corner—now
bursts the city on my sight—here is the very spot where I had
intended to pause and pray—no, I dare not, but rush past,
the foe getting nearer, till I overtake a company of peasants
carrying vegetables to market. I was now within hail of the
city, which I entered, every thread soaked, but in time to dress
for church and enjoy the morning service on Mount Zion. I
was reminded of our Lord's words, "Ye shall neither on this
mountain, nor yet at Jerusalem, worship the Father." "Every
place is holy ground," and heaven is near to every contrite
and believing heart.

Holman Hunt told me I had done very unwisely to venture
alone to the precincts of Bethany, inhabited by thieves, and
that I narrowly escaped losing watch, purse, even clothing,
and perhaps life in case of resistance.

After visiting Jericho, and bathing in the Dead Sea, we
cleansed ourselves in Jordan from salt-incrustations, and
returned to Jerusalem. Next day we rode past Bethel and
Nain; afterwards across the valley of Esdraelon to Nazareth,
where, in the English Church, I preached from "He came to
Nazareth, where He had been brought up." Here we met the
Bishop's daughter, who zealously conducts a mission. Thence
to the Lake of Gennesareth.

We encamped near Tiberias, close to the sea, and held
an evening service in a little semicircular bay, such as might
have been the scene of our Lord's narration of the parable of
the sower, and I gave a short address from the question to
Peter—"Lovest thou Me?"

Here we spent a delightful day—partly in a small boat,
thinking of the apostolic fishermen—and visited the ruins of
Capernaum. Next day across a spur of Hermon, whence a
glimpse of Damascus; and on the banks of a stream we
pitched our tents. At our usual evening worship my subject

was—" Are not Abana and Pharpar, rivers of Damascus, better than all the waters of Jordan ? "

At Damascus we spent several days. St. Paul wrote, warning against heretical teachers, "Beware of dogs." On my first stroll I was followed by fierce dogs barking and snapping at my heels. The next day, having bought an ordinary Damascus cloak, I walked about with comfort, the dogs respecting me as a native! On Sunday, at the English Mission School, I preached from Saul's conversion at Damascus—"Behold, he prayeth."

On the slopes of Lebanon I took a sketch from the famous eminence whence Mohammed beheld the city with raptured admiration. How its white houses, and scores of mosques with lofty minarets, shone out amid its palm-groves and gardens! Encamped on a spur of Lebanon, we were assailed by a snow-hurricane, which blew down our tents one after another, and the occupants had to run, lightly clad, through deep snow to the shelter of the kitchen-tent, which, screened by a rock, was the only one that stood the tempest. After a days' detention, lodged in peasants' huts, we pushed forward, our horses often up to their girths in snow. At length we reached Baalbek. Wonderful ruins! I measured three well-cut stones in the wall, each sixty-two feet long and fifteen broad. In a quarry, about a mile off, we saw a similar stone, somewhat larger, one side of it remaining unsevered from the solid rock. I suppose the stones were removed by constructing an inclined road, up which by rollers these immense blocks were moved into their places some twenty feet high in the wall. We marvelled at the seven Corinthian columns remaining of the colonnade of the vast temple seventy feet high, the shafts in three pieces, each piece seven feet in diameter, and about twenty feet long. Amid the ruins some of us—an Anglican bishop, a Presbyterian pastor, a Baptist evangelist, and others—held a prayer-meeting, and sang "Crown Him Lord of all."

On returning from our first visit, we rode down the ante-Lebanon valley, and encamped. Next day was Sunday, and the majority of the party voted to proceed to Beyrout in order to make sure of the weekly steamer, which was to start on the Monday. Some of us strongly objected to this, as the entry of a party with nearly one hundred horses and fifty drivers and servants would cause a great excitement, and discourage those who were endeavouring to inculcate Sunday rest. A few resolved to start on Monday early enough for the boat. We watched our large cavalcade start, with baggage-mules and attendants, in long line of march, and then we settled down in a rough restaurant for the day. We held an interesting little service, a range of Lebanon, topped with snow, on each side of us. My text was—" I pray thee, let me go over, and see the good land that is beyond Jordan, that goodly mountain, and Lebanon." The substance of my sermon was expressed in the following verses, written on the occasion, alluding to various features of the mountain:—

SUNDAY ON LEBANON.

Soon let me cross the stream and see
The land beyond that beckons me,
So fair above comparison,
"That goodly mountain, Lebanon."

I long to tread its fragrant fields,
To taste the ambrosial fruit it yields ;
I long to meet, to embrace once more,
Dear fellow-travellers gone before.

No lion fierce, no ravening bear,
No wily serpent harbours there ;
No murderous thief in ambush lies,
The incautious traveller to surprise.

No fierce sirocco's burning breath
Shall bring decay, disease and death ;
No summer droughts the fountains dry,
The streams flow everlastingly.

No locust-cloud shall dim the air,
Leaving the hopeful branches bare ;
No wintry frosts shall nip the bloom,
No blazing heat the fruits consume.

Those stately cedars ne'er shall feel
The stroke of wasteful woodman's steel ;
Those peaceful pastures ne'er shall dread
The thunder of the foeman's tread.

> Those heavenly heights I long to climb,
> To reach those glittering peaks sublime,
> Still up those shining slopes to press,
> The mountain of God's holiness.
>
> There "Carmel's excellency" blends
> With all the charms that "Sharon" lends :
> O for that never-setting Sun—
> The "Glory of" that "Lebanon !"

Baalbek, April, 1886.

Next morning our little company of a dozen, with as many muleteers and guides, climbed up the snow-covered road, on which were some recent wild-beast tracks, and enjoyed a grand view from the summit, looking down over a wealth of cultivation to our port and the Mediterranean. From frigid to torrid zone, through a succession of varied verdure, flowers, and fruit, we reached Beyrout in good time, welcomed by some of the Christian residents, who thanked God for answering their prayers that two preachers of the Gospel, whom they expected, had not discountenanced their protests in favour of Sabbath rest. Here I was hospitably entertained and doctored by my friend Stuart Dodge, of New York. Mr. Dodge took great interest in the American missions to the East, and especially in the Protestant College at Beyrout, where he held an honorary professor's chair. On my second visit, I spent a Sunday there, preached to the students, and was most kindly welcomed by the Principal, Dr. Bliss. The students are not limited to professed Christians, but they all attend Christian worship in the college and are instructed in the Bible. Many of them become Christians, and all of them go forth to occupy, by virtue of their advanced education and knowledge of English, influential stations, in which their appreciation of Christianity becomes widely useful.

We landed at Smyrna, observing the ancient cypress tree marking the site of Polycarp's grave, and went on by train to Ephesus, where within the ruined theatre we read how Paul was there in peril as the infuriated craftsmen shouted "Great is Diana of the Ephesians!" After a few days in Constantinople and a very short hour in the Black Sea, we reached the Piræus.

At Athens, on Good Friday, I preached in the morning at the American Episcopal Church from "The Greeks seek after wisdom," and in the afternoon on Mars' Hill from "The Unknown God." Pointing successively to Salamis, the prison of Socrates, the grove of Academe, the Parthenon, I proclaimed Christ Jesus, made known on that very rock by the apostle as a wiser teacher than Plato, a greater hero than Miltiades, a more illustrious martyr than Socrates, the only Saviour of mankind. About thirty English and twenty Greeks were present. Paul's great speech was read by my brother, "All hail the power of Jesus' Name" was sung, and the Episcopal chaplain pronounced the benediction. A resident Englishman remarked that perhaps the service then held was the first on that spot since St. Paul's visit. We spent a few days in Sicily, viewing Etna from Taormina, a charming prospect, and visiting Girgenti, with its massive Greek temples, and Syracuse. Then, after a hasty revisit to Naples, Rome, and Como, we reached home, with many sketches and many more memory-pictures to look over in after years. On leaving Athens, I wrote the following sonnet:—

MARS' HILL.

Athens! How grandly beautiful art thou!
Thy dignity, in death, retaining long,
In spite of centuries of cruel wrong;
In spite of earthquake, lightning, war, e'en now
Riseth sublime thy queenly, peerless brow.
What names and memories to thee belong!
Poets and statesmen; fields, renowned in song,
Where Athens guarded Greece from tyrants' thrall:
Demosthenes; eventful Marathon;
Plato and Socrates; great Salamis;
Still awes the soul thy pillared Parthenon,
Thy glittering, temple-crowned Acropolis:
But of thy glories this surpasseth all—
Rough, naked Areopagus, and—PAUL!

Athens, Easter, 1870.

Snowdon recalls one of the most interesting incidents of my ministry. I started one afternoon to sleep on the summit. When half-way up heavy rains fell, and I turned back; but when I reached the bottom, the sky cleared, and I resumed my climb, and slept on a plank in the then wretched little hut. During the night I was charmed by the hymns and anthems of companies of quarrymen who were giving up their rest to see the grand sunrise which their knowledge of local signs foretold. My " landlord " roused me early, and I sat on the top of the cairn that I might enjoy the phenomenon undisturbed. No words can describe it—the reddening sky, the first level rays goldening a hundred peaks, the shadow of our mountain slowly creeping over Anglesey, and a score of lakes gleaming in the sunshine. But I was recognised, and entreated to descend from my pulpit and preach to about a hundred Welshmen and a dozen Englishmen. I replied that God was preaching to us, and we had better hear *His* voice. But I offered prayer, and when I closed I noticed that several men were shedding tears. The miners, in groups, marched away, singing in their thrilling minor key.

A year afterwards an Englishman accosted me at Penzance, saying he was one of the congregation on Snowdon, and was there led to Christ. He was now a Sunday-school teacher.

Two years afterwards, when I was knapsacking near Snowdon, a man driving a cart, containing cheeses and a live pig, pulled up and asked if he might give me a lift. I felt it a good opportunity for conversation. He had recognised me, and, speaking of that sunrise, said it resulted in the conversion of fifty people. I said that I had only offered prayer. He said, " Yes ! and as they only spoke Welsh they did not understand a word you said ; but the effect was a revival in the village churches near."

Some may misinterpret this fact as showing that the Christian religion is unreasonable. But these converts had been taught the fundamental truths of the Gospel from childhood, at home, school, and chapel. The fuel had been carefully and continuously laid, and all that was needed was the " Holy Ghost and fire " to kindle the flame. The human instrumentality was that of many and various teachers, and not of the individual who, without effort, and without special prayer, had simply given utterance to the desires of the congregation.

The Rev. John Parry, pastor of a Welsh church at Llandudno, was known by the bardic name "Gwalchmai," and
had won several prizes at the Eisteddfodd. He was learned
in the history and tradition of his native land, and had
stories to tell of all the valleys and hills where we walked and
climbed on many an excursion. He was known and welcomed
at every outlying farm where we called, and we were regaled
with inexhaustible love-offerings of delicious Welsh bread and
butter, and milk in many a "lordly dish," which I learnt
from him to call "Llefrith," to distinguish it from sour milk.
I was a dull scholar, and told him I should never be able to
speak Welsh, to which he replied, "Then you will find it
very dull in heaven."

My brother and I were seated near the bank of the
torrent at Pontaberglasslyn, when we heard warning shouts,
and had only just altered our position, when big fragments of
rock were cast by a powder-blast on the very spot quitted.

Climbing Snowdon with Gwalchmai by way of Glasslyn,
our route near the summit lay along the ridge of what
is appropriately called Crib-y-Ddysgyl, "edge of the plate."
Both sides are precipitous, descending a thousand feet at
an angle, often termed perpendicular, so sharp that a stone dislodged by either hand would roll to the bottom. We put one
leg over on the right and the other on the left. A thick fog
prevented our seeing more than a yard or two below, behind,
or in front. But we crept along diligently while cautiously,
knowing that this was the only but certain way to the summit.
Thus we walk by faith, not waiting till we can descry the way
long in advance, nor understand the depths below and around
Our duty is to "go forward." Six feet or less in advance
suffice for the next step, and we can only go one step at a time.
We attain the knowing by the doing. "Then shall we know,
if we follow on to know the Lord."

One Saturday evening, in the same company, I was sketching at the foot of Conway Mountain, when a small boy went
by carrying a large book. To my inquiry, he said, "Dim
Saesnag, sir" (no English). My companion told me it was
a Welsh Bible. Within half an hour we heard, far above us,

a voice as of a child or woman in trouble pleading for succour Gwalchmai climbed up to ascertain whether we could be of any service. He returned saying, " It is that little boy with his Bible on the top rock, and he is kneeling before it, praying to God for ministers, that they may convert sinners to-morrow." I said, " Bless God for His little priest! and for multitudes of such priests, old as well as young, for the sick and helpless who can do nothing else, but are habitually doing their best thing! ' Ye are a holy priesthood.' " Twenty years afterwards I heard that this poor boy had become a preacher and was now gone up " to the hill of the Lord."

I have had many preaching rambles in Wales, often in company with an aged Welsh pastor named Owen, whom I used to designate as my archbishop. He would take me under his episcopacy during a week, making engagements for many consecutive days—two or three sermons each, indoors or out of doors. So I have preached often in South Wales, visiting Cardiff, Neath, Carmarthen, Llanidloes, Montgomery, Aberystwith, Whitchurch, Newtown, Oswestry, Pwllheli, and Tan y Bwlch. I have frequently taken a month's " duty " at beautiful Barmouth and Llandudno, and have climbed many of the peaks—Cader Idris, Carnedd Dafydd, Tryfan, Penmaenmawr, and Y Wyddfa (Snowdon)—in all directions. On my last visit to Llandudno, a lady with grown-up daughters told me that, as a child, she had heard a sermon from me on the beach there which she had never forgotten.

I have greatly admired the religious zeal of the Welsh, and their diligent attendance at public worship, but I have sometimes thought their denominationalism excessive, causing too great multiplication of churches. This is partly caused by the existence of two languages. Instead of one building being used at different hours for both English and Welsh, it is thought necessary to have a separate building for each.

At successive periods of life admiration of different authors, amounting to a passion, takes possession of some minds. After Walter Scott's poetry, that of Wordsworth was my fascination. I loved to write appropriate extracts over against my sketches, and to store in memory favourite passages. How I longed to see him. From a cousin of his I asked an introduction, but she advised me to accost him without one, for he was weary of these formal interruptions by strangers.

I reached Ambleside on a Saturday, and that same evening saw him, wearing his shepherd's plaid, chatting to a workman in a quarry, during a shower of rain. " To address him now would be a rude interruption. I'll try to-morrow morning at Grasmere church." As the small congregation went out I sauntered carelessly beside him, expressing my great joy in the scenery. He at once pleasantly responded. Then I thanked him for the poetry which had given me so much instruction and delight, and he spoke of the pleasure it gave him to depict characters under imaginary personalities. After a long stroll he invited me to his garden and walked up and down his favourite terrace. I have no distinct remembrance of what he said, but I cannot forget the charm of his speech, the beauty of the sentiment, his courtesy to a stranger, and my delight in conversing with the poet himself, surrounded by his beloved mountains and lakes, which his poetic soul had spiritualised for ever. From Hull I wrote thanking him for his kindness, and begging the great favour of his name, which I treasure on the title-page of his poems.

A personal friend was Ritson, a small farmer and keeper of a little hotel for tourists. One day he guided me among the precipices of Scafell. Walking beside a small stream, he said he thought he could get a trout there. So he lay flat on the bank, and put his arm down into the water, moving it a little to and fro. Presently he lifted his hand, grasping a fine trout. He told me he knew the pools they frequented, that they liked to feel the gentle movement of the hand till they were so enchanted that they became an easy prey. I have often used this instance of " tickling trout" as an illustration of the devices of a worse enemy, quietly approaching, touching, gratifying, enchanting, capturing, destroying the silly human fish.

One day, at the top of Black Sail Pass, I was arrested by the cry of a little lamb, which looked almost starved· and seemed to cry, " Pity me! save me! " Unresisting

L

it let me carry it to its supposed mother, but the old sheep
ran away, and the forsaken one repeated its cry. I tried
again, with the same result. Then I said, "I will carry
thee to the nearest cottage. But that may be three miles
off, and, if I meet the shepherd, what shall I say if he
accuses me of sheep-stealing? Never mind, I won't leave
thee to perish, after crying to me for help."

I sat to rest on the edge of the slope, and, looking down, I
saw a man climbing up. It was Ritson. He held some letters,
delivered soon after I left; he thought he could catch me up:
"Oh, Ritson! look at this starving lamb!" He said when
pasture was scarce the mothers often forsook their lambs, but
he knew the owner, and would take it home and soon feed it
up. As he carefully folded the young thing in his big
arms, and stalked down the mountain with giant stride
could I avoid thinking of the words, "He shall carry the
lambs in His arms"? If I, a poor selfish tourist in search
of pleasure could not desert the feeble lamb that cried
to me, could the Good Shepherd neglect the cry of any
poor wanderer from the fold entreating pardon and pity?
He never did, He never will, He never can. A year afterwards I called at Ritson's and asked about my lamb. He
said it was now the fattest of the flock. This mountain
parable illustrates the fact that many a wanderer who seemed
utterly lost has become one of the most holy and useful
members of the fold of the Good Shepherd. "Who hath
despised the day of small things?"

I took refuge at Ritson's one night after a whole day of
pouring rain. My friend, the Rev. R. Dawson, diligent and
able secretary of the City Mission, started with me early
from Ambleside, but we were soon soaked through and
through, water creeping down our backs and spurting up from
our boots. I remember how at midday we stopped at a
cottage for food, but at once changed our raiment for the dry
things in our knapsacks. I even now feel the shock when we
again, piece by piece, invested ourselves with soaked shirts
and other clothing, replacing the dry raiment in our knapsacks, and then starting amid a deluge of rain and through

frequent streams, till, reaching Ritson's in the dark, we were soon comforted as to the inner and the outer man. Rain and wet are harmless if you never remain inactive while wet, but keep up the internal fire by exercise.

Many were the anecdotes Ritson told me of mountain adventures, travellers, and shepherd dogs. Among the last he told me of one returning from the fair, in charge, alone, of a flock of sheep. On the way she littered, but instead of neglecting both family and flock, she carried one of the pups home, when the shepherd returned with her to provide for the rest of her family! How very near to intelligence, reason, and morality is what we call instinct—often affording a lesson and reproof to humanity!

Alas, poor Ritson! The last time I was there he had left his farm and small inn, having fallen into the snare of his trade, and was living in an obscure cottage, where I found him in a sad condition. He just recognised me, and listened to my expressions of sorrow and counsel.

My brother Arthur and myself, after a swim in Grasmere, were resuming our march with knapsack and alpenstock, when my dear friend Spurgeon drove along with secretary and deacon in a carriage and pair. Pulling up, he said, "What seems pleasure to you would be pain to me." After a short chat, I asked him what some of his congregation said of his driving thus to his church on Sunday? "Oh, I tell them my horses are Jews. I always make them keep the 'seventh day' so that I may keep my 'first day'; for if I walked, it would be the hardest work of the week to me, while they enjoy their exercise after their Sabbath rest. 'The Sabbath was made for man, and not man for the Sabbath.'"

A few years ago, without absolute concurrence in every utterance, I greatly enjoyed one of the Keswick conferences, where we met many devout fellow-believers, in whose estimation union at the cross of Christ was far more than identity in formularies. I preached on Sunday evening, and at other services enjoyed the ministrations of Webb-Peploe, Evan Hopkins, Moody, and Meyer. One fine morning I varied the place, though not the experience, of

"communion of saints" by climbing with two missionaries
to the top of Skiddaw, from a loftier temple blending our
prayer with dear brethren in the tent, and with them, though
in a lower sense, enjoying the "higher life."

I have often been entranced by the quiet loveliness of our
English lakes. How absurd to compare them with the Alps
and to depreciate them because Skiddaw would not be noticed
if it stood near the Weisshorn. Mountain *beauty* does not
consist in magnitude, but in form. Magnitude causes wonder
and awe, but form inspires admiration and delight. The forms
of some of our hills are as beautiful as some of those of Switzerland, and often more so. Certainly the view is more varied.
We may travel far before the Matterhorn is out of sight. I
have gazed at it day by day till I have felt overawed by its
unchanging outlines and terribleness. Often we spend a
whole day in reaching a Swiss mountain which has frowned
on us from morning till night, while half a dozen lovely hills
have smiled upon us during one half a day's journey among
our lakes, presenting new aspects of loveliness. A wild rose
has its distinctive beauty, which is not lessened by contrast
with the highest culture of the conservatory. Nor is the
silver birch less graceful because of the grandeur of the oak.

How often I have been enchanted while roving around the
placid lakes, meditating, musing, and perhaps weeping with
very joy at the beauty, and the voice of God in all. With
such emotions I penned the following sonnet at Ullswater :—

How deep, how pure, how tranquil is the lake !
Lowly beneath the great hills it doth lie,
Yet looketh day and night unto the sky,
Whose tints and glorious radiance it doth take.
The sun and stars a matchless mirror make
In its calm bosom, bending from on high ;
Yet none the less, earth's objects that are nigh
Are seen reflected there—the ferny brake,
The bending birch tree and the steadfast pine,
The daisied meadows where the cattle feed,
The tiny pebbles on the beach that shine,
Each tuft of moss and every trembling reed.
Lord ! to my soul be such pure calmness given,
Reflecting all things fair in earth and heaven.

CHAPTER XII.

My first personal interview with Mr. Gladstone was in 1858, when he was Chancellor of the Exchequer. I was one of a numerous deputation in reference to the liquor traffic. After their address had been read earnest advocates of abstinence pressed round the Chancellor with various questions and suggestions. One of the appellants asked him to take a chair! One after another was answered so promptly and conclusively that I seemed to witness a noble stag being baited by eager hounds, each in turn being tossed aside. One of the leaders appealed to me to come to the front and keep up the assault, but after what I had witnessed prudence forbade. One gentleman was trying to argue with him on a certain plea exactly contradicting a passage in our own address. Mr. Gladstone quietly asked the secretary to read it, and remarked, "You contradict your own appeal." He seemed to know more of the existing legislation on the subject than any of the deputation who were there to appeal for alterations. As several spoke at once, he remonstrated, "One at a time, gentlemen, and I will try to answer you all." The deputation pressed closer and closer, he gradually moving backwards, till, being nearer his private door, he suddenly and courteously bowed adieu, and disappeared, after an hour's discussion.

Soon after the commencement of the Civil War in the United States an exciting dispute arose on the occasion of some delegates from the Southern Confederacy, who had taken refuge on board the English vessel *The Trent*, being claimed by the Northern Government as prisoners of war. Popular passion here was so roused that there were many demands for war and some danger of its outbreak.

Troops were embarked for Canada in anticipation. I felt so deeply the miseries which would be caused, and the guilt which would be incurred, that I convened a special meeting of working-men for the advocacy of peace, and delivered an address to nearly 2,000 men in Surrey Chapel on December 9th, 1861. The following is quoted from a newspaper report of my address, afterwards printed as a tract:—

"War with the Northern States would be fratricidal. They are engaged in a war which is practically against slavery, and to attack them would be to side with the oppressors. Our two nations are allied champions of freedom—the hated of despots. Should we not reserve our strength for the common cause? Working-men have no special motive for desiring war; they supply most of the cost, and suffer most of the wounds and slaughter. But were our liberties assailed, you would guard your cottage as valiantly as the prince his palace, and shed your blood as readily as the descendant of a hundred earls. (Cheers.) But is the present an occasion for so great a sacrifice? You feel indignant that, as you suppose, our flag has been insulted. But should we, all at once, talk about fighting?

"Some people seem to imagine that Britannia has a right to rule the waves, that the ocean is her freehold, and that other nations must not be allowed to act in a manner quite justifiable in ourselves. Let us first ascertain what the law is, referring the dispute to an impartial referee. But it may be urged—'Must we not at once vindicate the honour of our flag?' What! is our flag of so recent invention, with so poor a history, enriched with so few memories of glory, that it will be dishonoured by a short and dignified delay?—dishonoured by not at once fluttering defiance against the free men of the North? But would it not be more dishonoured by floating side by side with the flag of slave-traders— (repeated cheers)—slave-breeders, slave-drivers? If there must be one or other dishonour, oh, spare us this latter! Never, never let the meteor flag of Britain be hoisted on the side of tyranny and oppression. (Great cheering.) I have been astonished at the opinion that we must either have redress or retaliation. Is there not a third alternative—forgiveness? (Hear, hear.) What is the law of Christ?—'Forbearing one another, and forgiving one another, if any man have a quarrel against any: even as Christ forgave you, so also do ye.'

"We feel it our duty to act on this law in our individual capacity. Is it less our duty as citizens and as nations? Alas! Christian nations seem to think they may do as communities what would be wicked as individuals. (Hear, hear.) But there are not two rules of conduct. If I am to forbear and forgive as regards you, my family must do so towards your family, my town towards your town, my nation towards your nation. What has our religion done for us as a country, if we are to appeal as hastily and angrily to the sword to settle a quarrel as if we

never had seen a Bible and never listened to the Gospel of peace?
(Cheers.) Oh, that God, in whose hand are the hearts of all, would
dispose the people and the rulers of both countries to peaceable counsels!
I beseech you, make earnest prayer to Him, that we may be patient and
gentle, 'forbearing one another, and forgiving one another, if any man
have a quarrel against any.'

"I am not one of those who condemn war under all circumstances,
but I consider in this case war would be most wicked. Let us listen to
the earnest pleadings which I can imagine the fair spirits of humanity,
of freedom, of religion, with weeping eyes and tones trembling with
emotion, are now, amidst the din of angry threats and warlike preparations, addressing to our reason and our heart. Oh, by all the
untold horrors of angry war—by the tenfold terribleness of a war
between brothers—by the sufferings of a negro race, who look on with
alarm lest you should join their oppressors to rivet their chains—by the
aspirations of the long down-trodden people of Hungary and Italy,
whose enemies will exult if the champions of freedom contend with each
other instead of making common cause against tyranny—by the interests
of the world, which will look on aghast to see its civilisers, its evangelists,
engaged in mortal combat, instead of prosecuting, in holy rivalry, enterprises of benevolence—by the example of Jesus—by the law of God—I
beseech you cast in your influence on the side of peace, and loudly proclaim, 'We will have no war with America.'"

The vast audience of artisans enthusiastically expressed
their approval. The prayers of peacemakers were heard; the
affair was amicably settled with honour to both countries.
The war between North and South raged several years
with terrific slaughter on both sides. I deeply lamented that
the great problem of emancipation could, seemingly, thus only
be solved. I mourned for the war, but as it was a reality I of
course sympathised with those whose victory would be freedom
and union instead of slavery and separation. During the discussion in Parliament, Mr. Gladstone was understood to favour
the opinion that, as Jefferson Davis had established the
Confederacy, humanity required that this should be recognised,
and that a war so destructive should cease at once, because it
could not, however protracted, terminate otherwise than in
victory for the South.

Regretting that this great statesman and champion of
liberty should have expressed an opinion which might be
misinterpreted as opposed to the cause of the North, I ventured to send him a copy of my tract, and also of my lecture

on the whole question of the war. I received a reply, from which I make the following extract :—

From the Rt. Hon. W. E. Gladstone, Chancellor of the Exchequer.

"11, Downing Street, Nov. 8, 1862.
"The Chancellor of the Exchequer begs to return his best thanks for the lecture and tract, read by him with great pleasure. . . . While he heartily concurs in the condemnation pronounced on the declaration of Mr. Vice-President Stevens, he hopes that there is no great difference between the author and himself on the subject of the war. On his own part, he can certainly say that he would not have taken opportunities, as he has taken them from time to time, to state in public his opinion that the issue of the bloody struggle (whether desirable or otherwise) is, humanly speaking, certain, had he not believed it to be quite as much for the interest of the Northern as for the Southern States that this condition of things should be understood and admitted."

This letter fully vindicates the writer from being indifferent to the cause of negro emancipation. In that early stage of the struggle he deeply lamented the horrors and woes of such a war. His study of history led him to the persuasion that a nation assailed, as was the South, and threatened with the loss of independence, could never, in the long run, be conquered, and therefore the continuance of the war was useless, and should be arrested by recognition of the Southern Confederacy. This is still more evident from the following extract :—

"Downing Street, February 2nd, 1863.
"DEAR SIR,—Believing that negro emancipation cannot be effected, in any sense favourable either to black or white, by the bloody hand of war, especially of civil war, I deeply lament the act of those who, not swept along like the Northern Americans by a natural and scarcely avoidable excitement, undertake, from an impartial position, to favour, in the interests of the negro, the prolongation of this dreadful conflict.

"You will, I am sure, forgive this frank expression of opinion, and believe me, with sincere respect.

"W. E. GLADSTONE."

To this letter I sent a reply, from which I extract the following :—

To the Right Hon. the Chancellor of the Exchequer.

"March 7th, 1863.
"HONOURED AND DEAR SIR,—I am deeply indebted for your kind letter—not the less because it so frankly expresses disapproval of what

seems to you the course which, with others, I have felt it a duty to take. An adverse opinion from yourself should make any man reconsider his own. After such reconsideration, I beg most respectfully to submit the following suggestions. In expressing sympathy with the North, we should no more be regarded partisans of the war than should those who withhold such sympathy be regarded as partisans of slavery. No one hates slavery more than yourself. I trust that I also am sincere in the conviction that 'war, unless the greatest necessity, is the greatest of crimes.' Any mitigation of abhorrence of slavery might impugn the consistency of England—at least of the religious portion of it—and weaken her moral influence.

"Had we so good a plea in the Chinese or Crimean War as the Government of Washington in this ? If our West Indian planters had rebelled rather than submit to our Act of Emancipation, we should have fought to maintain our *Empire*; but not the less would such a war have been for the liberation of the slaves ; and had the planters massacred them, as Jef. Davis threatens, the responsibility would not have been ours. They would have been the exterminators, we the emancipators. But our present argument is not to defend the war, but to condemn the cause for which the South fight—*i.e.* the setting up, as Professor Cairnes shows, of a vast slavery principality. The war is a fact apart from our agency. On which side shall be our sympathy ? It has seemed to be not only on the side of the South, but of slavery. The *Times* and *Saturday Review* have just defended modern slavery from the Bible. It looked as if injury to our cotton trade revealed that we had been hypocritical in former denunciations of slavery. Bitter disappointment in the North is breeding bitter ill-will, which may develop in a war at which liberty and humanity would stand aghast. Surely it is time to show that, whatever our differences respecting parts of the Lincoln policy, the people of England abominate slavery as much as ever, and therefore can never have sympathy with a selfish, cruel oligarchy, plunging a whole continent into war, with the avowed purpose of treating four millions of people as mere chattels, and of extending the unparalleled atrocity 'wherever' (as Dr. Palmer said at New Orleans) 'Nature and Providence lead the way.' For this reason some of us have felt impelled, not only as citizens, but as ministers of a Gospel of righteousness and peace, to prevent the people from being misled into any mitigated abhorrence of such a concentration of all villainy. The character of England must not be impugned before the world, and her moral influence weakened. We may not be able to stop the war between North and South, but we may prevent war breaking out between the North and ourselves.

"Still, as regards this war, it must be remembered that (1) the South began it, (2) without just cause, (3) treacherously, (4) with the avowed purpose not alone of maintaining slavery, but of extending it. Thus, if ever a Government had just cause to fight for its honour and empire, the United States had such right. Thus the responsibility for the sufferings caused by the war rests on those who began it and have not yet abated their claims, not on those who so reluctantly accepted the challenge. If it is lawful to fight for the preservation of empire, it cannot be wrong to fight for it because associated with philanthropy. Pardon me for intruding at such length on your attention, but the importance of the subject, and the swelling tide of national interest, are my excuse. —I remain, honoured and dear Sir, with sentiments of profound admiration and respect, etc., NEWMAN HALL."

I received this reply :—

"Carlton House Terrace,
March 27th, 1863.

"DEAR SIR,—I do not think I thanked you on receipt for your letter of March 7th, but I paid it and its inclosure the best compliment in my power by taking care to make them known to all my colleagues.

"More I fear I cannot say. My desires are still for peace, and in longing for its arrival I am conscious of no distinction between the interest of races or of sections.—Believe me your very faithful and obedient servant, W. E. GLADSTONE."

A short time after the preceding correspondence I had the privilege of meeting Mr. Gladstone on Penmaenmawr. I had been gathering oak-fern on the side of the mountain, and saw two gentlemen approaching engaged in interested conversation. As they drew nearer I heard that their subject was " Spanish Proverbs." I addressed Mr. Gladstone with thanks for his courteous letter. He then shook my hand heartily, thanking me for my letter, and introducing me to Dean Trench, whom I thanked for the benefit I was frequently deriving from his books on the Parables and Miracles. Mr. Gladstone expressed a desire to hear from me again.

The dreadful war continued. At first, the North, very much unprepared, suffered reverses in battle, but, with defeat in arms, enthusiasm increased for union and emancipation. For a considerable period the public opinion of the higher classes in England—wealth, commerce, and literature—was on the side of the South, because it was considered that the stronger were oppressing the weak, that ambition for empire was the real motive of the North, that the South were fighting in self-defence, and that free England should take their side.

I went to the House of Commons to try and influence some of the Liberal Members. I specially appealed to the

Radical member for Hull, being one of his constituents, but he said he would rather be a slave in the South than a free negro in the North. Then I resolved to go on a mission to the northern counties, and, with others, endeavour to persuade the voters to "teach their senators wisdom."

I remember in one single week, between the Sundays, addressing five great public meetings in Birmingham, Hull, Sheffield, Manchester, and Liverpool. The largest halls were densely thronged. My argument occupied two hours, heard by all present, and at each meeting a resolution was unanimously passed expressing sympathy with the Northern cause—union for the States and emancipation for the slaves.

Difficulty was anticipated in Liverpool, for the *Alabama* privateer was being fitted out, and Southern sympathisers abounded. A muscular friend of mine insisted on sitting close to me on the platform to defend me from the threatened assault, of which I had no fear. Long before time the great hall was packed with an eager crowd. I began with saying I hoped some were present who favoured the South. This elicited repeated roars of applause. "I appreciate and honour your motives, though I may not agree with some of your sentiments. You admire the culture of the Southerners" —(applause)—"their love of liberty"—(applause; renewed roars of applause after each clause)—"their bravery, their perseverance, their resolve to preserve self-government against ambition, against aggression." So I went on enumerating all the favourite pleas of the South, each clause eliciting a fresh demonstration, till the Southern sympathisers must have been weary of hearing their own sentiments repeated, and still more weary of applauding them. Then I said, " You see, gentlemen, that I am not ignorant of your arguments, and that I appreciate your honourable motives. Now, then, indulge me with your attention while I endeavour calmly to explain in what light we, on our part, regard this terrible conflict." My argument was listened to with respectful silence, then with increasing applause, till at last I denounced the abettors of *Alabama* privateering as supporters of slavery, foes of our constitution, breakers of law, and traitors to the Queen. The resolution was passed with extraordinary enthusiasm.

Amongst the distinguished sympathisers with the North and promoters of peace were John Bright, the Duke of Argyll, Milner Gibson, W. E. Forster, Edward Baines, C. Gilpin, Tom Hughes, P. Taylor, Professors Newman, Cairnes, Rogers, Goldwin Smith and John Stuart Mill; Benjamin Scott, City Chamberlain; the Hon. L. Stanley, H. Potter, M.P., H. Cosham, M.P., and the Rev. the Hon. Baptist Noel.

For several weeks I felt urged by a call I could not disobey; and, in opposition to ordinary laws of health, I travelled far and wide, and consecrated all my time and energy, except for my Sunday work of preaching the Gospel, to allay the perilous passion for war against America, which would have been the greatest folly, the most stupendous crime of this or any age. Having aided to calm the war-tempest at home, I resolved to cross the Atlantic to do similar work amongst those who were equally bellicose in the opposite direction.

I did not go with the authority of any society as a delegate or as representing any church, but I was armed with a kind letter from my friend, John Bright, and with the following introduction to Senator Sumner from Mr. Gladstone:—

To the Hon. Mr. Sumner.

"Finchley Road, Hampstead,
"July 23, 1867.

"MY DEAR MR. SUMNER,—I have many friends going to the United States this autumn. Among them, Mr. Newman Hall has requested of me an introduction to you. Mr. Hall is one of the most eminent and respected Nonconforming ministers of this country, and his manners and character are in all respects such as I am sure will lead you to excuse the liberty I take in recommending him to your kindly notice.

"I watch all your proceedings with great interest, and with the most earnest desires for the greatness, goodness, and happiness of your country.

"I remain, very faithfully yours,
"W. E. GLADSTONE.

"I write from Mr. Hall's house."

In response to this introduction, Mr. Sumner invited me as a guest, and in the Senate proposed that their hall of assembly should be granted for me to deliver an address on our international relations. The proposal was received with favour, but the difficulty arose that if so unusual a step were taken in the case of a foreigner, there would be difficulty in considering similar requests from American citizens. It was therefore decided that I should be asked to deliver such an address in the largest Presbyterian church. There was a full assembly of members of both Houses. Chief Justice Chase presided; General Grant sat in front, Senator Sumner and other prominent men near. I spoke for two hours to a most attentive audience. I maintained that, while many of the upper classes and some of the leading journals had advocated the case of the South, the great mass of the people, with some of the most eminent authors and politicians, were advocates of " Union and Freedom." I told them that our cotton manufacturers, whose interest was to secure cotton, were willing to suffer to any amount rather than fasten the fetters of the slave, and that, while crowded meetings were held all over our land in favour of the North, not one had been called on the other side, because an open meeting would have been crowded by advocates of the North, while those who convened the meeting would have been responsible for the cost. My address met with cordial response, except when I attempted to palliate, while condemning, our action in reference to the *Alabama*, and even here doubt or disapproval was expressed only by silence. This address, delivered in substance in Boston and other cities, forms one of the chapters in my volume "Divine Brotherhood."

It was a token of the general approval of my pacific mission that I was invited by Mr. Speaker Colfax to open with prayer the first assembling of Congress in 1867. After asking a blessing on the President of the Republic, I offered prayer for the Queen of Great Britain, which was heartily responded to. I was also invited to preach on Sunday before the two Houses in the Hall of Representatives, and I was told that, with very few exceptions, the whole of the Senators and Representatives were present. Speaker Colfax presided ; General Grant, the Chief Justice, Senator Sumner, and other leading men were present. The invitation came to me on the Friday, and notice being so short, I had to spend most of Saturday night in writing my sermon, as I wished that on so important an occasion it should be thoroughly prepared. My text was, "Stand fast therefore in the liberty wherewith Christ has made us free, and be not entangled again with the yoke of bondage." I alluded to the national freedom of the United States, then to the freedom of all citizens alike, then to religious freedom from political control, and then to spiritual freedom through Christ, from condemnation, sin, and self. "The truth shall make you free."*

In New York I was conducted to Wall Street, and taken into the Stockbrokers' Hall. In the midst of business, and of the loud shouting of prices as the figures were being displayed and changed, the president rapped with his hammer to call silence, and in the sudden hush announced my name and asked me to speak. A warm cheer, followed by cessation of business, encouraged me to say a very few words on the hearty goodwill of the English nation, their desire for that of the American people, and their resolve that our international brotherhood must never be broken. When my three-minutes' speech ended, someone started our National Anthem, a verse of which was enthusiastically sung, and then the shoutings of prices of stock recommenced.

I met General Sheridan on his public entrance into Boston, and paid an interesting visit to General Grant. At Washington Mr. Seward, Secretary of State for Foreign Affairs, did me the honour of inviting me to two of his receptions, as well as granting me a private audience, at which he listened with great attention to all I had to say in extenuation of any mistakes of our Government and in proof of the cordial goodwill of the great masses of our people. His face bore marks of the murderous assaults made on him at the time of Lincoln's murder. He took me to the White House and introduced me to the President. In the entrance-hall I admired a conspicuous marble bust of John Bright.

At Boston I was honoured by a public reception at the

---

* This sermon is also included in my volume, "Divine Brotherhood."

great monument on Bunker Hill, in Charleston. The Mayor presided. The Commodore of the Arsenal was present with the Government band, which played our "God Save the Queen" alternately with "Yankee Doodle." Judge Warren, President of the Monument Committee, delivered an address of welcome, full of good feeling towards our Queen and country. An immense multitude listened to my speech, and loudly cheered when I pointed to their flag floating above me and said, "There is not a flag in the world so glorious as the Stars and Stripes." Here the applause was overwhelming and delayed me some time; but I had not finished my sentence—my hand was still outstretched—and when I then pointed to the British flag waving side by side, and added in my loudest tones, "*excepting* that of the Clustered Crosses," the cheers were renewed and intensified, with the waving of hats and handkerchiefs, showing generous enthusiasm for the Old Country. As soon as this applause ceased and I resumed my seat, a venerable man, above fourscore, an apostle to sailors, greatly esteemed in Boston, ascended the platform, and with much emotion shouted to me: "Give my love to your Queen. Tell her she's my sister, and all her foes are mine and yours." The old man's words seemed to find an echo in every heart of that great multitude as the band struck up our National Anthem, and three cheers were given with an enthusiasm I never saw surpassed at home.

I was earnestly invited to deliver addresses on "International Brotherhood" in most of the great cities of the United States of America. As my time was very limited, I could comply with only a few of them, including Chicago, St. Louis, Springfield, Buffalo, New Haven, Albany, Boston, Philadelphia, Brooklyn, New York. To avoid misunderstanding, I ought to state that, though collections were made in accordance with custom, whatever remained beyond the necessary local cost, without any deduction for the lecturer or his personal expenses, was paid to a committee in New York towards erecting an international monument in London to be called "Lincoln Tower." This was suggested by my friend, the Hon. William E. Dodge, who started it by a spontaneous gift of five hundred dollars.

At New York the Union League Club honoured me with a public reception, and my portrait has been placed among those of other friends of their cause.

At the Union League Club, also, it was resolved to send fifty copies of "The Rebellion Record" to Europe as presents to selected individuals and to public libraries. This work was in six large octavo volumes, handsomely bound, filled with documents and narratives, and enriched by a large collection of portraits of eminent American statesmen and soldiers. To each copy was prefixed a letter of salutation, signed by fifty citizens, for the purpose of "conveying to influential gentlemen and libraries in Europe just views and accurate information of the great struggle." Four were addressed to the monarchs of Great Britain, Russia, France, and Italy; six to English newspapers, viz. *The Daily News, Star, Manchester Examiner, Liverpool Post, Leeds Mercury,* and *Caledonian Mercury;* fourteen to public libraries and societies; nine to public men in France and Germany; and others, in the following order, to sympathising friends in Great Britain: Cobden, Bright, Mill, Goldwin Smith, Thorold Rogers, Cairnes, Newman Hall, Milner Gibson, the Earl of Carlisle, the Duke of Argyll, W. E. Forster, the Rev. the Hon. Baptist Noel, Dr. Massie, George Eliot, Harriet Martineau, F. Freiligrath, and A. Langel. I felt it at the time, and shall always feel it, a great honour to have had my name thus associated with others of such far higher repute, in upholding the cause of American union and emancipation, at a time when that great cause was so little appreciated except by the multitude of humbler rank.

I must also thankfully acknowledge the unsought degree of D.D., conferred by a University of deserved renown—Amherst. As this was given on the ground of my political efforts rather than as the result of academic examination, and also because degrees other than those of British universities had been somewhat discredited, I did not, outside the United States of America, adopt the title given in 1864 till 1892, when I was similarly honoured by the University of Edinburgh.

With the certificate I received the following letter from the President:—

"Amherst College,
15th July, 1865.

"It gives me great personal and official pleasure to forward this communication to you. I have long known, in common with many educated men of America, something of your ability and influence as a faithful preacher of the Gospel of Christ ; and in the recent years of our nation's agony of your warm sympathy and earnest efforts on behalf of the integrity and entire freedom of our Republic. And now in these days of returning peace and prosperity, the damning blot of slavery for ever erased, and the National Government re-established to the extent of the Federal Constitution over all our states and territories, we take no little pleasure in expressing our grateful recognition, in such ways as we can, of those strong friends of the Republic who have stood nobly by us in those dark days of anxiety and anguish. And while we shall never forget the honoured names of Cobden, Bright, the Duke of Argyll, and many others, we feel particularly grateful, my dear Sir, to yourself for the distinguished sympathy, encouragement, and co-operating efforts which have marked your course on behalf of our struggling nation. May God preserve and bless you, and give you yet many good years of influence both in the Old World and the New.

"Very respectfully, etc.,
"W. A. STEARNS,
" President of Amherst College."

With a copy of "The History of the United States Sanitary Commission" came the following letter:—

"New York,
"March 27th, 1867.

" MY DEAR SIR,—I have the pleasure to transmit herewith a copy of 'The History of the United States Sanitary Commission,' being a general report of its work during the War of the Rebellion, and beg to ask your acceptance of the same in the name of the Commission and in recognition of your claim upon our grateful regard as a distinguished friend of our National cause.

" With assurances of the highest esteem, etc. etc.,
"F. S. BLATCHFORD, General Secretary."

During my short tour, endeavouring to allay unfriendly feelings, I was deeply grieved, though not surprised, by the strong condemnation of our Government in the matter of the *Alabama*, and on my return I ventured to write to our Foreign Secretary, saying that, as I had visited many of the chief cities, and had been a guest with many of the principal

M

clergymen and merchants, I had special opportunities of knowing what was the general sentiment of the educated classes and of those whose social influence made it important to secure their friendship. I should therefore consider it an honour and privilege to be allowed an interview. His lordship at once responded, and I called to see him, as proposed.

"December 26th, 1867.
"DEAR SIR,—If you can call at the Foreign Office on Saturday next at two o'clock, I shall be very happy to see you, and shall be glad to learn anything you may have to tell me as regards public feeling towards this country on the other side of the Atlantic.
"Yours truly,
"DERBY."

I was received with cheerful courtesy, his lordship listening to all I said with deep attention, sometimes interposing with a relevant question. I said that, although I endeavoured my utmost to extenuate our action in regard to the *Alabama*, there remained, along with a deep love for England, a deep sense of injury, which might for a time be buried, but which would be only dormant, and at some future occasion of difference might revive and provoke hostility. I presumed to urge that in some way, without disparagement to our own Government, there might be the expression of regret for any inadvertence and of willingness to redress any injury resulting. I said I felt sure that such an expression of opinion would be hailed in America, met in a cordial spirit, and the wound be healed which otherwise might fester. When I rose, his lordship pressed me to remain a little longer in converse.

The Geneva Conference and Arbitration followed soon after. I do not presume to think it was owing to my interview. All that I said may have been anticipated, but I rejoice that our Government achieved the most important work of the century in thus removing the cause of America's displeasure, linking more closely the two nations, and setting a priceless example of arbitration before the world.

CHAPTER XIII.

BESIDES my first visit to America, which was chiefly political, though the advocacy of peace and freedom is essentially religious, I have paid two visits, chiefly for the purpose of preaching the Gospel and obtaining funds to assist in building a monument to the memory of Abraham Lincoln and of his advocacy of emancipation. To describe the many and varied incidents of these tours would require a whole volume, so I must content myself with a brief summary.

In every place were loving hearts, grasping hands, open doors. I soon forgot I had crossed the ocean; I felt I was still in Old England, though they called it New.

I preached thrice every Sunday—sometimes four times—and nearly every week-night, for Presbyterians, Baptists, Methodists, Independents, and sometimes Episcopalians, without distinction. One Sunday, at Brooklyn, the sermon preceded worship, that I might reach the Episcopalian church before the evening service of prayer was finished. I heard of no difficulty in such intercommunion.

Amongst a hundred others of whose generous hospitality I was the grateful recipient, let me mention the Hon. W. E. Dodge and Mrs. Dodge, whose mansion in New York was my home, and who welcomed me as though I were a brother or a son ; Dr. Theodore and Mrs. Cuyler, with whom was my Brooklyn home, who, with his venerable but in spirit youthful mother, also overwhelmed me with affection ; the Hon. George Stuart, the eminent philanthropist at Philadelphia, chief promoter of the " Christian Commission " ; Mr. J. Tappan, a veteran emancipator ; Governor Claflin at Newton ; the venerable Mr. and Mrs. Ropes at Boston ; Mr. Toby, postmaster

there; Dr. and Mrs. Smiley, of the Mohonk Lake, a sort of
Paradise, where a picturesque crag bears my name. I frequently met Cyrus Field. The first occasion was when he
came on board our Cunarder, in 1867, on his arrival from
Newfoundland, whence he had sent the first cable message
to London. He related with enthusiasm how, as soon as
communication between New York and London was completed, he had wired thanks to Mr. Gladstone for a speech
delivered the same evening—thanks which reached the
statesman next morning at breakfast.

On my first journey, Dr. and Mrs. Calkins received me at
Buffalo on occasion of the Annual Convention of the American
Board of Foreign Missions. There was much excitement in
preparation for the "Board." When I entered the house, one
of the children exclaimed, "The Board has come!" and early
next morning a child's voice at my door kindly asked, "Will
the Board like some coffee?"

The Misses Irving received me courteously at Sunnyside,
near "Sleepy Hollow," on the Hudson, in the home of their
uncle, Washington Irving, and showed me some interesting
relics.

I spent a memorable afternoon with Longfellow at his fine
old mansion, once the headquarters of Washington. How
charming was his reading of some few stanzas of his new
translation of Dante! I afterwards met him in London at
dinner with Dickens, Russell of the *Times*, and other *literati*.
A refined gentleman, modest in manner, winning in feature
and voice, in full accord with his muse.

At Hartford I was hospitably housed by Professor and Mrs.
Beecher Stowe. A long forenoon was spent quietly together,
she finishing a drawing, and I colouring a sketch I had just
taken of their picturesque, English-looking, many-gabled
abode, erected from the proceeds of "Uncle Tom's Cabin." I
was told that while thus occupied she was most disposed to
converse. Dr. Bushnell called, and remained two hours. I
was charmed by their discussion of theological and political
questions. My memory does not retain the particulars, but
only that I was spellbound.

Mrs. Stowe told me how her tale of Uncle Tom originated. She was at a Holy Communion service, when suddenly the death-scene of the story was presented vividly to her mind. She seemed to see it as a reality. This was the germ of the whole. It was first described, and suggested the rest of that marvellous book which, more than any other influence, led to the great event of emancipation.

Either Mrs. Stowe or Dr. Bushnell related to me the following incident witnessed by a friend many years before, when the Niagara Falls were little visited, and the natives were in possession of the forests around. He saw a canoe moored to the American shore, opposite Goat Island. An Indian was lying down in it, fast asleep. Suddenly an Indian girl darted from the thick foliage, and, quick as thought, unfastened the rope, pushed the canoe out into the current, and disappeared. The sudden motion of the boat and the roar of the rapids awakened the sleeper, who started up and looked for the paddle with which he had often battled with the tide, now his only hope for life; but he looked in vain, and the canoe was hurried madly down the torrent. Calmly the Indian folded his head in his blanket, and, standing upright, was carried over.

I spent some hours with the famous authoress's famous brother, Henry Ward Beecher, and heard him preach at Plymouth Church on Thanksgiving Day. Logic, humour, passionate declamation, poetry, tender pathos, were marvellously blended, and I joined with the eagerly listening crowd both in laughter and tears.

From Mrs. Beecher Stowe.

"Sunday Eve., Jan. 29, 1871.

"DEAR MR. HALL,—Your little volume of poems was a pleasant reminder of a time we have not ceased to look back to as bright in our family annals, when we had the pleasure of seeing you under our roof. We are all as we were in the homestead of which you took away the memorial in your sketchbook. My husband desires his kindest regards to you, my daughters also. It seems to me that now, during this most unhappy war, will be the time to flood France with the Bible. After such wounds of heart there will come a craving for something, and the Bible must take the place of the poor old worn-out superstition. All these troubles speak of the coming of our Lord ; they are the signs of His approach. How wonderful a year this is ! We should all be so happy to see you once more in America. Shall we not some time ?

"Truly and faithfully yours,

"H. B. STOWE."

I spent a day at his country house with the famous orator, John Gough, of temperance fame. How musically sound in my memory the silver bells of the horses that play-fully drew our sleigh over the snow-covered track as I was driven by Mrs. Gough from the neighbouring town where I had been preaching ! How long we sat up into the night, Gough being as fascinating in table-talk as in platform oratory ! With what interest he showed me over his farm next morning, rejoicing in his rural retirement after many years of continuous and most useful labours.

Another eminent pastor and theologian whom I met was Albert Barnes, whose commentaries are perhaps more generally useful to ordinary readers and Christian workers and more widely spread than any others. For this work he rose very early all through the year, and in overtaxing his eyesight induced partial blindness, and by excessive toil and too little sleep shortened his life. I felt it a great honour to preach in his church at Philadelphia, while he sat with me in the pulpit and spoke of my mission in loving words.

Amongst other preachers and authors whom I remember with much interest were Professor Hodge, of Princeton, with whom and his students I witnessed a marvellous display of meteors at midnight; Professor Park, of Andover; Dr. Cox, Dr. Cheever, Dr. Wilkes, of Montreal; Dr. Patten, and Edward Everett Hale, of Boston, who invited me to a large recep-tion of clergy in his church parlour, and also to his pulpit, in which he sat with me on the eve of my return, while I preached to a crowded congregation from the text, "God so loved the world," after which he warmly grasped my hand and said, "Thank you for preaching for me, and from that text."

By the honour of introductory letters from Mr. Gladstone and Mr. Bright I had the privilege of meeting with many distinguished statesmen. Secretary Seward seemed surprised at what I told him of the sympathy of the great masses of our nation with those who had been struggling for union and emancipation.

Chief Justice Chase narrated to me the following incident:—A friend of his, who had been a slaveholder, went to visit his estate and his now enfranchised slaves. The Chief Justice accompanied him, and was surprised to see the "darkies" crowd round their old master, clinging to his arms and almost embracing him. He said, "You seem to love your old master. Don't you wish the old times again?" The reply was, "We lub de old massa, but we lub de Free more." Then a kind of religious service followed. One man with a good voice acted as precentor, singing in recitative, "I see Abel sittin' on de tree ob life." Then all the others joined in loud chorus, "I see Abel sittin' on de tree ob life." Then followed the same reference to the tree with other names—Enoch, Noah, Abraham, Daniel, etc. Then came final compliments to their visitors—"I see Massa Chase sittin' on de tree ob life," and "I see de old massa sittin' on de tree ob life."

At Richmond I was the guest of Governor Pierpoint, who conducted me over the city, which bore marks of the recent siege, and to the battlefield at Petersburg, fifty miles off, where the final victory was won, and where many signs of the fight were still visible in ruined stockades, battered accoutrements, and some bleaching bones protruding from heaps of soil. In the evening I preached in the " Black Bethel Church " to some two thousand negroes rejoicing in their new freedom. In the pulpit sat with me the Liberation Governor, the protector of those freed men, and successor to the Confederate Governor who had held them in bondage. My text was, " Let the brother of low degree rejoice in that he is exalted," and in the excitement of the auditors a perfectly black giantess mounted her seat and, with emphatic action, exclaimed, "When I feels de lub ob God in my heart I knows I'm one ob de royal family."

The Hon. John Wanamaker, late Postmaster-General,

gave us an interesting reception in his beautiful home near Philadelphia, where on Sunday he took me to his great Sunday school, the largest in America, with some 2,000 children assembled under one roof. During his tenure of high office, and his daily attendance at Washington, he never neglected his duties as superintendent of the school. His generous treatment of his workpeople is in harmony with the vastness of his business, the chief centre of which, at present, is one of the greatest of commercial palaces in New York.

I remember my hospitable host and hostess at Boston, Mr. and Mrs. Ropes; also Mr. Toby, postmaster there; and the Rev. Stuart Dodge—worthy of his name, zealous for the Gospel—at Beyrout, and New York, faithful friend and devoted to every good work. I have a well-remembered colleague in Dr. R. Thomas, pastor of an important church in Brookline, a wealthy suburb. I counted also among friends Philips Brooks, the bishop, who honoured me with coming to a clerical reception at Hampstead, and whom we visited at Boston. But I must pause, fearing lest, in what might seem a full enumeration, I might—with memory weakened —forget some true friends.

At Brooklyn I rejoiced to hear the fervent, pointed eloquence of my dear friend, Dr. Cuyler, for whom I preached several times in his Lafayette Avenue Church. Here, also, I delivered a lecture to young men on temperance; and, to illustrate the insufficiency of high education alone, I related the following incident :—

A young man of intelligent face and gentlemanly manner, but very shabby in appearance, followed me after sermon to the vestry in Surrey Chapel in great distress. I asked him what had brought him into such a condition. He said: "The drink! I can't keep from it. I've respectable relatives, but all they give me—cash, clothes, watch—all goes for drink. Tell me what to do." I told him that for him total abstinence was essential, and that I was an abstainer in order to encourage such as he. I signed the pledge again, for him to follow, which he did. I then said : "But we must pray for help."

He said he did not believe in God—yet he knew the Greek Testament, and had "coached" men at Oxford for Bishops' examinations! He only believed in the Spirit of the Universe. I said I believed also, and so we could both unite. We knelt down, and I prayed to the Great Spirit of the Universe to pardon him and help him to conquer this temptation. With tears, he said : " Oh, that my mother had seen this signature, to make her death more happy."

At the close of my lecture to the young men, a middle-aged gentleman, with an elegant young girl on his arm, came up to speak to me. " Don't you remember me ? I'm that young man, and this is my daughter. I'm editor of one of the chief journals here, and a member of the Episcopal Church, and I wish you would call on my wife and see our happy home, by God's blessing on your counsel." I shall never forget that lecture in Dr. Cuyler's church at Brooklyn.

I called next day, and took tea with him and his wife and daughter in a beautifully furnished house, pervaded by an atmosphere of refinement and domestic happiness. Not long afterwards I read of his funeral, attended by a large number of literary and other friends, in token of the respect in which he was held.

At Hamilton, Canada, I was invited to be a guest to a Mr. Pearce. Having written to accept his kindness, I received from a wealthy citizen a remonstrance to the effect that my expectant host was in a very humble position as an engine-driver, and it was hoped I would decline his presumptuous invitation and go where I should be properly entertained. Of course, I adhered to my promise, and was enthusiastically met by Mr. Pearce, who took me to his small but comfortable cottage. He led me into a bedroom called " Newman Hall," the walls of which were decorated with my likeness and the bookshelf furnished with my publications. After my sermon next morning there was a baptism of a child of his, and the name announced was " Newman Hall "! He told me his history. Just before starting from England, almost penniless, he heard me preach in Surrey Chapel

about Jacob and his stone pillow. The first night at New
York he slept on a plank, and thought of the sermon, and
prayed the God of Jacob to help him. When he reached
Hamilton he had not a dollar. He began work as a cobbler
of shoes. Soon he was asked to do a job of cleaning engines
at the railway. One day a driver was wanted for a luggage
train, and he was asked to make a first attempt. He did it
so well that he soon became a first-class engine-driver at
three dollars a day. A teetotaller and Christian, he avoided
costly follies, and bought the freehold house where he
entertained me. A few years afterwards he invited me
with my wife to be the guests of himself and wife, who left
the kitchen range, where she had been cooking the dinner, to
take the head of the table and entertain her guests.

One evening a large company of clergy were invited to
meet me—of several denominations—and they evidently
respected their humble host and hostess, who had prepared
for this occasion by the purchase of a good piano and the
laying down of a new carpet. When we came away, he
presented me with a very handsome and rather ponderous
walking-stick made of hickory wood, heavy and strong, with
an open book carved on it entitled "Come to Jesus," above
which is a hand pointing to it, and beneath, well cut, "It
is I." There is also an inscription on a silver plate engraved,
" Rev. Newman Hall, from W. Pearce, Hamilton, 1873."

Being suddenly called upon to preach in the great hall of
the Mountain House, on the Catskill Mountains, I took for
my text, "The mountain of the Lord's house . . . shall be
exalted above the hills." Spending a Sunday in a large hotel
on Lake George, I received a request to preach a sermon to
the guests. When all preparations were made, I asked where
the servants were placed—they were all coloured people.
Some excuse was made for their absence; I declined to
proceed without them. They soon appeared, and behaved
as devoutly and listened as intelligently as their white
brethren.

At Chicago I preached several times, but remember
more vividly a funeral sermon I heard from a young

negro pastor. In front of the pulpit was an open coffin, in which was the corpse, round which all the congregation slowly walked. The sermon was a solemn warning to young men to beware of sin, because the sins of people here would be their companions hereafter!

A very well-dressed coloured gentleman offered to show me a little of the city. We met a very fashionably dressed negress, in light blue skirt with long train, white satin bonnet with veil, white silk parasol with lace border, and so forth. They exchanged polite salutations. I asked who was his acquaintance. He said she was the wife of a friend, a carpenter. I expressed surprise at her costume—for, as far as I could judge, it was fit for Hyde Park or a flower show. He replied, " You know, sir, that all people like to distinguish themselves. The prejudices of the age shut against us the doors of advancement in many directions, and of fashionable society; but there is one mode of becoming distinguished, and of that we are capable—dress!" Then, when I thanked him for his courtesy, he stretched out his hand in an oratorical attitude and said: "Sir! Chicago is the most marvellous manifestation of modern civilisation now extant!"

On my way to Chicago my train was delayed by snow. It was past seven o'clock, and a large assembly was waiting to hear my lecture. The Rev. Dr. Collier kindly undertook to interest them till I arrived, by racy tales about Rowland Hill, my predecessor. About an hour after I was due, I was received most cordially and listened to for another hour.

Besides delivering occasional lectures, I generally preached six or seven times weekly. From New York and Boston to Maine in the north, Chicago and St. Louis westward, Baltimore and Richmond in the south, and in most of the intervening cities round about them—such as Rochester, Albany, Detroit, Worcester, Niagara, Hertford—and, in Canada, Hamilton, Toronto, Montreal, Quebec, Ottawa, and others. Everywhere the churches were crowded. People of all grades were not, as I well knew, attracted by originality, learning, wit, eloquence—for these qualities their own American pulpit is renowned through the world—but (as I read in some of the papers), by ease and simplicity of style, by clear exposition of Scripture, and by earnestness to exalt Christ and win souls. This was verily my aim and prayer. I did not seek the praise of men or fear the censure of critics.

At Washington we spent a week at the home of Chief Justice Drake—a fine old English-American gentleman—a Presbyterian elder, conducting family prayers every day, and often preaching in churches. He took us to see the magnificent State palaces of the Government, the White House, where he introduced us to the President, and the vast white marble Capitol, with its Senate Chamber and House of Representatives, and lofty dome. Here I preached, as already mentioned, to · two thousand Senators, Representatives, and others, and also to a congregation of coloured people, whose rapt attention, broken only by ardent responses, increased the energy of my delivery and my hope of spiritual results. During my prayer,· when I asked God to send the arrow of conviction into some hearts, a negro loudly shouted—"Do, Lud! shoot 'em! shoot 'em quick!"

I have no space to describe all the beautiful and grand scenes I visited. I confine myself to the grandest of all, and transcribe what I wrote at Niagara :—

"Small things and small minds show best on first acquaintance, while what is great continually increases its impressiveness, because it cannot be all seen at once, and the first view is, therefore, necessarily a partial one. Who, on his first visit, ever understood the vastness of St. Peter's? Who, on first perusal, ever appreciated the majesty of Milton, or the genius of Shakespeare? Who, at the first beholding, ever understood the grandeur of the ocean or of the Alps? Who, on first knowledge of Christ, can fully comprehend what eternity cannot exhaust—' the breadth, and length, and depth, and height' of the love of God, 'which passeth knowledge'? The true conception is composed of a multitude of impressions, which can only be received one by one, and therefore the first must needs be inadequate. I had, however, been so emphatically warned of disappointment that no such feeling was experienced. That long line of snow-white foam, stretching from bank to bank, with the lofty pillar of cloud soaring above it, with the solemn, steady, all-pervading, overwhelming, yet tranquillising music of the cataract, has left an impression on the mind never to be effaced."

Although I spent about ten days at Niagara, I felt the time hurry away with cruel rapidity, and I almost grudged the necessary time for meals and sleep—there was always so much to see that was new, always so much to revisit. I will recall one day. Soon after five I was up to watch the sun rise on the Fall. Then I climbed a wooded cliff to a road which brought me, at a distance of two miles, to the "Burning Springs." Then I reascended the high ground and strolled homewards, till I reached a spot just above the Horse-shoe Fall, and attempted a sketch. I had never seen Niagara drawn from that point. You see no bottom to the abyss, no exit for the water, which fancy might suppose is plunging through the very centre of the earth itself. The only foreground is a crag which, with its rich verdure, appears to be bending over the cataract. I think, of all the aspects in which I beheld Niagara, this, on the whole, was the most sublime. I now began to think it must be breakfast-time; looking at my watch, I found it was noon! I had been just six hours on my morning stroll. The waiter was amused when I asked for breakfast; the time for that meal was long past. Refreshed with food, I started forth again, intending to be back by three o'clock, in time for dinner; but again I was utterly beguiled, and when I returned it was five o'clock, and dinner had been all cleared away. I went out again for an evening stroll in the moonlight. I went beyond the Fall, and stood in the forest alone, close to the cataract. I held my stick in the water, and the vibration caused by the current thrilled through me. The silence of the forest contrasted with the roar of the cataract, the wild rush of the rapids glimmering in the moon, the foliage dripping and sparkling with the spray—it was past midnight when I regained the hotel.

My farewell view of the Great Fall was symbolical. A rainbow was spanning the entire river. One limb seemed to rest on American, the other on British soil. Immediately under it the divided stream was foaming as in anger; but the waters soon reunited and flowed on together to the quiet lake. I took it as an emblem of international peace. For a

season public sentiment, in some quarters, seemed at variance
with American interest, and American feeling was naturally
roused in return. But over the temporary misunderstanding
there still rested the bow of a true and abiding friendship;
while the two nations, separated only in appearance, not in
heart, were speedily to reunite, and in greater harmony, let
us trust, than ever, pursue together their great career of prosperity, peace, and freedom, for the benefit of each other and
of the whole world.*

I stood within the most solemn of Nature's temples,
where the sublimest service, the most imposing ritual, was
being performed in honour of the Creator; where sacrifice
was ever being presented on an altar from which the curling
spray was ever ascending to meet and blend with the awful
overhanging cloud, which seemed, as of old, the visible symbol
of Jehovah's presence; and where the grandest psalm was ever
swelling in praise of the glory and greatness of the Eternal.
Other temples have disappeared, but this has remained
through many millenniums. Other services are interrupted,
but this continues without intermission—day and night,
century by century, its priests unwearied, its voices never
mute. "The floods have lifted up, O Lord, the floods have
lifted up their voice; the floods lift up their waves. The
Lord on high is mightier than the noise of many waters."

Wherever I preached, as already stated, the minister appealed to the congregation to contribute to a fund for raising
in London, alongside my church, a "Lincoln Tower," in
memory of the martyred President and emancipator. As
by a few lectures I defrayed all my personal expenses, there
was no deduction from the amount contributed, every dollar
of which was sent by the officers of each church direct to
Mr. Dodge, the treasurer in New York, who in due time sent
it direct to the treasurer in London. The sums thus contributed amounted to £3,500, half the sum required, the
other half being furnished by British donors, making the
memorial tower international. As this subject has been
misunderstood, I should explain, what I have already briefly

* See my volume, " From Liverpool to St. Louis " (1868).

AMERICA: EVANGELISING TOURS.

touched on, that the project was originated by the famous W. E. Dodge, when visiting me in London, who started it with a donation of 500 dollars (£100); two others following with smaller sums—not £200 altogether. I asked and received no individual subscription, but may say I really earned the rest by my preaching. I might have realised for myself a considerable sum by using the same opportunities for paid lectures. Considering the tens of thousands who flocked to my sermons, I reckon that on an average no individual contributed so much as sixpence, and I may reasonably hope they received the full value back again. Still, the collection was urged by the various pastors, with the distinct understanding that the money would be devoted to one-half the cost of an international monument to Lincoln, and so I have rejoiced to consider it as an expression of American fraternity.

Instead of regrets at my long absence of three months, the following welcome was accorded by my beloved flock to their under-shepherd :—

"We, the church and congregation of Surrey Chapel, offer you our most hearty congratulations on your return from America. We rejoice that you have been everywhere received with the greatest cordiality, and that you have so frequently proclaimed the truths of the Gospel, and endeavoured to strengthen the bond of union between the peoples of America and England.

"During your absence we have reviewed the happy connection between us as pastor and people during thirteen years, and we find so much to rejoice in that we confidently anticipate years of happiness should your life be spared and the Divine blessing continue to rest on your labours. The results of your ministry are apparent in the admission to the church of 1,350 members, the majority of whom had not been previously connected with any church, in the increased usefulness of institutions which had been in a languishing condition, and the establishment by yourself of other societies for the temporal and spiritual welfare of the working classes. We admire especially the wisdom which led you to originate the Rowland Hill Fund, to perpetuate his work at the expiration of the lease, now exceeding £6,000. Your personal contributions and appeals to others demand our warmest acknowledgment. We highly appreciate your services for other sections of the Church of Christ, evangelistic efforts, and Sabbath afternoon services at St. James's Hall. We admire your catholic spirit and able advocacy of civil and religious liberty. Your works from the press as well as pulpit labours have been so blessed of God that we, who are the special objects of your ministerial regard, especially express to God our gratitude for having made our pastor so useful.

"And now, dear Sir, we offer for your acceptance the sum of £500 as a token of affectionate regard, with our earnest prayers that every blessing, temporal and spiritual, may rest upon you, and that we, the people of your charge, may be your 'glory and joy' now, and at the coming of our Lord Jesus Christ, and that there may be in store for you the blessing—'They that turn many to righteousness shall shine as the stars for ever and ever.'

"Surrey Chapel, 27 December, 1867."

These affectionate greetings and prayers are a precious memorial, apart from the generous gift, so unexpected.

I may here quote some passages from *Harper's Weekly* for November 23rd, 1867, on myself:—

"At home he averages five sermons a week, and since he has been in America has delivered fifty sermons in a month. In Brooklyn he addressed ten thousand people on a single Sabbath, and after the fourth sermon showed no symptom of fatigue."

"Mr. Hall's reception in America has been a complete ovation. Such citizens as Longfellow, Sumner, Beecher, and Mrs. Stowe have been his entertainers; and the leading churches have been thronged to listen to his tender and beautiful discourses. The New York Stock Board invited him to address them, received his speech with hearty applause, and then struck up 'God save the Queen.' 'Only think,' said he to us, 'of the London Stock Exchange suspending their business to listen to a parson!' No other British clergyman has earned such a compliment from American civilians. He expects to preach before the House of Congress at Washington before his departure."

"The secret of this preacher's success seems to lie in three or four effective qualities. He has prodigious *heart-power*. He has great simplicity of speech. No diplomatist could have woven a more skilful argument in behalf of Great Britain than did Mr. Hall in his lecture on the relations of his native land to ours during the late struggle. If England ever finds herself embarrassed in her diplomacy with America, we would recommend her to send as her ambassador the warm-hearted pastor of Surrey Chapel.

"The memory of his persuasive voice and evangelical discourses will long linger with our countrymen. He has come as a messenger of peace between the two great nations of Christendom. The benedictions of our people will follow him to his home; and among all the philanthropists who have visited our shores not one has left a more beloved and honoured name than Newman Hall."

During my return voyage from America, in a three-days'

gale, I had the privilege of the companionship of the mother and two daughters of the editor of the *Independent*, from whom I afterwards received as a memorial a small table-stand of Plymouth Rock wood and an etching of their own, depicting the *Mayflower* sailing homeward and a young couple waving adieu from the rocky shore. Miss Ward thus wrote :—

"Newark, N.J., Jan. 9, '67.

". . . Knowing your interest in Plymouth and our Pilgrim ancestry, we had the little table made in the Old Colony, of wood that grew in Plymouth. The top is part of a beam from the house of Governor Bradford, the first Governor of the Plymouth Colony, from whom our family are descended. The design on the tile is adapted from Boughton's 'Return of the *Mayflower*.' The legend which my sister has written on it is from Longfellow's 'Miles Standish'—' O strong hearts and true, not one went back in the *Mayflower*.' Those are New England Mayflowers which are hinted at in the border—the trailing Arbutus—and it grows in its perfection in Plymouth.

"Yours, with many grateful memories,

"SUSAN HAYES WARD."

I may here quote the following letter :—

From Lady Augusta Stanley.

"Osborne, July 24, '68.

"DEAR MR. NEWMAN HALL,—I hasten to thank you for your most interesting reminiscences of your American travels, which could not have reached me at a more opportune moment, for I hope to have, while I am here, an opportunity of bringing them to the Queen's knowledge. Few things, I am sure, could be more welcome to Her Majesty than such testimonies, both as affecting her personally and as a pledge of the feeling which it has been the Queen's desire, as it was the earnest wish of the Prince, to witness the growth of between the two great families of our race. Such visits as that which you paid to the States must contribute powerfully to strengthen and promote the friendly relations between us and to remove misunderstanding ; and when we consider the great mission our two countries have in common, we can hardly exaggerate the importance of such efforts. This was so fully recognised years ago by those most dear to me, and so much of the energy of their too-short lives was devoted to the cause, that to me individually there is none dearer to my heart ; and for this reason I am doubly grateful to you for making me the channel for the conveyance of such welcome tidings.

"Yours sincerely,

"AUGUSTA STANLEY."

N

In addition to the honour of the degree of D.D. by
Amherst University, I received as the result of my visit the
following complimentary invitation to the pastorate of an important church, my declining of which must not be interpreted
as any disrespect to it or its senders, but simply as arising
from the pressure of special obligations in my own country.

" Chicago, Ills., May 4, 1870.
" The undersigned are a committee to procure a pastor for the Third
Presbyterian Church of this city. . . . Our church is a most inviting
field for a Christian minister. It is among the best of our denomination,
well located, with a good church edifice, and free of debt ; will seat
comfortably about 1,100 persons, and with extra movable seats about
300 more. Our people are well-to-do in worldly matters, and above the
average in intelligence and refinement, and are as willing to work for
the interests of Christ's Kingdom as the average of Presbyterian congregations. Should the present edifice prove too small for those who desire
to attend your ministry, the church will, at once, build one sufficiently
large. Chicago is advancing in population and wealth with unpre-
cedented rapidity, and assuming a controlling influence in the great
interior of our country. It is therefore of the greatest importance that
the moral and religious influence going out from us should be of the
best type. . . . We propose for your acceptance the sum of ten
thousand dollars per annum. . . . It is distinctly understood that
the church will ratify any action that we may take in this matter. If
you will visit us to look over the ground, we will pay your expenses out
and back. Please answer by telegraph.
" Your brethren in Christ,

" V. T—,
" W. W—,
" G. W—."

On receiving this, I telegraphed, " Thanks. Impossible.
Will write." I wrote to say I had no wish to leave a loving
and beloved people, and that I felt bound to complete the
transference of the institutions of the old Surrey Chapel to the
new church, and not to leave on the congregation remaining the burden of a debt which had been incurred mainly
by myself. The salary offered was consistent with American
generosity, and considerably more than double my own; but
had it been quadrupled the reply would have been the same.

From Diary.—At Clifton with Mr. and Mrs. S. Wills.
Entertained with stories of years ago. They greatly honoured
missions. Son died in India as a missionary. Another

son is now a missionary there. Daughter going out to help him. A third son studying medicine in view of the mission field. Greater honour than earthly title or worldly wealth. The following letter refers to my visits to Bristol during my Surrey Chapel pastorate, and to his companionship with me in the United States of America:—

"MY DEAR FRIEND,—I understand that you are preparing for publication some reminiscences of your long and very eventful life. . . . Perhaps a few incidents in my own experience may be not unworthy of record.

"What a host of pleasant memories cluster around your frequent visits to Bristol during the 'fifties and 'sixties! I can recall one of many such occasions which stands out very prominently—I think in 1862—when you were the special preacher at the old Bristol Tabernacle. The first part of the service was conducted by a local minister, and when you had to ascend the pulpit the throng was so dense that for some time the managers were at their wits' end to get you to it, and amid the commotion came the cry, 'We can't get Mr. Hall in!' But by literally stepping upon the shoulders of the people you managed to reach your place.

"How well I remember your kindness to and wise method with us boys; the pleasant walks and breezy talks; a leap over a five-barred gate—unusual to us then in a parson—and the remark, 'This does not make a man a worse Christian'—all exerting a wholesome formative influence, not without its effect long afterwards.

"You remember our voyage together across the Atlantic in September, 1873, in the Cunard steamer *Java*, and how, thinking we would not wait for the tender, we took a small boat and joined the steamer in mid-stream, then finding that the only way to board her was by a loose rope ladder, up which we clambered?

"How well I remember your talks with the sailors in the fo'castle, and their appreciation of your services day after day.

"Then our long, lumbering ride up the Catskill Mountains, in company with Dr. Stoughton and Joshua Harrison, now both received into spirit life.

"Our journey to Niagara, when, in the Pulman car, the strange lady told me that she was doing earnest home mission work, and the reason of it was a sermon you had preached on a former visit to the States. This she related without knowing you were then in the States. When I told her that you were not only in America, but in that very car, her delight was great. I introduced you to her, and, after a chat, you said to me that she seemed like an angel sent to encourage you on the threshold of your visit. Certainly her face looked as though she had been on the 'Mount.'

"Our Sunday at the Fort William Henry Hotel, Lake George, stands out in my memory. A deputation of guests came to me to ask if you would preach to them in the salon of the hotel, and they would get the guests from the other hotels to join them. This you kindly promised to do, on two conditions—that the hour fixed should be after the other services had finished, and that the coloured servants should be permitted to attend. This latter was promised, but when the time came they were not allowed to be present. 'Then,' said you, 'I shall not preach'; and I spent an unenviable ten minutes in marching through the large congregation to remonstrate with mine host, whom I persuaded to allow the coloured servants to listen, and so the service proceeded.

"I remember at Hamilton, Canada, one of the principal bankers invited you to be his guest, but how you preferred the more humble abode of your friend and former member of Surrey Chapel, the engine-driver, and his delight in welcoming you.

"Then last, but not least, the 'At Home' given you at Christ Church to commemorate your eightieth birthday, at which, through the goodness of the Rev. F. B. Meyer, I was a privileged guest.

"May God long spare your most useful life, and when the end comes, may it be like a 'brilliant sunset after a summer's day.'

"Yours affectionately,

"SAMUEL D. WILLS.

"Clifton, October, 1897.

An inestimable result of my visit to America has been the brotherly affection of Dr. Cuyler, who has several times been my guest, as I have been his. Most precious have been his sympathy with me in joy and sorrow. His wise counsels, his constant prayers, his fidelity to the Gospel of the Cross, his large-heartedness to all of every name who love the Lord Jesus Christ in sincerity, his womanliness in affection, his manliness of uttering what he knows to be true, and doing what conscience tells him is right, have secured to him the devotion of the whole Church, and the deepening personal love of all who belong to the inner circle of private friends. The groundswell of his conversation is the love of God in Christ—the surface wavelets dance and flash with humour, anecdote, and wit.

All along his ministerial life he has been a most zealous and eloquent promoter of total abstinence; during the War a leading champion of the North in its struggle for emancipation, and an enthusiastic lover of the Old Country, where by his sermons and his religious articles he is universally known.

During his thirty years' pastorate in Brooklyn he received

4,650 members into the church, of whom about one-half were on confession of faith. In 1890 he resigned his charge because parochial duties became too onerous; but his capacity to preach was not diminished, and in his now open ministry his services have been in requisition from all parts of the United States of America. A still wider ministry has been that of writing short, pungent, practical articles for the religious press. He generally sends forth three of these every week. Altogether these homilies are more than four thousand in number, reprinted in different languages, and securing an audience of at least half a million. Besides these newspaper articles, he has published some twenty volumes, among which may be mentioned " Empty Crib," " Heart Life," " God's Light on Dark Clouds," " Wayside Springs," " How to be a Pastor." The great secret of his success has been his constant visitation of his parishioners, poor as well as rich, and his faithful preaching of the central truths of the Gospel in language plain, terse, vivid, never vulgar and never obscure—the language of the people.

SPECIMENS OF DR. CUYLER'S TABLE TALK.

" People talk of this 'higher life.' The two chief graces are *un-selfishness*—'He pleased not himself'—and *submissiveness*—'Father, not my will! Thy will!' He who attains these is near perfection."

" John Bull goes slowly, but when he puts his foot down it is to *stay*. It would be well if American dash were mingled with English hold-on-it-ness."

" Conscience and custom are deeper than prohibition. Convince the conscience, alter the custom, and prohibition will be easy—not otherwise."

" The English tongue is the ligament binding England and America and one blood pulsates in both. Round every Jericho of oppression the English tongue will be a trumpet to bring down the walls."

" We men hold the reins, but the women tell us where to drive. They have power enough without the vote."

" Despotic monarchy is the best if-the angel Gabriel is despot, but if Beelzebub, devilish. All depends upon who is in the saddle. Dr. Cox said in prayer, 'O Lord, we are Republicans with each other, but all are Monarchists before Thee!' "

" Others may be eager to go to the Holy City at once. I am satisfied with Brooklyn, so long as my wife is there. I sympathise with the darky who had been singing about the angel Gabriel coming to take him to glory. One night a neighbour, to test his sincerity, knocked at his door. '*Who's dar?*' 'Angel Gabriel.' '*What want?*' 'Come to fetch Pompey to glory.' '*Mistake! dat nigger went ten year ago!*' As I shan't ever come back, I'll stay here as long as I can."

"Have any people been killed on this line? Answer: Two, on their wedding tour, died of old age before the train reached its destination!"

"God deals with us as painters, who put shade into their pictures to emphasise the lights."

"Parnellites talk of Home Rule, but act Imperial Rule. Their vote determines the policy of Government, like the box of chain-cable on board a ship, rolled first to one side and then the other, as the wind blows."

"Duff, preaching for missions in America, said, 'You tell me you are not so green as to risk money on so doubtful an enterprise. No; to be green is to be alive, fresh, vigorous. No, no—you are too dead and dry to be *green!*'"

"The *Pall Mall*, in its revelations of London vice, has tapped Vesuvius."

"A throne was never built which came within ten leagues of a pulpit where Christ is preached."

We had a grand, aristocratic old gentleman in the form of a handsome Pomeranian dog, also a very lively, self-assertive fox terrier. The Pomeranian wore a smart collar, to which a strap was sometimes fastened when we went for a walk. The delight of the terrier was to hold this strap in its teeth, and, keeping out of range, to drag the stately animal about in spite of evident reluctance. Dr. Cuyler said: "That's your aristocracy dragged by your democracy. Aristocracy don't like it, but can't help it."

"There is a tree in California so tall that it takes two men to see up it. One begins to look where the other leaves off. Another tree in California was sawn through and yet stood upright, and had to be pulled over—like some people who adhere to their old opinions when all their arguments are refuted and all their statements disproved."

"His sermons are as dry as remainder biscuits after a voyage. They remind you of the Scotch preacher who once reached his church very wet with rain. The sexton said, 'Never mind; ye'll be dry eneugh when ye get into pulpit.'"

"Coleridge told of a man who never spoke of himself without taking off his hat."

"A back-settler was very anxious because the Indians were troublesome. 'Trust in God, He is good and watchful.' He said, 'Oh, I believe all that, but it's them plaguey Indians I distrust.'"

The following fact has become a proverb in America—for brevity. A clerical friend of Dr. Cuyler was advised to marry, and to visit another clergyman who had several suitable daughters. The father said he thought Mary was suitable—to whom he was introduced, explained his object, but said he had no time for courtship, but would go and have another smoke with her father, hoping she would come and say "Yes" or "No." In a few days this reply actually was sent, "Rev. and Dear Sir,—Yes.—Yours faithfully, MARY S." She knew and respected his character."

"A man was asked to subscribe to a fence round the cemetery. 'What's the need? No one wants to get in, and they who are in cannot get out, if they would!'"

"Salisbury Cathedral is petrified music."

"You don't want the electric light on the clock tower of Parliament to keep saying, 'I'm an electric light.' What it has got to do is just to shine. So Christians have just to 'shine as lights in the world.'"

"The dynasty of the Stuarts may be thus classified—(1) The reign of bigots; (2) of strumpets; (3) of poltroons."

"Your England is lovely—so it ought to be; for it has taken eight hundred years in making. When our country has been at it six hundred years more, I shall look down and see how *it* is getting along."

"We speak of the Church militant and the Church triumphant. What we chiefly hear is the Church mendicant. He's a lusty fellow—in season, out of season—from a Bishop to a 'General.'"

"Salvation Army hymns are like negro melodies whitewashed."

"Speaking of sermons which have little relation to the text, Beecher said, 'A text is a gate into a field. When you are in the field you shut the gate; so a text is the entry into the theme, and may then be left behind.' But a good feature of English preaching is deducing the whole sermon and elucidating it from the text."

"A friend of mine said to a London publican, 'If your shops were all closed, there would not be much work for the police.' He replied, 'That won't be till the devil is dead.' A publican said to a prohibitionist, 'You're sending our trade to the devil.' Reply: 'It has been his a long while.'"

"There is not a stone in Old England that you turn up without finding history under it."

"Horace Greeley, when asked to reply to certain censures, said, 'No; it's hard kicking at nothing.' So I won't go to Z. church, for it's hard trying to listen, and hearing nothing."

"Truth may be so diluted that it's hard to see it. Let the shadow of a pigeon pass over a pail of water, and then take two drops of it."

"A negro, touching his own forehead, thus described an incompetent preacher—'De truble wid dat ar man is dat nobody lives in de upper storey.'"

"The gait of an old family horse was about five miles an hour. They whipped him to go faster, but he was thus put out of his own pace, and only went four. Moral: Let every true worker go his own gait."

CHAPTER XIV.

A LARGE portion of my industry and time has been engaged in writing small books intended to convey Gospel truth in simple language, and thus to extend the preacher's influence much further and more permanently than by his voice alone. I will occupy the present chapter with a brief enumeration of my various publications, with some correspondence that would hardly fall under any definite heading, and with some account of the recreations with which I have lightened my work.

"Come to Jesus" is the least of my publications, though by it my name is most widely known in forty languages and 4,000,000 copies; but God often chooses small things to subserve His great purposes. It was merely the heart-utterance of the simplest truths, so that its very weakness would render self-elation ridiculous. All praise be to Him who has made the Gospel it expounds the power of God unto salvation!

The Secretary of the Religious Tract Society has kindly sent me the following list of languages into which "Come to Jesus" has been translated and issued by the aid of that Society:—English (leaflets), French, Romany, Italian, Portuguese, German, Dutch, Swedish, Danish, Norwegian, Magyar, Slovak, Czech (Bohemia), Polish, Greek, Servian, Croatian, Roumanian, Bulgarian, Greco-Turkish, Armeno-Turkish, Arabic, Armenian, Urdu, Urdu-Persian (for the Mohammedans of India), Bengali, Hindi, Khassi (Assam), Orissa, Mahrathi, Tamil, Kanarese, Telugu (South-West India), Singhalese (Ceylon), Chinese, Chinese Mandarin, Japanese, Yoruba (Western Africa), Kafir, Malagasy. It has also been published by several Independent missions and Continental publishers, by the Stirling Tract Society in floral leaflets, and in very large numbers by the American Tract Society, New York.

Soon after my work began in London I published a small work, "Follow Jesus," as a sequel to my earlier tractate, "Come to Jesus." Its purpose is to teach the duties of those who accept the invitation, showing that sincerely to come to Jesus means constant coming, and this means *following—i.e.* habitual love and obedience. This is translated into several languages, and has a circulation of 250,000.

"The Holy Catholic Faith" was written chiefly for Roman Catholics, presenting cardinal doctrines free from controversial antagonism. When they find that Protestants agree with them so far, they may be more disposed to consider those questions on which they differ. This booklet has been widely circulated in Italian.

"Prayer and Praise" is a volume of prayers in the very words of Scripture, arranged for private and family worship during a month. Some books of "family prayer" have seemed to me too pompous, some too familiar, some too monotonous, some too theological; but the Bible, God's instruction as to what we should ask, furnishes matter for prayer certainly acceptable to Him who inspired it. Many have used this volume as an aid in family and public worship, and also in private devotion.

Small tractates have been published, some of them on passing events:—"Death in the Palace," in reference to the Prince Consort, many copies of which were ordered from Windsor Castle; "Death in the Coal-pit," "The Christian Philosopher" (30,000), "Call of the Master" (50,000), "Author of 'The Sinner's Friend'" (70,000), "Warning Cry from Niagara" (40,000), "Day of Small Things," "Christ for Everyone" (60,000), "Brazen Serpent," "Jehovah-Jireh," "Now," "Watch and Pray," "The Shadow of the Almighty," "Quench not the Spirit," "The Man Christ Jesus," "Hints on Preaching," "Plain Truths Plainly Put," "Words from the Workshop," being reports of speeches by working-men on the benefits of teetotalism (40,000); "Ready to Perish" (25,000), "Stop the Leak," "It is I; or, The Voice of Jesus in the Storm" (140,000), "Christian Victory." Larger works have been:—"The Antidote to Fear," "From Liverpool to St. Louis" (out of print), "The Forum and the Vatican; or, An

Easter Pilgrimage to Rome," "The Convent Case," "Homeward Bound"; a volume of sermons at Surrey Chapel, and various tracts. Subsequently came:—"The Lord's Prayer,"" Divine Brotherhood," "Gethsemane," "Lyrics of a Long Life," the aggregate number amounting to above two millions, besides "Come to Jesus," all of them in various methods bearing some testimony to the foundation fact of salvation by Christ.

I was in constant correspondence with my parents, but have very few of their letters or my own. The following is a specimen of my father's outpourings, ever stimulating and consoling:—

"Maidstone, July, 1850.

"Mercy, great mercy, all well, 'looking unto Jesus.' This is, indeed, a great mercy, to be found looking unto Him—having the heart turned towards God—delight in the ways of God—separation from evil ways—love of holiness—love *of* Christ—love *for* Christ—love *for* His people—love *of* His people—Christian friends we should never have known but for the love of Christ. Other mercies—deliverance *from* trouble—support *in* trouble. When we think of His mercies, we shall exclaim with David—'I will extol thee, my God, O King; and I will bless thy name for ever and ever' (Psalm cxlv.)."

A note found among my mother's papers :—

"*From Newman.*

"We do long to keep you on earth as long as possible. My love for you has been a *passion* ever since I was a child. Life would be so different without you. I wonder I endured so patiently those twelve years' exile at Hull. If you were to go to heaven, I should want to go too, and be tempted to wish to forsake my present appointed lot.. So you must try and keep well to save me from this temptation."

Samuel Wilberforce, Bishop of Oxford—whose illustrious father I had visited as a junior reporter with a proof of a speech—I met at Mr. Gladstone's breakfasts. He was sometimes censured for inconsistency between his High Church doctrines and his broad sympathies. To this the following letter alludes :—

"Oct. 28, 1858.

"Rev. and Dear Sir,—I thank you heartily for your very welcome note. . . . Small minds, and above all, it seems to me, irreligious minds, cannot comprehend how a man can be convinced (as I am, with as a complete intellectual conviction as my understanding can admit, and with as full a spiritual addiction to that conclusion as my reason and spirit can yield) that their own spiritual body is most of any in full accordance with the mind and will of Christ, and yet honour, admire, and delight in the manifestation of the presence of the Spirit of God working upon the souls of those who have not, as I think, been enlightened to see what I see. It is a matter of thankfulness that some at least are delivered from this thraldom, and can see as you see, and can write as you write.

> "Ever most truly yours,
> "S. Oxon."

In a newspaper report of a debate in the House of Lords it was stated that Bishop Wilberforce had accused Edward Miall of endeavouring to destroy the Church of England. I wrote to him, saying that, as an intimate friend and great admirer of Mr. Miall, I was sure he would disavow any such wish. He honoured Christians of all Churches, but considered that the establishment of any Church was contrary to the New Testament and injurious to any Church so established. His objection applied to the establishment of Presbyterian or Independent Churches as much as to Episcopalian.

I also wrote that, convinced as he was so strongly that his Church was founded on the Rock of Christ and the Apostles, I was surprised that he should think it could ever be destroyed by removing from it the earthly prop of State patronage. He at once thanked me, regretting to have used any expression capable of a meaning he utterly repudiated, and saying that on any future opportunity in debate he would avoid suggesting that enmity to the Establishment was enmity to the Church itself. I extract the following from a letter of his :—

> "Feb. 16, 1860.
> "I am much obliged to you for the kind tone of your letter. I most fully and entirely recognise the distinction you point out between the 'Church' and its 'relation to the State.' Indeed, so habitually is it present to me that I have not the least doubt that what I did say was that Mr. Miall avowed his purpose of destroying 'the Establishment,' and not 'the Church.'"

Services in theatres were now being held, in order to meet the objections of many to enter churches, who linked the buildings with the reputed action of the worshippers in

political and social spheres, thus excusing themselves for
not attending divine worship; they also considered that, as
these buildings were devoted to separate sects, their own
attendance might identify them with one or another. Therefore Lord Shaftesbury, Mr. Morley, and others, more anxious
for religion than for sect, arranged for sermons by preachers
of various Churches, to be held in theatres and other places
which the people were accustomed to attend. Several
eloquent Churchmen as well as Nonconformists preached to
immense congregations, chiefly of the working class. With
others, I preached with great enjoyment to crowds of attentive and devout listeners in the Britannia, Victoria, and
other theatres.

In a letter to me (January 21), 1861, Bishop Wilberforce
writes :—

"I ought honestly to say that I cannot look with pleasure on the
'theatre services,' because I believe the *lasting evil* to the sanctity
of worship will exceed the present good of sowing the good seed.
Will you also let me thank you heartily for a most interesting and
instructive memoir?

"Most truly yours,
"S. OXON."

A charge was delivered at Reading by Bishop Wilberforce
which gave great offence, because he had apparently linked
public-houses and Dissenting chapels as foes to the Church.
In reference to this he wrote me the following explanation :—

"Dec. 16, 1863.
"I venture to ask you to accept as a token of respect a copy of my
recent charge. I do this the more because, greatly to my regret, I understand that some passages in it have excited feelings of opposition in the
minds of some of my Non-Conforming brethren at Reading, and they
are holding, I am told, public meetings to condemn me and it. And
yet I venture to hope that you will not find in it one uncharitable word
as to those with whom we differ. Of course, these are my own principles, because I believe them to be the principles of my Church. There
is, I hope, no disproportion between them and the great truths of our
common Christianity. There is, I trust, no word which ought to wound
a conscientious dissenter from our communion. But if there is, I
heartily wish it unwritten, and I ask you to point it out to me."

To this I replied by quoting a sentence in which he said that " Dissent and the public-house were the chief antagonists to the Church." It was not surprising that this offended godly Dissenters. He courteously replied, explaining that he did not intend to class together drink and Dissent, but to point out that, though by totally different methods, both drew away many from attendance at the parish church. He regretted an expression capable of interpretation in a sense so abhorrent to his own feelings, and so opposed to what he had intended to express.

In reply to an appeal from me to use his influence in preventing Church of England missionaries entering on fields already occupied, the Bishop concurred in the general principle being acted on by all missionary societies, but made exception in the case of large populations, saying :—

"But when a nation is to be evangelised; when that work is but begun in the capital ; when from that capital influence must go forth to the whole island ; when in that capital, besides our own missions, Rome is seeking to propagate her faith—then it seems to me that not absence from the capital, but absence in the capital from anything like hostility to you or undervaluing your work, is the line our principles require of us. We believe that without what we consider as the apostolic form of Episcopacy, Rome cannot be successfully resisted. We therefore, as it seems to me, are compelled by the accidents of a capital to conduct at once our mission for the island there, lest, in fact, we yield the ground to that superstitious system by which Rome has to so fearful a degree disfigured the Gospel of our Lord. We should not address *your* converts but the unconverted.
"I am, my dear Mr. Newman Hall,
" Ever most truly yours,
"S. Oxon."

From Dean Stanley, on Disestablishment:—

"Deanery, Dec. 3, '77.
"I much regret I could not catch you after the service to have brought you into the Deanery. . . . Do not some members of the Liberation Society desire, by legislation, to destroy the existing institution of the Church of England as completely as the Parliament of 1662 proposed to destroy the existing institutions of Independency, Presbyterianism, etc.? The particular means may be different, but the end sought is the same. But I never meant to say that this programme was approved by all Nonconformists. I am quite aware that this is not the case. Nor did I intend to question the sincerity and conscientiousness

of those who do approve it. I always feel respect for those who do honestly adopt what seems to me a mistaken and superstitious objection to the Church of England, or those who, regarding it as a noxious institution, wish for its destruction as an injury to the country. There is a broad distinction that separates them from the political leaders who do not believe in these objections and yet encourage them as the means of recruiting a broken party. With the former I have some sympathy and much forbearance ; with the latter none whatever."

Cardinal Manning's interest in all efforts to instruct the working classes is indicated by the following :—

"York Place, April 4, '67.

" Rev. and Dear Sir,—I have seen in the papers a notice of some work in which you are engaged to provide the working classes with instruction on Sundays. The subject is of such common interest that I should feel obliged if you would kindly give me information as to its nature and extent. If it would save you trouble to do so in conversation, I should be happy to call upon you or to receive your visit. I am at home every day till one o'clock, or any afternoon after Tuesday next

"Believe me, Rev. and Dear Sir,

"Your faithful servant,

"Henry E. Manning."

I explained that my work on Sunday was preaching the Gospel out of doors or in theatres; my secular lectures were on week evenings.

Tom Hughes, as he was familiarly called, was one of my early public friends, with whom I was in full accord on social questions. He was once my guest in Hull, in company with Lord Goodrich, when the latter was canvassing for the representation. I value the following note as a record of the past :—

"Park Street, July 19th, 1865.

". . . . I am sure you will believe how much I value your good word, and hope we may often meet for fellow-work in the future, though I trust, for the credit of educated England, never in such a minority as we used to be in during the American war.

"Most truly yours,

"Thomas Hughes."

Allusion is here made to the comparatively few who manifested sympathy with the North in their struggle for union and emancipation.

I had the privilege of meeting Kossuth several times,

with Bright and others, at the house of my friend, Charles Gilpin, M.P. I greatly admired his correctness and fluency of speech in the English language. His public addresses were characterised by true eloquence. Crowds gathered to listen to him and applaud. I received from him the following letter in acknowledgment of a sermon of mine in Surrey Chapel:—

" May 30th, 1859.

" Receive my heartfelt thanks for your note and report of your sermon. It is approval of such earnest thinkers as you are which is most valuable to the cause of my country ; it is their task to keep the public right, to awake the consciences of such men as now govern by personal or class interest, not by the principles of freedom or the general interests of the country. I am much obliged to you for having spoken from the pulpit to the heart of the multitude, reminding them of their religious duties in the present crisis. I once more fervently recommend to you the cause of my country, which is the cause of civil and religious liberty. Being called to action, I have soon to leave England, but I trust the friends of freedom will not forget us, and that England should not forsake us in the struggle. Accept the assurance of my highest regards, and believe me

" Yours very truly,
" KOSSUTH."

I had the honour of being a member of the committee for Garibaldi's reception in London, and was in one of the numerous carriages in the long procession which attended him amidst enormous crowds of enthusiastic admirers. I was admitted to a private audience in the grounds of the Duke of Sutherland, and was afterwards present at the grand reception, when I saw a beautiful and stately lady kneel before him, and then salute him with a courtly kiss. I sent him a letter of congratulation, with a copy of my tractate on Divine Socialism, in acknowledgment of which I received the following letter :—

" Pisa, December 10th.

" General Garibaldi desires me to acknowledge the receipt of your book and letter, and to express his gratitude for the sympathy you show to him and to the Italian cause. No man more than Garibaldi admires those who struggle for civil or religious liberty.

" Yours truly,
" CLEMENTE CORTE."

I had the pleasure of entertaining an aide-de-camp of

Garibaldi, and rendering him some small service, and received
a letter from which I copy :—

"Spezzia.

"The General finds himself better since we came here. The
projectile is not in the foot, and the bone not broken. It is a grave
wound, but he has never complained, never reproached the enemies who
wished to kill him, never spoken evil of any person, even of those who
roused his indignation, which never extended to themselves personally.
I never knew such an accumulation of sanctities in one single human
heart. I told him of your taking me to the director of the Waterloo
Station, and the thirty shillings returned to me. Receive again my
thanks, and those of my poor Italy so maltreated by her children,
victims of that Catholic priestism, which is the cholera, the typhus, the
yellow fever, the scourge of Egypt for souls and bodies.

"Very affectionately yours,

"C. O. VIECHY, M.P. and Colonel."

Professor F. W. Newman was frequently my breakfast
guest at Hampstead, where he and his wife resided. We were
in such full accord in reference to temperance and other philanthropies, though differing so absolutely on religious doctrines,
that we respected each other's convictions and never indulged
in theological controversy. When he came to breakfast he
always remained, without any constraint, to family worship,
and I sometimes noticed that he seemed deeply affected. He
was with me on the committee for the trial of Governor Eyre,
by whom Mr. Gordon had been unlawfully executed on a false
charge of inciting the negroes to insurrection. Martial law
administered by soldiers was in operation in the disturbed
areas, but Gordon was seized at his own home, where he
claimed trial by jury, and carried off to the district where the
Habeas Corpus Act did not run, and the judgment was given
by officers strong in sympathy with the panic-smitten partisans
who knew that a fair trial would result in Gordon's vindication.
When the trial came before the grand jury in England, the
Chief Justice delivered a very strong charge, showing that,
whatever opinion were formed on Gordon's motives and conduct, the mode of his trial and execution was directly opposed
to British law, which the Governor was bound to administer.

In reply to a letter directing the attention of Mr. Gladstone to the subject, he wrote :—

"March 22nd, 1865.
"With respect to Jamaica, perhaps the less I say at this moment the better, but undoubtedly in my opinion, while the several parties are on their trial before England, England herself has been and is still on her trial before the world.

"Most faithfully yours,
"W. E. G."

I can find the following letter alone from Professor Newman, which has only a personal interest, as regards his conjugal affection. It was to me very touching to see him trudging by the side of Mrs. Newman on her visits to the poor, he carrying her bag of tracts and Testaments. During her illness he wrote respecting her sufferings during many weeks, adding (January, 1866) :—

"For nine or ten days she seemed to lie at the point of death. The doctors thought she could not live forty-eight hours. But by dint of indefatigable nursing we strengthened her to rally. My painful expectation is that a lingering death is her only future life ; and from that I am disposed to pray that anyone dear to me may be released, since it is that which of all things I deprecate for myself. On January 6th she first believed herself dying, and gave me very numerous charges, which I put down on paper. Not only relations and near friends, but the poor, were very prominent in her thoughts. She at first wished to live, for *my* sake, she said ; but distress of breathing and general misery soon reconciled her to die, and until a few days ago it has been her fixed, tranquil expectation. We have now only to possess our souls in patience, and while actively struggling to recover her, passively accept the high will of God, our blessed Father.

"I am heartily yours,
"F. W. NEWMAN."

From Mrs. Cobden, acknowledging a copy of my little book containing the sermon preached at Surrey Chapel, *in memoriam,* entitled " Cobden " :—

"Midhurst, May 15th, 1865.
"I return my warm and grateful thanks for your eloquent and instructive tribute to the memory of my beloved husband. I have derived much comfort from the little book you so kindly sent me, and shall ever value it, as having emanated from one who so well comprehended his pure and practical Christian character.

" Yours sincerely,
" C. A. COBDEN."

In reply to a letter of sympathy on occasion of the death

o

of Prince Albert, I received the following from Lady Augusta Bruce (afterwards the wife of Dean Stanley):—

"December 23rd, 1861.

"Lady Augusta Bruce begs to acknowledge the receipt of Mr. Newman Hall's letter and the poem accompanying it, and will take the earliest opportunity of laying these before the Queen, whose unutterable grief is soothed by the multiplied and touching proofs of the heartfelt sympathy of her people."

From Dr. Moffat, in reply to an invitation to meet Mr. Gladstone :—

"February 6th, 1874.

"I shall esteem it a very high privilege to meet the great Gladstone, of whom I have heard and read so much—the Gladstone who has fixed a thorn in the side of Pio Nono, which is affecting the hearts of millions and will continue to fester, till Babylon be thrown down and be no more found at all. As to remaining with you a day or two, it is, under a severe pressure of engagements, impossible.

"Very gratefully yours,

"ROBERT MOFFAT."

On a former page, relating to an open-air meeting on Calton Hill, I have told of an address I delivered forty years ago and its sequel. The following letter is from the clergyman, labouring among the poor in Glasgow, who was led to Christ on that occasion :—

"Ratherglen, December 9th, 1887.

"MY DEAR SIR,—It is a long time since we met on the Calton Hill, Edinburgh. You then helped me into the light of Life. I was about to refresh your memory in the anteroom of our City Hall when we were called upon to march to the platform. You will see from the enclosed what is being done through me in the East End of Glasgow.

"Yours very cordially,

"ROBERT HALL."

Fifty years after the conversion of "Sailor" Jackson at Hull,* I received the following letter from his daughter, dated Hull, 1892 :—

"As soon as my father adopted teetotalism, he remembered a favourite niece whose husband was in danger of ruining himself and family by intemperance. He had some trouble in inducing him to go to a temperance meeting. At length they went to one where you were lecturing. He signed ; went home and threw wine and spirits down the sink, but found he must either return to his grog or give up his pipe. One night he surprised his wife by throwing all his tobacco and cigars into

* *See* pp. 74, 75.

the fire, and breaking up all his pipes; and to the day of his death, last February, he never either drank or smoked again.

"JANE RHODES."

I desired to feel assured that the Crystal Palace of recreation, so full of objects of interest, historical, artistic, musical, natural, with its delightful grounds, was free from any objectionable feature. I had several times been there, and was glad to find this to be the case. But during the Christmas holidays of 1873—and for the first time—I witnessed a pantomime, and was surprised and sorry to see much that seemed to me unfit for public exhibition, especially to young men and women. I accordingly wrote a polite protest to the secretary and received a courteous reply, from which I extract a few sentences :—

"I am very much obliged by your kind letter. I feel the force of everything you say, and frankly admit that the pantomime of last Christmas was anything but what it ought to be, and I have taken the greatest care this year to prevent anything of the kind which I know offended, and justly offended, many of our best friends. I sympathise with everything you say about a pure theatre, but the difficulties appear to me to make it quite hopeless. But if you were to compare the Crystal Palace pantomime of this year with the theatres, you would find the difference so great that your objections would be very much lessened. The matter was very carefully looked after by Mr. W. and myself, and the restrictions which we enforced met with the greatest opposition from the people employed. It is there that the chief difficulty arises. You can control the length of skirts, but you cannot control the gestures of an actor or actress, and the public are so wedded to certain people that it is necessary to have them in order to ensure the success of the piece. However, I am so much encouraged by the kind, frank, and sensible tone of your letter, that we shall certainly endeavour next time to make still greater restrictions."

So much is said of the lack of courtesy between Churchmen and Dissenters that it gives me pleasure to narrate many instances of friendship shown me on the common grounds of Christianity, although my political and ecclesiastical opinions were never concealed. The following letters are illustrations.

From the Very Reverend Dean Vaughan :—

"The Vicarage, Doncaster, 21st April, 1869.

REV. AND DEAR SIR,—I venture to address you, not quite as a stranger, on behalf of the Young Men's Christian Association of this town, who are ambitious enough to ask of you a lecture in our Guild-hall, during the next autumn or winter. I fear that I am causing you trouble by an application which reaches you doubtless from all parts of England in turn. I can only plead, as a very inadequate excuse, my desire and hope to be favoured with your company at my house during your stay in Doncaster.

"Very sincerely and respectfully yours,

"CHARLES J. VAUGHAN."

"The Temple, 1st February, 1871.

"I deeply feel your kindness in asking me to undertake a service in St. James's Hall. Unequal as I should feel myself to be, in *all* respects, to that particular office, requiring gifts so marked and exceptional, I have the additional and fatal disqualification of being unable to add to my regular duties, always heavy enough for my strength, and of having laid down to myself the rule of preaching *nowhere*, except in deference to some very direct official compulsion. I am equally obliged by the kind and brotherly spirit which breathes in your request, and which I *heartily* reciprocate.

"Ever faithfully yours,

"C. J. VAUGHAN."

From the Rev. Dr. Boyd, late Moderator of the Established Church of Scotland :—

"When in London I shall certainly be most happy to preach for you. The time has quite come when those who are agreed on vital matters should do all they can to break down barriers raised by indifferent things ; and when you come to Scotland I hope to hear a sermon from you in our ancient church. Stanley was here, and spoke warmly of your kindness at the meeting of your Convocation. Whether you agree with him or not, you cannot but admire his liberal spirit. . . . By the way, when shall you and I be able to preach in Westminster Abbey ? Will it ever be at all ? If any man will bring that day, it will be Stanley. . . . I envy you the testimony God is giving you of the efficacy of your work. We here must work in faith, not seeing such results. But when we see people on their death-beds we often find that they are much more truly Christian people than we had thought. . . . In 1864 I came to your house from the house of my very dear friend Thorold, Rector of St. Giles', now Bishop of Rochester. Froude says when a friend is made a bishop you lose your friend. I have not found it so. Each May I spend some time with him. If I am at Selsdon Park next May I shall come and see you. One has not so many friends as to afford to grow out of acquaintance with one of them.

"Yours most sincerely,

"A. K. H. B."

Amid constant and varied activities, religious, ecclesiastical, philanthropic, social, I have not seldom been asked what my recreations have been. I am a strong believer in the need of rest for both body and mind; for pleasures to vary pain, for enjoyments which strengthen and fit for duty— really to renew and re-create, and thus deserve the name of Re-creations. I have advocated and endeavoured to procure them for the sons and daughters of toil—I have valued and given God thanks for them myself. The following favourite lines from Wordsworth's "Excursion" illustrate this subject of recreation :—

> "Truth has her pleasure grounds, her haunts of ease
> And easy contemplation, gay parterres
> And labyrinthine walks, her sunny glades
> And shady groves in studious contrast, each
> For recreation leading into each.
> These may he range, if willing to partake
> Their soft indulgences, and in due time
> May issue thence, recruited for the tasks
> And course of service Truth requires from those
> Who tend her altars, wait upon her throne,
> And guard her fortresses."

Among these recreations I enumerate literature, including history, fiction, poetry; music, as a listener; social intercourse, scenery, walking (for many years eight or ten miles daily sometimes thirty; now reduced to four or five).

Sketching has been a delight from the age of sixteen— since twenty in water-colours—self-taught, or rather Nature-taught. Wherever I travel I take a sketch-book and colour-box with me. I have now about one hundred books with about twenty-five sketches in each. The subjects include scenes in Egypt, Palestine, Jerusalem, Damascus, Lebanon, Baalbek, Beyrout, Constantinople, Cyprus, Sicily, Corfu, Tangier, Spain, Belgium, Germany, Holland, Norway, France, the Alps, Italy (including Rome, Naples, Florence, Milan), the United States of America, Canada (Ottawa, etc.), Sagony River, and, of course, England, Scotland, Wales, and Ireland.

These sketches are the spoils of my sporting excursions. They involved no death or pain to any fellow-creature. Those which I took fifty years ago retain their freshness, and still give pleasure to friends who care occasionally to partake of what to me are dainties, and enable them to listen with me to "songs without words."

Another recreation has been versification. I began when a mere child with a love-song to my mother. Then followed sacred rhymes until my first published small volume, entitled " Bolton Abbey Hymns," after the spot where some of them were composed, and dedicated to my mother in this sonnet:—

> Mother ! to thee, of right, this book belongs ;
> For, seated on thy knee, an infant weak,
> With lisping tongue, I learned from thee to speak
> " In psalms, and hymns, and spiritual songs."
> Oft didst thou stroke my head, and kiss my cheek,
> And weep for joy to hear thy child repeat
> How the Good Shepherd came from heaven, to seek
> His wandering lambs, and how His hands and feet
> Were pierced with nails—while He, the sufferer meek,
> Prayed for His foes, then mounted to His throne.
> With themes like these my years have still upgrown,
> Through thy persuasive teaching, tender care,
> Thine, and a loving father's life of prayer ;
> The book I offer thee is thus thine own.
>
> *Bolton Abbey, Sept.*, 1857.

A small volume followed, " Pilgrim Songs in Cloud and Sunshine." I have known both—cloud dark and long, sunshine bright and permanent. My verses have been autobiography, heart utterances, calling for no minute interpretation. Another booklet consisted chiefly of " Mountain Musings." Finally, I gathered all into " Lyrics of a Long Life," now out of print. I propose to republish most of the contents in two small books, one containing devotional " hymns," at a low price, and the other short " poems."

An ambition fondly cherished during many years has been that some hymns of mine might be considered worthy of a place in Christian hymnals and be used in public worship. This has been realised in collections of various Churches. The Church of England *Record* said:—

"Some of the hymns for public and private worship are as fine as any we know."

I must confess to disappointment that not one appears

in the hymnal of the churches with which I have chiefly laboured during sixty years, though several have been selected and kindly acknowledged by editors of Episcopalian and other hymnals.

The Sunday School Chronicle remarked that :—

"'A Little Child's Morning Hymn' is almost a model for a child's hymn";

and from *The Christian Leader* I may quote the following :—

"Some are to be found in almost every new collection. Those for the young include some of the most truly serviceable for children's meetings to be found in our language."

The following are not generally known :—

CORONATION.

Crown, crown Him ! Son of God;
   Crown, crown Him ! Son of Man ;
We'll blaze His boundless love abroad,
   Redemption's wondrous plan :
Our hearts, our lives we bring,
   And joyful tribute pay ;
With many crowns we'll crown our King,
   Through heaven's eternal day.

The Church He ransomed sings
   His vict'ry o'er the grave ;
O crown Him ! crown Him ! King of Kings,
   Who lives and reigns to save.
Crown Him ! Creator, Friend ;
   Sound His dear Name again !
Crown Him ! through ages without end,
   Emmanuel ! God with men.

A LITTLE CHILD'S MORNING HYMN.

Day again is dawning, Darkness flies away ;
Now from sleep awaking, Let me rise and pray.
Jesus ! tender Shepherd, Watching while I slept,
Bless the little lambkin Thou hast safely kept.

Help me, Lord, to praise Thee, For my cosy bed ;
For my clothes and playthings, For my daily bread ;
For my darling mother, For my father dear ;
For the friends who love me, Far away and near.

Robin blithe is chirping, Glad the night is o'er ;
Larks the light are greeting, Singing as they soar :
I'm Thy little birdie ; May I ever sing,
Goodness making music, Unto Christ my King.

I think that too much prominence has sometimes been given in children's hymns and addresses to early death and examples of godly children who never reached maturity. I demur to a hymn beginning "I want to be an angel," and as a protest I wrote the following:—

A BOY'S HYMN.

I want to live and be a man,
Both good and useful all I can,
To speak the truth, be just and brave,
My fellow-men to help and save.

I want to live that I may show
My love to Jesus here below ;
In human toil to take my share,
And thus for angel's work prepare.

I want to live that I may trace
His steps before I see His face,
And follow Him in earthly strife
Before I share His heavenly life.

Lord ! grant me this—to live and serve,
And never from Thy laws to swerve ;
Then, after years of service free,
In ripe old age to go to Thee.

Some of my lyrics are voices from the darkness. All of them are the utterances of a heart lamenting, praying, trusting, or rejoicing. I can in no other way be autobiographical here than by quotation.

DE PROFUNDIS.

Out of the depths I cry to Thee, O Lord !
  The hidden depths of darkness and of woe :
My only hope is in Thy faithful word ;
  Thy sympathy the only balm I know.

Give ear to plaints that from such depths arise,
  Nor leave me in the dark to grope alone ;
On my affliction look with pitying eyes,
  And answer prayers condensed in sigh or groan.

For many years I longed to depart from the overshadowed

valley, but God helped me to resist this temptation by thoughts expressed in the following verses :—

> We will not pine for death and rest,
>   Too soon from service breaking ;
> Fruit plucked unripe can ne'er be blest,
>   Our task beneath forsaking :
> Not till the course is run,
> Our Leader says " Well done ! "
> Not till the conflict's borne,
> The chaplet can be worn ;
>   The Cross the Crown is making !

> Our life on earth has tender ties
>   We should not wish to sever :
> Rich works of faith, sweet charities,
>   Which soon must cease for ever :
> To watch, and weep, and wait,
> By love to conquer hate,
> The flesh in curb to keep,
> To rescue wandering sheep—
>   How noble such endeavour !

> 'Tis gain if Jesus bids us die,
>   When young, mature, or hoary ;
> 'Tis loss to wish the fight to fly,
>   Foreclosing life's bright story :
> To battle for His laws,
> To suffer for His cause,
> To share His grief and shame,
> To vindicate His Name—
>   To live for Christ is glory.

I preached many sermons specially to comfort others. I tried to act on my own counsel, and crowded my life with work. To promote the cause of God and man I wilfully neglected no opportunity of service. Very likely I seemed too much engaged in mere outwardness. But next to communion with God it was this activity which enabled me to sing with David :—

> Not one of all who trust Him
>   Shall find His promise vain ;
> The feeblest of His servants
>   Shall reap eternal gain.

Then bless the Lord at all times,
  Nor let His praises cease ;
Praise Him 'mid din of battle !
  Praise Him in time of peace !

I'll bless the Lord at all times,
  In darkness as in day !
I'll sing glad Hallelujahs,
  All through my pilgrim way :
Until I cross the river
  I'll sing my Saviour's praise ;
And then in heaven for ever
  An endless song I'll raise.
                    (*Psalm* xxxiv.)

When I began my ministry in London, I feared that
my constant engagements and anxieties might destroy any
capacity for continuous and exact study which I might have
acquired at college, and therefore I resolved to read up for
the LL.B. degree of the London University. This should be
kept secret, because failure would have been a public dis-
credit.   I began a systematic study of Blackstone, and
Bentham.   I never travelled in trains or omnibuses without
my legal companion.   In a small pocket note-book I wrote
an abbreviated analysis, and by it kept up a daily examination.   At the close of a year, during which all my
preaching and pastoral work was carried on as usual, my
name appeared in the first class.   I then received strong
advice to go in for honours in Legislation. Only a week
intervened for specially reading up.   As my competitors were
young barristers, I was as much surprised as pleased when
informed that the parson was first in honours, and had won
the Law Scholarship, which meant fifty pounds for three
consecutive years.

CHAPTER XV.

THERE are many who remember the terrible scenes in front of Newgate, when large sums were given for suitable windows to survey the tragedy, when hundreds gathered in the evening, increasing to thousands till daylight—laughing, drinking, singing, gambling: the putting to death of the body of one, the occasion of deadly injury to the souls of multitudes.

When a boy at Maidstone, I used to hear descriptions of condemned prisoners being conveyed in an open cart to the gallows on Penenden Heath, with their arms pinioned and guarded by police—how the throng yelled or greeted—how the vast crowds waiting round the fatal tree were invited to drink a glass "of gin and water before the men are turned off," and how, at the fatal sign, the condemned men actually were "turned off" from the cart, to be suspended by the rope already adjusted.

About the year 1830 many were hung for "swing fires"— arson—igniting hay and corn stacks as a protest against agricultural machinery. I saw three hung on the Heath for rick-burning; one, aged eighteen, and another, nineteen, afterwards proved innocent. The people believed these youths were to be hung unjustly, and special precautions were taken against a possible attempt at rescue.

When acting as "reporter" to our paper, I remember standing on the scaffold in front of the jail, and seeing a man in a state of stupor, led along, while the burial service was read over a body still living, which, at a certain passage, dropped with a thud. Then, after a few heavings, it hung lifeless before thousands of eager spectators.

The man whose execution I witnessed was convicted of setting fire to a corn-rick at a time of agricultural distress and excitement. I have been in court when men have been sentenced to death for stealing a sheep, for forging a bank-note, for passing a forged note, for burglary, and often for arson.

A case of fatal mistake was that of a man condemned for administering poison to his wife, whom he dearly loved, on the evidence of his son, who swore he saw his father put some white powder into the tea-pot. The father, a man of excellent character, swore he was innocent. The chaplain was convinced, and made strong remonstrance. The people protested. Influential persons sent petitions. On the day of execution, the High Sheriff, strongly convinced of the man's innocence, hesitated to carry out the sentence until he should receive a reply to his urgent plea for further investigation. The victim was kept in suspense till the fatal decision arrived. A few years after, the son, under conviction for some crime, confessed to the chaplain that he himself administered the poison and, to screen himself, swore away his father's life. Such cases, which have often occurred, have convinced me that it is wrong, on fallible evidence, to inflict irreversible penalty.

The chief argument for capital punishment is its deterrent effect on others; but the uncertainty of conviction acts in the contrary direction. Certainty of punishment has been a more effectual deterrent than severity, jurymen being unwilling to pronounce a verdict which is beyond redress. In pleading for the total abolition of capital punishment, it has often been urged that if the criminal is impenitent he is not fit to die, but if penitent, he is fit to live. I do not say that this is a demonstration, but it is worthy of a place in the argument which embraces both sides of the question.

In January, 1860, a working-man, named Wright, industrious and sober, respected by his class, was suddenly roused from sleep at midnight, and pulled out of bed by a drunken woman. Half-awake, but enraged, he seized the razor prepared for his shaving, and drew it fatally across her throat. When thoroughly awake, he was overwhelmed with remorse, gave himself up to the police, and before the Central Criminal

Court then sitting, pleaded "Guilty," in opposition to strong remonstrances, because a plea of "Not guilty" would probably secure conviction only for manslaughter. He was sentenced to be hanged, and the execution was to be within a week or two. There was great excitement among the working-people of Southwark, who were convinced that his act was not premeditated. There was danger of violence should the sentence be executed. My friend Murphy and myself sought the help of members of Parliament. We were told that earnest appeals had been made by my friend, Charles Gilpin, and others, to the Home Secretary, to the judge who tried the case, and to others, but in vain. Then, though doubting success, we went to Windsor to seek, somehow, royal intervention. The following letters courteously express the impossibility and impropriety of our efforts, but we wished to feel and to show others that no possible means had been neglected. Late in the evening before the execution, an influential deputation waited on Sir George Grey, the Home Secretary. He listened patiently, but regretted he could not interfere with the course of law. Even then I dared to hope that, acquainted as I was with the state of public feeling, and dreading a popular outbreak which might cost many lives, I resolved to make one more effort. I was several hours before I could find out the address of Sir G. Grey, who was avoiding any further distressing appeals. At length my search was rewarded. Long after midnight I gave a thundering knock at the humble door, and requested to see the Home Secretary on urgent public business. His secretary said Sir George was in bed. I was so persistent that I was asked upstairs, and Sir George appeared in his dressing-gown, and listened to my pleas during a good half-hour. Oh, how I pleaded, knowing that in eight hours the death-knell would strike! Then I made a fatal blunder. I said I feared a breach of the peace! Then the responsible Minister's manner changed at this semblance of threat: "*We* know how to preserve the peace!" All was over. I could say no more. I had spiked my own guns. I thanked the Minister for his great courtesy and patience, and withdrew with a sorrowing heart.

On January 18th, 1860, I held a great meeting of working-men at Surrey Chapel, and spoke as thus reported next day in *The Daily News* :—

"THE CONVICT WRIGHT AND THE HOME SECRETARY.

" Newman Hall understood that at a meeting held on the evening of the execution the National Anthem was refused. This was a great mistake. The Queen had always acted most loyally to the constitution, which deputed the execution of law to responsible Ministers ; this was the security of liberty. In the former times of despotism the monarch did interfere in many ways. But who would like to be a responsible Minister if he was controlled by a superior who was irresponsible ? Besides, if the Queen interfered to save the life of convict No. 1, she would be regarded as responsible for the death of No. 2. The Home Secretary, when applied to, said he was only the administrator of the law. If the judge, who was the interpreter of the law, said that there were circumstances which would warrant a commutation of sentence in Wright's case, he (the Home Secretary) would commute it. He had received a deputation as late as half-past ten on Monday night, after which a personal stranger to him was prompted to make one more effort. Yet, though Sir G. Grey had gone to bed, after a day of unusual anxiety and toil, he rose to receive his visitor, and with perfect courtesy and patience listened to every argument which was urged. This one fact should be sufficient to vindicate him from the imputation of indifference or obstinacy. (Loud cheers.) Credit should be given him for the best motives in keeping to what he considered the law, though they might regret the decision. Public opinion had been so strongly expressed against the execution of Wright that there was danger of his crime being overlooked. It was very injurious, socially and morally, when the law was censured more than the law-breaker, and a sort of ovation given to a man who, in a rage, had cut a woman's throat. But good might come out of evil. Law must be upheld while it was law, but bad laws should be changed. And he hoped that a strong effort would now be made to abolish capital punishment altogether. (Loud cheers.)."

The following letters illustrate the case :—

"The Queen has literally no power in the matter. It seemed, therefore, to me to be causing Her Majesty unnecessary pain to appeal to her feelings on so distressing a subject, when such appeals could have no practical result. The responsibility of a decision on the life or death of a fellow-being is so awful that it must always be undertaken upon the deepest conviction that it is supported by its unquestionable justice and a stern sense of duty. Such a deliberate judgment should not, in my humble opinion, be altered by any appeal to the feelings and by any pressure of application from other benevolent persons, however much we may sympathise with their feelings. Such a concession would, indeed, acknowledge that the previous decision had been arrived at without sufficient consideration. Though I should not have been justified in withholding from the Queen any communication addressed to Her Majesty, it was, I think, my duty to endeavour to save the Queen from appeals upon so distressing a subject on which I knew that she was powerless, and to do my best to confine such applications to the proper constitutional channels. Mr. Woodward would, I am sure, have explained all this to you, and that you would not suspect me of want of respect in guarding myself carefully from the appearance of arrogating to myself a position which only belongs to Her Majesty's responsible advisers.—I have the honour to be, etc. etc.

"C. B. PHIPPS."

"Lieut.-General Knollys presents his compliments to Rev. Newman Hall, and is desired by the Prince of Wales to acknowledge the receipt this morning of his letter of yesterday's date, and to inform him that he has forwarded his representations on the case of the convict Wright to Sir George Grey, through whom alone, as Secretary of State for the Home Department, any effect can be derived from them, and by whom His Royal Highness is confident they will receive every consideration which a sense of humanity and justice can dictate."

"January 19th, 1860.

"Permit me to thank you for the kind and considerate manner in which, I see by the papers, you spoke of my conduct in reference to the case of S. Wright, at a meeting of working-men yesterday evening. It is gratifying for me to know that one for whom I entertain so sincere respect as yourself is convinced that I acted from a sense of duty, and my thanks are due to you for having publicly stated this.—Your faithful servant,

"G. GREY."

On June 4, 1875, there was a large party at my house to tea and supper to meet Lord Shaftesbury and the Bishop of Gloucester (Ellicott), and among whom were Bickersteth (now Bishop of Exeter), Llewellyn Davies, Dr. Lee, Freemantle, Minton, and other Churchmen; Drs. Allon, Kennedy, Raleigh, and other Nonconformist clergy; Samuel Plimsoll, M.P., and other Christian workers. An interesting discussion on the expediency, as regards Ritualism, of Disestablishment. Bishop Ellicott urged that divergent parties were held together by Establishment, as spokes by an iron hoop, without which they would fall asunder into schism. Allon replied, "So much the better, if nothing but an iron ring binds them in unreal union." Davies and Lee urged the sad condition of rural parishes without the support of Establishment. In reply, Wales and Scotland were adduced as, although districts of comparative poverty, they are well supplied with church edifices, parsonages, and pastors by voluntary offerings. Dr. Patten asserted the ample supply of religious instrumentality in America. The Bishop admitted the strength of the reply, but considered that Ritualism and sacerdotalism would be more successful and arrogant with Disestablishment. Others said that Establishment gave Ritualism prestige, and shut out the Gospel from many parishes. Lord Shaftesbury expressed no opinion on the abstract question, but considered that the Establishment, as such, would be at an end in twenty years from causes within itself. We talked most amicably and candidly from eight till nearly eleven, then sang the Doxology, and the Bishop offered an earnest and appropriate prayer.

Bishop Ellicott said he had so enjoyed the conference that he thought such a one might be held monthly, for a better understanding between Episcopalians and Nonconformists; and by his appointment I met him at his rooms, and a day was fixed, but the proposal was afterwards adjourned *sine die.*

Since then several similar conferences have met at my house, attended by Dean Farrar, Archdeacon Sinclair, and others.

Dr. Berry, ex-Chairman of the Congregational Union, on his return from a visit to the United States, said :—

"Two things impressed me greatly. The first was that the absence of a State Church made for the compacting of all the forces on the side of religion and humanity ; and the second was that in no country I had ever visited had the Christian Church a more potent voice and a more potent hand in respect of national affairs than in the United States."

I know Dr. Berry as a friend, as a distinguished preacher, and also as a man of singular independence of judgment and freedom from party prejudice ; and from my own three visits to the States, and intercourse with the leaders of religious thought and work of all the Churches, I fully confirm Dr. Berry's opinion, in further endorsement of which I may say that I met with no one, not even the clergy of the Episcopal Church, who desired Establishment, or would not strongly oppose it.

In August, 1874, I had a very delightful excursion with nephew J. to Norway. I preached at Nerofjord—congregation of three, and was invited to breakfast by the wife of the "priest"—so called by Lutherans. Looking towards a fine view of mountains, she said, in response to my "Beautiful," "Beautiful!—yes, very! No sun three months. Husband gone to funeral of a member—one day to go, another to return. Three days to get doctor, if ill. Beautiful!"

We were hospitably entertained by Sir Thomas and Lady Brassey on their yacht, the *Ocean Queen*. One morning the cook, stewards, and most of the crew, were sent several miles to see a fine glacier. Lady Brassey, who had passed the cooking examination at Kensington, prepared a breakfast of three courses. Lord Brassey was his own captain, and also assisted the men in raising the anchor, etc. One of the crew, in many words of praise, specially referred to his Sunday services and the good sermons he preached.

Instead of prose descriptions of scenery, I quote a sonnet I wrote at the time :—

"THAT YE MAY BE FILLED WITH THE FULNESS OF GOD."

> In winding gorges of Norwegian hills
> Flows the full Fjord : wedding sea and land,
> And linking each small creek with ocean grand.
> Watching the tide each rocky creek that fills,
> The mountains opening, reverently stand,
> And offerings give with no reluctant hand :
> Mosses and ferns, and flowers of every hue,
> All that they can, to greet the dark-blue wave,
> That loves these crags and verdant nooks to lave :
> From beetling cliffs that pierce the curtain blue
> The foaming torrent leaps, and seems to say—
> "It is thine own, O Sea ! we give this day."
> Thus, Ocean infinite of Love Divine,
> Enter and permeate this soul of mine.

P

I knew a farmhouse, some two miles from the post-office, to which a Newfoundland dog went every morning for the leather bag containing the letters. After delivering them, it used to lie down and sleep on the rug. One morning, instead of resting, it ran off quickly. Why? When the bag had been delivered by the post-office clerk, a butcher's dog had attacked the messenger, who took no apparent notice, but performed its office, and then ran back to punish the assault of "an officer in discharge of his duty."

I was in a train where was a lady with a big retriever, with wistful eye, which lay at her feet. She said it always slept in her bedroom. She had been from home two days, and the dog would not leave her room. It knew all that was said. "Is he gentle?" "Yes, to humans, but not to dogs, but would fly at anyone who might seem to strike me." I said, "Then he would not resent my stroking him?" The dog immediately rose and placed his big head between my knees, as if asking for a pat, wagging his tail.

One day I was chatting with a farmer about the best method of self-defence when attacked by a savage dog. "Take off your hat and hold it in front of you. The dog will at once bite the rim. Then kick violently under your hat, and, the distance being exactly that of the length of your leg, the toe of your boot will strike the lower jaw of the dog, which will at once go off in great pain." The very next day I was crossing a large field, when a fierce dog rushed at me. There was no refuge near. I had no stick. I remembered my lesson. In an instant the dog rushed howling round the field, and I went my way.

The husband of a dear old friend, a colonel in the Indian army, lost his life at Agra during the Mutiny. He had a favourite Newfoundland, which he left behind when ordered with his regiment to the front. This dog was chained up during several days to prevent him following. When at length loosened, he disappeared. Several days elapsed, when he was found lying exhausted under a tree near the camp, several hundred miles distant from home. When rested, the dog reached the camp, entered the officers' mess-tent, and fainted at his master's feet. The dog must have followed the trail of the regiment, and crossed several rivers by ordinary passenger boats.

The widow of this Colonel Thomas was a devout seeker after salvation, and it was my privilege to help in directing her to a clearer apprehension of the "truth as it is in Jesus." With this view, I wrote the following hymn, which she much valued as explaining her difficulties and strengthening her faith. She had several times asked for my hymn to be read to her, and, at her request, the copy I wrote for her was fastened to her shroud in the coffin. She said I had given her much comfort. She understood what I said—it made it so plain without being tedious—one of the most pleasing tributes to my verse that I have received:—

SEEKING THE SAVIOUR.

Lord ! I come because Thou callest,
    Not because of worth in me ;
Thou the Saviour, I the sinner,
    This my earnest, only plea.

Thou the Healer, I the wounded ;
    Thou the Finder, I the lost ;
Thou whose whisper calms the ocean,
    I the trembling tempest-tost.

Hand that graspeth mine is mighty,
    Though my own response is weak ;
Trust is not in my own finding,
    But in Him who came to seek.

Thou didst stoop from heaven to find me,
    I am eager to be found ;
Grace of Thine is overflowing,
    Let that grace to me abound !

I am burdened, doubting, fearing,
    Great Deliverer, set me free !
Words of mine are weak and halting,
    Speak, O Saviour ! speak to me.

Let me know my sins forgiven,
    Feel Thy love within my heart ;
Make me Thine, for earth and heaven,
    Thine—and never more to part.

For some years I knew personally many members of the House of Commons, by whose kindness I frequently obtained a seat in the Strangers' and sometimes in the Speaker's Gallery. I have heard O'Connell speak, Sir R. Peel, Lord John Russell, Cobden, and frequently Bright and Gladstone. I observed that the speeches securing the largest audiences and most fixed attention were generally those of a high conversational character rather than those of elaborated rhetoric. These studies in some degree helped to form my style of preaching—not in imitating any particular speaker or the dulness of the great majority, in what is known as Parliamentary style, but, in a very humble sphere, endeavouring to preach the Gospel as one man in earnest, addressing other men so that his meaning may be understood and his earnestness appreciated. From law courts I have also profited by observing that successful counsel do not strive to please the jury, but to secure their verdict.

Once I had the pleasure of hearing the Queen open Parliament by reading her own speech in the House of Lords. An Honourable Member suggested that as they marched in a body across the central lobby it was possible to take a member's arm, and thus pass along through the crowd. So when, at the word of command, the column moved forward, I saw my friend looking out for me, and, taking his arm, I was hurried along, and found myself in the House of Lords, being addressed as one of Her Majesty's faithful Commons. I cannot forget her dignified demeanour and sweet, articulate voice.

I may quote from Sir Wemyss Reid's "Life of the Right Hon. W. E. Forster, M.P.":—

"A meeting between Mr. Gladstone and some Nonconformist opponents of the [Education] Bill led to a conference at Mr. Newman Hall's house, Surrey Chapel Parsonage."

To his wife, November 21, 1871:—

"A call from Newman Hall—fixed to go to his house Friday evening, Dec. 8. I told him I could prove to any reasonable person that I had worked the Act fairly."

Two of the representatives of our League declined to come, though they had brought the strongest public accusations against him. Amongst those who came were Dale, W. Arthur, Binney, S. Morley, and Raleigh. The friendly discussion lasted till midnight, but failed to reconcile the League party.

This meeting at my house took place while I was under the deep sorrow of my mother's death a few days before, and her body was to be interred in a few hours. Had I loved her less, I should have been conventional, and put off the party, thus to exhibit my love. But a very important national question needed consideration by leaders of two parties— invitations had been sent out weeks before and accepted, a Cabinet Minister had fixed to come—so I felt a private sorrow should not intervene. I did not honour my mother and grieve for her the less because on this occasion I might seem to love public interests more. I did not even indicate to my guests the sorrow oppressing me.

At St. James's Hall I preached to a large congregation sermons in memory of Canon Kingsley, Dean Champneys, Dr. Macfarlane, and the Rev. Luke Wiseman. Wiseman was a popular preacher of the Wesleyan Church, lately President of the Conference; Champneys had spent a long life of consistent service as an Evangelical clergyman of the Church of England. Macfarlane, who died on the preceding Sunday, had been an eminent minister of the United Presbyterian Church. Kingsley, known during thirty years wherever the English language was spoken, was the friend both of the Court and the cottage. These four men represented different schools of thought, but they also showed that there was "one Lord, one Faith, one Baptism." Macfarlane, a Presbyterian by tradition and conviction, was opposed to prelacy and liturgy, which Wiseman the Methodist partially adopted, and Champneys and Kingsley gloried in. Macfarlane was opposed to a State Church; Wiseman preferred to labour outside of it; Champneys upheld it, but would have confined it to his own school; Kingsley clave to it, for the very comprehensiveness which Champneys might regard as a betrayal of its trust. Macfarlane was Calvinistic, Wiseman was Arminian, Champneys preached the sacrificial death of

Christ, Kingsley directed attention chiefly to the sanctifying influence of the life of Christ. Yet all served the same Master, and in His Name strove to lead men to righteousness. Why should not the fellowship of faithful servants of Christ be recognised here, since to all, irrespective of rank or sect, and with reference only to their fidelity, the same salutation was accorded in heaven—"Well done, good and faithful servant"?

The *Daily News* on Stanley's presiding at Surrey Chapel at my lecture :—

"If all the clergy of the English Church followed the example set by the Dean of Westminster at Surrey Chapel the other evening, we should hear little about the encroachments of Dissent. The pastor of Surrey Chapel is the Rev. Newman Hall. The place is a stronghold of Dissent, and ought therefore, in the opinion of good Churchmen, to be avoided by the orthodox as if it were an unclean thing. A Churchman so distinguished and devoted as Dean Stanley thinks differently. On Monday night he took the chair in the chapel, when the pastor delivered a lecture on 'Jerusalem and its Neighbourhood.' Mr. Hall explained that the meeting was entirely unsectarian, and the Dean gave a bright preface to the lecture by describing the Holy Sepulchre, which he himself had visited, and he dwelt on the interest with which any account of the sacred scene was heard by Englishmen. Thus Church and Dissent shed their blended lights on a spot which is equally consecrated to both, and the sturdy members of Surrey Chapel, we do not doubt, went home with a newborn feeling of kindness for the Establishment. But a Dean—a Dean of Westminster—who is so independent of episcopal authority as to be himself a sort of bishop, presiding in a Dissenting chapel! Many good people will be appalled by the idea. Some High Churchmen, who long for communion with the Greek Church or with the Church of Rome, will be horror-stricken at the large Christianity of the Anglican dignitary. Nevertheless, Dean Stanley is a far better and safer Churchman than his critics. He sees that if the Church is to retain its influence it must once more become the Church of the English people. He sees that Dissent must be fought with the weapons, not of intolerance, but of conciliation and goodwill. Happily, he is only one out of a large and growing band to whom that truth is visible. The late Dean of Canterbury was guided by the same broad Christian principles, and, although he was an ardent Churchman, his memory is venerated within the pale of Nonconformity as a divine who strove to heal the unchristian enmities of generations."

The following address from the working-men of the Steam Boiler Works, Southwark, dated April 17th, 1861, greatly encouraged me, and is here produced as an evidence of the usefulness of the weekly lectures to working-people, and an encouragement to others :—

"Permit us, and in the name of many others of our fellow-workmen, to render you our heartfelt thanks for the interest you have taken in our welfare, in getting up the Monday evening lectures, and your untiring efforts to enlighten our minds and teach us that which is just and true. Our thanks are echoed by thousands of other working-men and women, who feel benefited and happy by having so earnest a teacher. We not only feel grateful for the instruction on various subjects (of which we were ignorant) delivered by you and other talented gentlemen, but that you have been the means of establishing the glorious principles of Temperance in many of us, and the which has been the means of leading us to your house of prayer. Through teetotalism and these lectures many of us have been induced to give up the public-house custom and its companions, and like men enjoy ourselves in a much more happy and Christian-like manner, at the Surrey Chapel; and likewise attending there on the Sunday to worship our Maker and hear His most Holy Word. We not only feel ourselves more happy by this, but we have made our wives and children happy, for which we feel much indebted to your untiring labour of love for the working-classes. We earnestly pray God to preserve you for many years, and then hear the call of the Great Master to receive the wages due to all who labour for Him truly. In giving you our best thanks, we are not unmindful of our much-valued friend, Mr. Murphy, your brother Arthur, and the other gentlemen who have so kindly contributed talents and time for our instruction.—We most respectfully subscribe ourselves, your obedient and humble servants, S. BONN, J. BALDWIN (and many others)."

A handsome silver inkstand was also given, with this inscription :—" Rev. Newman Hall, LL.B., presented by the working-men of London, as a token of gratitude for his efforts for their welfare (1861)."

A letter from my brother Stephen, dated November 5th, 1868, contains the following incident, illustrative of the benefits resulting from these lectures to working-men :—

"At Croydon, a gentleman got into the carriage who spoke of the memoir of our father and said that to you, its compiler, he was much indebted. He said, 'I used to attend his lectures to working-men. On one occasion he said : "It was the fashion for men to say, I hope something will turn up some of these days. Now, suppose, instead of waiting for something to *turn up, you* were turn up something for yourselves. Nothing can be done without exertion, and I am sure many of you are capable of better things. Suppose you were to try and turn up something for yourselves." I took this to heart, and took it home with me, and thought, "Am I to be a working-man all my life? No, I am capable of better things, and I will try." The result is that, instead of being a working-man, I am superintendent of a large establishment. I owe my present position entirely to what Mr. Hall said at a Monday evening lecture.'"

My brother adds :—

"I was delighted to find my companion had not only improved his *worldly* position, but had also found the pearl of great price, and was labouring to make known the Saviour to all with whom he had any influence."

With great thankfulness, I received the following letter from my brother Stephen, after a short visit home, when he heard me preach one Sunday evening in Surrey Chapel :—

"Hong Kong, January 12th, 1863.

"As long as you are able to preach I wish very much that you would preach every year, on the second Sunday in November, that sermon from: 'Abide with us, for it is toward evening, and the day is far spent.' I never in my life heard such a sermon, and I am sure the angels in heaven must have rejoiced as they heard you give utterance to those few words, and saw the many melting hearts on that day. I trust you will often hear from new members that they date acceptance of the Saviour from your exposition of the words 'Abide with us.' O those beautiful words! Never, dear brother, be less earnest; I do not think you can be so, but I beg of you to *persuade* men and women to come to Christ—persuasion is the charm—much better than bullying people, which only makes hard hearts harder. I wish all ministers were alive to the necessity of *fervency*. As an inducement, I shall send a subscription yearly to the funds of Surrey Chapel."

I publish this, not because of it praising my sermon, but because it illustrates how a very simple discourse impressed my brother's heart because of its earnestness in persuasion to accept the call of Divine Love.

An Evangelical Church paper having inaccurately stated that at a meeting of the Protestant Alliance I had "reflected strongly" upon Episcopal ordination, the editor published my reply, from which I quote :—

"This would have misrepresented my view, as I have always admitted the validity of ordination by Bishops, no less than by Presbyters. If I 'reflected strongly,' it was only on Romanistic notions associated with any ordination, whether Episcopal or Presbyterian, and not on the ordination itself. If succession through centuries of Roman priests be considered essential, so that a Romish priest is admitted to the Anglican ministry without re-ordination, while a Protestant, ordained by a Presbytery, must be re-ordained, though he may have been preaching the one Gospel faithfully all his life, with evidence of the Holy Spirit working by his instrumentality—if sanction is thus given to Popery and withheld from Protestantism, this explains the perversion of many who have been taught by their own Church to recognise the validity of a priesthood which denies their own. I expected that all Evangelical Protestants would agree with me, believing with Bishop Latimer that 'It is not the imposition of hands by the Bishop that gives grace, but grace which authorises the imposition of hands.' Thanking you for your constant vindication of Protestant truth, I remain, etc."

January 26th.—Telegram from Moody to help him at Birmingham. A convention at Bingley Hall, 6,000 present in afternoon. I spoke on " How to Reach the Masses." In the evening Moody preached to 15,000, and multitudes vainly tried to enter. Hundreds rose in token of a desire to be prayed for. Afterwards I addressed a crowd of young men in a neighbouring church.

February 1.—Again summoned by Moody, and addressed 7,000 the following night. Kindly entertained by Dr. and Mrs. Dale. Much impressed with his strength of character, learning, genius, and piety.

February 5th.—Moody invited all the London clergy to meet him at Freemasons' Hall, which was crowded. Among many questions, a clergyman said : " Please tell us what your object is ?"—" *To preach the Gospel.*" "What do you do with converts ?"—" *Leave them with Christ to take care of.*" "Would it not be well to print your views of the Gospel, that we might know ?"—The evangelist replied, " *They're in print already ; you'll find them in the Fifty-third of Isaiah.*"—Ritualists, Evangelicals, and Nonconformists of all sorts crowded the hall.

March 15th.—To Moody and Sankey's service at the Agricultural Hall. 20,000 present. Till nearly midnight busy with him in the " Enquiry Room " trying to guide anxious seekers to Christ.

I had once a valuable conversation with an eminent Christian author and editor. Substance as follows :—Peter by the

Spirit meant what he said: that, when put to death in the body, Christ in His Spirit went into the invisible state, Hades, and proclaimed the good news of salvation to spirits in safe keeping, who in their earthly life had been · disobedient. Christ has " the keys of Death and Hades "—Lord of the invisible world, is He inactive there ? Is the time between death and resurrection wasted ? Judgment, not death, is final arbiter of destiny. Are fourscore years of earth the only season of possible improvement, and four thousand years of Hades useless ? Are the multitudes who did not, and could not, hear on earth of salvation, never to hear in the unseen state ? Final condemnation will be at the judgment day. Of all who then are penitent, we may cherish hope ; the resolutely rebellious will die—self-destroyed. Would Christ " see of the travail of His soul, and be satisfied," if He gathered the gleanings alone, while Satan reaped the harvest ? " Who is worthy to take the Book "—the awful book of human conduct and destiny ? The Lamb of God, the gracious Saviour, the Man of Calvary !—and then they cried " Hallelujah !" These are simply suggestions—not assertions.

I once visited an admiral in his last sickness, and frequently prayed with him in the name of the "Sinner's Friend," trusting simply in Whom he departed in peace. His widow, in expressing her thanks, spoke of me as " so very good." I replied I was only one of others, both good and bad, trying to be better, hating what is bad—more of the latter known to myself than to anyone else. " But you know that Dissenters have not the help of the Holy Spirit. If, then, you are so good without such help, you must be very good indeed."

The following terrible instance of alcoholic mania was reported to me through our clerk by a trustworthy member of Surrey Chapel, who was about to pass a pawnshop near Kennington Park one cold evening, snow descending and covering the ground. A woman was standing against the railings, without shoes, stockings, bonnet, or dress—covered only by a cloak drawn tightly round her shivering frame. She politely accosted my informant, earnestly asking a great favour. Her wretched appearance and eager tone induced the passenger to inquire what she needed, the reply being, " Please take this umbrella into that shop and try to get five shillings on it." This was done, when the shopman, examining it, said it had been brought some time before by a child, and he had refused it. " But now I will take it from *you.*" And he gave five shillings, which the poor wretch, who was waiting, received with a profusion of thanks, and took her new friend to the nearest liquor-shop, drank a glass of gin, and, taking an empty bottle from under her cloak, ordered it to be filled with gin—spending all the five shillings. She then went to a respectable-looking house in Kennington Oval, and explained that her husband, anxious to keep her from drink, had locked up her day-clothing and kept from her all money, but that, unable to abstain any longer, she had rushed from her bed, covered herself with the cloak, and appropriated the umbrella. The narrative was ended when they reached the door, which was opened respectfully by the servant, and the melancholy scene closed.

Anticipating a few years, I here insert my reply to the *New York Herald,* asking what habits might conduce to a " vigorous old age " :—

"To remain in health to threescore and ten, and possibly, by reason of strength, to fourscore, I would say : Live according to the laws of God—temperately and virtuously, soberly, righteously, and godly— ' abstain from fleshly lusts, which war against the soul,' was Paul's advice to young Timothy. As regards my personal habits, I have never smoked, and during sixty years have wholly abstained from all intoxicating drinks. I generally sleep from half-past eleven or twelve to seven or half-past. I sleep seven hours without waking. I take a cold bath every morning throughout the year. On an average, I walk four miles a day. I can still walk ten miles without fatigue. I generally have three services on Sunday, and am never Mondayish. On an average, I preach four times weekly, and neither suffer from pain nor fatigue. As to overwork of brain, I would say : Give up working as soon as it is a weariness, and do the chief brain-work early in the day. Do not work the brain late at night if you wish to sleep ; and as to worry, do your duty and cast your care upon the Lord, content with His approval and a good conscience."

At the funeral of my humorous old college friend, De Kewer Williams, I am reported to have said that "some disesteem humour because destitute of it; but it is surely a gift of the Creator, conferred only on intelligent creatures. Mental culture favours it. Society would be happier with more of it. Some of the most godly, learned, and useful Christian divines and preachers have been thus richly gifted. On the Christian path there is more sunshine than shadow, more singing than sighing. The Bible says there is 'a time to weep, and a time to laugh.' The Psalmist records, 'Thou hast turned . . . my mourning into dancing.' Are we sure it is excluded from the bliss of the life to come? If eloquence, poetry, music, and song develop yonder, why not humour? Our friend's wit never wounded by its keenness, never scorched by its brightness. No joke was ever uttered to injure or grieve. He never degraded humour by ridiculing righteousness, by manufacturing cheap fireworks out of Scripture texts, by desecrating the golden vessels of the sanctuary for carrying about and displaying vulgar samples of self. If humour sometimes appeared in the pulpit, he suppressed far more; it was holy pleasantry to illustrate and impress truth, not to dilute or disfigure it, or turn solemn worship into pleasant entertainment. His lectures and general demeanour eloquently denied that religion is an enemy to cheerfulness, and that godliness means gloom."

I record the following incident, vouching for its absolute truth, but suggesting no explanation:—A dear friend and earnest Christian fellow-worker, Mrs. A., was, with her husband, much interested in a young man, B., whose engagement with their daughter had been broken off by his misconduct, and of whose whereabouts they were ignorant. One midsummer Sunday evening she was on her bed sleeping, her husband sitting near her, reading. Suddenly she awoke with a cry of distress, and said, " I have seen B. ! He has a house on the shore of the Clyde. He was sipping coffee in a room with low windows opening on a lawn, up which that beautiful but bad person was walking, and, stretching out her arms, exclaimed, ' I have found you, B. !' B. was rising to greet her, when I earnestly remonstrated with him, and he answered me so angrily that I awoke in terror. This seemed to me a reality, but it must have been only a dream." On Tuesday morning a letter was received, to their surprise, from B., dated from the shores of the Clyde, and saying, "Last night, as I was taking my coffee, with the windows opening on the lawn, that person came up to greet me, when I saw you at the door in a white dress, and you so reproved me that I resented your interference with anger, and you, with a scream, vanished out of sight. But your reproof went to my heart, and I intend never to see her again." The vision was narrated to her husband at the time, and two days after came the letter, dated from two hundred miles distant, after all communication had ceased several years.

After a long interval, Mrs. A.'s daughter, who had been engaged to B., walking in a suburb of London, came home and told her mother, with considerable emotion, that in the street she had met B., who looked at her with a fixed gaze and passed on. She felt so afraid of meeting him again that she refused to go out with her sister to a party that evening. Next morning they received intelligence that B. died at the time when she saw him in the street.

Without speculations respecting the spirit world, it is surely not scientific to denounce all such phenomena, although testified by credible witnesses, as merely imaginary or superstitious, and, with our imperfect knowledge of the universe, to declare that whatever is beyond the limits of ascertained laws of nature is contrary to nature and incredible.

CHAPTER XVI

ONE Sunday morning, when preaching in Christ Church, I saw a man suddenly enter the middle aisle, and with determined step march up the church towards the pulpit, holding something in his hand. He did not seem to be looking for a seat, but intent on the pulpit. I immediately felt his errand was to myself, and mentally resolved, if he threatened to attack me, to place my hand on the side of the pulpit and leap over to the floor, which was only a few feet below. I did not stop in my discourse, but fixed my eye on the stranger, who began to ascend the pulpit steps. I turned to meet him, holding out my hand in friendly greeting, when the verger came in from behind the organ, and, with the organ-blower, led him away to the vestry. He had only a short stick in his hand. His object was pacific, though his manner was hostile. He said afterwards he had come to deliver to the preacher a message from Christ. He was evidently deranged, and was taken care of by his friends. Until the man actually ascended to the pulpit there was no just cause to stop him, and when he came up to me there was no time to do it. I went on with the sentence I had begun, and not one of the congregation stirred. Two ladies were sitting together, one of whom had been so frightened that she was unable to stir when the service closed. Her friend asked what was the matter? She said it was the shock of seeing the minister in danger of being killed! The other was surprised to hear this, for she had witnessed nothing but a man walking up the aisle, and had observed no pause or interruption in the sermon. Her companion suffered so much from the fright that for several weeks she was unable to walk. It is wonderful that while tens of thousands of preachers are every Sunday liable to such interruptions, they so seldom occur.

I was one evening preaching near Surrey Chapel in the open air in a back street, verily a " slum," when a gentlemanly dressed man came up and ridiculed. Very unwisely I uttered a few words of rebuke. This enraged him, and he bribed a drunken man to break up the meeting. Swinging his arms in a threatening style, the assailant rushed among the listeners, seized the chair on which I was standing, and brandished it to the peril of the poor men and women around me. Instantly some " navvies " carried him into a cottage, where he smashed the windows. I returned to my post, and continued the service. At the close one of the "navvies " came up to me and walked alongside till I emerged into the broad " New Cut "—then he held out his hand for a hearty shake and said, " I resolved to see you safe, and if anyone tried to injure you I would have fought for you !" The assailant was visited by our missionary and became a Christian.

On a certain anniversary occasion at Bedford I preached to a crowded congregation on the text, " Is it nothing to you, all ye that pass by ?" and drew a series of pictures of persons who pass by the Cross—the sensualist, the worldling, the covetous, the self-satisfied, the procrastinator. On the following Sunday a lay-preacher of the town went to a neighbouring village congregation, and said that, having lately heard Newman Hall, he could not do better than reproduce his sermon. Then he presented his own copies of the preacher's pictures, and these were much appreciated. The next Sunday a request was again sent for a preacher. Another one came and gave his own version of the same theme, but forgot to acknowledge his indebtedness. The congregation were amused to listen again to the same sermon, knowing it was not the preacher's own. It would be good, both for preachers and hearers, if sometimes the teaching were varied by using both the thoughts and words of others—of course, with full acknowledgments.

At an evangelistic mission week at Torquay, shared by both Church and Dissent, there were a large number of professed converts to Christ, among them five young men and women from the same drapery store. I attended one of the morning services in an Episcopal church, where Mr. Aitkin preached a sermon so impressive that I resolved to use it in an address to workmen which I was to deliver at noon. This I did forthwith before a large concourse of artisans. At the close I told them that they had been listening to a Churchman, who had thus been occupying a Dissenting pulpit. Then I explained how in my poorer words I had given them the substance of the great missioner's discourse just delivered in the parish church. Until we may occupy each other's pulpits, may we not reciprocate by availing ourselves of each other's discourses, with due recognition, and thus demonstrate Church unity? When walking away, I was accosted by a workman returning from the meeting, who said how glad he was I had explained, because, while I was addressing them, he wondered to hear the same sermon he had himself been hearing from Mr. Aitkin. I have very seldom used the liberty I justify.

Those who cannot preach can repeat what they hear, and so become " workers together." At Maidstone, when I was about twenty years of age, I occasionally went to hear the minister of a small Baptist church. My sister Mary, in 1896, when dying, told me that she remembered my coming in one evening and repeating what I had just heard from Mr. Cornford—that if anyone really desired to be converted, he or she should make a point to ask it of God, and read a few verses of Scripture every day, and that before a year was over the prayer would be realised. She told me that she said nothing at the time, but resolved to begin that very night. Before many months she herself had found Christ. This was the beginning of her spiritual life, but she had never mentioned it before. She was at that time sixteen.

Bishop Wilberforce had been preaching on St. Thomas's Day in the parish church near Surrey Chapel. He was eloquent and thoroughly evangelical, except that in pleading for the enlargement of the *chancel* he dilated on the sanctity of that portion of the edifice. On the following Sunday I gave my version of the sermon, omitting what to me seemed superstitions, telling my people that in Rowland Hill's pulpit a bishop, son of the great Wilberforce, who was Rowland Hill's friend, had been preaching by deputy the common salvation.

I remember a good illustration I heard in Regent's Park from an unlettered but eloquent open-air preacher. He said that an infidel contradicted him in declaring that an unbeliever never died happy. He said he once knew a man who had no belief in Christ, and yet he died very happy. "What! died happy, and an infidel?" Yes, he was an infidel, and died happy. "And did not believe in a better life after this?" No, he did not believe in God, or Christ, or heaven. "And yet went out of this world quite happy?" Yes, quite happy. "Then, if quite happy to leave the present life he couldn't have been quite happy in it. But the religion of Christ makes us happy to stay here while it is God's will, and happy to go where we shall be happier still; so our faith does better for us than your unbelief for you."

Leicester, October, 1889.—Speaking at a Gospel mission, I referred to a special encouragement in connection with a former visit. I said, "Some eight years ago I spent a week here on a mission, holding services every afternoon and evening. No 'inquirer' came to me, and I began to fear no good had been done, and that I had no qualifications for mission work. On my last evening I was asked to speak to a gentleman of about twenty-five years of age who was lingering in the aisle. I sometimes unwisely hesitate to address individuals, but, urged as I then was, I asked him to join a few friends in the vestry. He had lately returned from hunting wild beasts in South Africa. He was non-religious, but the subject of the most earnest prayers of his parents, who had urged him to come and hear one sermon. My text was my favourite and earliest theme—'God so loved the world.' Next morning, on entering the breakfast-room, he said to his parents, 'I mean to be a Christian—out and out —and to go back to Africa as a missionary.' They were over-powered with surprise and gratitude. He at once applied to a great missionary society, who counselled college and long training. But he knew the language; he had received salvation; he wanted to go at once. He applied to Grattan Guinness, who recognised his fitness and divine call, and sent him at once as head of a mission up the Congo, where he

Q

founded several stations—now centres of usefulness. On his return voyage he took fever, and joined the noble army of martyrs."

Some years after I was again at Leicester, and spoke of this as the only but great result of my former mission. On leaving I was addressed by a gentleman holding a collecting-box—"Don't say it was the only case; I was then converted through you, and so was my wife." Thank God!

One Sunday evening I was delivering a written sermon on temptation, and suddenly felt that my address was unlike my usual style, and too argumentative for many of the poorer people. I suddenly paused, looked away from my manuscript, and, appealing with a loud voice to the more distant of my audience, said, "Perhaps among those pressing in at the door there may be someone so miserable as to think of throwing himself over yonder bridge, saying, perhaps, 'It's too late to tell me not to enter into temptation. I've done it—I'm in it. There's no hope for me.' Stop! stop! there is hope. Christ died for thee. He will pardon, He will save, even thee." Then I resumed my manuscript. Some critical hearer might say, "What a fool the preacher is to interrupt his argument for a bit of rant like that!"

A few weeks afterwards one of my district visitors told me, "I have called to see a woman who was intending to throw herself over Blackfriars Bridge one Sunday evening; but she thought it was too light, and a policeman might stop her, so in order to wait for darkness she went into Surrey Chapel, and stood in the crowd inside the door. Just then you seemed to call to her to stop and come to Christ, and she went back to her home to pray, and seems to be a true penitent and a Christian."

What I said was entirely unpremeditated. I had never before made such an appeal. I knew nothing of the woman. Am I wrong in the belief that the Spirit of God both directed the woman to enter the church and prompted the preacher to utter those words at that very time? All preachers pray that the Spirit of God will help them to say what may do good. Must this guidance be confined to the study, the manuscript, or the memory? Should not we feel at liberty in the pulpit to utter what the Spirit suggests during the service in the presence of a congregation uniting with the preacher in appealing to the chief Bishop? Do we sufficiently *realise* what we profess to believe—the real presence of Christ in His Church: "Wherever two or three are gathered together in my name, there am I in the midst of them"?

September 19th, 1893.—Preached at Clifton for London Missionary Society. At the close suggested these questions:—

(1) Whether the great religious revival of the world is to be expected on the occasion and as the immediate result of our Lord's second advent.

(2) Whether the conversion of all men living at that period would be an adequate fulfilment of the prophecy of Christ's universal reign, if all the generations preceding, who had died in sin, were to perish eternally.

(3) Whether, when He went and preached to "the spirits in prison," He preached the gospel of His death for sinners; whether by His preaching many repented and were saved; and whether He thus preached to all the heathen represented by those impenitent in the days of Noah.

(4) Whether believers in Christ, when they die, may, in like manner, be missionaries to former generations, or to the inhabitants of other planets.

(5) Whether a period may not arrive when every intelligent creature in the universe shall obey and rejoice in Christ, in conformity with the Apocalyptic vision, *Rev.* v. 13. Will the reign of Christ be universal as long as any remain in rebellion? Will the crushing under His footstool be true victory while those crushed continue to curse? May not a future hope suggest either ceasing to curse or ceasing to exist?

The "Ancient Merchants' Lecture" was founded in 1672 for the advocacy of Puritan Christianity in opposition to Popery and infidelity. Richard Baxter and John Howe were among the original lecturers. Our Hon. Secretary, son of the veteran Evangelist Dr. Wilson, has kindly sent me the following particulars :—

"Memorial Hall, September 20th, 1898.

"Your connection with the Lecture is rather ancient history. I have searched the minute book and ascertained that you were appointed Lecturer October, 1862, and gave your first lecture in December, 1862, having as your colleagues at that time, Davies, Spence, Samuel Martin, Binney, and Raleigh. Vacancies were subsequently filled up by Allon, Baldwin Brown, Kennedy, and Edward White, and now the present lecturers are as per list at the head of this circular : Newman Hall, LL.B., D.D., J. Guinness Rogers, B.A., D.D., Alfred Rowland, LL.B., B.A., J. Morgan Gibbons, W. Hardy Harwood. I have also ascertained that it was due to your persevering advocacy that the monthly was changed to a weekly lecture. Next month you will renew your acquaintance with the Dutch Church in Austin Friars, where you lectured on May 27th and July 1st in 1872 when the Weigh House was under repair.

"Yours truly,
"J. KNOX WILSON."

For some years my name has headed the list only as the longest on the rota of the "Ancients." I remember when the lecture used to be given in the vestry of the old Poultry Chapel. Here and everywhere, however varied the occasion or subject, I have kept in mind my mother's parting charge in a letter dated 1867, when she had accomplished her threescore years and ten—"Stand up for Jesus. Preach Christ everywhere—in the perfect loveliness of His human character, in the dignity and love of His Divinity. May the Lord help you, and while attempting to teach others, may the Holy Spirit fill your own soul with joy and peace, and may you delight more and more in your Master's work."

CHAPTER XVII.

REFERENCE to persons I have known will naturally be expected
in an autobiography. Disregarding dates, I will put together
various cherished memories.

Arthur Penrhyn Stanley, D.D., Dean of Westminster, and
Lady Augusta—I link the two names, for they themselves
were inseparable. Wherever one was, the other was sure to
be. It was a joy to see the lovely grace and beaming
features of the Queen's great lady friend distributing prizes
to the poor on occasion of a window-flower show, greeting
each person with an individual smile of recognition. How
dearly loved by the parishioners! And also when doing
the honours as hostess at the Deanery, where it was the
delight of herself and the Dean to welcome together dignitaries
and other ministers of the Established Church, together with
Nonconformists, in social intercourse. I remember Lady
Augusta's thoughtfulness at one of her afternoon "At Homes,"
when she took me aside for some more solid food, saying she
knew how often I had evening engagements and perhaps had
to leave the Deanery for some meetings which would occupy
me till late in the evening; which was the fact that day.
She accompanied her husband to tea in my study at Surrey
Parsonage, when he came to preside in the chapel at a lecture
I delivered on my recent visit to the Holy Land. During my
chairmanship of the Congregational Union a breakfast was
given by my congregation to 300 ministers, whom the Dean
in a hearty speech greeted as "Nonconforming ·Members

of the Church of England," a designation which has had a wide publicity.

The following extract from one of his letters expresses what has been called his Erastianism :—

"You of course know that whilst gratefully acknowledging the kindly tone in which the address * speaks of the Church of England, I am one of those who consider its connection with the State, and its control by the laws of England, one of its most valuable characteristics. I think that all Churches and sects have their secular side, and that the secular element which has the most ancient and the most legal basis is the best. I only say this to avoid misconstruction."

He seemed to rejoice in difference of opinions as illustrating unity of hearts. At a large clerical meeting at my house, and elsewhere, I have heard him say emphatically, "There is nothing more stupid than only to meet with those who echo your own sentiments." This catholicity was illustrated at his wife's funeral, to which he invited men of various opinions and Churches.

He once asked me to bring to the Abbey a company of artisans, and I well remember the Saturday afternoon when with eloquent tongue he led us round, explaining the most interesting of the monuments, and with what geniality he entertained his company at tea in the Jerusalem Chamber. He was, with several other Deans, a cheerful subscriber to the erection of our "Christ Church, Lambeth." He told me how he regretted he could not invite me and other Nonconformists to preach in the Abbey. When he died he was under promise to lecture at Surrey Chapel. Whilst Dr. Cuyler was in London he went to hear the Dean at the Abbey, and wrote a respectful and appreciative letter, rejoicing that such a voice made known such important truths in that historic church, but regretting that the great subject of salvation by the cross had not been referred to. The Dean replied most kindly and said : " I agree with you as to the place the Atonement occupies in Theology and in all ecclesiastical history, but I make it a rule to keep to the particular subject in hand, and on that occasion it was not in the text." But should not

* Chairman's Congregational Union address.

every subject be viewed in relation to the central truth, as planets to the sun ? Doubtlesss this great truth was precious to his own soul, and his Christ-like life due more to its power on his own heart than to the sweetness of his natural disposition, which was pre-eminent.

While the invited guests for the Dean's funeral were assembling, I was told by an intimate friend of his that when a boy of fourteen at Rugby, it was his custom to retire to his room after hearing Dr. Arnold preach, and write out the sermon from memory. Also that in his bedroom at the Deanery, on the wall opposite the bed, so that he could see them first on awaking, were the words of his favourite hymn, " How sweet the Name of Jesus sounds ! " It was his custom to give a threefold benediction—" The Lord bless you and keep you," " The Peace of God," and " The Grace of our Lord Jesus Christ," Lady Augusta greatly admired this triple blessing, and begged him always to think specially of herself when pronouncing it. No one who was present at her funeral can forget the tremulous yet decided voice, the suppressed emotion, the triumph of love, as, standing at the end of the nave, the Dean closed the service, and with quivering accents made this benediction of prophets and apostles heard throughout the Abbey.

Not long afterwards the same benediction closed his own funeral ceremony. There I met Lord Shaftesbury, Stopford Brooke, Huxley, Lecky, Carlyle and Browning, Stoughton the venerable Nonconformist historian, as a pall-bearer, and Gladstone. To the solemn strains of organ and choir we moved on to Henry VII.'s Chapel, where the body of the beloved Arthur was laid beside that of his dear Augusta, both already re-united in the presence of " the Resurrection and the Life."

I need not enlarge on the noble features and form of the Earl of Shaftesbury, on his lifelong labours for humanity and religion, or on his disregard of mere party preferences in co-operating with all of every political and ecclesiastical opinion who were engaged in any enterprise to promote the glory of God and the good of men. I will confine myself to personal recollections.

He very often came into South London to encourage the teachers of the various Sunday schools connected with Surrey Chapel, and to aid us in our missions to the working classes. He has gone to little rooms in obscure courts with as much readiness, and has spoken with as much power, as when presiding at grand meetings in Exeter Hall and addressing three thousand people. He spoke to the poor folk as one of themselves, understood and appreciated by them all. I fancy that by nature he was proud, but grace had conquered and made him meek and lowly in heart, and no respecter of persons.

At the funeral of Dean Stanley (July 25th, 1881) I met Lord Shaftesbury in the Abbot's Parlour some time before the other guests arrived, and enjoyed a memorable conversation with him and our common friend, Joshua Harrison, on the efforts of the Dean to overcome the alienation of working men to Church ordinances. Lord Shaftesbury said that "many were truly religious, though they would not attend church, and that we were not told in the Bible that church-going was necessary for salvation. A deep and wrong prejudice kept them away, arising from the faults of all Churches in past times alienating them; they would receive visits thankfully, and listen to preaching out of doors, but not commit themselves to systems by worshipping in regular churches." A company of representatives, both of Church and Dissent, once spent an interesting afternoon at my house to discuss whether the establishment of religion tended to such alienation. Lord Shaftesbury presided, with some apprehension that such discussion might lead to acrid controversy, and he seemed surprised as well as gratified that it was conducted with Christian gentleness as well as candour. He was gratified by the conviction that both parties in the controversy were animated by sincere desire for the true interests of religion.

The last time I met Lord Shaftesbury was on May 20th, 1888, at Grosvenor House, on occasion of a meeting on behalf of ragged schools. I quote from my diary:—

" Dear old Lord Shaftesbury in the chair, looking haggard and ill, but spoke twenty minutes, giving pathetic illustrations of the power of sympathy to win the hearts of the poor and reclaim the wicked. At the close of his speech he left the room, and I followed him into the picture gallery to render any service. There he honoured me with a long talk. I alluded to the emphasis with which the Evangelist Mark speaks of the *hand* of Christ : 'He took the blind man by the *hand.*' He then related to me the following incident, his eyes moistened with emotion : ' The chaplain of a gaol sent to me a young man who was just out of prison for burglary, hoping I might say something to encourage him in his professed desire for a better life. He had seemed incorrigible, having been in gaol twenty-two times. Rather a formidable visitor for a private interview ! Some time afterwards the chaplain told me that the young man was really reformed, and had related the interview, and added, " But it was this broke me down—he slapped me on the shoulder and said, Jack, we'll make a man of you yet." ' "

This record in my diary closes with a presentiment soon verified :—

" I don't expect to speak to the dear old veteran of humanity and take his hand again—one of God's nobility."

I used to meet John Bright at the house of his friend, Charles Gilpin, and was in full accord with him on great public questions. I have rambled with him on the Orme's Head, Llandudno, where he showed me, in the ancient consecrated Episcopal churchyard, the simple grave of his dearly loved boy, with the words, " There shall be one fold and one Shepherd." When visiting the spot with this boy for the last time, the boy, then quite well, said, " Father, I should like to be buried here."

In service for others he had found solace for grief of his own. He described how he had been thus prompted to labour for the cheapening of the staff of life.

" I was at Leamington, in the depths of grief, I may say of despair. All that was left of my young wife—except the memory of a sainted life and too brief happiness—was lying cold in the chamber above me, when Cobden called on me as a friend to condole. He said, ' There are thou-sands of homes in England at this moment where wives, mothers, and children are dying of hunger. Now I advise you, when the first paroxysm of grief is over, to come with me, and we will never rest till the Corn Law is repealed.' "

Then, impelled by a heavenly inspiration, he buckled on the armour in this holy crusade. And not only in this. He was the eloquent champion of Temperance, Peace, Reform and Freedom. Never was the House of Commons more thrilled than when in 1853 he raised his warning voice against fighting Russia in the Crimea, and said, " The Angel of Death is abroad in the land ; you may almost hear the beating of his wings." He thus apostrophised all the clergy :—

" How will an after-time look back on this quarrel ? Were there no churches in 1853 ? no ministers of the Gospel of Peace ? What were these men doing all the time ? Were they splitting hairs ? disputing whether baptism should be by sprinkling of an infant or immersing of a grown man ? whether it was lawful to burn candles on the altar ? or the precise amount of labour a man might do or not do on the Sabbath ? What were your ministers about ? Why were they not rather awakening the people to this gigantic and incredible evil."

As popular and party opinions varied, he was in turn subjected to all manner of abuse—" Ignorant! fanatical! destructive! revolutionary! reactionary! youthful! impetuous! senile! imbecile!" He was even burnt in effigy. His advocacy of peace cost him his seat in Parliament, but, instigated by conscience, " seeing the Invisible," he was as little frightened by the curses of the mob as he was delighted by the smiles of the great. And because he continued the same amid surrounding changes, all parties, whether they had agreed with or opposed him, concurred in admiring his honesty.

In reply to my inquiry how he prepared for his public speeches he said that he might have uttered things which some persons censured, and perhaps afterwards himself regretted, but he never said what he had not beforehand considered and purposed to say. When he was intending to speak he spent several days in reading and thinking about the subject ; then he arranged what he wished to say in proper and effective sequence, and on small slips of paper wrote brief, suggestive notes ; then wrote fully the last short sentence or two that he might feel sure about the winding up of his address. Then, pacing his room or garden terrace, he talked it all over to himself, leaving himself freedom for fresh suggestions at the moment.

In the House of Commons and elsewhere I have been enchanted with his oratory—calm and deliberate, but mighty with suppressed emotion, now and then rising to the supreme heights of eloquence, and always impressing you with absolute sincerity in all he said, and the suppression of self-display in the obvious eagerness to win the convictions of his audience. I remember once, as I was seated in the Speaker's gallery, close to the front, being so excited as he denounced the suspension of the Habeas Corpus in Ireland, and appealed to both great parties led by Gladstone and Disraeli to combine their influence to do justice to that country, that I was about to stand up and shout approval when I remembered the sergeant-at-arms.

From John Bright, M.P. :—

"November 12th, 1862.

"DEAR NEWMAN HALL,—Thank you for your lecture on the American struggle, which I have read with great pleasure. It is glorious to see the black nation coming to the front. History will tell what the war was for and what its result. But our middle and rich classes are depraved by our aristocratic institutions, just as America has been depraved by slavery, and there is little morality in the public view of any question. . . . Wishing you all the good that is good for you. . . . I watched your progress in the States with much interest. . . I am uncomfortable at our differences with the Government at Washington. I think they press their claims with some harshness. . . . The evening we spent with you at Llandudno we remember with pleasure.

"Always very sincerely yours, J. B."

Mr. Bright's remark that the Washington Government "press their claims with some harshness," reminds me of an incident when I met the American Minister, Mr. Adams, at dinner at the Duke of Argyll's. It was rather a grand affair— Highlanders waiting in native costume, and the dinner-service of gold. After the ladies had withdrawn, conversation became excited, and the Duke having urged Mr. Bright's objection to the exaggerated claims of the American Government, Mr. Adams put his arm round the Duke's neck, exclaiming remonstratively, "My dear SIR! my dear SIR!" The Duke throughout was a strong supporter of "Union and Emancipation."

"July 7th, 1874.

"I am glad that anything succeeds in which you take an active interest. I am rather amused at the pictoral grandeur of your church. I do not suspect you of any desertion of your great principles, and can only hope that your success will give you more room to enforce them upon a larger body of hearers, and upon the world. Wishing you every success, etc.   J. B."

In reply to an invitation to preside at a lecture on Peace with America :—

"June 26th, 1876.

"I must decline all offers of work. I only get through indifferently well my duties as an M.P. by resolutely refusing all other engagements. I have often to make this explanation, but never with more regret than on this occasion. I am sorry to have to refuse you anything."

May 4th, 1877.—I told him I was sorry to be a dissentient from Gladstone's Irish policy. He lamented that Gladstone was now under the influence of Parnell, whom he had previously denounced as "advancing through rapine to dismemberment"; that some of Parnell's party friends had given him up because his word was worthless; that two millions in Ireland out of five were against him, and, therefore, Parnell did not represent Ireland; and that it was suicidal to allow one part of a nation to rule itself as it pleased, since it might please to annex itself to U.S.A. or France, or any foe to England.

"Piccadilly, April 23rd, 1884.

"DEAR NEWMAN HALL,—I hope the time may come when the Christian feeling of the country may check the folly of our Governments in their dealings with foreign affairs. Every war is condemned after it is over—the result is loss of treasure, and loss of blood—and yet the people are led into the next war as if they could learn nothing from the past.

"I hope this Egyptian business may teach them something. The end of it is not yet, and the way out of it is not yet apparent.

"Sincerely yours, J. B."

May 16th, 1887.—Returning from Windsor after memorialising the Queen, we had a saloon to ourselves, and I enjoyed a long chat. In substance he said, "Parnell and Co. mean what they always meant: absolute separation from England. They are and have been intimately associated with conspirators who avow their evil deeds. Gladstone is

hampered by alliance with Parnell. He must submit to Irish
terms or lose the Irish vote. If there were a Parliament in
Dublin, Ulster would not submit : there would be civil war,
and English troops would have to fight against loyal
Protestants." We talked of the Egyptian war. He said
that he had told Ministers there was no reason for it—if
they made war he must quit the Cabinet. He considered
that Gladstone had yielded to pressure against his better
judgment; he was astonished that Chamberlain had
supported Gladstone in this. I said I hoped he (J. B.)
would soon speak in the House of Commons on Ireland.
" No, I don't think I shall ever speak in the House of
Commons again." He spoke with much admiration of Gladstone, and with manifest grief at their difference of opinion.
In March, 1886, Gladstone had sent for Bright, who found
him on his couch, poorly. They spent two hours together.
When Gladstone explained his notions, Bright told him he
could never carry them out.

Death of John Bright, March 27th, 1889. I feel deeply
his departure. Known so many years, honoured by his
friendship, admiring his whole career; with him, heart and
soul, in free trade, reform, anti-slavery, temperance, free
churches, peace, opposition to the China, Afghan, Zulu, and
other wars, anti-capital punishment, cause of the North and
emancipation, and now Unionism. One after another old
comrades taken! But Truth "goes marching on!" I
preached a sermon *in memoriam* from the great feature
in the character of Moses, "He endured as seeing the
Invisible." I always thought of the familiar lines of Horace
as applicable to him :—

> "Justum et tenacem propositi virum
> Non civium ardor prava jubentium
> Non vultus instantis tyranni
> Mente quatit solida . . ."

He honoured the laws of God as applicable to all men of
whatever rank, and to governments as to individuals. He
said, " The moral law was not written for men alone in their
individual character, but also for nations, and if they reject it

penalty will inevitably follow. It may not come at once; it may not come in our life-time; but rely on it the great Italian is not a poet only but a prophet when he says:

> "The sword of heaven is not in haste to smite,
> Nor yet doth linger."

John Bright lived before his time, and was often censured for dangerous opinions, because these were in advance of the fashion of the day; and when this fashion rolled onwards beyond his deliberately formed convictions, he was censured as a renegade for simply adhering to what he had always professed.

Many a pleasant hour I spent with William and Mary Howitt at their Highgate home. She was all and more than all the Mary Howitt of literature. At one time they were greatly interested in the subject of "Spiritualism." They had heard knockings on the table and wall unsought, and believed that the spirit of their son held communication with them. He had disappeared in Australia, and they had sorrowfully concluded he had died, but they knew not how. They told me it had given details; and that, travelling over a wide tract of country on horseback, he had been carried away by a torrent he was trying to ford. Every evening, sitting at a table, they believed that they conversed with him; they asking questions vocally, and he replying by taps. There can be no doubt of their veracity and full belief in the facts. But in after years they doubted the explanation of the phenomena and the rightfulness and utility of the practice, and so relinquished it altogether. In her Autobiography Mrs. Howitt says:—

> "With constant prayer for guidance we experimented at home—the teachings were often akin to Gospel truths; at other times more obviously emanations of evil. I was thankful for assurance of an invisible world, but resolved not to neglect any common duties for Spiritualism."

Some years after their decease, I received from their daughter at Innspruck a reply to some inquiries of mine, in which she said that her father had been regarded as a leading pioneer in a new reformation which was to usher in the triumphant reign of the Holy Spirit; but the anti-Christian views of some Spiritualists and of Theosophists pierced him to the core, and he became convinced that the spirits professing to be his two sons, Claude and Charlton, were emanations of evil in the form of angels of light. She added the following interesting evidence :—

"A fellow-believer in Spiritualism with my uncle, Dr. G. Howitt, wrote to my father saying that the spirits had solemnly predicted to him the death of Dr. Howitt on a certain day—say, July 17—ten days afterwards. On the 17th my parents, after reading the Bible and prayer, seated themselves at their indicator, and, their dear departed children annexing themselves, they inquired whether their uncle had arrived in the spirit land. With great piety and unction they answered in the affirmative, adding that they could not yet converse with him, for every soul entering the spirit land slept for some time, watched over by the spirits that loved it ; and that only gradually it awoke to a consciousness of its celestial surrounding. Evening by evening Claude and Charlton (the deceased sons) arrived to report the progress of their uncle's gradual awakening to the new and better existence. Finally, he himself came with them, and described joyously and piously his spiritual birth and present bliss. All these days, almost weeks, my parents were deeply affected and edified by their holy communications from their spirit-children and spirit-brother. You can, therefore, better imagine than I can write it the thrill of relief to their natural affections, coupled with an awful shock to their spiritual belief, when a letter arrived from Melbourne written by my uncle Godfrey, still in the flesh, after the portentous 17th July, and I may add he lived for a considerable period after his supposed death. When the pious spirits of Claude, Charlton, and Uncle Godfrey announced themselves on the evening of the day when the letter had arrived, and my much-grieved parents solemnly, in the name of God, called them to account, the spirits rudely, almost jocosely, averred the whole to be a hoax, and intimated that my parents had well deserved it for their credulity. From that date the habit of consulting their dear departed children was given up. It left a deep scar on both their souls.

"I ever remain, dear Mr. Hall, yours faithfully and, for auld lang syne, very gratefully,   "MARGARET HOWITT.

"P.S.—Thanks for Mr. White's 'Modern Spiritualism.' I have always entertained a high respect for a name familiar from the days when I lived with my parents at West Hill Lodge. I admire his persevering championship of the Word of God and his detestation of demonology My dear father never sat down to consult the spirits without first praying and reading the Bible. It was his daily companion, but to him it appeared to sanction these manifestations, as the second coming of Christ. The evil side was a terrible blow to him, and embittered his last days on earth. Mr. E. White unites himself with us in believing that apparitions of spiritual beings, coming uninvited by men, do not rank under the category of prohibited intrusions. Many such have occurred in past times, unless overwhelming testimony is to be rejected."

In 1872 I met Dean Ramsay, of Edinburgh, at breakfast at Mr. Gladstone's, when a very interesting conversation took place on the subject of interchange of pulpits. On the one side it was urged that this would much lessen the lamentable alienation between the various Churches; would promote as well as exhibit the true unity of all who believe in Christ, who join in the Apostles' Creed and the Lord's Prayer, and would lessen much of the alienation of the working classes. Mr. Gladstone considered that the Established clergy were under certain legal obligations, both of belief and practice, which would be inconsistent with the opening of their pulpits to preachers not pledged in the same manner. Moreover, the laity of the Church relied on those pledges so as to expect no other tenets from their pulpits than those to which those pulpits were restricted, and might object to other teachers on whose orthodoxy they could not so authoritatively rely. The conversation ceasing to be general, I found myself engaged in an unequal duel with the most accomplished debater of the day. I tried to reply by saying that the various orthodox Dissenting clergy preached for each other without any doubts or difficulties; that Methodists, Presbyterians, Baptists, Congregationalists, held firmly their various views on secondary and ecclesiastical questions, but that ordinary courtesy kept them from debating differences in pulpits devoted primarily to expounding doctrines common to them all—that each minister was responsible not alone for what he himself preached, but for the preacher who by his invitation was his representative—and that the only result was the strengthening and exhibition of catholicity. Of course, I felt, that though I advocated what to myself was the truth, yet I was no match for my opponent, who with the greatest possible courtesy listened to all I said.

This was the commencement of a very pleasant but brief friendship with the Dean, who wrote as follows (1872):—

"6, Queen's Gate, S.W.

"Dear and Rev. Sir,—I look back with much pleasure and much interest on the Premier's breakfast where we met. In the talk about exchange of pulpits I agreed with you—not with the P.M. But is he not a skilled talker? Oh dear, you would suppose he had all his chief time been a polemic rather than a politician. Few Prime Ministers could have talked like that—Disraeli could not, nor Palmerston, nor Wellington. To show how much I agree with you, I send you 20th edition of my "Scottish Reminiscences." You will see I take up the question in a small way. At page 316 you will see a discussion, but not a discussion conducted with the skill and acuteness of the talkers at breakfast on Thursday at Mr. Gladstone's. What a mind to embody, what a tongue to syllable forth the ideas which come under his mental inspection he has. I have known him well since he was quite a boy, and I have known him under very peculiar and trying circumstances. He is a sincere and true man. He is a faithful Christian man.

"If anything brings you to Edinburgh, come and see me—that is, if I am still there. But I have entered upon my fourscore. I am more and more convinced on the point you argued on Thursday.

"Believe me yours sincerely and truly,

"E. B. Ramsay."

"June 24th, 1872.

"Rev. and Dear Sir,—I should have accompanied you to Cheshunt with much pleasure, and I am gratified by your proposal—but, alas! to say nothing of other engagements, years and infirmities render such gratifications beyond my physical powers. I have all my life, and since in orders especially, taken an interest in Christian men not members of my own communion. I am proud to call Lyndsay Alexander a friend. He dedicated to me his nice work, 'Paul Preaching at Athens.' A dear friend of forty years I have in John Sheppard, of Frome, and Thomas Chalmers I was proud of as a friend of years—as a Scotsman and great and good man. I delivered a notice of him before the Royal Society of Edinburgh, and I have been chairman of the committee which is getting up a bronze commemorative statue. I remember long, long ago hearing of Lady Huntingdon's preachers. She *began*, I think, by having them exclusively of the Established Church and her own chaplains. Whitfield was one. I hope to see you again, and next time in Edinburgh.

"Yours very sincerely and truly,

"E. B. Ramsay."

"Dear Mr. Hall,—I have had a most kind *following up* of your proposal to attend the Cheshunt anniversary, but I have not the

R

physical strength to carry me through such a day as that must be. I am sorry, for I should have much enjoyed it. The additional invitation you will have been aware, is from Dr. Reynolds, and I am proud in this my *last* (?) visit to London to have made two such friends. I do venture to hope I may see you both under the roof of 23, Ainslie place, Edinburgh. I have a tie with Newman Hall which he knoweth not of. I lost a dear brother six months ago—Admiral Sir William Ramsay, K.C.B., a Christian man if there were ever one ; a man of benevolence and works of charity which had the testimony of all Scotland. He never missed his opportunity of hearing you preach in St. James's Hall. What a loss he was to me and what a loss for Christian edification I cannot say. Your volume of poems has been appreciated by my nieces, who have enjoyed it. Some things in it have specially pleased me, say dedicatory sonnet. But I need not specify where there is so much to edify and to console. I could not help feeling how strong a resemblance I could trace between the tone of the volume and what I had marked in the tone of the author's manner and conversation at Mr. Gladstone's. At least I should have been disappointed and surprised to find the poetry of the volume of a hard, stern, and exclusive caste. I return, please God, to Edinburgh on Friday.

" I am, with much respect,
" Yours sincerely,
" E. B. RAMSAY."

" Rev. Newman Hall."

" Edinburgh, July 3rd, 1873.

" I noticed your kind present of your charming verses ; I have not noticed to you the other, ' Come to Jesus.' I am an old man, and feel the effects of age upon mind and body. I am disturbed, I confess, sometimes in a manner most trying, on the subject of our approaching God as a friend and saviour—the perplexing questions of election and reprobation—the question of special grace through sacraments only, and of ordinary grace and favour through high ritual—daily, nay, hourly, prayers—frequent celebrations, etc. etc. Disturbed and anxious, your little book came home to my heart, when you say, ' Come to Jesus— come to Him personally, directly, as Adviser, Friend, Consoler, Comforter. It was good of Dean Hugh McNeil, in a sermon, ' Show thyself to the Priest'! Yes ; but let the Priest be himself, not merely his church or clergy. Show *thyself* to *himself.* Need I apologise for sending this vague hint ? I would not (after our meeting at Gladstone's) willingly suppose we were to think of each other no more.

" I am yours sincerely in Christ Jesus,
" E. B. RAMSAY."

It was my privilege during many years often to meet Samuel Morley in public and private intercourse. With delight he contributed money, time, and influence to the spread of the Gospel and all kinds of philanthropy. He is too widely known, the memory of him too fresh and fragrant, to need any detailed account from me. His personal kindness was great and generous. He was the first contributor to the building of our new " Christ Church."

I cannot omit reference to helpers within our church. First I mention John Bun Benn, the well-known clerk at Surrey Chapel—a veteran official when I came to London. Surrey Chapel was a " three-decker," but the " decks " ranged side by side, the pulpit in the middle, the prayer-desk on its right, and the clerk's on the left, sacred to Benn. He led the liturgical responses with an emphasis peculiar to himself, gave out the notices, and then, in a perfectly different and most solemn tone, announced the number of the hymn and of the tune. I cannot forget the gravity with which, at a Sunday service, as if pronouncing the fatal sentence, he exclaimed, " Hymn one hundred! Tune—Die John ! " (Dijon). In the evangelistic meetings following the sermon I often invited him to offer prayer, and worshippers of Christian culture and deepest piety might sometimes feel that the desk rivalled the pulpit.

He was secretary to our Band of Hope. Once, when Lord Shaftesbury was presiding in the church, Benn described how his grandfather became an abstainer. He, like the grandson, was a tailor. In his first engagement in London as a journeyman, he expressed admiration of a coat another man was braiding, and said he had never done that kind of work. Accepting the invitation to add a few stitches, he was greeted with the word " Pints ! " which meant giving a pint of beer to each of the men. Next day he was told that the foreman was a wonderful man, who could hold his leg in a pail of boiling water. This he declared impossible. " Will you bet pints ? " " Certainly." The boiling water was brought, the leg was immersed, but its owner did not cry out or wince. The leg was of cork ! " Pints " again ! Disgusted, grandfather took the pledge, and left London next day.

One Sunday Benn was missing from his post. I visited him next day. He was poorly, but quite hoped to resume his services the following Sunday. "But it was only in a dream." Humorously, he said he hoped he had not violated Sabbath rest by sitting on his bench mending a coat. We talked of the Sabbath of Heaven, and he promised me that, if he was called first, he would deliver to my father and mother my message of love, and tell Rowland Hill that we were diligently carrying on his work. After prayer, he opened the door for me, in hope of meeting again very soon. I went at once to our prayer-meeting, in the midst of which a note was brought to me, saying, "Our Brother Benn has just passed away." A large number of the congregation attended the funeral. At the entrance to the cemetery we removed the coffin from the hearse, that his friends might, with their own hands, carry it to the grave. My assistant minister, Mr. Grainger, and myself walked at the head followed by others two and two, holding two ends of pocket-handkerchiefs, singing favourite hymns of Brother Benn's, till we reached the grave, where, in "sure and certain hope of the resurrection to eternal life," we deposited the small body of which the great soul had been the temporary tenant, till we should again "join our cheerful songs with angels round the throne."

I have often felt that much more credit has been given me for various works of evangelisation and philanthropy than I deserved, because so much connected with my name was done by the agency of many zealous fellow-workers. Among these, during twenty years, was George Murphy (1856–1876). He had been a temperance missionary in Birmingham, strongly recommended by John Angell James, and became an Evangelist for the "Southwark and Lambeth Mission to Working Men." This name suggests the most fruitful of all the agencies connected with my Surrey Chapel pastorate—all praise to God, and deserved honour to His servant! He began his labours with us in June, 1856, conducting Sunday evening services in our Hawkstone Hall, Waterloo Road, preaching out of doors almost every Sunday evening during half the year, outside the Surrey Chapel and elsewhere, and visiting the sick. So many converts resulted from his labours that they desired he should become their pastor. With this we cordially

concurred at a church meeting, when ninety-four Surrey
Chapel members volunteered to join the 132 from Hawkstone
Hall Mission. We held a social tea meeting on December 16,
1866, and then commended to the blessing of the Great High
Priest and Bishop of souls these 226 believers, and recognised
as their pastor the Rev. George Murphy. I presided, and
delivered an address commending this indefatigable and richly
endowed minister of the Gospel to the combined sympathy
and co-operation of the whole church. Several pastors and
elders of the neighbourhood took part in this ordination
service, including my beloved elder, William Webb, hon.
secretary of the mission. The building to which they
migrated had been the chapel of the Rev., vulgarly known
in the district as "Sammy," Wells, the famous hyper-
Calvinist. The newly-formed church commenced their
regular services there on January 28, 1866, when I preached
a free salvation for all sinners in the afternoon, and the new
pastor preached morning and evening.

Murphy and his friends sometimes overlapped our older
institutions, and attracted some of our people to their services; but we rejoiced in them as helps, not hindrances—not
as invading our parish or diocese, but as co-operating with
us in one common war against the powers of evil.

The pastor of this new church habitually frequented the
prayer-meetings at Surrey Chapel, and interested us by
describing his work. His was essentially a working-men's
church. All his seven deacons were artisans. The sittings
were all open, expenses being met by voluntary offerings.
Murphy was emphatically the people's friend. He was an active
member of the London School Board from 1873 till his death.
He instituted adult educational classes, and promoted every
effort for the welfare of the "masses." Temperance, education,
improved dwellings, enlarged political privileges, had in him
an earnest advocate. The confidence the multitude felt in
George Murphy, his social and political sympathies, and the
various lectures given for their amusement and instruction,
attracted the populace to his ministry of the Gospel. His
labours at the Borough Road Church were united with a

variety of efforts in the Lambeth Baths, the rent of which was supplied by Mr. Samuel Morley. Here three times on Sunday religious services were held adapted for working-people, who were invited to come in any dress they preferred, to sit where and to leave when they liked.

He was the originator of exhibitions for the display of the productions of working-men. The first was held at his lecture-room, Hawkstone Hall, in the Waterloo Road. It was opened by the Prince of Wales, who was attended by the Archbishop of Canterbury, Lord Shaftesbury, and others. Amongst the articles exhibited were carvings, paintings and drawings, mechanical contrivances, and needlework by workmen's wives and daughters. As president, I had the honour of conducting the Prince over the exhibition and explaining some of the articles. Here his Royal Highness purchased Prince Albert Victor's first perambulator. At the opening of another similar show I had the honour of assisting to his carriage Lord Palmerston, then infirm with age—this being the last, I understand, of his public functions. On another occasion Mr. and Mrs. Gladstone visited the show, and afterwards asked me to bring some twenty representative workmen exhibitors to early dinner at their house.

In reply to an invitation to open the workmen's exhibition, Mr. Gladstone wrote:—

" 11, Carlton House Terrace,
" Feb. 13, '64.

" MY DEAR SIR,—I regret very much that the day and hour at which it is proposed to open the Industrial Exhibition will render it impossible for me to attend, as I must always reckon on its being necessary for me to be in my place at the commencement of public business in Parliament. I hope and presume the exhibition will support itself; but if aid should be necessary from others, I shall be happy to appear upon the list.

"Allow me to mention that it is our practice to see our friends at breakfast on Thursdays after Easter at ten, only begging the favour of a previous intimation ; and I shall be very glad if you will sometimes write to say you will give us the pleasure of your company.

" Yours faithfully, etc.,
" W. E. G."

" Carlton House Terrace,
" March 19, '64.

" MY DEAR SIR,—I went on Tuesday evening with my wife, having snatched an hour from the House of Commons, to the exhibition, and was sorry to find it closed.

"Would it be agreeable to you to send or bring to my house a few of the exhibitors on some day in Easter week, to see such things as I have? I should be glad to spend an hour or so with them. I have not much, but it would be well meant, and so they would take it. I should say from twelve to twenty of them. If you like this idea, I will ask you to call and settle details.   "Yours faithfully,

"W. E. GLADSTONE."

In accordance with this kind proposal, Mr. Murphy and myself brought about sixteen skilled artisans, who had contributed their own works, to Carlton House Terrace, where we were welcomed with great cordiality, and, after a hearty one-o'clock dinner of roast beef and plum pudding, were shown an interesting collection of curiosities, natural and artificial, by our host, who astonished our workmen by his thorough acquaintance with the work of sculptors, carpenters, gold- and silversmiths. Our friends were charmed with Mr. Gladstone's questions and answers, and his painstaking to enable them to understand and appreciate his varied and extensive collection. Mr. and Mrs. Gladstone evidently enjoyed the visit as much as their guests. Not a word of politics spoken.

The work at the Lambeth Baths well deserves to be regarded as a poor man's church. It was superintended during a quarter of a century by Murphy, the work comprising 3,650 meetings, with an aggregate attendance of above 2,000,000, and the taking of more than 23,000 pledges. The Baths were thus utilised from November till April every year every night in the week besides special meetings on Sunday; Saturdays, readings from newspapers, singing, and recitations, 2,000 working-people being present. These Saturday meetings were the first of the kind, and have been widely imitated, with most useful results in affording, on a leisure evening, recreation safer than the public-house.

One Saturday evening Murphy was all alive at a people's meeting; the next morning his congregation, waiting for him, were told that he was in heaven. Tens of thousands of people thronged the streets and the cemetery at the funeral of their friend. At the service I closed my address by reading a letter of warm appreciation and condolence from Mr. Gladstone to the widow.

Murphy was followed at Surrey Chapel by Benson, ever diligent in aiding the various works of the church and labouring for the poor. The Rev. V. Charlesworth was for several years our faithful and devoted assistant pastor, but his varied qualifications were the cause of our losing his services, for he was invited by Mr. Spurgeon to superintend his famous orphanage, where for many years he has enjoyed the full confidence of the managers and the love of the children. Mr. Spurgeon greatly respected and loved him.

During twenty years my assistant-pastor, Henry Grainger, has, with a friendship uninterrupted, aided me in all my work, and won the abiding respect and affection of rich and poor, old and young. I have had the loyal devotion of trustees and elders, who, during my thirty-eight years of pastorate, have comforted me by their sympathy, and carried out my plans by their counsel, prayers, and generous contributions.

David had pleasure in remembering the names of his mighty men who helped to win his victories—"Adino the Eznite, and after him was Eleazar, and after him was Shammah," and the rest—names little known now, but once honoured by many; so I take pleasure in the names of some "unknown, yet well-known," men and women, mighty in prayer and faith and love, battling with the sin and misery around us, and aiding to build a temple for God—such as Freeman, Rider, Ruck, Pigott, Hadland, Earl, Atley, Goodman, Dunning, Frederick, William Webb, Williams, Heffer, and many others, of whom the chief during the whole of my pastorate was senior elder, honorary secretary, collector of subscriptions, never weary in well-doing, honoured and beloved by all—William Webb.

Of these, Hadland was a teacher in our Hawkstone Sunday school fifty-nine years, including forty-eight as superintendent, and Earl fifty-three years; William West was the " veteran Sunday-school teacher" of whom I wrote a brief memoir, who was teacher in our school in Kent Street seventy years, during which he was superintendent fifty years—examples of " patient continuance in well-doing."

CHAPTER XVIII.

I THINK it will be easier for me, and more interesting to my readers, to put together most of my recollections of Mr. Gladstone and of our correspondence, rather than to scatter the records under their proper dates among all manner of topics.

I have recorded our first correspondence in reference to the American War. Of subsequent letters preserved, the earliest is one dated May 14th, 1864, in which he says :—

> "I thank you for the promised address (Chairman's of the Congregational Union) which I shall read with the utmost interest. Myself in profession at least, a somewhat stiff Churchman, I value beyond all price the concurrence of the great mass of Christians in those doctrines and propositions of religion which lie nearest the seat of life. And this description applies practically, though indirectly, to the question of the Sacred Volume. Many thanks for your reference to my speech. I have unwarily, it seems, set the Thames on fire. But I have great hopes that the Thames will, on reflection, perceive that he had no business or title at all to catch the flame, and will revert to his ordinary temperature accordingly.
>
> "I remain, with sincere regard,
> "Very faithfully yours,
> "W. E. GLADSTONE."

When Mr. Gladstone was Chancellor of the Exchequer the following incident was related to me by my friend, Sir Francis Crossley, told to him by the Rector of St. Martin's in the Fields, Trafalgar Square, whose church Mr. Gladstone attended. The rector had visited one of his parishioners, a street-sweeper, who was ill, and being asked if anyone had been to see him, replied, "Yes, Mr. Gladstone." "What Gladstone?" "Why, Mr. Gladstone himself. He often speaks to me at my crossing, and missing me, he asked my mate if I was ill, and where I lived, and so came to see me, and read Bible to me." Less busy and distinguished people may learn a lesson of personal service to the poor and suffering, equally impressive whether we agree or differ in political opinions.

At Wigan where I was preaching, my host told me that in the neighbourhood of Hawarden a young woman entered the train carefully carrying a bouquet of beautiful flowers. In response she said to my informant, " Mr. Gladstone has just given them to me. It is their custom that when a servant marries from their house she pays them a week's visit in turn. I was coming away from my visit when Mr. Gladstone came across the garden to wish me good-bye. He was carrying these flowers which he had been gathering, and when I admired them he asked if I loved flowers, and gave them to me."

My friend told me of another young woman he knew at Wigan. Her birthday was the same as Mr. Gladstone's, and she was working a book-mark for him. But she was far gone in consumption, and feared she might die before the birthday. So her doctor sent the little present, explaining its history to Mr. Gladstone, who at once wrote his thanks to the sick donor, and sent a fine bunch of grapes which he had himself cut for her.

In reply to an invitation to a conference breakfast on the subject of the University question came this reply :—

"Carlton House Terrace, February 4th, 1865.
" My DEAR SIR,—I much regret that I am obliged on account of the daily pressure of business to decline all invitations to breakfast out, or I should gladly have availed myself of your hospitality.

"No doubt there is much to consider in relation to the point which I placed before you. But I think there is little likelihood of any early recognition of a claim of persons other than the members of the Church to share in the governing bodies of the colleges at Oxford and Cambridge, a considerable number of which it is material to bear in mind, were founded by and for members of the Church of England only, since the period of the Reformation. However, I have no doubt you will obtain a careful and judicious consideration of the whole matter.

"Very faithfully yours,
"W. E. GLADSTONE."

"June 18th, 1865.

" I am much concerned about the Oxford tests. The announcement that the Dissenters will not consent to enter the University except on a footing of equality, which, abstractedly reasonable or not, means, I think, in practice two things : first, the removal of the guarantees for its definite religious teaching, and secondly a long adjournment of the settlement of the controversy. I cannot draw a distinction in principle between the exclusiveness of the University and the exclusiveness of the Established Church ; and I believe the day to be distant when England will consent to separate them. Both may in the abstract be infringements of religious equality ; but religious equality is, I think, a principle to be applied according to times and circumstances, and I confess very deep regret that when everything, except what is withheld for the sake of maintaining the religious character of this place, may probably be had, the policy of all or nothing should be pursued. However, in lamenting I do not presume to find fault, and am thankful to you for giving me the benefit of a most charitable construction.

"I am, my dear Sir,
"Faithfully yours, W. E. G."

In reply to representations I presumed to make respecting distress in the paper trade, arising from taking off the duty on foreign rags, while foreigners continued to tax British paper, Mr. Gladstone wrote :—

"March 10th, 1865.

"DEAR MR. NEWMAN HALL,—I have read the periodical you gave me with great interest. It is full of important information. I am obliged to believe that many persons engaged in the paper trade are suffering much distress. From the facts before us we learn that they export more British goods than they did, and that they import more material from abroad. The question is influenced by the results of the cotton scarcity ; but on the whole it seems far from proved that the *body* is in distress. But whether it be so or not, I myself and all my colleagues are equally desirous to use every effort in our power for improving their access to raw material of every kind. A good deal has already been effected, and I am glad to see that in the opinion of this journal more is likely to follow.

"Yours faithfully, etc."

In the old days of Surrey Chapel Mr. Gladstone met some friends of mine at tea in Rowland Hill's study at the "Surrey Parsonage," and was the last to leave. As he preferred to walk I had the privilege of his company to Carlton House Terrace. When crossing the old toll-bridge at Charing Cross, I stepped before him at the turn-stile to pay the fare, and said jocosely, "The Chancellor of the Exchequer owes me a ha'penny."

"Carlton House Terrace, Feb. 26, '66.

"MY DEAR SIR,—I am very sensible of the spirit of candour which has prompted your remarks on the Irish University question. With regard to the English one, as long as nothing is offered to those in possession but the successive breaking down of all the fences of the system both as to the universities and the colleges, my opinion is that little progress will be made. I do not well see how the question can be settled except it be by some composition agreed upon by moderate men on all sides. On the one hand, the present state of things is unsatisfactory and untenable. On the other hand, it is no unreasonable or immoderate demand on the part of parents belonging to the Church of England that, forming as they do at least nine-tenths, or some such proportion, of those who would, in any circumstances, send their children to Oxford or Cambridge, they shall have full security for the rearing of those children in the principles and practices of their religion. I cannot help thinking you will feel there is force in this. Indeed, I must say that when the subject was briefly mentioned during the pleasant evening at your house, a great spirit of equity was shown.

"Very faithfully yours,
"W. E. G."

One day, in conversation on education in the universities, I remember Mr. Gladstone saying that the best improvement would be to teach divinity students how to read the Bible, with allusion to the manner in which the greatest of books is often read in churches.

Mr. Gladstone on the Congregational Union and education :—

"September, 1866.

"Thanks for your most interesting letter. I am deeply concerned at Mr. Morley losing his seat, and I have written to him to say so. Please to remember our breakfasts on Thursdays at ten. I thank you for the (Congregational Union) address. It had not escaped my notice, and I have read it with much interest, and with sincere desire that subjects in themselves controversial may always be handled in as kindly a manner. We have to look forward to 1867 as an arduous year. May its issues all be ruled or overruled for good. What I feel myself *most* to require at this juncture is a perfect truthfulness and integrity of mind in relation both to the measure and the men. May it be given me."

"March 8, '67.

" I avail myself of a free moment to thank you for communications which have in no case passed without thankful if silent notice. The position of the Government with respect to reform does not mend, but my hopes of a good and not very remote issue are sanguine. What I feel myself *most* to require at this juncture is a perfect truthfulness and integrity of mind in relation both to the measure and the men. May it be given me. "Very faithfully yours, etc."

I wrote to Mr. Gladstone from New York respecting the great meeting of the Evangelical Alliance, and received the following reply:—

"Downing Street, January 11th, 1873.

"DEAR MR. NEWMAN HALL,—I am not, as you know, one of those who think any of us should make light of any matter of religion which we conceive to belong to its integrity or to tend to edification ; but I shall ever thankfully remember and endeavour to attach full weight to the wonderful unity of Christians in the central truths which have with-stood so many storms, and will, as I believe, outlive those which are still to blow, or are now blowing. "W. E. G."

June 26th, 1873.—Breakfast with Mr. and Mrs. Gladstone. I sat next Street, the architect of the Law Courts. Spoke to Mrs. Gladstone about the Shah of Persia, regretting that while he had been taken to see our army, navy, and opera, he was not taken to Westminster Abbey and to Spurgeon's tabernacle to see how multitudes come together for the worship of God, and not merely to see the Prince of Persia, reviews, and spec-tacles. Mrs. Gladstone acquiesced, and doubtless spoke of it to the Premier. She narrated several amusing anecdotes of the Shah. Conversation had turned on the City com-panies, their vast wealth, and methods of spending it; and that if they ceased to exist as corporations, their funds would be more usefully employed in such objects as training artisans than in feasting wealthy citizens. At noon Madame Neruda played exquisitely on the violin, to which the Premier, with closed eyes, was listening with delight. At three he was with the Queen at Windsor. I had met the Shah at a grand evening reception by the Lord Mayor, at Guildhall, and all I can remember is that from head to foot he was ablaze with diamonds. But there seemed no pity in his face.

Mr. Gladstone and Dr. Dale:—

"November 23rd, 1871.

"I thank you very much for Mr. Dale's letter, which I shall keep as one of the important documents of the education question. I see

Mr. Dale is alarmed about Ireland, but I believe in his candour and love of the golden rule; and I think he will not find reason to condemn us in the matter of Irish education. I wish I could see my way as well through the difficulties of the English question. My duty for the present is to watch and reflect."

"Downing Street, Oct. 30, '73.

"DEAR MR. NEWMAN HALL,—I have received the numbers of the *Tribune.* I had already read some reports of the meetings of the Evangelical Alliance, not only with the respect ever due to upright and fervent zeal, but with great sympathy, inasmuch as the object and spirit of the meeting seemed to be positive rather than polemical. Your kind gift will enable me further to extend my acquaintance with the proceedings. Your account of the reception given to the Queen's name is truly gratifying to us, and praiseworthy on the part of the Americans. It is a time of much heaving and stirring; none of us, I think, know what it will bring forth.

"Believe me, dear Mr. N. Hall,
"Very faithfully yours, W. E. G."

Reference to the Lincoln Tower of our new Christ Church :—

"July 17, '74.

"The memorial tower promises to be one of a beautiful and striking character, and I am sure that your own interest in the question of negro emancipation has well entitled you to all the interest and all the gratification which the work must afford you. I am at present overwhelmed, but shall be glad when the time arrives which may permit us to have another quiet and friendly conversation.

"W. E. G."

Mr. and Mrs. Gladstóne asked me to convey to the Negro Jubilee Singers an invitation to breakfast at Carlton House Terrace. This took place in the large drawing-room, where three round tables were arranged. The guests were placed alternately, coloured and white side by side. If I remember correctly the Duke of Argyll was present, with some other persons of distinction. The servants, of course, ministered to all alike. In conversation Mr. Gladstone seemed well versed in negro affairs. After breakfast the choir sang several of their pieces, both humorous and pathetic, Mr. Gladstone listening intently while receiving telegrams, etc. After a while he quietly left the room, and the next day we read that he had an audience of the Queen, and then went to his place at the opening of business in the House of Commons.

February 16th, 1875.—Mr. Gladstone honoured me with his company to spend the evening. Among other guests now passed away were the venerable missionary Moffat, Dale, Edward Baines, Sir Charles Reed, Henry Richard, Donald Fraser, Henry Allon, Baldwin Brown, Joshua Harrison, Henry and Russell Reynolds, H. Cosham, Edward Cecil, William M'Arthur, etc. Mr. Gladstone declined to take the chair arranged for the chief guest, and insisted on the venerable missionary occupying it. For two hours we discussed Papal decrees and Disestablishment. The chief topic was "Vaticanism," the theme of Mr. Gladstone's recent pamphlet. On this he and Rev. William Arthur, writer of "The Tongue of Fire," maintained a long, learned, and lively dialogue. Here the Premier, as seldom occurred, found his match. His courtesy and marked attention to every question and remark won all hearts. He seemed thoroughly acquainted with every topic discussed. In the name of my brethren, I thanked him for his presence, recognising his great public services, and reminding him of what he knew well—that Nonconformists asked for no advantages for themselves alone, but only for the nation; that they never asked nor would receive any that were exclusive; that they asked simply for religious equality in the interest both of the State and the Church. Dissenters regarded him with respect and affection, not because of theological identity, but of loyalty to the same Divine Head, which was a stronger bond of unity than agreement in forms. Mr. Gladstone, in reply, expressed with much emotion his gratitude for the kind appreciation by Nonconformists of his motives and public services, the confidence and kindness he had always received from them, and their desire to put the best construction on what he said and did. He could say nothing of the future; he had retired into more private life. He then asked that, as on a former occasion, we might have a hymn together. He heartily joined in singing four verses of "Sun of my soul." Then we had supper and general conversation. I took him into

my study, where he sat in my mother's chair. I introduced
to him my " Royal Friend, King Robert Bruce "—a fine collie,
who seemed to appreciate the honour of the Premier's pat.
Mr. Gladstone remained till midnight, talking chiefly about
Moody and Sankey. He listened with much interest to Dr.
Dale narrating how Moody, after bidding affectionate farewell
to his converts at Birmingham, said, " You are sorry to part;
but we must part. You would like to tell me this, one by
one. Now, if ever you think of leaving Jesus, go alone with
Him, and tell Him that, though you don't forget what He has
done for you, yet you have resolved to leave Him, and go to
the world. Could you *thus* leave Him ? " Sir Edward Baines
wrote afterwards, saying, " What a charming conference we
had at your house with Gladstone. It was an historic evening."

We had conversed on the subject of eternal life bestowed
on believers through the life of the Lord Jesus. I had mentioned my dear friend Edward White's book on the subject.
On a postcard he asked for the title of it. I think I forwarded my own copy. From Mr. Gladstone's great work of
notes on Butler it is evident he had given much consideration
to this subject.

In reply to a suggestion that Mr. G. would write a hymn
which might identify him with the worship of all the Churches,
he replied on a postcard :—

"Your request is most kind and acceptable. But I am concerned
to say my answer is *nil*. The gift is a high and peculiar one, and is not,
I fear, in my possession. I hope you will announce yourself for breakfast on some Thursday at Harley Street.
"March 21, '76."

On a previous page I have alluded to an interesting
discussion with Mr. Gladstone, Dean Ramsay, and myself
on pulpit interchange.

From a letter by Mr. Gladstone dated October 12th,
1876 :—

"With lively pleasure I witness from day to day the exertions made
by the Nonconformists in the cause of humanity and justice for the
East ; while the clergy (though I must say in this matter they have
been well led by many of their Bishops) seem to be much divided, some
going with Dr. Liddon, some dumb, and some—Low Churchmen, too—

denouncing ' sentiment ' in the matter ; a denunciation of which we all know the meaning.

" I thank you for your explanation about the Blackheath meeting ; but be assured no explanation from you on such matters can ever be needed *for me.* I was disappointed at not hearing you, but was sure you had a good reason, and it was an act of self-denial on your part.

" The ' Upper Ten Thousand ' and their organs are working hard for Turkey. Unhappily that on any one great occasion—Reform, Emancipation, Free Trade, Irish Church, Irish Land, Italy, or any other, less than a minority of that body has been found to sustain in its day of difficulty the cause which, long after, all admit to have been right.

" W. E. G."

February 20th, 1877.—Breakfasted at Mr. Gladstone's, at Carlton House Terrace, with Lord Lyttelton and the newly appointed Governor of Fiji, and others. Conversed on Papal claims. Mr. Gladstone indignant at the decree that all marriages not celebrated by the Roman Church are held to be invalid, so that anyone married otherwise might, by professing to be a Catholic, be married again. He had called it " monstrous," but the proper term would be " wicked." Speaking to myself, he said solemnly, " I desire that every word " (in his work on Papal decrees) "shall be *within* the line of exact truth, and that I may not by heat of controversy say anything I might regret." We talked a little of the " eastward position," and I referred to the practice in the Lutheran Church I had witnessed in Norway, when it was explained to me that in that service the Pastor was one of the people and so turned in the same direction. Mr. G. said that was reasonable. Lord L. said, " No! the people are to hear what is said, and how can that be if the speaker turns his face away ? "

July 6th, 1877.—Mr. Gladstone spent the evening at my house, Hampstead. About fifty gentlemen to meet him—till 11.30. General conversation on the Eastern question, and various opinions. We might be led by our Government to annex Egypt in some form. This might alienate France—might lead to war—our empire was already too large—large empires were in danger from lack of brain-power to manage—as businesses might overgrow capacity—we should be responsible for no more than we can properly and consistently control. The

8

opinion of the Continent was that we were drifting towards war. The last blow of Turkey had been delivered in Montenegro, which was now safe. Zeal for Irish Church Establishment was in great degree not for religion but for ascendancy. Parties within the Church of England were hastening disestablishment. It was unwise to institute legal proceedings against ritualism—this would excite the sympathy of the laity, who did not care about the ritualistic practices. As long as there was an Established Church he considered it was an advantage and not a detriment that the House of Commons was composed of members of different religious views.

Amongst others present were Sir W. M'Arthur, M.P., Sir H. Havelock, M.P., Sam. Watts, George White, Henry Bompas, Q.C. (now Justice), Baldwin Brown, Edward White.

Extract from letter touching upon Greece :—

"November 17th, 1877.

"I fear the people of the Hellenic provinces will suffer for the follies of their leaders. Those leaders have done everything in their power to damage the Slavs and Russia. Who can expect that Russia, which can in no case have strength to spare, will weight herself with provisions on their behalf? All her promises, you will observe, are to the Slavs. I do not see that any of the other Powers care a rush for the Greeks. And yet I do not believe that the people are to blame, but the leaders grievously. Meantime let none of us forget the poor Easterns, either in prayer or otherwise."

Extract from letter :—

"Hawarden, January 3rd, 1878.

"I need hardly say I am not surprised at finding you both staunch and active at this crisis. The upshot is that while I am resolved to do my utmost against war or what tends to war, I am desirous not to act until the indications are such as to give proximate cause for alarm. But constant vigilance is necessary, and I do not see that meetings for neutrality, where desired, can do harm. We can have no rest as long as Lord Beaconsfield is Prime Minister and the Eastern question open."

"February 23rd, 1878.

"Our struggle in the Eastern question is not yet over. Hope predominates in my mind over fear, thankfulness over both, for the slavery broken down cannot be set up again. But there is something terrible in that mixture of levity, indifference, and positive appetite, with which some of our countrymen, who ought to know better, dally with the idea of a causeless war."

June 2nd, 1878, Whitsunday.—Christ Church. Mr. Gladstone quite unexpectedly and uninvited entered with the general congregation unrecognised. He took vocal part in all the responses and hymns. My text was Acts i. 8, " Ye shall receive power, after that the Holy Ghost is come upon you: and ye shall be witnesses unto me." I said that the disciples, by the gift of the Holy Spirit at Pentecost, were qualified to bear witness for Christ many years prior to the existence of the New Testament Scriptures ; in that sense the Church witnessed prior to the Book, which was written to confirm the testimony already given; and that all who shared the gift were bound to fulfil the obligation, viz. by their confession of Christ, their zealous testimony, their holy lives, to be witnesses, " martyrs " if need be, for Jesus. Every Christian a witness ; if not a witness is it possible to be a Christian? I had no thoughts of the bearing of my argument on the question of Church authority, but only on the present duty of every individual to fulfil his personal responsibility, " Ye shall be witnesses unto me." To this Mr. Gladstone referred in conversation at his house a few days afterwards.

June 13th, 1878.—Breakfast at Harley Street. Dean Church, Freeman the historian, the Editor of *North American Review.* For an hour and a half Mr. Gladstone spoke almost continuously, pouring out in eloquent language opinions on various topics, with such vivacity, emotion, variety of tone and manner, that I was entranced. His memory of facts, dates, and persons was remarkable. In my own poor language I recall, according to my best recollection, some of his sentiments.

" In proportion to the House of Commons, the House of Lords has more men of culture and ability ; but it is averse to work and does it carelessly. It legislates in favour of *classes* rather than of the *nation,* and originates little for the people's welfare."—" *But is not a drag on the wheel useful when going down hill ?* " " But the coach of reform is going uphill, which is hard work and wants *helping* not *hindering."* " *But is not the House of Lords useful in preventing too hasty legislation, and so preparing the nation for the change ?* "

"That has been already done. Great questions are agitated throughout the land and discussed in Parliament, so that there is no need of further delay. Tell me, if you can, what good measure during fifty years has the House of Lords ever originated ? What has it not sought to hinder? It only passes great reforms when the nation has been fully roused, and they yield to the irresistible. All great measures of improvement have been carried in the House of Lords in the *wake* of some great national excitement. Thus after the Irish Disestablishment the Irish Land Tax," etc., etc. Mr. F., "*But a House of Lords saves us from a nobility !*" "You speak enigmatically, explain!" Mr. F., "*Our aristocracy is condensed in the Peerage, others are actually commoners. In other countries there is a vast noblesse with special privileges, and our House of Lords saves us from this.*" American Editor: "Americans admire your House of Lords as giving dignity and stability, preserving from many abuses prevalent in America." Mr. Gladstone : "Don't misunderstand me. Mr. Ruskin some time ago seemed alarmed lest I should become a leveller, and was pleased when I coined a word to express my opinion. I said I was an 'INEQUALITARIAN.' I believe more and more in HEREDITY. Qualities are inherited. The aristocracy spring from people, who, good or bad, were mostly men of *power*. This they inherit, and with wealth, leisure, and culture, no wonder superior faculties are developed, and may be very influential for good or bad. But as a rule the House of Lords upholds class and not national interests." I understood him to mean that there is an inequality in aristocracy, not confined to the Peerage. "How is it that Bishops in the House of Lords do not exercise more influence there?" Mr. G. : "They may not have as much *learning* as Bishops of a former age, but on the whole are better men and administrators. The claims of their dioceses keep them away. They do not feel much interest in the proceedings." The Dean : "*They think the Peers regard them as of a lower caste— not regular Peers, and so they abstain from debating, except the Primate.*" Mr. G. : "I asked a popular Bishop why he did not speak on this Eastern question, and he said the atmosphere was so chilling he could not contend against it. The Bishops are not so united as they were, and so their Bench loses influence."

Of emancipation Mr. Gladstone thought " the results in our empire inferior to those in the United States." He had predicted that good results could not be expected from freedom obtained by war, but he confessed he was mistaken. The negroes were more industrious in the United States of America than Jamaica, and could be entrusted with political privileges which we could not safely grant to our own free blacks. The American editor spoke of their inferiority as a race, at the best not rising above mediocrity and without organising power.

To myself Mr. Gladstone said afterwards : " At your church the other Sunday evening, I so admired the playing of your organist (Mr. Edwards), so practical, not to display self or instrument, but to promote worship. Let me also say I admired your boldness in stating that the Bible must be tested by it practical effects, and that it was not intended to teach science, and that discrepancies between its language and modern discoveries did not weaken its testimony to God, salvation, and righteousness."

It was mentioned that all the plenipotentiaries at the Congress opening that day spoke French except Beaconsfield, and Mr. Gladstone repeated as a joke a reported saying of his —" *Le tabac ! est le tombeau de le mot.*"

July 12th, 1882.—In the morning casually met Bright in the street, Camden Town. He seemed very depressed about public affairs. He greatly objected to our going to war in Egypt, and obscurely hinted that he might feel obliged to retire from the Cabinet if the Government decided to interfere by force of arms. I was grieved that an absolute engagement made me decline his earnest desire that I should accompany him to his rooms.

That Wednesday afternoon news reached Government of the fateful step being taken by the bombardment of Alexandria. Before it was publicly known I went to the House of Commons, where a debate was going on about Irish rents. To Gladstone, earnestly listening, a despatch-box was brought, which he eagerly opened, and while attentively reading a letter, started up suddenly, and turned to Mr. Shaw, member for Cork, who was then addressing the House : "I beg the hon. member's pardon, but what I said was so-and-so." Then, sitting down, he resumed his examination of despatch papers. I had noticed his eager attention to these, yet he was evidently conscious of all Mr. Shaw was saying, and ready to reply. When the House was about to rise I left, and, walking near the arcade outside, saw, seated in her victoria, Mrs. Gladstone, who beckoned me to her. After kind greeting, I said there were many who prayed for Mr. Gladstone in these circum-stances of anxiety. Just then he hurriedly came up from the inner court, holding papers. I instantly backed, just raising my hat to him, who abstractedly returned the salute and was driven rapidly away. I deprived myself of the privilege of a hand-shake in consideration of the Premier's evident anxiety and haste. I afterwards somewhat regretted my self-abnega-tion, though pleased, under special circumstances, with his wife's marked kindness. Next morning my surprise was great at receiving a letter directed in Mr. Gladstone's own handwriting, with his signature on the envelope. The letter is as follows :—

"Downing Street, 12 July, 1882.

"DEAR MR. NEWMAN HALL,—How rude you must have thought me ! My sight gets weak, especially in recognition. I was in a great hurry, and rather avoided personal inspection ; but had I seen who it was, I should not have failed in greeting, and asking how you did in these anxious and oppressive times. Pray, forgive me.

"Faithfully yours,

"W. E. G."

Astonishing that with all the cares of State, especially this very day, he took pains, by a letter in his own hand, to prevent my being pained by so trifling a circumstance—a striking illustration of character. So great a man, yet so mindful of small courtesies to small people ! I replied thus :—

"Hampstead, July 14, '82.

"HONOURED AND DEAR SIR,—I cannot express the feelings excited by the considerate kindness of your letter, which I shall always treasure.

But the explanation was quite needless. I purposely withdrew at such a time, lest by your courtesy I might possibly be the occasion of detaining you even for a moment. I must confess, however, that afterwards I felt some selfish regret that I had missed so great a pleasure. Under the circumstances of the day, the Prime Minister might pass without recognising the highest in the land, much more so humble a person as myself, who, however, yields to none in affectionate reverence, or in deep sympathy with you in the anxiety and pain caused by the events of the last few months, and more especially by this Egyptian trouble. Permit me to assure you that your old friends, the Noncons., have unabated confidence—that whatever can be done consistently with the honour and safety of the empire will continue to be done both at home and abroad, in the interests of peace and freedom. Not less than others on whom the authorised form is incumbent do they pray, both in public and private, for "the Lords of the Council," and especially for him on whom rest the chief toil and responsibility.

"I remain, honoured and dear Sir,

"Yours most respectfully, N. H."

In a letter inviting Mr. Gladstone to my house, naming several days for selection, I enclosed a card for reply, and, to save his time, I asked him simply to fill up or erase one word. The card I sent was :—

"Convenient."

"Not convenient."

The card returned to me had the "Not convenient" crossed through, with this added in very small letters—

"With thanks.—W. E. G. July 8."

One morning my friend Dr. Cuyler went with me to breakfast at Mr. Gladstone's, when several eminent Episcopalians were present, and the question debated was "Reform in the Church of England." Some urged that this was necessary to avoid disestablishment; others that reform could not be effected without it. Dr. Cuyler told of a woman in America who, on her death-bed, begged her husband to remember certain necessary improvements : A new pane of glass in a certain room ; a fresh carpet in another; their little boy to go earlier to school, etc. etc. ; to each of which he promised attention, but at length, wearied with so many pieces of advice, he said, "Yes, yes, my dear, but get along with your deeing!" Mr. Gladstone's laugh was the heartiest in the company.

So fascinated was I by Mr. Gladstone's oratory that one Wednesday I left my study to hear his great oration at Birmingham. I was in the crowd which welcomed his arrival, and was near him when he spoke for nearly two hours. It was a mental inspiration quite equivalent to the proverbial "midnight oil"; and I secured several hours of sound sleep prior to my usual duties.

June 7th, 1874.—Breakfast at Gladstone's, Harley Street. Prebendary Irons (Rev. Irons from Servia). Memories of Gladstone's table talk :—

"Great physical effort at Birmingham—unfavourable to thought and expression—never addressed so many—Bingley Hall good for demonstration, but too large for effective speaking—need to watch Government lest involved in war with Russia—the romantic interest is in Montenegro —200,000 inhabitants—resisting Russia 300 years—longevity—knew of seven generations living together under one roof—the eldest 107 (or 117 ?), youngest two years—very tall—live on oatmeal—scarcely any meat—we used them in war with Napoleon, and forgot them in treaty of peace—bravery—in battle each man often killed his Turk—no commissariat—wives carried food to husbands day by day—domestic virtue —atrocious that the Pope ordered prayer for success of Turkey—laity of Armenia demanded ancient right to elect their bishops—Pope refused and sent his own — people refused and held the churches — Pope covenanted that if the Turkish Government handed over to him the buildings, he would advocate cause of Mohammed against schismatic Christians—about jokes in the House of Commons—weariness at poor speeches—disposed, as a relief, to welcome poor jokes—Horsman's were got up beforehand—best retort he knew was by Lord John Russell— Burdett had turned off to the Tory side on some occasion and denounced as the worst kind of cant, the cant of patriotism. Lord John Russell in reply said, ' I also hate cant, but I disagree with the hon. baronet when he says the worst kind is the cant of patriotism—there is one worse : the re-cant of patriotism.' The conversation turned to the wit of London boys. He spoke of a tall friend to whom a boy exclaimed, ' I say, old fellow, if you was to tumble you'd be half way home.' I told of a shoe-blacking boy near the Westminster Clock Tower. Looking up to it, I said it had lost time. The boy responded, ' O, there ain't no go in that there 'ouse.' Mr. G. gave me his pamphlet on Montenegro, and promised to spend the evening of Friday, July 6th, at my house."

On the publication of my volume on the Lord's Prayer, I

forwarded one of the first copies to Mr. Gladstone, who replied as follows:—

"Hawarden Castle, December 11th, 1883.
"I thank you much for your note and for the volume. On its arrival I read the first chapter and thought that you had there stated the arguments *pro* and *con.* between form and no form with impartiality as well as with care and ability. I remember hearing extempore prayer used with excellent effect in a parish church in Naples. The preacher worked up his people by a feeling sermon, and then ended it by praying in accordance with it from the pulpit.

"Very faithfully yours,
"W. E. G."

I spoke at several meetings protesting against war against the Arabs in the Soudan and wrote with respectful urgency to Mr. Gladstone, who thus replied:—

"Downing Street, February 24, 1885.
"DEAR SIR,—I am desired by Mr. Gladstone to thank you for your letter of the 21st, and to say that he values highly your kind words and the good will of your community. He notes what you say as to their feelings in respect to the Soudan, and it is painful to him to find himself under the necessity of doing anything which is not in harmony with the views and principles which they apply to the consideration of these important matters. "Yours faithfully,

"H. W. PRIMROSE."

To W. E. G.—Home Rule :—

"January 21st, 1886.
"MY DEAR SIR,—I asked your indulgence for expressing the very deep regret with which some of your most devoted friends have been unable to accept your Irish policy. Speaking for myself alone I may say that though I read all you spoke and wrote with a very strong bias in favour of whatever you might propose, it has been a daily grief to be still unconvinced. This result may arise from my own ignorance or misconception. I am convinced that all Nonconformists are anxious to grant to Ireland the redress of every wrong, and allow her every facility for regulating her internal affairs, subject to the supreme authority of the Imperial Parliament of a united Empire. If on your return you should feel disposed to gratify some of your most devoted friends who wish to have their difficulties removed, I shall feel it an honour to make the necessary arrangements as on former occasions.

"Most faithfully and respectfully, N. H."

This proposal Mr. Gladstone courteously declined on the ground of pressure of engagements, and his hopelessness of any good result of such a conference at the present time.

In a letter of mine in 1880 I referred to a newspaper

article seeming to require some explanation, and offering to give it. Having received no reply I thought my letter had miscarried, and I wrote again repeating my offer, and received a very satisfactory reply, from which I quote:—

"Carlton House Terrace, August 19th, 1886.

"DEAR MR. NEWMAN HALL,—My intercourse even with my oldest and closest friends, has from the immense pressure of my occupations, and from the growth also of years, been extremely intermittent and even shadowy, except in cases when public duty brought them across my path. Hence, perhaps, may sometimes have arisen the appearance of an indifference which I did not really feel. . . I can most truly say that I never attached the smallest credence to any imputation on you, or believed you capable of any act at variance with a Christian or a pastoral character. I hope that this explicit statement may efface from your mind any shade of misgiving, and I remain, with best wishes and sincere respect,

"Most faithfully yours,
"W. E. GLADSTONE."

June 16th, 1887.—Mr. and Mrs. Gladstone at Dollis Hill. Garden party—Lord and Lady Aberdeen. Missionary convention. Many American friends. Syrian bishop from Smyrna. Met Shaw Lefevre, M.P., T. B. Potter, M.P., Sir C. Foster, M.P., Queen of Hawaii, some Indian magnates, and others. Spoke to two domestics at the tea-table, who smiled recognition, and said they always attended my church when staying in Downing Street, in company with an elderly lady who had lived with the Gladstones fifty years. I had a quiet opportunity of speaking to them spiritually. They said they had enjoyed my ministry. One was the housekeeper. From Jaffa I had sent anonymously a large case of Jaffa oranges. Speaking of oranges, she said they had once received a case from the East, and had wondered who sent them. "How good they were!" I did not gratify her curiosity. Long chat with Mr. Gladstone in drawing-room. I said that though I grieved at inability to agree with his Irish policy, I honoured his motives. I suggested that it would be difficult to pass for all the Irish a measure against which one-third protested. He said the minority did not exceed 600,000, and these of the Orange faction. But did not the majority belong to the opposite faction? Will the Irish party be contented

with such local government as that of England? No—
this would not be granting management of her own local
affairs. Then Local Government in Ireland means more than
in England. If this includes Imperial matters, those who
insist on Imperial unity are repelled; if not, then Parnell and
his dynamite allies revolt. This is only a hasty record of
a long conversation, and may not be verbally accurate. I
said our personal regard for him was no less than when we
agreed with him more fully. He said he was very desirous
that Allon, Dale, White, Spurgeon, and others agreed with
him. I said, " May God spare your life to become leader of
the united Liberal party and settle Ireland." He replied, " This
is farther off than ever. I've made every possible advance
without recognition." He spoke under great emotion. I
told him I had recently recognised a correct natural profile
of him on the upper part of the Acropolis from Schliemann's
housetop.

" Hawarden Castle, June 22nd, 1887.

" DEAR MR. N. HALL,—I thank you for your kind and considerate
letter. Naturally I have observed and lamented that want of active
support from the Nonconforming Ministry on the great Irish question,
of which you supply a new indication. I am not sure that a meeting
such as you are good enough to propose, offers the precise way in which
it is now requisite for me to proceed. I have been too much in the front,
and such a meeting still keeps me there. My desire is to recede and leave
the question, under God, to the teachings of reflection and experience.
I think that what is called the People, in a proper sense, is on the side
I have taken; nay, that the polls at the last election prove it, when
we consider the immense number of votes that are under influences, the
proportions in which that influence is divided, and also the powerful
effect of plural voting. When I consider what England—my Scotch
blood makes me happy to add, ' not Scotland '—has been to Ireland for
nearly the whole of seven hundred years.

" Most faithfully yours,
" W. E. G.

" April 15, '88.

" DEAR MR. NEWMAN HALL,—I will pass over some questions
relating to the Irish policy to discharge the more agreeable office of
thanking you for the great and generous indulgence with which you
have treated my character and conduct generally. You say, however,
that you are in favour of some safe scheme of Home Rule. But on the
day before you wrote, Mr. Smith announced in the House of Commons
that not even any measure of Local Government could be extended to

Ireland until the Irish people had shown that they would use it in a loyal and constitutional manner. This declaration is the severest trial yet imposed upon Liberal Unionism by the ministers, its despotic masters. With many thanks.

"Most faithfully yours,

"W. E. G."

On occasion of the Handel Festival in the Crystal Palace, I was walking in the rear of Mr. and Mrs. Gladstone as they went out during the interval, and saw two ladies fashionably attired go up behind him, one of whom hissed in his ear. On returning to our seats I happened to be near them, and heard one exultingly say to her companion, "Didn't I hiss in his ear?" In my clearest, loudest tones I said, "And you should be ashamed of yourself, madam, whatever your politics, for daring thus to insult a man of whom the whole nation should be proud."

On Mr. Gladstone's birthday at this time I wrote a congratulatory note, "in the prayerful hope that a life so precious might be spared to lead a united Liberal party in establishing the unity of the empire on the permanent basis of the true welfare and loyal contentment of every part of it; and also to be instrumental in the fulfilment of the prayer, 'Give peace in our time, O Lord!'"

To Mrs. Gladstone, on her golden wedding :—

"July 25, '89.

"MY DEAR MADAM,—Permit me to blend my respectful and heartfelt congratulations with those of multitudes. The occasion of your golden wedding permits the expression of what I have long felt in reference to a domestic love as beautiful as the public life is illustrious. On such a day the wife of the foremost man of the age may well be congratulated, and also the husband in having a wife worthy of himself —companion, counsellor, and friend. It is well for the world to see that the most arduous labours of the Statesman are consistent with all the tender assiduities of conjugal affection, and that the most public and absorbing functions may be blended with the most sacred enjoyments of home. May you be spared to enjoy together many such anniversaries in preparation for the life to come, when all that is pure and precious here will have its full development, with no change but progression, and no fear of ending.

"I remain, honoured Madam,

"Yours very respectfully,

"NEWMAN HALL."

To W. E. G., for birthday, 1890 :—

"DEAR SIR,—I cannot fully express my congratulations and desires. Those who cannot at present coincide with all your political *methods*, possibly through misunderstanding them, deeply lament such inability and none the less reverence the purity of the motives and generosity of the sentiments which now, as in the past, prompt every action and purpose. Each year added to your honoured life increases the nation's debt, and by divine grace matures meetness for the perfected life in which blessedness blends with service.

"I remain, with respectful affection, etc."

To W. E. Gladstone, on Sunday closing :—

"Feb. 24, '91.

"Having been during fifty years actively engaged in promoting sobriety among the people, I know how greatly the opening of public-houses on Sunday encourages the chief cause of the pauperism, crime, and irreligion which disgrace our nation. I do not ask legislation to promote church interests, but Sunday closing seems to be demanded by justice—justice to other trades, whose shops are closed, though drink-shops are open when working-men have most cash to spend, most leisure, and most temptations, so that the privileged trade unfairly deprives other and useful industries of their due proportion of custom; justice to the families of the men whose drinking on Sunday, just after receiving their wages, deprives them of many of the comforts and even necessaries of life; justice to those employed in the trade, who need and would rejoice in obtaining a day of rest—the only losers being the rich brewers; justice to the ratepayers, whose taxes are considerably increased by Sunday drinking; justice to philanthropists, whose efforts are thus impeded. I heard a man say last Sunday at a meeting of artisans, 'We want the nation to be entirely wise. We are almost so, Wales is, Ireland is, Scotland is. We now want to be altogether wise.' Pardon this expression of the hope of multitudes that you will feel able to support the Sunday Closing Bill, etc. etc."

To this Mr. Gladstone replied on a postcard :—

"I have voted for all the Sunday Closing Bills, and I constantly supported the Irish one which was fiercely opposed. I shall be very sorry indeed should I be obliged to alter my course. I hope not."

December 29th, 1891.—In reply to a letter of birthday congratulation, with a copy of Prof. George Adam Smith's "Isaiah," I received the following reply:—

"Jan. 2, 1892.

"It is, indeed, extremely kind of you to repeat your former kind-nesses, and not only to write to me on my birthday, but to minister to my mental sustenance by sending me the work of Mr. Smith. The anniversary, always a solemn thing at my advanced age, suggests much that you can hardly put on paper. The work of Mr. S. is already known to me by repute and citation, and I hope at once to make myself better acquainted with it. Viewing it from outside and without authority, I expect to find it less affirmative than I should be inclined to desire ; but I am aware of the high eulogies it has received from persons to whose opinions their special studies largely give weight.

"I remain, with reciprocal good wishes,

"Faithfully yours,

"W. E. G."

This letter I felt bound to deliver to the learned expositor—the only one from Mr. Gladstone which I have not carefully treasured for myself.

To W. E. G. :—

"1892.

"Sympathy results from community in motive more than from identity in method. My earnest prayer is that the great aim of your life may be realised—the glory of God in the welfare of the nation and of every part of it. That in your most high position you may be instrumental in this, may He sustain your strength amid accumulated cares and toils.

"With great respect, etc., N. H."

September 15th, 1892.—Gladstone at Barmouth. I was invited to join the reception committee, and wore a rosette. It was pleasant to be the first he recognised on leaving the car. To Mrs. Gladstone I presented a large bunch of heather I had just gathered, and said, "The hills of Wales salute you," which she received very graciously. Both seemed very pleased to meet me, though increasingly and sorrowfully opposed to his measure of Home Rule. I stood near him on the hotel platform as he spoke for thirty minutes with great fascination on the country and people of Wales and his early connection with it. Mrs. Gladstone frequently waved my bunch of heather After speaking, he entered the hotel, and in five minutes reappeared in altered costume, sat in the bow-window opening letters, while a secretary read telegrams, and Mrs. Gladstone tossed a grandchild in her arms, 2,000 people looking on from the adjacent sands, he absorbed, sitting half-turned towards them. Two days after, I left my card and my new book, "Divine Brotherhood," having written on the cover "No acknowledgment"; but at once he sent a note of thanks, saying he hoped to look into it next day (Sunday). What a wonderful man for attention to little things, while so abundant and diligent in the greatest!

To the Right Hon. W. E. Gladstone, on his 86th birthday:—

"December 29th, 1895.

"MOST HONOURED AND DEAR SIR,—Honoured and dear inversely to the rarity of my expression of a prayer that a life so dear to the home and so precious to the world may be spared to enjoy many 'happy returns.' There is seldom a day when my best thoughts do not mingle with your name; and now my heart aches with yours in contemplating six great Christian Powers, through mutual jealousies and mistrust, looking on helplessly while the roaring lion is hourly watching to mangle and devour an ancient race, who celebrate the same Christmas with ourselves, but look to us in vain for rescue. In my 80th year I feel it an honour to be associated in the same decade. With increasing years, and nearness to the coming of our Lord, may we, spite of all mysteries, have confidence in the King, who shall 'rule in righteousness and break in pieces the oppressor,' and humbly but surely say, 'I know Him whom I have believed.' Permit me to congratulate you most heartily on the recovery of your 'angel of the house,' to present to her my most respectful and best New Year wishes, and to assure yourself of the increasing respect and affection of your humble but faithful friend.

"N. H."

My eightieth birthday: Mr. Gladstone's card to Rev. F. Hastings, convener and hon. secretary of the celebration:—

"May 21st, 1896.

MY DEAR SIR,—On the one hand I have received marked personal kindness from Dr. N. Hall; on the other have had the misfortune to differ from him seriously. Putting both these circumstances out of view, I cannot but rejoice that his prolonged and devoted labours on behalf of his religious profession should now receive the warm acknowledgment of his friends.

"Yours, etc., W. E. G."

Reply of N. H.:—

" . . The difference to which you allude so gracefully is one of plans alone, not principle; of method, not of motive; of the road, not of the goal. Nothing in my public life caused me such distress as my failure, after great effort, to agree with one whom I so reverence, and from whom I have received so much kindness. But this diversity of view has only emphasised true unity of heart. None of those who have zealously followed your lead in every particular, have sacrificed more in

this agreement than I have in this variation. May your life be yet
spared many years, the light of your home, the pride of your country,
the friend of the oppressed, and now, in this well-earned leisure the
vindicator of those foundation truths which unite all Christians, and
which will abide when all ecclesiastical disputes will be buried for ever
with Catholic hallelujahs and a universal Te Deum. I remain, with
profound respect, and permit me to add with warm Christian affection,
"N. H."

On our return from Italy in 1896 I sent Mr. Gladstone a
duplicate set of admirable photographs of the old Christian
churches in Ravenna, and received the following acknowledgment:—

"Penmaenmawr, October 29th, 1896.
"DEAR MR. NEWMAN HALL,—I have received those most interesting photographs with a mixture of pleasure and regret ; for, while they
are highly desirable to possess, I have certain misgivings upon the question whether I ought to deprive you of them. However, I can assure
you that they will be much appreciated, and they revive, with some
freshness, my recollection of a place, Ravenna, which I have not been
able to visit for 64 years. I thank you very much for your kindness. A
recollection not quite so old as the other, but yet of a mature age,
reminds me of having seen you, perhaps for the first time, on the hill
behind the village of Penmaenmawr. I hope your walking power holds
out better than mine (as no doubt it ought), and I remain, with every
good wish,   "Faithfully yours,
                  "W. E. GLADSTONE."

To this I replied, saying that I possessed duplicates now
much more valuable as being duplicates of those possessed by
himself, and thanking him for his kind remembrance of our
first meeting, which remembrance, of so trifling an incident
was as remarkable as my forgetfulness of it would have been.

May 9th, 1896.—To Dollis Hill, where Mr. Gladstone was
resting at Lord Aberdeen's. I took a copy of the most recent
photograph, asking his simple signature if not inconvenient.
It was soon brought back, the ink still wet, with a message
regretting medical order not at present to see any visitors. I
wrote expressing thanks and saying I called chiefly to report
with what enthusiasm a resolution had been passed at the
Congregational Union expressive of sympathy and prayer. I
thought that he would be interested by the evidence in the
chairman's annual address that our churches are faithful to

the gospel of a crucified Saviour, which alone can give peace to the individual, brotherhood to the race, and abiding impulse to all good works.

Wednesday, January 27th, 1897.—Gladstone was travelling to Cannes from Hawarden. I knew the platform at Euston would be crowded, so I went to Willesden Junction, where all trains stop for tickets. After waiting two hours the train drew up—no other person on the platform. I saw him leaning back in the corner of an ordinary carriage with Mrs. and Miss Gladstone. Mrs. Gladstone drew Mr. Gladstone's attention, who warmly shook hands. I said, " To avoid the crowd I came here in hope of greeting you and saying that my whole soul prays that the Peace of God may keep your heart and mind. I bless God for your glorious past, and still more glorious future." Mrs. Gladstone beamed with kindness as she gave me her hand, which I respectfully saluted. Another grasp of the veteran's hand and I closed the door, bowing " Farewell." I paced up and down till the train moved off, when I waved my hat, to which Mrs. Gladstone responded with her handkerchief.

W. E. G. looked far older than when we last met, at Barmouth, four years before. He seemed wearied with the journey. Though I might have enjoyed five minutes' conversation, I would not intrude beyond this greeting. I felt I should never speak to him again—he looked so very worn and haggard. What a marvel of learning, eloquence, statesmanship! what a history—what a loving and what a godly heart!

I sent copies of his letters to Mr. Gladstone, asking permission to use them in these Reminiscences, and received the following reply—his last to me—in somewhat trembling handwriting, six months before his decease:—

" Hawarden,
" November 13th, 1897.

" Dear Dr. Newman Hall,—Forgive my brevity, which is due to circumstances of health.

" You little know how sore a subject this of publication of my letters has been to me. There has been so much of it, that a wise friend admonished me I was undergoing *piecemeal* biography.

T

" The utmost I can agree to now is—

" 1. The publication of letters of mine which concern not myself but the person addressed.

" 2. Reference and general, not detailed, description of my letters at large (when not confidential).

" You will, I dare say, be able to give not only readable, but some-times important descriptions of the very interesting evening meetings which I have at various times attended under your roof.

" With all best wishes,

" Very faithfully yours,

" W. E. GLADSTONE."

I have endeavoured to observe these wishes of my honoured friend as if he were still with us.

To the Right Hon. W. E. Gladstone, on his eighty-eighth birthday, December 29th, 1897 :—

"MOST HONOURED AND DEAR MR. GLADSTONE,—Permit me to express my early thought and prayer this morning, that God may yet grant you many happy returns of the day, enjoyed together with the beloved and honoured life and heart companion of so many years. I cannot forget the great privilege I have occasionally enjoyed in your society, and some small share in your friendship. With countless others I unite in admiration of your genius, gratitude for your services, and sympathy in your unchanging love of justice, liberty, and progress.

" We are both advancing toward the limit of the present stage of human life ; but though in spheres far apart, we rejoice together in the full assurance of hope for the undying development of our life in Christ —when all that is pure and beautiful and good, and the best joys of friendship and love, of thought and action, will be glorified in the cloud-less light of Him we have tried to serve, whose grace we have rejoiced in, and in whose more immediate presence we shall experience ' fulness of joy ' in perfect obedience and unwearied service.

" I remain, honoured and dear Sir, with sincere affection,

" Most faithfully yours,

" NEWMAN HALL."

When Mr. Gladstone was rapidly declining, I wrote :—

" To MRS. GLADSTONE.

" HONOURED MADAM,—Every day during the last few months the illustrious sufferer has been in my sympathies and prayers. In thousands of our Free Churches as well as in those of the Establishment, such petitions are presented. If life may be measured by conscientious devotion to the welfare of mankind and the glory of God from youth to age : with unswerving trust in Christ, and years brightening by the nearness of the unending life of love and service, and of renewed intercourse with those whom death cannot sever—then the promise is indeed fulfilled : 'With long life will I satisfy him, and show him my salvation.' Though far behind in all else, I hope that the nearness of fourscore years and two may excuse this intrusion on your hours of mourning and anxiety. Relying on this, without response, I remain, honoured and dear Lady,

"Most respectfully, N. H.

" Hampstead, April 30th, 1898."

To William Ewart Gladstone, shortly before his decease:

"Now holdest thou converse alone with Him
Who reigns the King of Kings ! and fade away
The pomp of Courts and Powers thou hast known ;
They pass in vision and in vista dim.
Yea, nations who have waited for thy word,
While England's fiat was oft voiced by thee,
Great Leader eloquent of vast array ;
And nobles thou hast coroneted, grown
In statesmanship now grey. But thou hast heard
The herald-call to *rest.* By length of years
Is earth's frail cup of life filled to the brim,
And overflows into that boundless sea
Which laves God's Throne.
                    In sympathy and tears
All discords die—He Heaven's own music hears !"

HARRIET M. M. HALL.

To Mrs. Gladstone, on the death of her husband.

"June 1, 1898.

"HONOURED AND DEAR MADAM,—I have purposely delayed the expression of my ever-present sympathy. Beyond the innermost circle few have felt more deeply. I passed with the reverent multitude around the object of a nation's honour in Westminster Hall ; I stood close to the historic procession of princes and peasants in the Abbey ; I joined in the solemn hymns that arose from around the open grave ; and I spoke last Sunday in the Park, in the presence of a hundred thousand of the people ; but the one object indelibly fixed on my memory is the heroic widow who suppressed the exhibition of her agony to manifest to the end her true love, and to brave a heartless fashion. While praise is offered constantly for such a gift to the nation, prayer is also offered, fervent and tender, for the chief mourner. To those who are approaching the same age grief is allayed by the near hope of reunion in the presence and service of the Lord of Life."

CHAPTER XIX.

I HAVE filled several pages with memories of the greatest Statesman of the British Empire; I shall now refer to the greatest Preacher of the Church of Christ. This epithet has been questioned, other names have been mentioned as far more illustrious. Possibly—as orators, writers, rulers, but my statement relates to *preachers*. I thank God for all the varied gifts of His servants, and do not depreciate because I do not possess. I thank God for those who, in a former age or now, are celebrated for learning, genius, logic, imagination, wit, administrative or other power, all of which may be incidentally helpful to preaching; but if preaching is to be estimated by its adaptations to its special ends, then I consider that Spurgeon's preaching has no rival in the present day, and scarcely any in the past. Consider the length of time during which his ministry has gathered many thousands several times a week in one building; the steadfast setting forth of Gospel truth, the evident aim to exalt Christ and not self, the multitudes converted to God, and the fruits of such conversion in the abundant evangelistic and philanthropic labours carried on—then I think my estimate capable of defence. A barrister, as such, excels not by the admiration he receives from the court, but the verdict he wins from the jury; a doctor, not by the honours he claims, but by the patients he cures; a general, not by the decorations he wears, but the victories he gains; and so a preacher, for success, not in the commendation of critics, the laudations of the press for eloquence or popularity, but for successful endeavours in turning sinners to God, and strengthening Christians in holiness and usefulness. This success is not restricted to Spurgeon's work here or now—week by week during thirty

years his sermons, just preached, and fresh sermons from
old notes, are multiplied in myriads through the press, in
various languages. "He, being dead, yet speaketh."

We were near neighbours ecclesiastically, and still nearer
in true brotherhood. His Tabernacle was within a mile of
our church. We never grudged one another any transference
of members, and I rejoiced that so many of mine regularly
attended his Thursday ministry. The question of baptism
became a link of fellowship, for, whenever any of my flock
told me their doubts on the subject and desire for immersion,
I lost no time in trying to alter their views, but gave them a
note to Mr. Spurgeon, asking him to grant them satisfaction,
and this involved no alteration in pastoral and church
relationship. Half my church officers were Baptists, and I
never made the method a topic of controversy, though always
practising infant baptism myself, the custom of my predecessors in the pastorate. The subject never gave occasion for
controversy.

In some other matters Mr. Spurgeon differed from me, but
always lovingly. One day he spoke of my Temperance work
as using a wooden saw instead of the Gospel steel saw. I
replied by retorting—"I, like yourself, use a steel saw, but
mine has a special tooth in it which yours lacks." Happily,
he soon after, and to the end, used with great efficiency this
Temperance tooth included in the old and comprehensive
steel saw. He controverted my styling our new building
"Christ's Church," as if asserting exclusive or superior
position. I showed him that it was not "Christ's Church"
as if solely belonging to Christ, but Christ-Church for com-
memoration of Christ, as others to commemorate Peter or
Paul, Wesley or Rowland Hill, for preaching Christ, and
serving Christ, just as others, and his own. Once, on his own
platform, he pleasantly criticised the term "church," to which
I replied that some Christians, like infantine Israelites of old,
delighted in a tent or "Tabernacle" in the wilderness; some
belonged to a more advanced Jewish people, settled in a
"Temple"; while others loved "Mount Zion" and the
"Church of the first-born," applying the name of the

assembly also to the place. At a meeting at which he presided he questioned the use of printed prayers, and of
liturgics " meant for everybody but fitting nobody," to which
I replied in the course of my speech that some people even
used printed prayers composed in artificial rhyme and sung
to elaborate tunes, as " Jesu ! Lover of my soul." He seemed
much amused at the retort. When I was preaching to young
men a course of sermons on Butler's " Analogy," he referred
to them from the pulpit as delivered by a brother who, he
considered, did not understand Butler, nor did Butler understand the "Analogy" himself. I mention such trifling differences to show that our mutual affection did not result from
identity of opinion on all matters. We did not express our
views on several important truths in the same terms.
Diversities only accentuated agreement. An emphatic illustration was sending £100 for our building fund :—

"March 17th, 1873.
" DEAR FRIEND,—I beg to hand you the collection of yesterday with
the love of all of us. Please receive it as token of true fellowship in the
Gospel of Christ Jesus our Lord.—Yours, for all the Church,
"C. H. SPURGEON."

I was glad to reciprocate with a surplus of value in surren-
dering my very efficient assistant in the pastorate, Rev.
V. Charlesworth, to become the greatly valued secretary of
Spurgeon's orphanage, with the oversight of several hundred
children.

"December 28th.
" May you have a good year. I greatly need your prayers. May we
not look for far greater things if we have faith ? We are neither of us
too old to reach something higher yet if the Lord help us, though I, for
one, am weaker and more unworthy than ever. ' The Lord liveth.'
" Yours heartily,
"C. H. S."

On two successive years Mr. Spurgeon preached on
Monday at our anniversary. He took the same text both
times and expounded it in the same manner. I was very
glad, for I had myself been recently, but undesignedly, guilty
of the same indiscretion elsewhere.

February 5th, 1875.—Found Spurgeon on sofa in bedroom. Though suffering pain, he made me smile by wit mingled with wisdom. Speaking of the teachers of Christian perfection—" They are chiefly half-pay officers and single women in good health and no cares. Let them have a touch of gout, and ring for something which is not brought at once, and see if there isn't a bit of devil left in them. There's our dear friend X. I always thought him perfect till he himself told us he was." " Going to preach for a brother, I stopped to vote, and thus was a little late. He reproved me by saying, 'I thought your citizenship was heavenly.' ' Yes ; but I'm told to mortify the old man ; but he is a Tory, and so I mortified him by voting for a Liberal.' "

In reply to an invitation to take part in the opening services of our church :—

"April, 1876.

" Do take the will for the deed this time. You do not need me, for your opening will secure an audience from its own interest ; and I will, if the Lord gives me strength, serve you on some humbler but not less needful occasion. I am sure I would help you if I could, but now I am so weak that to stand an hour is such a trial and makes me tremble so that I shall be obliged to give up altogether unless I can have the half-duty of a cripple.

"Yours ever heartily,

" C. H. S."

May 9th, 1877.—Mr. Spurgeon preached in our church during the great annual meetings of the London Missionary Society. This sermon has always been regarded as a great function, in preparation for which some of the best preachers of the day have spent their best hours during several weeks. Mr. Spurgeon told me he could not fix his mind on his text till 7 o'clock the same morning, when he made these notes on a single leaf of note-paper, which he gave to me :—

" Joshua vii. 3. : ' Let not all the people go up.' Joshua viii. 1 : ' Take all the people of war with thee.'

" I. An error to be carefully avoided, caused by secret sin—presumption. Forgetting their commission—forsaking first model—carnal wisdom—running counter to divine design.

" II. A command to be earnestly obeyed, else evil to the inactive themselves. Hunt out the sin. Urge personal obligation—unity of the whole body—importance of the enterprise—practical work ourselves. Pray for more grace. Who has hitherto been an idler ?

"III. Results to be believingly expected. Increased life and unity. Strength adequate. Overflow for larger enterprises. Eagerness to complete the conquest of the whole world by missionary operations."

Two thousand people listened to the sermon preached from these notes, which occupied an hour in delivery. I feel sure many will be interested in this sample of the great preacher's notes, and may wonder at the smallness of the "brief" compared with the greatness of the oration ; for it was admitted by all—a large proportion of the hearers being preachers—to have been a deliverance of the very highest character for adaptation, impressiveness, and usefulness. Although the discourse was long, no one went out or seemed weary.

After some gap in correspondence :—

"I never expect an answer merely as a matter of form. When I perfectly agree with a brother I neglect mere etiquette and send no reply. Time is too precious to us both to care for form. Hearty thanks for your letters, and sevenfold for 'The Shadow of the Almighty.' I have been feeding on it, and must go through it again. . . . I want you to give my students a solemn address on their work, which may do them good as long as they live. There are not in England more devoted young men than the most of them, but we need daily arousing, and you can do it. I greatly bless God for your success in winning souls, and while I gird up my loins to run side by side with you in this good race, I pray that you may take even greater strides, and that by grace I may also maintain rank *passibus equis.* Pleader with men, O come and plead with us, that we may be more earnest than ever."

"Jan. 29, 1887.

"I am full of rheumatism and other mischiefs, but will say nothing about it if I can keep on my legs. I don't know how to preach ; I am a poor bungler. We shall both do well so long as we still feel that we are learners.

"Yours ever heartily."

May 21st, 1887.—Visit to Spurgeon, and referred to the great speech, an hour long, the week before in Exeter Hall. "How long did it take you to prepare it ?" S.: "I could do nothing that morning—bothered by a caller. Only time to select three or four anecdotes from scrap-book, which, on my way, I threaded together. A deacon said afterwards,

'You did well, and felt happy. I knew you would. I was up early, and from 5 to 7 was urgent in prayer that God would give you a message.' That deacon hunts for souls as dogs for the hare. He accosted a prostitute one evening—raining —knocked at a door and asked shelter—mistress listened while he spoke to the girl and prayed. Both are now members of the Tabernacle." Replying to question, he explained how he spent his time :—

Diary.—Visit to Spurgeon, who told me his method of work. Monday morning : Correcting report of Sunday sermons. In vestry at 3 with inquirers. Church-meeting at 6. Prayer-meeting 7 to 8.30. Tuesday, 5 to 8, inquirers. Wednesday, for preaching elsewhere. Thursday, prayer-meeting and sermon. Friday, 3 to 5, with his students. Visiting confined to cases of affliction—cannot undertake funerals. Reading—always some scientific book ; also travels, history, sometimes fiction, for illustration. Showed us scrap-books full of humorous anecdotes and caricatures of himself—"good and bad, getting ready for my burial"—strong against G.'s Home Rule—declined a certain invitation to confer as allies respecting Gospel truth and conduct because his own views were opposed to those of H. W. B., and because he disapproved of Christian ministers sanctioning by their presence the theatrical exhibitions of the day. He objected to receive as members theatre-goers.

Diary.—May 20th, 1888.—Now closes my seventieth year. Much refreshed by this visit to Spurgeon. I praise God for undiminished faith in the Old Gospel—sympathy with such a zealous servant of Christ. It is difficult to realise my age. I eat, sleep, preach, study, walk as well as ever, only that I do not climb a hill so fast as once. But how little I do compared with Spurgeon and others ! God forgive an unprofitable servant !

"Beulah Hill, 1888, July 4.

"DEAR FRIEND,—I have only just heard that the fourth of July is your anniversary. I congratulate you, and I pray that you may have a right good day. If I had been well enough, I would have accepted your invitation, you may be quite sure.

"I thank you and your friends for many kindnesses by way of help in my hours of sickness. The Lord bless *you* who preached and the people who spared you! In these days we are two of the old school. Our experience has taught us that both for conversion and edification the doctrine of Christ crucified is all-sufficient. A childlike faith in the atoning sacrifice is the foundation for the purest and noblest of characters. As the hammer comes down on the anvil ever with the same ring, so will we preach Christ! Christ! Christ! and nothing else but Christ. Our friends leave us for the suburbs, but I trust the Lord will raise up around us another generation of faithful men. God bless those attached brethren who stick to us and bear the brunt of the battle with us. I feel a deep gratitude to all such, both at Tabernacle and at Christ Church. To you I desire continued health and joyous communion with God.

" Yours very heartily,

"C. H. S."

June 22nd, 1889.—Wife and I, with our dear friend Cuyler, to see Spurgeon. He told us that the Archbishop of Canterbury (Benson) added the word "Reverend" to the envelope for reply sent to the Archbishop with the address, " C. H. Spurgeon." The Bishop of Rochester (Thorold) took him into his private chapel, and asked that they should pray together. He spoke with much animation of the true interpretation of Christ preaching to the spirits in prison, which had lately flashed on his mind. The antediluvians in the days of Noah found themselves between the rising flood and the closed ark. They were in terror, and by the Spirit of Christ, preaching to them by Noah, they repented and were saved. He was " quite sure this was the explanation, and so simple"! But is not the plain statement still more simple— that Christ himself, after he was put to death in his body, went and preached to spirits in safe custody, who in the days of Noah were impenitent?

We spent an hour with him in his grounds. We saw his cart with name painted, " Charles Haddon Spurgeon, licensed to sell milk." He told us that as he was informed milk could not be sold at the usual price without temptation for the vendor to put water in it, he sold his milk to a few neighbours at a proper price' and gave the produce to two elderly Christian ladies in very reduced circumstances. They had no notion from whom the cheque came to them every month, and it was a constant delight to himself to think of their wondering gratitude.

At a cheerful "high tea" with him and Mrs. Spurgeon, I asked what text he would preach from next day. He had no idea. When his friends left him about seven o'clock, he would take a turn and think over a number of texts. When one struck his mind he came to his desk, and on a single leaf of paper wrote a few heads; then enriched his own meditations by reading what others had written, and trusted to God for enlargement. So for the evening sermon, which he began to prepare on Sunday afternoon. But he said he was storing up materials all the week, and so saved the time others spent in laborious writing. He asked me for a text, and I gave him what he said was quite new to him: "And we are" (see R. V. 1 John iii. 1). After tea, family prayer. Marvellous was his prayer—such nearness to God, such reverential, familiar communion of a child with a father!

"Westwood, Oct. 10, '91.

"DEAR FRIEND,—Your love to me is never a matter of question with me, but far rather a theme for wonder. The Lord be with you in the service of love which you have undertaken to-morrow morning (Sunday). It is His wont to aid those who, in His name, deliver a true message, and that you always do. May you have a joyous sense of Divine aid. I desire my kindest regards to Mrs. Newman Hall, a crown of many gems to her husband. I am decidedly better; a poor weak creature, but mending. Everyone seems bent on pleasing me. The Vicar of Eastbourne called, and we had prayer together. The Mayor also called, and is to come again. I see an 'open letter' appears. What next? Yours in our Lord Jesus,

"C. H. S."

He absolutely insisted that his friends should make no reply to this "open letter," or take any notice of it.

My wife and I frequently spent part of Saturday afternoon with Mr. Spurgeon. I regret I have so few memoranda of these visits. I remember his speaking of Job's comforters, "They often tell us of folks worse off—as if that was any comfort. A man said to me, suffering from gout in the legs, 'I know a man with no legs at all.' I replied, 'Do you take

me for a *demon*, to be pleased that others are worse off? Tell
me of others who are *better* off.'" Another, who had never
known pain, coming to comfort him, "seemed like an elephant
trying to dance." God afflicts His servants to enable them to
comfort others by sympathy. He told me they expected
five hundred conversions every year at the Tabernacle—
there was scarcely ever a service without one led to Christ.
He asked me to pray, and then he followed, earnestly
beseeching blessings on our new church. Pressing my hand,
he said, affectionately, "I take it so kind of you to come and
see me." His face often twinged with pain as he uttered
sayings both humorous and godly.

Mr. Spurgeon's increased illness excited great sympathy
and anxiety. Prayer-meetings were held day by day in the
Tabernacle. In some of these I took part, and in one of
my addresses I affectionately warned my hearers against
praying even for so dear a life, apart from resignation to
the Divine Will. We ought not to ask for anything so
importunately as to be tempted to disbelieve in prayer and
in God, in case our prayers were not answered xactely as we
wished. Should it be the will of the Master shortly to
release His faithful servant from the pains of the body
and welcome him to his eternal rest with the welcome,
"Well done, good and faithful servant," we ought, in the
true spirit of prayer, to be prepared to say with our Lord,
"Father, not my will but Thine be done."

June 29th, 1891.—One of the newspapers thus referred to
the occasion :—

"It was peculiarly fitting that the Rev. Newman Hall, the friend
and neighbour for so many years of Mr. Spurgeon, should bring to
a close the day of prayer at the Metropolitan Tabernacle on Monday—a
day that will henceforth be regarded as perhaps the most memorable in
the interesting history of the great Nonconformist edifice. Mr. Hall
said he regarded Mr. Spurgeon as the greatest preacher of the day, the
greatest preacher in the truest sense of the term that England perhaps
had ever been favoured with. The marvellous hold Mr. Spurgeon had
of the people, maintained for a long series of years the freshness
and vivacity with which he proclaimed the 'old story'—a freshness
of style which pervaded the printed page in a manner almost equal
to his matchless oratory, extorting admiration from those who were

unfavourable to his theology, his philanthropy, the universal esteem in which he was held by all denominations, and the fact, of which he was personally cognisant, that Spurgeon's sermons were read every Sunday in many parish churches, were briefly touched upon. The prayer-meetings on Monday, fitly closed by the Rev. Newman Hall, Mr. Spurgeon's old and trusted friend, were characterised by real earnestness and simplicity of feeling."

June 29th, 1891.—Short address at prayer-meeting for Spurgeon at M.T. In my prayer a sudden thought came to me: There are some here who love Spurgeon, but do not love Spurgeon's Christ! O may this illness make them consider and repent! O let not his faithful ministry rise up to condemn them!

Next day I received the following letter :—

" June 30th, 1891.

"I feel constrained to thank you for your inspired prayer at the Tabernacle last evening, for it went direct to my heart. Christ had been to me an ideal, but not, as I rejoice this morning, *my Saviour* These words, 'some here do love their Spurgeon, but do not love his Saviour.' These words by God's Spirit touched my heart. Thank God for your loving entreaties, for now I know that I both love the Saviour and dear Mr. S., whose words ever set my heart in a state of condemnation and unrest ; but now I can say, 'I am the Lord's and He is mine.' I felt constrained to thank you for the inspired line of thought you took, which, by God's Spirit, has led me to, I trust, a whole-hearted life-surrender, to the service of Him who is now my Saviour.

" A. D."

This was a prompt answer to Him who can use as instrumental in conversion not only the sermon but the prayer. I at once sent this letter to dear C. H. S. as a first-fruit of good from his affliction.

1892.—Spurgeon's decease and burial. January 31st.— Had seemed better at Mentone. Sudden chill—in four days at rest. February 7th.—The body, in coffin of olive wood, placed in Metropolitan Tabernacle. Palm branches around ; open Bible on lid ; 60,000 persons walked round it. Great service in the afternoon, men alone : pastors, missionaries, and students on platform with Canon Fleming, Monro Gibson, James Spurgeon, Meyer, Pierson. Admirable and touching address from Dr. Maclaren. February

10th.—Funeral. Tabernacle crowded. Archibald Brown read. N. H. offered prayer. Crowds outside all the way to Norwood Cemetery. All shops closed and blinds drawn. Dear friend, true brother, great philanthropist, grandest preacher of the age, if preaching is estimated by its fitness for its own object, and its success in converting sinners and feeding the flock of God. Special services were also held at Christ Church, where my heart dictated a memorial sermon.

Letter from the Baroness Burdett-Coutts on the death of Spurgeon :—

"Stratton Street, February 8th, 1892.

"DEAR DR. NEWMAN HALL,—You have been much in our thoughts during these days which have brought you and Mrs. Hall so much sorrow. I remember in last summer when you were at Holly Lodge you did not indulge much hope of your great and your dear friend's ultimate recovery, and perhaps, knowing how much he must have suffered, you scarcely wished the stay on earth prolonged ; and now, he may not seem very far from those to whom he was in heart and spirit united in such close bonds. Still you must 'sorrow' you shall see his face no more, and both I and Mr. Burdett-Coutts offer you our very sincere sympathy. Your narrative of his 'Dairy Charity' has remained impressed on my mind, and I shall never see the word 'dairy' without feeling a wish (and more than a wish only) to do something after his fashion. We are invited to attend the service in his Tabernacle, and we are gratified to be thus able to render tribute to the work of one of our century preachers and brightest beacons of a pure and unswerving faith.

"Believe me,
"Dear Dr. Newman Hall,
"Very sincerely yours,
"and in most true sympathy with your affection for the friend who has gone before, but at whose grave you must weep such tears,
"BURDETT-COUTTS."

Dr. Henry R. Reynolds, Principal of Cheshunt College, was one of my oldest, nearest and dearest friends. A wonderful combination of learning, godliness, humility, and tender heartedness. In every student's heart he had a home. While admiring his intellect and prizing his instructions, they confided in his counsel, and shared in the friendship he felt for every one of "his boys." Cheshunt was an impersonation of Reynolds. What he was as a friend may be inferred from his letters, from which I venture to make a few extracts.

"Cheshunt College, September, 1880.

"MY BELOVED NEWMAN,—Love is very wonderful and blessed, and when it ministers to us the Divine fulness and is its very image, how can we do other than make our life a psalm of thanksgiving. . . Just read through your 'Grace and Glory.' Your words have the old ring and fire in them. May our Divine Lord bless them to kindle hope and strengthen faith in the lovableness of our Eternal God."

"December 6th, 1883.

"I have read ever so much of your Lord's Prayer, and feel sure it will go right to other hearts as it does to mine, and lift many of us into the Father's everlasting arms. It is wonderful uplifting when we can appropriate our Father's Name, call it ours, and be honoured best in its hallowing. . . . I have your portrait over our door, with Gladstone and Wordsworth and others, and I greet you and think of you every time I enter the room, God bless you and dear Mrs. N. Hall, and be thanked for having given me such a friend."

"May 21st, 1883.

"Every morning strikes us with a fresh sense of wonder, at the inestimable fulness of God's goodness! What will it be when our eyes and hearts are purged! . . I hope your brother's boy Arthur will be really helped here in his preparation for the work for which he seems wonderfully and hereditarily—avicularly and avuncularly and parentally predestined. So prays lovingly your affectionate brother-friend."

"February 17th, 1884.

"I am going steadily forward with my commentary: at all events it is a blessed exercise for oneself, whether anyone will ever read it or not. How clear it is that we have only specimens and hints of the abundant life and inexhaustible teaching of the Word manifest in the flesh."

Referring to certain hymnals :—

"June 7th, 1887.

"How extraordinary the omissions, and new ones which do not convey either in felicitous rhyme, poetical touch, or freshness a solitary advantage over some which have been discarded."

Referring to his commentary :—

"December 30th, 1887.

"I am deeply thankful that God has permitted me to see almost to the end of this long but happy task. You can imagine how intense the feelings are which every verse and almost every word excites. I sometimes dare to hope that the commentary may be of some help to my brethren. It comforts me exceedingly that you and a few others will read it with loving eyes. Would that we could meet a little oftener, not only in thought, love and prayer, but hand to hand."

On the death of his wife :—

"October 22nd.

" It would be unfilial to rebel against the Infinite Goodness that has taken my dearest one from me that she should be with Him. I cannot write the throbbing words that press to be said. God knows what He is keeping for me. I am trying to praise and to read His word *with her* still. But I feel that she has climbed a long way up the mount of God. How fond she was of you and dear Mrs. Hall. My dear love to the sister. I thank you both for your dear tender love, like dew upon the flowers.

"Your loving brother friend to both,

"HENRY R. REYNOLDS."

Funeral of Dr. Henry Allon, eminent as pastor, preacher, essayist, my true friend of many years :—

"Cheshunt, April 23rd, 1893.

"BELOVED BROTHER FRIEND,— . . . The only compensation to us, his old friends, is that the grace of God which reached us through his loving, magnanimous nature and robust sense and tender heart, may come to us direct from the great Giver and Lover and Father.

" I was too agitated to speak for the first time in the dear fellow's pulpit, with his coffin just below me, not himself there, but in the rest and the light above. When two or three times I felt I should break down I saw your dear face and knew you felt with me, and asked for the strength I needed.

" It delights me unspeakably that the University of Edinburgh has honoured itself by bestowing the D.D. God bless you and give you years yet to wear this entirely honourable tribute. I do greatly rejoice in it. With dear love to you both from us both,

"Your very loving friend,

"H. R. REYNOLDS."

He told me that his brother, Sir Russell Reynolds, on his death-bed, when unconscious to things visible, said: " I see father and mother, and Henry's wife; but where is Henry and where is my wife ? " So that he saw mentally dear ones who had entered the spirit world, but not the living.

November 30th, 1894.—To Cheshunt. Dear Reynolds, through illness, obliged to resign his office as principal. He spoke in sympathy with Dale, who in a recent letter lamented his own imperfections, while rejoicing that God deigned to use for His loving purposes unworthy instruments, sending streams of grace through channels so stained.

September 9th, 1896.—My dearest and oldest friend went home. He had been in Yorkshire visiting friends and returned on Monday, September 7th, weary and weak. Wednesday, 9th, sank gently to sleep in Jesus. That afternoon I went to weep with the two loving sisters at Broxbourne. We gave thanks together for his manly strength and womanly tenderness; his learning, wisdom, usefulness, and humility; above all his entire reliance upon and consecration to Christ. How he sympathised in grief, and rejoiced in joy as his own! He was an Apostle John. What a treasure is the memory of his love, the consciousness of its perpetuation, and the assured hope of its endless perfection in the love and glory of the Elder Brother.

The Reverend Edward White was for nearly forty years one of my dearest and most honoured friends. For a combination of learning, secular and sacred, godliness and manliness and human sympathy, beautiful thinking, heavenly communion, and eloquent expression, searching of the Scriptures and profound reverence, along with a never-failing fountain of refined humour, I have never known his equal. At the beginning of his ministry at Hereford, fifty years ago, he published the result of much contemplation and prayer in his volume, "Life in Christ." In these pages he dared to differ from the dogma of the old philosophy—natural immortality. Instead of basing his belief on the indivisibility of mind, and therefore its indestructibility, he made the resurrection of Christ the foundation of the Christian hope. Christ lives for ever; therefore all who are united to Him by faith are partakers of His life. This immortality is not conjectural, but actual; not merely future, but present. To understand his argument his own book should be studied. It has been reproduced in several languages, and has much influenced theological opinion in the Churches.

But his strong arguments and boldness in publishing them caused him to be regarded by many as heretical. Because he

U

differed from a long-prevailing mode of explaining the great mystery of the future, it was assumed that he questioned the truth of the Bible on other and fundamental questions. His book was strongly censured by some who refused to study it, and many doors of ecclesiastical advancement were thus closed upon one of the most worthy. This has long since passed away, and he has been for many years regarded with admiration even by those who have not accepted all his opinions. I feel personally indebted to him, more than I can express, for "Life in Christ"—a wider hope for the race, a stronger personal hope for each believer, without accepting every detail. I also owe to him my change of view respecting the second advent, which I no longer postpone till the completion of the millennium, but contemplate as possible in our own day, to bring that millennium to pass. But this is not the place to discuss these questions.

I extract from my diary a few scattered notes of my intercourse with him and some of his observations :—

Edward White knew how Darwin had opened a room for the villagers where he lived, for lectures, reading, and recreation. There were some drunken, dissolute fellows he could do nothing with. Some gentlemen were associated for evangelisation, and obtained permission to occupy the room on Sunday evenings. Some of the wildest fellows were converted, and became sober and courteous. Darwin was astonished. What evolution is this? He went himself to the service—wondered at the result from such simple means. "But seeing the man who was healed standing by, he could say nothing against it."

Darwin's inquiry of one of the evangelists how it was done gave an admirable opportunity of explaining to the scientist the great facts and doctrines of the Gospel, and the work of the Divine Spirit in connection with the truth.

Edward White was one of a "breakfast-fraternal" to which we both have belonged thirty years. His deeply devout prayers, his reverence for the Bible and knowledge of its contents, his critical and, at the same time, practical and devotional interpretations, interspersed with flashes of wisdom and wit, gave special charm to our brotherhood. I transcribe from my diary some remembrances of his sayings :—

"Many readers do not understand the teaching of my 'Life in Christ'—which is not a theory of punishment of the wicked, but of the eternal life of believers. More than pardoned, they have a new existence —a condition of oneness with Christ, uniform abiding co-partnership— a communion which infirmity and faults do not sever. Am glad Dale held the same views."

"Can we imagine that in the Apostolic Church there could have been such a thing as half a dozen Baptist and Congregational Churches in one city, all separate from one another, each with its own independent pastor, officers, treasury, membership? Are not all Churches departures from primitive practice ? While criticising each other, may we not all confess that we have erred and 'come short of the glory of God'?"

"We see evolution in certain ecclesiastical regions. In the appointment of highest offices in the Church, 'natural selection' often begins in the school. To be a head master is a strong qualification for a head bishop. Ecclesiastical evolution."

"Plymouth Brethrenism makes one think of cream turned sour."

"Like Peter, when a disciple is 'warming himself,' he is often in danger of denying his Lord."

My dear friend's health declines. Unable any longer to undertake many preaching services. Visited him at Hilda's Mount. Asked him to pray with me. O what a prayer it was! profound, reverential, grateful, affectionate ; thanks to God for early nurture in the Gospel, for saints we have known, for benefit received from others, clearer views of Scripture, steadier effort, etc.

July 31st, 1898.—Yesterday the body of my dearly loved Edward White was laid in the grave, aged eighty years. He had appeared to be restored to comparative health. He was present at the opening of the new chapel of Mill Hill School a fortnight before. On last Sunday he heartily joined at public worship in singing "There is a land of pure delight." A few days after he was suddenly transported across the narrow sea, and welcomed by the heavenly host, and by the Lord he loved, honoured, and preached. I am grieved that I was unable to be among the friends who surrounded the grave. But I am glad I had recently been with him. On returning home a few weeks ago from a distant journey, I learned that he was dangerously ill—perhaps had left us—and early next morning hastened to Worthing to see him. For two days he had seemed to be dying, and by medical orders none but his family were allowed to see him. But he was then resting after long pain, and in such profound slumber that I was allowed to see him from behind a screen. How grandly peaceful that head and those features, so expressive of his humanly divine soul! I might remain a few minutes only, but I shall always retain the memory of what then was impressed on my heart.

Since then he rallied, travelled home with comfort, received his friends, seemed likely to survive for months, if not years. We went over to see him twice, walked with him in his garden, listened again to his wisdom and wit, his godliness and affection, and came away for two months' preaching in Scotland, fully expecting to rejoice again in his earthly fellowship.

I am to-day looking over a number of letters and records which aid my reminiscences, and come upon a letter which my friend wrote to my "deacons" on occasion of the celebration of my eightieth birthday. I hesitate to republish it; but from such a friend it is very dear to me, and expresses what I myself would in substance say of himself:—

"*From Rev. Edward White, to the Deacons of Christ Church.*

"I much regret that the state of my health prevents my presence at the celebration of my beloved friend's eightieth birthday. He needs no spoken or written praise from those who have known and loved him for thirty years. Yet these are the very persons who wish to praise him, if only to satisfy their own affection. . . . The *English public* owe to him a prolonged, faithful, and loving proclamation of the Gospel of salvation both by word and writing, as well as a manful support of every righteous public cause. The *Church of Christ* owes him an indefatigable life-service and a consistent example. His *friends* owe to him an unshaken and unshakeable friendship and life-long sympathy, and they believe that such friendship will be *eternal.* I heartily join in all the loving wishes which will be expressed both for him and his dear wife, who shares in all our love and honour for her husband.

"E. WHITE."

Letter to Mrs. Rundell Charles, the writer of "The Schönberg-Cotta Family." I have very seldom taken copies of my own letters, but I happen to find in my commonplace book notes of a letter to our dear friend on the death of her mother, who for many years had lived with her, a constant companion:—

"April 30th, 1889.

"DEAR MRS. CHARLES,—Permit me to express my sympathy, I will not say in your loss, but in the temporary suspension, not of spiritual communion, but of that personal intercourse which has so long been your delight. I have passed through a similar experience. It is easy to say that departure, long expected, and at so ripe an age, need not much grieve us; but the lengthening of the life has made it more dear, and the removal makes a darker blank when lives have been so long illuming each other. The home is so different when a familiar occupant is no more with us, and habits of daily life are broken. Yet sadness is almost eclipsed by joy in contemplating a long life of love, the ripeness of the corn, the certainty of the bliss, the greetings of the larger circle, and, yonder, the hope of the speedy reunion and the welcome of the Lord Himself, and perfected resemblance and service; these are a bright 'silver-lining' to the cloud. The sorrow itself helps in its measure to fill up that which is behind of the sufferings of Christ and His Body, the Church, the allotted trials prior to the completed glory. I feel I should apologise for seeming to suggest this to one who has given solace to such multitudes of sufferers. 'The God of all consolation' will make your consolation 'to abound by Christ,' that you may be still more able to 'comfort others by the comfort wherewith you yourself are comforted of God.'"

It was Mrs. Charles's habit to spend one day in the week in the East-end, near her husband's factory.

Mr. and Mrs. Charles came once to our evening service, chiefly liturgical, and were pleased with the singing together of the vast congregation; and then by visiting some of the after "people's services." Mrs. Charles expressed her sorrow that such work by congregations outside her own Church were so much ignored and sometimes opposed.

A.'s eldest boy said, "Father, do babies grow in heaven?" Calling on Mrs. Charles, I asked her this, and she replied, "Of course they do; a baby that never grows is a deformity. A mother in India, sending an infant to be nurtured in England, would not expect to find it a baby after ten years. Growth is the law of life." Then I called on the Vicar, Rev. E. Bickersteth, now Bishop of Exeter, who said, " Of course *not.* Heaven without babies would be very deficient; what so sweet as a baby's voice ? Imagine the effect of myriads of babies praising God!" "But is not growth a law of life ?" "Yes, but it is growth in the beauty of babyhood—they do not cease to be babies. There will always be children in heaven." Curious diversity between two thoughtful persons within an hour !

We always felt it a privilege to meet Mrs. Charles at her house on afternoons when she laid aside her writing and books to commune with her friends. Her pleasing voice and manner gave due expression to her well-stored intellect, her large-hearted benevolence, her comprehensive and scriptural piety. I remember a delightful summer afternoon, spent on her sloping lawn at "Combe Edge," when I introduced the "Jubilee Singers" from America, whose thrilling songs and choruses gave intense pleasure. Throughout the States she is well known by her books, and beloved.

She had a little dog between which and herself there was a strong attachment. She thought the great intelligence and strong affections of dogs are suggestive of a spiritual nature which may survive the body.

March 3rd, 1896.—Afternoon tea at Mrs. Charles's: Edward and Mrs. White, Dr. Horton, self and wife. Two hours' talk : Cardinal Newman's piety ; Manning's subtlety and ambition ; Dean Stanley's natural truth, fun, breadth of heart, and illegible writing; development of Roman doctrine and ceremony in second century; attractiveness of the idea of one historic church and the chief bishop. Why did not the early Church protest prior to the Reformation ? It did; but the protestors were few and weak, their testimony overlooked and forgotten. The great future. Mrs. Charles cannot concur in the extinction of any creatures made in the image of God. Those who pass away without the knowledge of God may receive instruction and "find grace to help in time of need" hereafter. "The wicked will be punished till they become good." Christians will grow in knowledge, goodness, happiness ; saints will improve ; sinners may—multitudes will—repent and be saved. Query: If no one created in the image of God—*i.e.* having individuality—will be annihilated, the wicked must exist for ever, and either be bad and in hell for ever, or repent and be saved? Revelation v. 13, 14 suggests a period when, without exception, all human beings then existing will unite in holy worship of God and Christ: "And every creature which is in heaven, and on the earth, and under the earth, and such as are in the sea, and all that are in them, heard I saying, Blessing, and honour, and glory, and power be unto Him that sitteth upon the throne, and unto the Lamb for ever and ever. And the four beasts said, Amen." Dr. Bickersteth, Bishop of Exeter, introduces this scene into his poem, "Yesterday, To-day, and For Ever." To join in this anthem with the heart is salvation. Can any who sing it be, at the same time, in hell?

These are rough notes of topics discussed *pro* and *con.*, and must not be regarded as the words of the whole party or of any one. We felt the solemnity and difficulties of the subject.

A few days after this conversation I happened to meet Mrs. Charles, with her little dog, walking towards her home, Combe Edge, on Hampstead Heath, when her conversation was wholly on the blessedness of departed saints, and how there should be joyful thanksgiving rather than oppressive lamenting when those who are partakers of eternal life in Christ join the blessed company of the redeemed in glory.

A few days afterwards we started for Switzerland, where I received the following note from Edward White:—

"Ap. 2, '96.

". . . It is only three weeks after our call on her that the angel of death—let us rather call him the angel of everlasting life—came for her, on March 28. When we saw her then there were no signs of decay or drooping spirits. Yet now we shall see her no more till the resurrection, when she will be clothed in far finer singing robes than she possessed on earth. A great company in the church and at the grave came to pay their last loving respect."

A public subscription was promptly raised as a memorial to endow an additional bed in the Consumption Hospital, in which Mrs. Charles had taken a deep personal interest as a visitor.

CHAPTER XX.

To the incessant claims of my large congregation to direct its various operations, to study, preach, and visit, the varied demands of the church at large, and frequent journeying in all directions to preach anniversary and other sermons, there was now added the anxiety and toil connected with erecting a new church. To this I devoted my best energies, and to the unremitting labours thus demanded I attribute under God my help to bear and sometimes to forget other troubles. With Samson, when he found honey in the carcase of a lion, I could say, "Out of the eater came forth meat." From bitter seed grew a tall and beautiful tree.

I think it well to place on record a brief but complete history of the building of Christ Church.

Surrey Chapel was founded by the Rev. Rowland Hill in 1783, who was pastor till 1833, when he died, leaving a considerable sum for the perpetuation of his work at the expiration of the lease in 1883, either by purchase or renewal of the lease. After the retirement of his successor, the Rev. J. Sherman, in 1854, I became pastor. There being some doubt about the legality of the bequest, the trustees consulted the Vice-Chancellor, who decided that by the Statute of Mortmain the bequest fell to the residuary legatee, Hackney Itineracy (now Hackney College), to which a similar bequest had been more correctly made, both institutions being specially dear to Mr. Hill. Our trustees thus lost his provision for the permanence of his church. After serious consideration it was decided that it was our duty to provide for this loss and fulfil the purpose

Photo.   Cassell & Co., Ltd.

CHRIST CHURCH, WESTMINSTER BRIDGE ROAD.

of our founder. The "Rowland Hill Fund for the perpetuation of Surrey Chapel" was thus instituted in 1861, and it was decided that on every Sunday an offertory should be taken at the doors for this express object. The first financial report to December, 1862, shows a total amount of £475 16s., in sums from one shilling to one hundred pounds.

With the weekly offertory and personal donations, we resolved to raise £1,000 yearly, in trust, to be invested in Consols. In 1873 our fund reached £16,000, considerably more than the original bequest would have amounted to. In 1874, as the result of special efforts by the pastor for the tower, we had £22,550. This included more than two hundred purses, holding £5 each, laid on the memorial stone, and £5,370 special donations for that occasion.

The freehold site, for which funds were specially given, was transferred by Messrs. Oakey for the moderate sum of £8,200. This was subscribed within six months, and the site was dedicated by a continuous service in the open air from ten a.m. to ten p.m.

The Hawkstone Hall—so named from Rowland Hill's birthplace—cost about £5,000, and the Lincoln Tower £7,000, the cost of the latter divided equally by contributions from America and England. In March, 1875, I stated that £7,000 were still needed to pay the contract of the builder; that I made myself responsible for raising £5,000 of this, relying on the congregation to contribute the remaining £2,000 during the year. This was done within the year, with great rejoicing.

The architects of the building were Messrs. Paull and Bickerdike. The builders were Messrs. Perry and Co. The contracts, including £2,000 for foundations, were £40,000. The entire cost, including land, organ, fittings, commission, etc., was about £62,000.

Within four years of the opening the total cost was cleared. The whole was raised by voluntary contributions, excepting about £2,000 received from the sale of the former Hawkstone Hall, which also had been obtained by voluntary contributions when the old school was built.

THE TRUST DEED.

By the trust deed, the financial affairs of the Church are managed by trustees, whose nomination by the body of trustees must be confirmed by the vote of the Church members. The elders are appointed in a similar manner, and their function is to aid the pastor in the spiritual affairs of the Church and in the care of the poor. In the appointment of pastor, the trustees and elders form one body to nominate a candidate for the approval or otherwise of the Church members. Pastors, trustees, and elders are required to sign the following

SCHEDULE OF DOCTRINES.

As I am responsible for this schedule, it should be noticed that while the essential truths of Evangelical Christianity are stated, opinions on which believers are divided are left open, such as theories of atonement, modes of baptism and worship, methods of church government, and theories of the everlasting future. Thus differences of opinion on these subjects are no hindrance to church fellowship.

1.—The Divine inspiration of the Holy Scriptures of the Old and New Testaments, and their supreme authority in faith and practice.

2.—The Unity of God—the Father, the Son, and the Holy Ghost.

3.—The incarnation of the Son of God in the person of the Lord Jesus Christ ; the universal sufficiency of the atonement by His death ; and free justification of sinners by faith in Him.

4.—The depravity of man, and the necessity of the Holy Spirit's agency in man's regeneration and sanctification.

5.—Salvation by grace ; and the duty of all who hear the Gospel to believe in Christ.

6.—The resurrection of the dead, and the final judgment.

7.—The sole priesthood of the Lord Jesus Christ in the sense of mediation ; ministers of the Church, priests only in the sense in which all believers are " kings and priests unto God ; " the sacraments means of grace, and not efficacious of themselves, or by any virtue in the administrator ; the brotherhood in service of all ministers of the Gospel of all communions ; the unity in the one Church of "all who love the Lord Jesus Christ in sincerity."

As the bond of union of Church members is not agreement in forms or creeds, but in personal repentance and faith, the following "Solemn Covenant" is

RENEWED AND PUBLICLY RATIFIED AT CHRIST CHURCH BY THE COMMUNICANTS OF THE LORD'S SUPPER ON THE FIRST SUNDAY MORNING OF EVERY YEAR.

On this first Sabbath of the new year, and assembled round the table of our Lord, we do hereby, before God and one another, renew our solemn Covenant.

We confess that we are guilty, ruined sinners, deserving the righteous punishment of God. But we declare our confidence in His mercy, as revealed by Jesus Christ, who is " the propitiation for our sins, and not for ours only, but also for the sins of the whole world." We trust in that atonement ; we plead the merits of the Redeemer. By Him, the only way to the Father, we draw near, with penitent, yet confiding hearts, saying—" God be merciful to me a sinner." And we desire anew to yield up ourselves entirely to our Triune Jehovah. We would look up with filial love, and say—" Our Father, who art in Heaven—hallowed be Thy name !" We would live as His adopted children, trusting, obeying, rejoicing in Him. We yield ourselves to the Son of God. We would be taught by Him as our Prophet ; we rely on His sacrifice as our Priest ; we would obey His commands as our King. For this we seek the aid of the Holy Spirit, the Giver and Preserver of the life of godliness in the soul ; and we declare our sincere purpose to give heed to His counsels—not wilfully to grieve Him—but daily, through the year, to cherish His presence in our hearts.

We declare that we are not our own, but bought with a price. We desire to present ourselves—spirit, soul, and body—time, property, influence—a living sacrifice unto God. We will endeavour in all things to prove that we love Him by obeying His commandments. We will endeavour in private and public, in our households, in our business, in daily life, in all places, in all companies, to act as becometh the Gospel —to promote true religion in the hearts of others, to help the needy, comfort the sorrowful, and to diminish vice, ungodliness, and misery in the world, "looking for that blessed hope, the glorious appearing of our great God and Saviour, Jesus Christ." And knowing, from numerous past failures, how unable we are of ourselves to do anything that is good, we do earnestly implore the help of Him, without whom we can do nothing—but who has said, "My grace is sufficient for you."

In the name of the Father, and of the Son, and of the Holy Ghost, to this our solemn Covenant we do now severally and unitedly assent— with a solemn and a hearty—*Amen.*

I was advised by a very influential and wealthy friend not to take up the burden of rearing a new church, but confine myself to the work of an evangelist and pastor, leaving to those who should follow the work of their own day. But I felt that in accepting the pastorate I ought to help in bearing the burden already cast upon us. Worldly policy said : " Rest and be thankful." The necessities of the district, the goodly fellowship of zealous believers, the traditions of the place, the memories of the departed, the voice of conscience said : " Arise and prepare to build." Many said : " Change your locality—nearly all the wealthy have gone—the need of the district increases, the capacity to meet it diminishes; go to the West End, or to Clapham Common." But my elders, trustees, and people said that we should remain on the ground, among the poor. We prayed year after year for God to find us a site, and after long fruitless search we consider God provided a place in which to pitch our tent, moving only from one end of the notorious "New Cut" to the other; at the junction of the Kennington and Westminster Bridge Roads, in middle distance between Waterloo or Westminster Bridge and the "Elephant and Castle," on highways to West-minster, the City, and the southern suburbs, and in a network of poor people's dwellings.

Many years before our new church could be commenced it was in our thoughts. I was very desirous that it should not only be commodious but beautiful, and resolved to consult Professor Ruskin, to whom I wrote for advice and received the following characteristic reply :—

"Denmark Hill, S.E., 20th January, '72.

"MY DEAR SIR,—I am sincerely obliged by your letter ; the paragraph flattered and amused me, and I wished it had been true. Not less, because it never can be true in any sense. I wish I could either design a church, or tell you a workman that could build one, or that I saw good cause for such building. So far from that, I believe all our church building, all our preaching, and all our hearing, is as great an abomination to God as ever incense and new moons, in days of Jewish sin. I believe you clergymen have but one duty to do, to separate those who believe from those who do not; not as wheat from tares—but as fruitful from fruitless. You cannot look on the heart, but you can on the deeds, and when you have gathered round you a separate body of men, who will not cheat, nor rob, nor revenge, it may be well to build a church for them ; but I think they will scarcely ask you. I would be at home for you after Monday, whenever you liked to call, but I fear I should only pain you, by what I should endeavour to say.

"Always faithfully yours,

"J. RUSKIN.

"The Rev. Newman Hall."

I gladly availed myself of this courteous invitation, and told Mr. Ruskin that we should be glad of any hint from himself in carrying out our purpose to erect a church, which should not only be commodious but beautiful; not only sheltering from rain and sun, but inspiring happy thoughts

and holy emotions. He replied—as he had already written—
that we should not build up stones, but gather together a few
people who would not steal or tell lies. I said that we had
many hundreds of such, and needed a building where under
shelter they might worship and be taught. He repeated his
opinion, and I said I had made a mistake in troubling him, as
I thought I was speaking to the author of the " Stones of
Venice." He said, "No, you are not. Everyone who does
something in teaching men passes through three stages of
life. At first he teaches what is inaccurate ; then he unlearns
it ; and lastly, he teaches the Truth—which stage I have now
reached." Of course I accepted this dictum, with due consideration of the speaker's genius, and with assent to what he
meant—that vast sums are spent in building churches which
are not needed, which are never filled, sums which might be
better spent in instructing, civilising, and evangelising the
practical heathen outside our own doors.

From boyhood I had great delight in architecture,
especially " Gothic." I used a special sketch-book entirely
for arches, windows, clustered columns and towers. I disliked bad imitations of Roman and Greek heathen temples,
which my Hull experience had strengthened. I longed
for a church suggestive of Christian worship, in harmony
with general Christian usage and the days of old ; so
I hoped for a Gothic structure. At the same time I
desired the new building to remind us of the beloved old
chapel. So I began my scheme with the eight wooden
columns in the centre of the sixteen-sided " Round House."
Let eight marks represent large columns. From one pair
mark out two other pairs of smaller columns in line, and let
this be the nave, with three arches and west window. Let
the two opposite columns flank the chancel, with east window.
Let the four remaining columns be entrances to two transepts,
each with an outward pair, two arches, and window. In one
of the corners outside, between nave and transept, there will
be space for tower, in another for stairs to gallery floor, in
another for verger's house, in the fourth for vestries. Let the
eight central columns support a groined dome, surmounted

by a flèche, for ventilation. I showed this to our proposed architects to work out the details. The arrangements for the various adjuncts were admirably suited for the ground at disposal. The style of architecture—early thirteenth-century Gothic—was carried out perfectly. When Sir Gilbert Scott saw my rough sketch, he said, " You got that from Ely, the only English cathedral with octagon centre." I replied that I had never been at Ely, and that the plan was my own, suggested by Surrey Chapel.

I dislike a great organ facing the congregation, which a heathen visitor called a golden god. So our organ was to be placed on one side of the chancel. Instead of a choir gazing at a congregation gazing on them, as at a concert, let the singers be ranged in the chancel, sideways, facing the organist, and the prayer-desk in the first row of the seats for the choir, the reader being the head of the singers. Let the table for Holy Communion be in the centre under the east window, and in front of it a lectern for the Lessons, and the pulpit on one side against one of the big columns, which will act as a sounding-board, the preacher facing diagonally from the table of Communion, and, as it were, beckoning the people to come to it in confession and self-surrender, " showing forth the Lord's death."

There is a large lecture-hall for the school and meetings, for 700 children or 500 adults ; under it a mission-hall for prayer-meetings, seating 150, with six classrooms and infant school ; two vestries for clergy, a large deacons' room, a ladies' room, and a committee room, and comfortable house for verger and family. The tower, on its basement, serves as an entrance to the gallery. Above this are two large classrooms, one named " Washington " and the other " Wilberforce," consecrated to Freedom. The entire structure was designed for various philanthropies, and a working church has from the first availed itself of these facilities, rooms and church used every Sunday and often on week nights.

Over the tower entrance at the apex of the arch a large stone is inserted bearing the title, " Lincoln Tower." Under the paved basement is the coffin of Rowland Hill, removed from below the Surrey Chapel pulpit. A tablet is on the wall above it on which his name, etc., is cut, removed from the front of the gallery in the chapel. There is another similar tablet in memory of his successor, James Sherman. A still larger memorial stone gives the name and purpose of the tower—to commemorate emancipation by the martyred Lincoln, the contribution of half the cost of the tower by American citizens, and as a pledge of international brotherhood. As a visible sign, the steeple is decorated by structural stars and stripes in red stones upon white. I had the honour of putting the last stone in its place—the point of the spire, 220 feet high.

The Lincoln Tower is regarded by good judges to be second to none of the church towers and steeples erected in London during the last hundred years. The material is Portland stone and Kentish rag outside, and Bath stone within. The front porch has over it a carved representation of an angel holding a scroll, with the motto of the church, "Christ is all and in all."

I particularly desired that the ornamentation should be structural and not supplemental, true and not fanciful. Let, then, the carving on cornices and capitals represent real and not conventional flowers and foliage. Thus we have an abundance of copies of real ferns, roses, and ivy or oak leaves. The elaborate carving of the capitals of the eight columns were private gifts in memory of departed friends, one of them bearing the name of William Wills, whose house used to be Rowland Hill's Bristol home. The capitals were carved after models I selected. The column on the north side of the table bears ears of corn, with the motto, "I am the bread of life"; on the opposite side grapes, with "I am the true vine." The other columns—roses, with "The rose of Sharon," and lilies, "The lily of the valley"; passion flowers and "The man of sorrows"; pomegranates and "The resurrection and the life"; ivy wreaths and "The same yesterday, to-day, and for ever"; oak leaves and acorns, "The mighty God." The windows are, or will be, decorated in a similar style. The large north window has pictures of Christ's miracles—healing the leper, calming the storm, raising the dead, transfiguration. Below I placed two small windows, in one of which is a memorial of my father. " The sinner's friend receiving sinners," and of my mother, Christ blessing infants, "Suffer little children to come unto Me." In the chancel are three small windows representing the Death, Resurrection, and Glory of Christ. One of these is a memorial by Canadians, another of an officer of the church by his widow, and one of the chief contributors, C. Ruck.

On Tuesday, July 4th, 1876, Christ Church was opened for divine worship. The members met for praise and Holy Communion at 8 a.m. At 11 a.m. the consecration service, chiefly in accordance with the Prayer-book arrangement, at which I preached from "Christ is all and in all." The Lincoln Tower was then inaugurated by Sir Fowell Buxton, Bart., and the Rev. Dr. Thompson, of New York, delivered an international address in the church. In the afternoon the Rev. W. H. Aitken, the eminent mission clergyman of the Church of England, preached from the words, "How good and how pleasant it is for brethren to dwell together in unity." In the evening the Rev. Donald Fraser, D.D., of the Presbyterian Church, preached from " The grace of our Lord Jesus Christ be with your spirit." The opening services were continued almost daily during a month by the following preachers:— Spurgeon, Raleigh, Rogers, Mellor, Allon, Parker, Stoughton, Parsons, Balgarnie, Chown, Graham, Wilson, Tucker, Baldwin Brown, Joshua Harrison, Arthur Hall, Dykes, D. Fraser, Paterson, Smith, Wilson, Penrose, and Rees in Welsh. The following ministers of the Established Church preached or gave addresses:—Revs. W. H. Aitken, S. Minton, H. S. Warleigh, A. Price, J. Kirkman, R. Maguire, and the Rev. the Hon. W. Fremantle. These brethren aided us most cheerfully, without any hindrance or censure from the other authorities or the Archbishop, whose palace garden extends immediately under our steeple, who knew and sympathised, but made no sign. Thus the preachers represented the Independent, Baptist, Presbyterian, Methodist, Primitive, as well as Episcopal Churches, in happy sympathy with this non-denominational and truly Catholic unity.

In responding to the request to preach one of the opening sermons, the Rev. Hugh Aitken said he had well considered the kind proposal; that had the application been for the consecration of one of the Established churches, he would probably have declined it as not in his line, but that he felt so strongly the importance of witnessing to the principles of Christian charity and mutual respect which should characterise the dealings of Christians with each other, he felt constrained to accept the invitation, wishing success in the work.

Diary.—January 1st, 1872.—A great day commenced in Surrey Chapel; crammed in every part at the watch-night service, after which seventeen persons received from me the temperance pledge card. At noon Mr. Oakey met our committee and offered a very eligible site for £8,000 (several thousands less than I expected), with a donation of £200. Filled with gratitude and hope, I went and told my friend Samuel Morley, M.P., who at once gave £500; R. Sturgis and K. Hodgson gave £200; — Morgan, £100; James Spicer, £100; I added as a thanksgiving £100, and thus on the first day £1,200 was given towards the site. Bless the Lord, O my soul! I could scarcely restrain my joy within decent bounds. Then a crowded prayer-meeting, at which I had the privilege of proposing sixty-six for Church membership, chiefly young men and women, some children under twelve years who had given good evidence of intelligent and sincere conversion. Then we distributed several hundred New Year tickets to members whom I thus had the opportunity of taking by the hand with New Year benedictions. Afterwards, from 9 to 10.30, I delivered a lecture in the Surrey Chapel on my journey to the Pyrenees, to a great crowd of working men, concluding with the Doxology.

January 3rd.—To personal calls this day the following responses:—Kemp Welch, £100; H. Dunn, £100; H. Thompson, £100; Tarn, £100; M'Culloch, £50; Moreland, £100; Ruck, £50; promise by our generous friend, T. Rider, £500; so that on this third day we have £2,300 specially for the site, the bargain for which at £8,000 was ratified by our committee this day.

v

On the first Sunday after the site was our own we consecrated it, as I have said, by an all-day service. I preached at ten a.m., and others continued prayer, praise, and exhortation without a pause till ten p.m., when 2,000 were present, and I preached again. Many thousands heard the glad news of salvation during the day; and services were held there constantly till building commenced.

January 7th, Sunday.—At the morning service I asked the congregation to consider what they would subscribe towards the site. After evening prayer I stated the whole case, and then paused for five minutes, asking the people to pray silently and fill up the cards. I engaged personally to collect £5,000, outside the congregation, by midsummer, if they would subscribe the rest. The emotion was great. All were eager to secure cards. Plates were handed round and were returned filled up. While I preached from "Who is willing to consecrate his service this day unto the Lord," and pleaded for the surrender of hearts, the committee were counting up the promises. Just as I closed my sermon the figures were handed to me. I could scarcely believe my eyes as I read £2,600. The Doxology was sung in a scene of holy excitement such as I have never before witnessed. Next day the amount was made up to £3,000, so that my own part of the contract has now to be completed.

Monday, February 5th, 1872.—The whole of my £5,000 is already subscribed. God has, indeed, blessed my labours which have been abundant. I have written a hundred letters enclosing circulars, and have made many calls on city merchants and others. I narrate two specimens. Mr. R. Moffatt had given £100 some years before. As I stated my case a carriage stopped at the door, and a card was handed in. As I rose to retire Mr. Moffatt said, "This is the richest man in London. I'll have him in; go on with your story." So I did, repeating some facts. Presently Mr. Moffatt said, " I'll give you another £100," and, turning to his friend, added " I'd recommend you also to help." As I left I said, " I came with my hook baited for a particular fish, which I have

caught. If another should unexpectedly come to my line
I shall be doubly thankful." Next morning came a cheque
for £100 " with Mr. C. Morrison's compliments."

I went to St. Mary Cray, to see an old friend of my father,
Mr. Joynson, the great paper-maker. He was taking his
morning drive in his carriage and four. When he alighted,
espying me, he said good-naturedly, "The last time I saw
you (ten years before) I gave you £100, and you've the
impudence to come again. No use! Won't get anything
—can't—I tell everyone so now." I replied, "Never mind,
let me help you off with your overcoat." Then we sat down,
and I patiently listened to his chatting on his own affairs,
his poverty, that he was not worth above half a million, and
how many claims he had to meet. I said, "Like yourself,
I am a man of business, and my business to-day is to state
my case, and yours to resolve whether or not to help." He
repeated that he could do nothing, having recently given
large sums to various religious and philanthropic objects.
This was true. He was a very generous giver—but he selected
his own objects, and gave in his own way. Two brothers,
Messrs. Spalding, came to dinner. They were friends of mine,
and I was invited to remain with them. As we walked in the
conservatory, which, Mr. Joynson said, was about three hundred paces long—one for each day of the year, he referred to
my appeal and his own inability. In a jocular way, I said it
was a shame to come begging to a man so poor, and who had
just been obliged to spend several pounds in repairing some
glass injured by a hailstorm! At dinner, when one of the
Spaldings gently said a word for me, Mr. Joynson in a sort of
jovial roar exclaimed, " What business is it of yours? What
have *you* done? Whatever you'll do I'll double it." Mr. S.,
"I'm giving £50." Mr. J., "Then I'll give £100." Mr. S.,
"I'll give £50 more." Mr. J., "I'll give £100 more." Mr. S.,
jun., "£50." Mr. J., "Another £100. Go on! I'll go on if
you will." Mr. S., "Another £50 in twelve months." Mr. J.,
" No! it must be cash." Then, calling for pen and ink, he wrote
a cheque for £300, and seemed as much pleased with giving
as I was with receiving. Within two days the £150 of the

two friends was sent, so that this one call produced £500, including the deferred £50.

I stated my case to a godly Nonconformist banker, who refused me when I told him I had read Tennyson's "May Queen" on a Monday night to a crowd of artisans in Surrey Chapel; another banker, nearly next door, when I told him the same, warmly commended, and at once gave me £100.

March 3rd.—The subscription for the site by the congregation is now £3,300, and my list exceeds the pledged £5,000 by £500; so that in two months after purchasing the freehold site we have the whole cost of £8,000 and £800 over. Praise the Lord!

But amongst these large gifts there was another which most of all touched my heart. A young woman, a lady's attendant, neatly but very inexpensively dressed, laid a small brown paper parcel on the vestry table, and asked me to accept it for the church. It contained twenty sovereigns. I thought it far too much for her circumstances. She said she had been long storing it for the Lord, and wept when I declined to take it. I then asked her solemnly to promise that if ever she were ill and unable to work she would let me know. This she at once promised, and rejoiced that her little offering was accepted. The giver was unknown, and the only entry on the subscription list was "B. B., £20." The Divine Treasurer, estimating subscriptions, declared, "Verily I say unto you, That this poor widow hath cast more in than all they which have cast into the treasury." A few years afterwards, "B. B." brought another £5.

The foundation stone was laid by Mr. Samuel Morley, June 26th, 1873, just ninety years after the opening of Surrey Chapel—June 8th, 1783. Ministers of various churches assisted in the service, in the presence of two thousand persons. On July 9th, 1874, the foundation-stone of the Lincoln Tower was laid by the American ambassador, His Excellency General Schenk.

June 18th, 1876.—Last Sunday in dear old Surrey Chapel. Lord's Supper morning and evening. Last sermon same subject as my first, "God so loved." With much emotion bade farewell. Yet it is ugly, dirty, inconvenient; neighbourhood so increasingly bad that it is necessary to remove unless it might become deserted by all but the very poor, who would then have none to help institutions for their special benefit. Moreover the lease will soon expire, and the owners would demand £800 yearly rent. Though we leave the old building, I trust we take with us the old blessing! To my great joy the Primitive Methodists take the remaining five years of the lease at ground rent of £40. May they gather a large congregation and establish a permanent church.

As in connection with public funds of all sorts, vague notions are afloat, or at least questions are asked which suggest doubts of correctness or disinterestedness, I feel bound in justice to myself and the chief promoters of this enterprise to explain that while a large number of outside friends generously aided us, much the larger half was provided ourselves by an offertory every Sunday during twenty years, without any deduction; by repeated donations from our own members—in several cases of £1,000 each; and by collections in hundreds of churches where the pastor preached on condition of receiving half, sometimes the whole, of the collection, without any deduction for time and service, except mere cost of travelling. As I have been charged with undue extravagance in the style of the building, I may be forgiven if I recall that, with frequent appeals to others, I was myself the largest contributor, in instalments during over twenty years—and thus comparatively small and easy; that the years of extra work, the distances travelled, the sermons preached, the visits paid and letters written, were enough to prove that if responsible for excess of expenditure in erecting a church of which the size and the architecture are in excess, I bore the chief burden of the care and cost and toil, not one iota of which I regret, but thank God for the honour and privilege, and for the zealous co-operation of friends without whom this temple of truth, this home of benevolence, this church of God, this place for the union of all Christians, would not have been raised.

I may add that the accounts were all carefully kept, the

books open for inspection, the accounts scrupulously audited, passed by public meeting of the congregation, and published in an annual report. I acted as assistant-secretary, receiving and depositing donations—all the donors being recorded in the bank-books, and on the final winding up, not a shilling discrepancy was in the total account. For this accuracy in this great business I owe something to my business training at Maidstone.

Saturday, July 7th, 1877.—Closing meeting of the Rowland Hill Committee, in my study, Hampstead :—

" On this seventh day of the week, and on this seventh day of the seventh month of the year 1877, this Committee, after seventeen years and upwards of continuous labour, having built the church and settled the accounts, dissolved—with devout prayer and praise, and singing he Doxology." (*Mem.*—This remarkable concurrence of dates of "seven"—the sacred number of the Old Testament Church—was not preconcerted, and was not noticed till after the meeting.)

The buildings were then handed over to the possession and care of the trustees, and the management of the affairs and worship to the pastor, elders, and members of the congregation.

May 22nd, 1878.—This day my beloved congregation presented to me—*i.e.* to the church in my name—a very beautiful alabaster pulpit. It is about 10 feet by 5 feet inside, and is built entirely of various kinds of alabaster. The style harmonises with the architecture of the church, and has about fifty small Gothic arches and columns. Round the top is a row of ornamental inlaid stones. Some of these are Labradorite, and the central one is crystal from Mars' Hill. The base of it is Welsh marble. A chair inside is one block of alabaster, too heavy for me to move, with my name engraved below the seat. Within the shadow of one of its arches in the rear is the inscription: " This pulpit was erected by the congregation in loving recognition of the labours of their pastor, the Rev. Newman Hall, LL.B., by whom the greater part of the funds for the erection of this church and adjoining hall was obtained, and to whose faithful ministry, under the Divine blessing, they attribute the prosperity of the Church and its institutions.—May 22nd, 1878. 'We preach Christ crucified.'" This memorial was entirely spontaneous, and the cost (£800) contributed by the unsolicited offerings of all the people. No mark of respect and affection could have taken a form so congenial.

Wednesday, March 16th, 1881.—Farewell. Next week Surrey Chapel will be surrendered to the freeholders. The Primitive Methodists have continued divine worship there during the last five years of the lease. At this, our last service, the building was crowded. I took the text from which Rowland Hill preached when the chapel was opened, ninety-eight years ago, during the whole of which time no other than the one Gospel has been heard there—"We preach Christ crucified." God be praised that the good work has not declined. At Rowland Hill's decease there were 500 members; now, in the new building, which is correctly designated "Christ Church perpetuation of Surrey Chapel," there are 1,000 members; the 2,300 scholars are now represented by 5,000, and the buildings are of twice the former capacity. We had reason for singing "Praise God." From the very pulpit occupied by Rowland Hill and J. Sherman, and occasionally by Venn, Scott, Chalmers, Irving, and others, it was my privilege to preach during twenty-two years. I closed my sermon somewhat in these words: "Christ was crucified but not conquered, and they who truly worshipped here triumph with Him. O ye who formerly preached and worshipped here, we, God helping us, will hand down unimpaired the traditions we have received—we still will preach and live 'Christ crucified' till we join with you in singing 'Worthy is the Lamb that was slain.'" After service I took leave of the little vestry in which I had conversed and prayed with 2,800 applicants for membership, besides many other seekers for counsel and comfort; and where week by week I had met with the elders on Mondays—my father among them—Jones, Ruck, Freeman, Hadland, J. V. Hall; then to the old parsonage; to the study where I visited Mrs. Sherman in her last illness, and where Rowland Hill passed to glory. But the work remains.

Sunday, March 20th.—I attended a united Communion

Service. The Primitive Methodist pastor, Mr. Senior, preached. For the last time I mounted the old pulpit. Visions of the past floated before me—standing in the crowded aisle as a student, listening to the sententious utterances of Jay, the cumulative periods of Parsons, the tender pathos of Sherman; then of my occasional visits as "supply" from Hull; then of my first Sunday as pastor there from "Brethren, pray for us"; then of twenty-two years' happy ministry without intermission from illness except on two Sundays. I peopled the pews with dear friends in their old seats, especially my beloved parents, looking lovingly and prayerfully at me. I thought of Rowland Hill preaching there within a fortnight of his decease, at eighty-eight, urging teachers to be "stedfast, unmovable, always abounding in the work of the Lord"; and I thanked God that substantially I had preached the same Gospel. Preachers pass away, buildings perish, but "the Word of the Lord endureth for ever."

CHAPTER XXI.

MARRIAGE AND HOME.

In 1869, bodily and mentally exhausted, I was ordered by Dr. Winslow to leave the country instantly. On February 5th, 1870, accompanied by my brother Arthur, I went to Italy to join a party of pilgrims to Jerusalem, under care of Mr. Cook. At Milan a lady, Miss Knipe, hitherto a total stranger, joined her old friends of the party, and was cordially greeted by Mr. B. and his sister.

In the preface to "A Modern Pilgrimage," written by this lady on her return, dated April, 1871, she relates how she was led to undertake this journey :—

"One Sunday evening at Cannes I was reading in Isaiah, and singing over the words, 'O Jerusalem, the Holy City,' when a letter was brought to me from E. B., commencing thus: 'Dear Friend,—Can you come to Jerusalem? C. and I are thinking of going. Answer as quickly as possible.' It was a singular coincidence, that at the very moment I was thinking of that 'Holy City,' and half wondering whether I should ever behold it, this invitation came. I was inclined to look upon it as a sort of sign that I *ought* to go, and it came to pass that after a few preliminary arrangements and a telegraphic despatch from L—y Park, which put the finishing touch to my hesitation at setting forth, I resolved to risk all and go. Although doubting the advisability of going with rather a 'mixed multitude' of strangers, I could not but feel that with such friends as C. and E. B. it would be 'all right,' and that we would make up our minds to share in the advantages and disadvantages of joining Mr. Cook's party. We found it altogether a most easy and agreeable way of being conveyed about the world, by the care and forethought with which everything is arranged. There are so many, that you are able to make your little *coterie* rather apart from the others ; and how agreeably ours was formed, and how friendship was strengthened by the pleasures and perils shared in the course of our 'pilgrimage,' will be seen in the following pages."

At Venice they presented a letter of introduction to me. To my brother I expressed regret at receiving this letter, obliging me to pay some courteous attentions, when I desired to travel unrecognised. He said I should consider it an honour for people to desire my acquaintance, and a privilege to give pleasure to others. He wisely considered that converse with others would help to take me out of myself.

During three months we five were together as fellow-pilgrims all day and every day. The three were godly Evangelical Episcopalians, but such differences were not thought of in the true unity of faith in Christ. We were associated in Bible study, prayer, singing, sketching, adventure, and varied talk; beside the Pyramids, on the Red Sea, at Joppa, Jerusalem, Jericho, Jordan; hymns on the Mount of Olives, kneeling in Gethsemane, at the Sepulchre, and at Bethlehem; at Jacob's Well, Nazareth, and in Galilee; crossing the spurs of Hermon; rambling in Damascus, amid the ruins of Ephesus, singing " Crown Him Lord of all " at the Parthenon; worshipping together on Mars' Hill, climbing the crater of Vesuvius, in the blue grotto of Capri; musing amid the ruins of the Forum, in Firenze la Bella, the Duomo of Milan, the lovely promontory of Bellagio. These two ladies, honoured me by calling me " Padre." I had no feeling but that of travelling friendship towards her who is now the life of my life.

I had left England in danger of misanthropy. I went abroad resolved to bury myself in myself henceforth. I still loved my mother with the passion of childhood, but her fine intellect was becoming obscured, and she could no longer be the companion and counsellor of former years. These two ladies, by their modesty, gentleness, unspoken sympathy, perfect refinement, unostentatious piety, interest in all things beautiful, applied the very balm which my wound needed. I began to forget my sorrow in their society. They intensified the interest of every scene. They were to me as messengers of God to solace me in my bitterest need. I regarded them with respectful admiration and gratitude. But I knew that such wayside, casual acquaintance did not justify any hope of an abiding friendship, and my brother and myself parted from them at London Bridge as a final separation.

Of course, I was delighted in the August following to receive an invitation from the Rev. W. Bathurst to Lydney Park, on occasion of a Christian Convention at his mansion. There I again met my three fellow-travellers, and a delightful week we enjoyed together, with a number of clergy and others, meeting daily in a tent for worship and conference.

Miss Knipe, having lost her mother in early life, had been chiefly brought up by her godly aunt at Bath, in the most exclusive school of Evangelical Church-of-Englandism. Both aunt and niece knew nothing of Dissenters, but felt it right to avoid intimacy and never to enter their chapels. Some years previously, when Miss Knipe was with these very friends visiting in Hastings, they asked her to go with them to hear Mr. Newman Hall give a lecture in the Congregational Chapel on his visit to America, when she replied, "No ; I do not care to go and hear a Dissenter, and in a *chapel*, too."

My mother was with me no longer. Here was one worthy of her, on whom I could fully rely for counsel and sympathy. I felt that this was as a boon from God, enabling me to trust, and pray, and preach, and rejoice.

Diary.—February 26th,1880.—To Metropolitan Tabernacle, together with H. and friend Cecil. After a grand sermon from Spurgeon, I introduced her to him. Several times he warmly grasped her hand with benedictions. H. asked his prayers. He said that after my trials I should be in danger of worshiping such an one, and warned me of idolatry. Sunday at Christ Church, where she sat with my sister Susan, and for the first time was seen by several of my friends.

March 9th, 1880.—Mr. and Mrs. Spalding, of Ore Place, near Hastings, were confidential friends whose house, with its beautiful grounds commanding extensive views, was often my recreative home. She was a daughter of the celebrated philanthropist and sister to my only surviving schoolfellow, Rev. Andrew Reed. They invited to meet me this lady, whose acquaintance they wished to make. Calm sea, blue sky, song of birds, spring flowers, sympathising friends, reflected our joy.

Easter Sunday, March 28th.—Preached twice as usual. Evening, "Peace be unto you"; then Holy Communion.

At 9 convened Elders, and informed them that at 9 next
morning I hoped to be married in the church. I had kept
my plans to myself to avoid any public demonstration. They
might inform a certain number of representative members
and special friends, rich and poor. The bride would have
preferred to be married quietly elsewhere, but I was desirous
of being married in the church for the erection of which I
had so diligently laboured, and among a people whose pastor
I had been thirty-five years.

Amongst those visitors, my precious, long-loved brother-
friend, Dr. H. Reynolds, was present in spirit, as expressed in
the following letter, written on the eve of the day :—

"Easter Day, 1880.

"BELOVED NEWMAN,—I am so far from well to-night that I dare
not hope to be present at C. C. to-morrow morning. You know how I
shall be present in spirit, and join in the praise your hearts render over
the newly-planted flowers of love to Him who is the source of their
beauty and fragrance. My amen to the benediction and my warmest
congratulations for the days of brightness that we trust are to come.
Seeds of joy watered with tears may fructify and be very beautiful.
God bless you *both*, to-morrow and for evermore, with the light of His
presence, doubling your love to each other in your common love of Him.
Our own Lord and Light and Love Eternal watch over you and your
beloved, and us, too, now and evermore.

"Yours most affectionately,
"HENRY R. REYNOLDS."

Easter Monday.—All the church officers, with about 200
members, had assembled, entering by the vestry, not exciting
notice. The bride was given away by her father, accompanied
by her brother, Mr. Henry Knipe, barrister-at-law, J.P. My
brothers were present, with wives, nephews, and nieces, and
many old friends of the bride. The Rev. Dr. Allon, with Rev
H. Grainger, performed the service. My friends, Revs. E. Cecil
and Samuel Minton, stood by, and Rev. E. White pronounced
the benediction. We sang part of the hymn, "The voice that
breathed o'er Eden," and at the close "O rest in the Lord and
wait patiently for Him" was played on the organ. Afterwards
I led the bride into the large vestry, and introduced to her
the officers of the church and their ladies and chief workers,
amongst whom the cake was distributed.

After singing together the Doxology, when the visitors all had departed, my bride and I knelt at the communion table and consecrated our linked lives anew to the giver of every good and perfect gift.

In due course the papers announced, among the list of marriages :—

"On Monday, 29th inst., at Christ Church, Westminster Bridge Road, by the Rev. Dr. Allon, assisted by Rev. Edward White, Rev. Newman Hall, LL.B., to Harriet Mary Margaret, eldest daughter of Edward Knipe, Esq., of Elvaston Place, Queen's Gate, and of Water Newton, Hunts."

During many years I have known sorrow beyond words to express, but now God has given gladness still more ineffable. "When the Lord turned again the captivity of Zion, we were like them that dream." When we knelt together at the Communion Table I remembered a night when there alone, and in the pulpit, I committed the church, my ministry, and the future to God. Now to have knelt there with her in the presence of God, with the loving sympathy of family, friends, and congregation ! If there are "groanings" there are hallelujahs " which cannot be uttered." A new stop was heard that day in the organ, Vox Angelica.

April 4th, Sunday.—In the grand cathedral of Canterbury. Sang the Te Deum, and together at the table of the Lord. To Nice, Rome, Venice. Sunday, May 9th.—Bellagio. Changes of locality have only been the shifting distances of the abiding fore-ground. It was such a joy to re-visit as a unity scenes familiar as only to separate persons. We climbed the cone of Vesuvius, which we ascended ten years before as casual fellow-travellers. Again re-visited the blue grotto of Capri, and lovely Sorrento, mused amid the ruins of the Forum, stood beneath the solemn dome of the Pantheon, saw greater beauty in transcendent works of art because seen together, gliding in gondolas in and out among Venetian palaces, and now in the paradise of Serbelloni on Lake Como. Upon a wooded eminence commanding a glorious view of the lake, while nightingales sang an accompaniment, and spring blossoms flung around their incense, we blended our praises and prayers to Him who through the wilderness had brought us to Beulah.

At Lugano symptoms of measles suddenly developed in H., possibly caught from an invalid with whom we had travelled in the train, and wo were detained about ten days. On her recovery we went out in a boat, when the water was without a ripple, and the sky without a cloud. A sudden thunderstorm—torrents of rain on the soaked awning—terrific blast —pull to nearest shore—refuge in gap of wall—carried H. to a hut—procured carriage from the town.

I might well fear such an exposure when recovering from such an illness! " Bless the Lord, O my soul—who healeth all thy diseases." Sunday, May 30th.—Milan—Duomo together —poem in marble. Sunday, June 6th.—Lausanne. I should have preached at home but for this sickness. The Gospel for the day with unfortunate opportuneness contained the words, "I have married a wife, and therefore I cannot come."

Wednesday, June 9th.—Home! home, indeed: the best part of all our journey. Dear relatives to welcome us— little dog Fido beside himself with joy. Together praising God, and seeking benediction on our dwelling.

The trustees and elders of the church sent us the following congratulation:—

" We, Trustees and Elders of Christ Church, avail ourselves of the earliest opportunity to offer you a very cordial welcome, and repeat the assurance we have on former occasions given you, that we deeply sympathise with you in all your joys and sorrows; and we do so especially at the present time, when you return to us relieved of the heavy trouble which had long pressed upon you, and with the prospect of future years of domestic happiness in loving companionship with her whom you have recently made your wife. We earnestly pray that God's richest blessings may rest on you both—that His love may fill your hearts, and that your home may be made bright by His abiding presence. Although Mrs. Newman Hall is almost a stranger to us, we are prepared to welcome her, as the wife of our Pastor, with the greatest cordiality. We hope she will find herself happy in association with us in all the work and worship of the Church; and that she may not only be a loving helpmate to her husband, but a zealous co-worker with us in the various works of usefulness in which we are engaged. Her presence amongst us, we anticipate, will be an influence for great good, stimulating to energy and combined effort to make the message of the Gospel acceptable to those among whom we labour, and for whom our prayer is that they may be saved.

"We hail with joy and gratitude your return to us as our Pastor, in your present happy circumstances. The affection we have always felt for you, and the confidence we have had in you are unabated. We increasingly value your ministry, and while we would not forget how much we owe to those who minister to us in your absence, we assure you no one is so acceptable to us as our own Pastor, upon whose stated ministry, we deeply feel, the prosperity of the Church chiefly depends. We cannot look back upon the twenty-six years of your Pastorate without feelings of devout thankfulness for your faithful proclamation of Evangelical truth, the stimulus you have given to Evangelical labour, and the efforts you have made to render the services of the sanctuary attractive and profitable. For these, and other characteristics of your work, we have as a Church to acknowledge our indebtedness to you ; and cannot but rejoice that now, as it were, a new epoch has arrived, when, under happier circumstances than formerly, you resume your duties of the Pastor of Christ Church, an opportunity for increased usefulness seems to present itself. We have every facility for carrying on the work of God, especially in the possession of a beautiful church, capable of containing thousands who flock to hear the Gospel, and which we trust will be for ages the spiritual birthplace of souls, and, erected as it was mainly by your efforts, a standing memorial of your marvellous energy, noble self-sacrifice, and spontaneous liberality. We know, dear friend, how earnestly you desire the welfare of the Church, that there may be a spiritual awakening in our midst, that souls may be saved — that those who do love Christ may openly confess it, and that the Church by united, earnest, persevering prayer may obtain an abundant outpouring of the Holy Spirit, without which no progress will be made in sanctity. We shall always be happy to aid you in any steps you may see fit to take to accomplish these results. The words we use but feebly express our sentiments, but you will accept them, as indicating, at least, how ardently we desire the increased usefulness and happiness of our Pastor and the growing prosperity of the Church.

"Once more, accept our hearty congratulations upon your marriage, and our best wishes that you and your dear wife may live together for many years in the enjoyment of every temporal and spiritual blessing. Most sincerely do we adopt the words of an ancient salutation, as aptly expressing the feelings of our own hearts and say, 'The blessing of the Lord be upon you ; we bless you in the name of the Lord.'

"June 5th, 1880."

A PORTRAIT.

Instinct with goodness ; sensible, refined,
Both grave and gay, wise, witty ; native grace
More natural by noblest culture made ;
A charm enhancing beauty in a face

The earthly mirror of a heavenly mind,
Perennial charm, in autumn ne'er to fade ;
Fair landscape varied, sunshine, pensive shade ;
With nooks where friends sweet hidden flowers may find ;
A steadfast, tender, sympathising heart ;
Crowning man's strength with beauty, counterpart ;
An angel forming but a woman still,
Happy all woman's holy place to fill :
Far wealthier than by widest empire's throne,
The man who calls such treasure all his own.

March, 1880.   N. H.

Bonchurch, March 29th, 1881.—Bless the Lord, O my soul ! Day of days ! Grateful to the Giver, I look back on a year of happiness more intense than I thought possible in the world, and still less dreamed that I should ever experience. Without irreverence, I say—" Next to the gift of Christ, ' thanks be unto God for His unspeakable gift ! ' " We came to " seaside cottage " for the brightest day in the calendar. From our window we look across a little lawn, beyond the low wall of which we see only the ocean, whose tiny waves murmur on the beach below. No one passes. A few days alone together—rambling on the shore, the cliffs, and the wood in the landslip. I sometimes ask why I have never known till now what I am capable of enjoying ; now I may hope for it during a long evening of life.

Within doors we have the companionship of books :— Carlyle, George Eliot, Homer, Cowper, Tennyson. At intervals I write in shorthand memories of my child-life, which H. copies out. When she reads to me, I fill up the sketches taken in wedding-tour.

Sunday morning, service in the ancient church. How lovely is the scene—the greenest turf radiant with the golden stars of celandine and tufts of primroses ; rocks draperied with ivy ; graves lovingly decorated with daffodils, each with its daisied turf, or marble cross ; the sea glimmering through the branches, the " ivy-mantled tower." But I feel it needless to describe it when I have before me lines of my H. :—

Within sight of the seas,
All encircled by trees,
With a mantle of leaves,
Made of ivy that weaves
Its dark verdure around.
There is never a sound
Of the strife of the day :
'Tis a spot where you pray.
That like peace may be won,
When your own day is done :
For a churchyard more fair
I know not elsewhere.

From centuries hoary
The church stands in story ;
Not far from its wall
A shadow doth fall :
By a cross it is made,
That in sunshine or shade
Lieth low on the grave,
As the emblem to save.
Blest he who there sleeping,
His soul in God's keeping—
Beyond moan of the sea,
Beyond shadows that flee.

And so all the dead lie,
Within sight of the sky,
'Midst the circle of trees,
Within sound of the seas.

H. M. M. H.

CHAPTER XXII.

RAMBLES TOGETHER.

SHORTLY after our marriage we visited Chamounix, and by way of the Flegère were approaching the Brévent, when we suddenly came to a gap caused by the fall of a rock. The path was not wide enough for the guide to walk by the side of the mule. To my horror I suddenly saw the hind legs of the animal beginning to slip, the front legs having crossed. It was only by a vigorous pull of the chain of the mule by the guide, who was in front, that a most terrible catastrophe was averted. For some years I could not speak of it, but now I record it with special thankfulness. My wife merely remarked to me as I came up to her full of emotion, "That was a very awkward place!" Yet she told me afterwards that when she felt the mule slipping, and looked to see if it were possible to jump off from it, she saw only air beneath her on the left side of the saddle.

Diary.—1886. May 22.—Home from Holy Land—delightful fellowship with ministerial brethren, and a wife in perfect sympathy with nature, art, and sacred scenes. Can it be that this day I reach my threescore years and ten, yet feel only fifty? Responsibilities increase with lessening opportunities.

Wedding counsel.—My niece was married at our district parish church, Hampstead. I acted as father. At the close of the service the vicar, Rev. G. Head, invited me to address the congregation, which I did from the Communion steps, much as follows:—

"Love is the fulfilling of Law. Love will eclipse authority in the husband by solicitude for the best welfare of the wife. Love will supersede obedience in the wife by the alacrity that anticipates the wish of the husband. Love blending two lives blends also two wills, so that the pleasure of each becomes the bliss of both.

"To others I say, If the physical glory of the man is strength, use it not to dominate, but protect; if the physical glory of the woman is beauty, let her above all seek the 'beauties of holiness,' the 'ornament of a meek and quiet spirit.' And to all, married or single, I would say, Accept Him Who woos us for His bride; 'love Him Who first loved us;' then He will be our Guardian and bliss here; and when this life ends will welcome us to His eternal home."

Bath, Oct. 21, 1886.—With wife to Blind Home. Wife in former days used to visit there frequently; had not been there for ten years. Her name not announced. She said, "An old friend has come to see you." There was a general cry of her name. Her voice had awakened heart memories. How their faces shone with joy as she took each by the hand! I never saw her face more radiant, or heard her voice more sweet than as she greeted these old blind friends. It was worth going to Bath to see.

March 29, 1887.—We are reading the "Life of Lord Shaftesbury," and I copy words of his which express my own heart:—

"It is a most bountiful answer to one's prayers to have obtained a wife, in the highest matters and in the smallest details, after my imagination and heart. Often do I recollect the very words of my entreaties that God would give me a wife for my comfort, improvement, and safety. He has granted me to the *full* all I desired, and far more than I deserved, praised be His holy Name." Amen.

1889.—It was at Riffel that we first met two choice friends. I was seated near an athlete, whom I regarded as a distinguished member of the Alpine Club. Another mountaineer called him "Smith," and something was said about his being a Scotch parson. "May I ask if you are *Isaiah* Smith? It is the book I was reading last, and it now lies on my study table." Here we both made the acquaintance of the lady who soon after became the angel of his home.

Dec. 18.—To the wedding of our Alpine friends. Though an Episcopalian, the bride became a pattern mistress of a Scotch manse at Aberdeen: with her husband, diligent in nurturing the church. So now (1895) helping him in guarding his time, revising his proofs, and visiting with him as missionaries amongst the poorest of the inhabitants of Glasgow.

He has lately published " The Minor Prophets," and is in the possession of two fine boys whom we designate by that title.

Hurried fear of the results of critical and scientific research reminds me of the word, " He that believeth shall not make haste." The second part of Isaiah, equally with the first, lifts up the soul to God, and reveals the Spirit's inspiration through human instrumentality, whether by one amanuensis or by two.

Dec. 4, 1891.—To Woodsford to visit an old servant, now the wife of a small farmer, volunteer verger of an iron mission room in their garden. They entertain freely the local preachers on Sundays. Special service this evening. H. gave a personal testimony about the love of Christ, alluding to several of the little company she used to know (now infirm and crippled) when she paid long visits to the then rector, her uncle, Rev. Wenham Knipe, and used to lead the singing. She then sang a hymn as a solo, and I preached to the rustic congregation. May the latent power unexpectedly indicated in their old friend be hereafter developed for much usefulness.

March 29, 1894 :—

TOGETHER.

(AFTER FOURTEEN YEARS.)

" TOGETHER ! O the rapture of the day
When two full streams that side by side had run,
With mutual gladness glided into one !
No longer twain—inseparable alway.
O blissful hope, though swift years pass away,
Never will set that daily brightening sun,
Never be lost this growing treasure won.
Together in the earthly, heavenly race,
In holy service as in fond embrace :
The life, bliss, work of love is never done.
Together now, dearer and still more dear—
Such blending of two kindred spirits here
Is pledge and earnest of the perfect love
Which constitutes the home of Heaven above."

Together in my preaching journeys and missions, in re-creative travels, and in home engagements. Referring to

" Recreations," on a former page I could not write as I do now, of many a time of refreshment, listening to piano improvisation, or hearing again and again the mellow music of rich hymns as " When I survey the wondrous Cross," to an old Hebrew methody, or rambling together, partners in sketching, and I am now greatly indebted to an adept in water-colours, who has many books full of interesting reproductions of places seen together.

In 1891 we again met our friends at the Riffel. They were forming a party, chiefly of Alpine clubmen, and asked me to join them "just for a ramble on the ice." As their ages averaged from twenty to thirty-five, and I was seventy-five, I pleaded unfitness, but as they kindly persisted I took my own guide, so as to be no hindrance. We were soon on the medial moraine of the Gorner Glacier, and then were clambering up seracs, piled in random confusion. Cutting every step on the steep slopes I thought, " When next I see a fly on the wall I shall say, I don't think much of your climbing, I've done it myself." But I should not have ventured to try it had not the strong and skilful Professor been next behind me on the rope. Climbing a specially steep ice crag, I anticipated that when we reached the crest I should be able to walk on a level top ; but the stride from the very last step was so long that I could not have stretched my leg sufficiently, but for the strong arm behind. Alas ! there was only a knife-edge, so that I had to use it as a saddle and straddle along. At length we reached a group of rocks in the middle of the ice, where a plentiful *al fresco* was followed by tales and songs. Wonderful that we ever got there ! But how to get away ? I suggested I should go off with my guide but they said it would be easier to go forward. And after an adventurous search for a passage through the intricacy of icy pyramids, we landed safely on the mountain-side after eight hours clamber. My companions went in advance to report what they kindly regarded as my memorable achievement. To my wife, who gladly greeted me, I proposed, after a cup of tea, a long walk together in the forest.

March 29, 1896:—

EXCHANGE NO ROBBERY.

(AFTER SIXTEEN YEARS.)

I CANNOT find a flower so fair
    That true expression can convey,
Of half this overflowing heart
    Would of that blissful morning say.

The sun had never shone so bright,
    The sky had never smiled so blue,
Until on that celestial day,
    As Bride and Wife, I greeted you.

The song of lark was ne'er so sweet,
    Its eager flight so near the sky,
As tuneful lay of mine did soar
    More and more rapturously on high.

And is all this o'erpast and gone?
    Does faint remembrance only stay?
Thank God! our lives themselves prolonged,
    Are a perpetual Wedding Day.

Impromptu Response.

Could I once exceed in passion
    All the love-songs ever writ;
Though such lines might be the fashion,
    Would they prove my love more fit
Than I do, in whispering low?
    All my *being* doth it show.

Diary.—Aug. 12, 1897.—Riffel again. To the Gorner Grat
to bid farewell. Heeding kind caution not to over-fatigue
myself I took mule to the summit, baked with sunshine and
no perspiration to relieve it. On my way down sudden sickness. When near hotel sank on the path. Soon in room.
"Mountain sickness." Fell fainting on floor. An hour of
anxious suspense. A clever young doctor at the hotel aided
my restoration, and told me afterwards that there was one
anxious half-hour. The tender care of my H. is a lasting
memory, which makes me thank God for this brief illness.
Dean Lefroy's kindly talk and prayer increased the gladness

of a sick room which I was able within four days to exchange for the mountain side and forest glade.

While I was recovering, a gentleman at the same hotel, thirty years my junior, was gradually sinking from a similar attack. To breathe an atmosphere less rarefied he was carried down to Zermatt, but died the next day, and his body was laid to rest in the English cemetery there. " One shall be taken, and the other left."

Hampstead Heath is the scene of our most frequent rambles together. Our home is within three minutes' walk of its summit, called Jack Straw's Castle. From this eminence we can see, in clear weather, Windsor Castle, Harrow-on-the-Hill, the lake-like reservoir at the Welsh Harp, Hendon, Totteridge, Finchley, Barnet, where Wilberforce once lived, Highgate, where the houses of Cromwell and Ireton still remain, and Lauderdale House with its contrasted memories of Charles II., and the site of Andrew Marvell's cottage, and the embowering trees of the home of the philanthropist, Baroness Burdett-Coutts, and the old house of Coleridge ; and then the vast metropolis of the world with its countless domes and spires, St. Paul's towering above them all. Near the summit are the recent residence of Mrs. Andrew Charles, and the old mansion at North End, where Pitt retreated for a time from the anxieties of State, and the dell where musical memories linger of Shelley and Keats, and the hotel which Dickens often made the starting-point of many rambles. Some know the Heath only as the resort of holiday crowds ; but there are glens and avenues and copses where you may wander for hours and meet scarcely anyone. In spring the May trees are a sight worth walking miles to behold, while anemones, celandines, blue-bells, golden gorse, and yellow broom beautify the scene which larks, black-birds, and thrushes gladden with their songs. Here I often met and chatted with our dear friend and neighbour, Hugh Matheson, venerated elder of the Scottish Presbyterian Church, known far and wide for his generous sympathy with all philanthropic efforts, and love for all who love Christ.

CHAPTER XXIII.

WHEN I accepted the pastorate, the government and direction
of the church and its affairs were legally in the hands of the
pastor and trustees. The new church had a new trust. The
constitution of the church is essentially Congregational, with
an element of Presbyterianism. A body of "trustees" regulate
finance ; a body of "elders" assist the minister in matters of
worship, discipline, visitation, relief of the poor. Both are
appointed by vote of the communicants. When a pastor is
to be appointed, trustees and elders form a joint committee to
select a suitable candidate, who is then proposed to a full
meeting of the members. If not accepted, another is nomi-
nated by the same "Church Council." This method avoids
competition, as there is only one candidate at a time.

The absolute and invariable practice is that every account
of every institution be properly audited, put to the vote, and
printed in an annual report of the church. Thus all the congregation and the public may know whatever monies are
collected and exactly how expended. During my whole
pastorate of thirty-eight years no money was collected for
which a full account was not rendered, and printed in the
annual report of the "Church and its Institutions."

I was responsible for drafting the trust—of course, with
the advice and concurrence of the officers of the old building.
That the area of choice of pastor might be as broad as possible,
while evangelical truth was essential, no assent was demanded
to any special mode of church government or fixed method
of worship. Thus Episcopalians, Methodists, Baptists, Presbyterians, as well as Congregationalists, are free to become
members and to take office.

"March 1, 1892.

" *To the Trustees and Elders of Christ Church.*

"With the deepest personal regret, and solely with a view to the interests of the Church, I give notice that I intend to resign the office of pastor at the close of the present pastoral year—*i.e.* June 26. Having commenced my pastorate work at Surrey Chapel, July 2, '54, this will complete thirty-eight years of happy pastorate and fifty years of service as an ordained minister. I cannot be too thankful for the undeviating respect and affectionate co-operation of my church-officers during all this period ; but at my age, in the near certainty of lessening powers and the increasing need of more varied and active service, I feel it my duty to make way for another—younger, stronger, and better fitted for the changed character of the times and neighbourhood—through whom not only the traditions of our church may be maintained, but the people of the district drawn in, to fill the building whose true glory must ever be the gathering of souls hungry for the bread of life.

"Your loving friend and pastor,

" NEWMAN HALL."

Diary.—June 27th.—Where shall we look for another pastor over such a church ? It was reported that the Rev. F. B. Meyer, pastor of Regent's Park Baptist Church, was being urged by Mr. Moody to join him in evangelistic work in America. Let us also appeal to him to evangelise in South London as president of all our operations, known as he is and honoured for godliness, eloquence, usefulness, and evangelistic zeal. Our "Kirk Session" unanimously made overtures, and after prayerful conferences with him it was decided to propose him to the communicants. After a fortnight's notice there was a great assembly of nearly eight hundred members, to whom the case was stated, with hearty recommendation by officers of the church and pastor. It was at once decided unanimously to invite the Rev. Frederick Meyer to the pastorate. All rose and sang the Doxology. Four elders at once drove off in quest of Mr. Meyer, whom they found in his vestry, and who promised his prayerful consideration. In conference all his proposed methods were cordially approved, and his difficulty respecting adult baptism met by a promise to provide a baptistery for those who desired immersion, while retaining the practice of infant baptism as before, according to choice. Bless the Lord, O my soul! If the church becomes fuller than ever, and my fainter light be eclipsed by his brighter one, my heart will overflow with gratitude.

Sunday, July 10th, 1892.—Farewell to Christ Church. Preached morning, "That fiftieth year shall be a jubilee " and " Thou shalt remember all the way by which the Lord thy God hath led thee "; "Ebenezer," a review of fifty years' ministry. An hour in delivery. Difficult to repress emotion. At the close I said that " all that I have ever been or done worthy the commendation of my brethren is owing to my mother, who, humanly speaking, is the author of my ministry." I then narrated what is recorded in earlier pages relating to my childhood and youth in connection with her influence. I thus concluded my last sermon as pastor:—

"The more I look back, it is with an increasing sense of my own unworthiness, multiplied omissions, much that might have been done for the Church that was not done, and for Christ. I need more and more that great atonement which I preach to others. Oh ! but for the blood of Jesus Christ that cleanseth from all sin, I assure you I should close my jubilee with a burdened spirit ; but I close it with thankfulness to a beloved congregation, a loyal and zealous band of church officers, a most helpful and beloved assistant minister ; to a wife devoted to God and His service, loyal to this church of her adoption, by birth a Church-woman, and by wise counsel, unfailing affection, constant care, and blended prayers, helping the pastor to perform duties and bear responsibilities which otherwise would have sometimes injured his health and oppressed his spirit, and so in the most effective and appropriate manner by helping the pastor ministering to his church. For all this I render hearty thanks to the Giver of all good, and say, ' Bless the Lord, O my soul, and forget not all his benefits.'"

In the afternoon I bade farewell to the Sunday-school. In the evening I preached from my first text, "God so loved the world," and then "That I may not have laboured in vain." After sermon, five hundred at Holy Communion.

Monday.—Farewell prayer-meeting.—" Keep yourselves in the love of God."

Tuesday.—Farewell meeting and presentation in the church chancel, filled with brother ministers and church officers. Touching prayer by dear Joshua Harrison. Deputations from Temperance League, Peace Society, Band of Hope Union, Sailors' Society, Lambeth Mission, Sunday-school, country churches, Albion Church, Hull, congregation of Christ Church. Then an address from the church, handsomely framed, written by the senior elder, devoted friend of myself and the church, Mr. Webb, read by Mr. Atley, the treasurer, with an elaborate service of silver, and a purse of £200, which I devoted to the institutions of the church, guaranteeing the cost of erection of a baptistery for those who might desire immersion. Sir George Williams, my very dear friend, from the beginning a trustee of the church, presided. Lord Kinnaird uttered hearty congratulations. Other speeches by my most dear friend, Henry Reynolds, by the noble-hearted Presbyterian Moderator, Monro Gibson, by my beloved "son in the Gospel," Robert Downes, editor of *Great Thoughts*, and others. Then I rose again, and referred to our anxiety and prayer about a suitable successor, and how the whole church had unanimously accepted the designation of the elders, and had invited the Rev. F. B. Meyer. I said, "This morning I received his letter of acceptance," which I then read, and called for him from the rear of the chancel. I took him by the hand, amid great emotion, all rising to greet him. Then I said, "I now welcome you, dear brother, as successor of Rowland Hill, James Sherman, and Newman Hall, the fourth pastor of Surrey Chapel, perpetuated in Christ Church." (Great demonstration.) "If you love me, my dear people, show it by loving him. The more the church profits under his ministry and outstrips any work of mine, the more I shall rejoice and thank God."

Diary.—Very remarkable has been the answer to our prayers in every respect. Resignation of a pastorate of thirty-eight years, and the welcome to his successor on the same evening—the church not one hour without a pastor —and the wall of partition between Baptist and Independent taken down by those who, using the font for babies, provide also a bath for adults.

Kind letters were read from the Dean of Norwich, the Archdeacon of London, Sir Fowell Buxton, Professor George

Adam Smith, and many others. It was midnight before we
could leave the church, so many waiting for another last
farewell. The occasion gradually recedes, but as a mountain
from which we retire reveals itself more and more, so am I
increasingly impressed with a sense of unworthiness of all
this commendation, and gratitude to God, His servants, and
my church. O what wonderful mercy God has shown me all
these fifty years—from what troubles delivered, in what
sorrows comforted, and enabled me during more than half
a century to preach the old Gospel with scarcely any interruption from sickness and with increasing joy! Hallelujah!

Having thus terminated my life-work as pastor of a single
church, in order to avoid the misrepresentations often made
in regard to the incomes of ministers of Free churches, I wish
to say that my average income from the churches at Hull and
in London did not exceed £500—for a few years larger, but
for many much less. Surely not exorbitant, considering the
various and constant applications from my own and other
churches and societies. Though constantly preaching, often
four times weekly, for other churches, I asked for no remunera-
tion for the extra work, considering my regular income from
pastorate adequate in my case to cover my ministries elsewhere. But whatever was voluntarily given me I devoted to
the institutions of my own church as some equivalent for the
loss of my time and service in other directions. These sums
were regularly audited in the annual accounts. For several
years I asked half of the collections when I preached elsewhere
in aid of our building fund, which thus was augmented by
more than a thousand pounds. But now that pastoral support ceased, I have felt warranted in asking the churches
served to take the place of the one which had acted on the
apostolic principle—" The labourer is worthy of his hire." But
I have made it a rule that, unless the excess of average collection covers the excess of average fee, I return the balance,
so that no church served by me should suffer financially.
In every case no loss has occurred, but almost always considerable gain. As some pastors need, deserve, and receive
fees for such extra service, and are often misrepresented in

receiving what in many cases is a most inadequate recognition I may be pardoned for stating my own experience, that in recompense for long journeys, often three days in the week, abstracted from literary and other work, preaching fees for forty Sundays in the year have averaged under £250. Of course, during the week and otherwise vacant Sundays I have served many poor churches freely. But in all cases I have been more than repaid by generous hospitality and brotherly love.

Friends wished that supplemental to the celebration of the jubilee of fifty years' pastorate, there should be a jubilee to celebrate my eightieth year of life, in which a larger constituency might share. It was resolved that a memorial present should be made to me in the form of a full-sized oil-portrait. This was well executed by Mr. Herbert Olivier, and was shown in the annual exhibition of the Royal Academy and afterwards at Liverpool.

Diary.—May 22, 1895.—Can it be true that I enter my eightieth year? I do not feel more than sixty. "Bless the Lord, O my soul: and all that is within me, bless His holy name."

"He forgiveth all thine iniquities."—Justification.
"He healeth all thy diseases, body and soul."—Sanctification.
"He redeemeth thy life from destruction."—Salvation by Christ.
"He crowneth thee with loving-kindness and tender mercies."

Love the crown of all the blessings of this life; the love of God, the "crown that fadeth not away." God should be praised for any wilderness that leads towards Paradise. May I be more diligent as opportunities lessen.

May 23.—Kept birthday by a preaching visit to Southminster, small village in Essex. Text—"Ye are my friends." Painted from life a true friend—disinterested, faithful, tender, reciprocal; each needing mutual intercourse; forbearance unchanging; but such friends die—our heavenly Friend ever present.

May 22, 1896.—Eightieth birthday jubilee. The *Christian* newspaper reported that:—

"The proceedings were a hearty acknowledgment of Dr. Hall's public work during a long period, and a testimony to the deep and

wide influence which he has exerted in the religious life of two generations. A large number of notabilities and others who could not attend,
wrote letters of congratulation; these included Mr. Gladstone, Sir
George Williams, the Duke of Westminster, the Archbishop of York
the Bishop of Exeter, the Bishop of Gloucester, Archdeacon Sinclair,
Dr. Guinness Rogers, Dr. Clifford, Dr. Rigg, Thomas Spurgeon, and
scores of others.

"Lord Kinnaird, who presided, spoke some hearty words, followed
by Dr. Horton, who said it was difficult to believe that Dr. Hall was
eighty years of age, but having been satisfied by statistics that such
was undoubtedly the case, he had gained a new impression of what old
age was; in fact, old age had lost its terror for him, and he would no
longer entertain his former fears regarding it. Then an address from
a Ministers' Fraternal, acknowledging Dr. Hall's contribution to
Scripture exposition. The members of this Fraternal included Andrew
Reed, Edward White, Monro Gibson, D.D., Robert Horton, D.D.,
R. Dawson, A. Connell, F. Hastings, S. Hawker, C. Horne, G.
Macgregor, R. Thornton, D.D., G. Hanson, F. Meyer, A. Ramsay.
The Rev. Henry Grainger spoke of having been for twenty-three
years a colleague in Christian work with unbroken harmony. The
Rev. F. Hastings—who had taken an active part in organising the
meeting and the presentation—followed with an address from the
United States, accompanied by an album of paintings. Many famous
names, of statesmen, divines, and philanthropists, were inscribed on
the document. He then, in hearty terms, unveiled and presented the
portrait amid loud cheers.

"After thankful acknowledgment Newman Hall said that he had
felt, with increasing years, how small are the differences of Evangelical
Christians when agreed on the fundamental doctrine of the Atonement.
He rejoiced that his successor was so faithful in this, and that his
ministry was greatly and increasingly blessed among a people so busy
in endeavours to benefit the ignorant and poor that denominational
differences were never discussed.

"The Rev. Edward White remarked that during the long course of a
fifty years' ministry he had received from no one such hearty and
supporting affection as from Dr. Hall. Dr. R. P. Downes gave a
striking testimony. At the age of nineteen, while 'tasting life' in
London, he was taken by a friend to Old Surrey Chapel, and there
heard sermons which turned the course of his life. The Rev. R. Balgarnie
described experiences of friendship with Dr. Hall many years ago; and
hearty addresses were also delivered by the Revs. Arthur Hall and
W. Mottram. The former adopted teetotal principles through his elder
brother's advocacy, and that was with him the first step to the cross of
Jesus Christ."

After the presentations I said:—

"Fourscore years! Solemn, but not sad. The milestone

does not record 'nearing grave,' but 'glory,' not foreshadowing the end of life, but brightening the beginning. 'Many happy returns' means 'May every return be happy in the service and love of God.' I am often saluted as old, but I do not feel old. Age weakens only capacity for playthings of childhood. The more abiding bounties and beauties cause fuller joy with increasing experience. Poetry, science, mountains, flowers, the human face divine, radiant with devotion to God and affection to man ; the Gospel studied and preached, the high purpose of seeking to save the lost, Christian intercourse, home bliss, communion with God, the 'Blessed Hope' nearing and brightening. Age can experience in these truer joy than is possible for youth ; and thus my heart thrills in response to your greetings by hand, eye, voice, and gifts." Then after some references to my childhood, " As my earlier days were bright with a mother's love, now my maturer years are brightened by one in whom all a mother's tenderness blends with that of a still closer tie, combining all that is meant by counsellor, comforter, guardian; helper in all my studies, prayers, and works. Thus the promise is realised—'At evening-tide it shall be light.'"

The following letter was read from the Rev. Dr. Cuyler:—

"176, South Oxford St.,

"Brooklyn, U.S.A.,

"May 8th, 1896.

"BELOVED BROTHER HALL,—For what shall I most heartily congratulate you on your eightieth birthday?

"Shall it be for the production of that immortal love-message, '*Come to Jesus*'?

"Or shall it be for a faithful ministry of the blessed Gospel for nearly threescore years?

"Or shall it be for all your abundant labors on behalf of Temperance, and Peace, and Freedom, and Righteousness, in your own and other lands?

"All these have been combined in your fourscore years of consecrated service—and, for all these, God's people honor and love you in every clime.

"To me and to the members of my former flock you are the beloved personal friend ; and our prayer is that the autumn of your long, useful, and Heaven-blessed life may be gladdened by the sweet sunshine of our dear Master's countenance!

"My dear wife joins me in loving salutations to Mrs. Hall and yourself; and believe me,

"Yours to the heart's core,

"THEODORE L. CUYLER."

The following is a copy of the American address, artistically decorated and enriched by coloured drawings of the head of President Lincoln, and the House of Representatives:—

"As Citizens of the United States of America we tender to you our most cordial congratulations on your

EIGHTIETH BIRTHDAY,

and we rejoice in the gracious blessings with which our Heavenly Father has crowned your long and beneficent public career.

"For nearly half a century your writings have made your name a household word among the Christian people of our land.

"At a critical time when the peaceful relations between Great Britain and America were seriously threatened, your voice was one of the first to be raised in protest against any hasty outbreak of popular resentment.

"During our sanguinary civil conflict you took your nobly resolute stand alongside of John Bright and the other unflinching friends of American Union.

"When your congregation erected its new edifice of worship it was your happy suggestion that its lofty tower should bear the name of

OUR BELOVED LINCOLN,

and should stand as an abiding memorial of

EMANCIPATION,

and a token of

INTERNATIONAL BROTHERHOOD.

"Throughout your whole busy and beneficent career we have recognised in you the eloquent champion of Bible truth, of Christian fraternity, of impartial freedom, of peace, of temperance, and of manifold measures of social reform.

"In the name of our countrymen we thank God for you, and for the splendid service you have wrought for our common humanity; and our fervent prayer is that your remaining years may be gladdened by the Divine favor, and by the grateful love of your fellow-men in every clime."

Amongst the signatures are those of Bishop Potter, Doctors Storr, Strong, Cuyler, J. Hall, Roberts, Ellinwood, Atterbury, Abbot; Messrs. Vanderbilt, Low, Stuart, Terry,

Ward, Field, Depew, Parkhurst, Morse, and others; and Mrs.
W. E. Dodge.

Diary.—April 13, 1892.—Invitation by Edinburgh University to receive the honorary degree of D.D. Guests of Sir T.
and Lady Clark. Dined at Sir W. H. Muir's, late Lieutenant-
Governor of Bengal, Chancellor of the University, with Professors and hon. graduates. Sat next Sir Charles Tupper, during
many years Prime Minister of Nova Scotia—interesting
conversation—laws repressive of drink traffic should not go
beyond public opinion, else they will be evaded; so his measure
for Nova Scotia required a majority of two-thirds of the
population. Canada most loyal to the Empire.

April 14.—Capping Day. Vice-Chancellor in grand robe
with mace, with three candidates for D.D., and eight for LL.D.,
and twenty Professors, among whom my old friend Blackie.
After prayers, the name of each candidate was announced,
and each stood before the Chancellor while the Dean read
the reasons for conferring the degrees. In my case notice was
taken of my London University LL.B., Chairmanship of the
Congregational Union of England and Wales, books written,
and fifty years of ministry. Over each graduate in turn the
Chancellor held a large black cap, pronounced the usual
Latin formula, while the Clerk placed the appropriate hood
over the shoulders of each candidate, who then bowed and
returned to his seat. Then a procession to St. Giles' church,
where solemn service, partly liturgical and choral, and an
eloquent and appropriate sermon by Canon Tristram. All
was over at 2 p.m. Our hostess took us a drive round
Arthur's Seat, with our dear friend, Mrs. George Adam Smith,
who had come from Aberdeen to represent her husband.

Christian Convention at the house of Lord and Lady
Mount Temple, Broadlands, with fifty other guests, among
whom were clergy very high and very low, Established and
Free, Quakers and Salvationists, Lord Radstock, Canon
Wilberforce, Antoinette Sterling, Countess Darnley, George
Macgregor, Andrew Jukes. Three days' fraternal converse on
central truths, with Bible reading, praise, and prayer. Ideal
unity realised.

x

CHAPTER XXIV.

LATER EVENTS AND LETTERS.

DIARY.—May, 5 1893.—Walking on our Heath, a gentleman and wife accosted me and said that he had once dreamed of being inside an unknown church and hearing an unknown preacher, and being deeply impressed. When afterwards he was taken to Surrey Chapel, he said, "Good God! this is the place I saw, and that is the preacher." This led to his conversion, and to his becoming a Baptist pastor, and instrumental in the conversion of a young man who entered the ministry of the Church of England, and another who became an eloquent Methodist preacher and editor of a famous religious periodical.

Though parochial cares were resigned in 1892, I never intended to cease preaching, which has been the vocation and joy of my life. Up to the present time I have preached on an average four times weekly, beside attending meetings and giving addresses. I have been welcomed indiscriminately to the pulpits of Presbyterians, Congregationalists, Baptists, Wesleyans, Primitive Methodists, and others; and I would have been equally happy to preach for Episcopal brethren if invited. I wish to express grateful thanks to the many kind friends who have welcomed us to their homes on the one basis of Brotherhood in Christ. I hope they will accept the following inadequate general acknowledgment, as well as friends in other years, for which I have not space. During the twelve months of 1895 I preached in the following larger and smaller places. I ought to add that the companionship of my wife was never at the cost of the church visited, and often a help at the after-meetings.

Beside "supplying" at many churches in London proper, there were visited in the following order:—

January, 1895, to January, 1896.

Hastings, Leicester, Lincoln, Torquay, Leytonstone, Brighton, Hornsey, Liverpool, Newcastle, Middlesbrough, Hanley, Rochdale, Cambridge, Sale, Tunbridge Wells, Broadstairs, Bath, Nottingham, Plaistow, Tredegar, Southminster, Leeds, Kilburn, Upper Clapton, Harringay, Exeter, Crewe, Henham, Birmingham, Finchley, Olney, Ashford, Bexley, Exmouth, Lewisham, Spalford, Barmouth, Hemel Hempstead, Cirencester, Taunton, Bristol, Malmesbury, Workington, Seaton, Yeovil, Smallbridge, Bury, Nottingham, Kilburn, Wolverton, Farnham, Sheffield, Brighton, Blackburn, Tottenham, Brentwood Marlpool, Clapton, Tonbridge, Dudley, Bow.

However deficient otherwise, I have never preached during sixty years without endeavouring to answer the question— "What must I do to be saved"? In every congregation there are persons unconverted, unsaved : perhaps who will never hear another sermon. Should they not be told of the Saviour of sinners ?

February 14, 1895.—Conference at our manse on "How best to cultivate true Christian unity in presence of prevalent sacerdotalism, scepticism, and worldliness." Amongst others, the following were present—Dean Farrar, Canon Girdlestone, Edward White, Dr. Thornton, Hugh Price Hughes, and the Editor of *Great Thoughts.* Dean Farrar gave us an eloquent and hearty address, and strongly urged that in the New Testament the term "priest," in its sacrificial sense, is applied to Christ alone, and in its subordinate sense of service to all believers alike.

I may here quote an old letter of my own :—

WHAT WILL DISSENTERS GAIN BY DISESTABLISHMENT?
TO THE EDITOR OF "THE TIMES."

"April 6, '87.

"SIR,—As a Dissenter, I heartily endorse the Rev. Llewellyn Davies's argument. We shall gain nothing. We wish to gain nothing. We seek no advantage over others, claiming equal rights for all. The question never was, 'What shall we get?' but 'What is true, what is just, what is best for all?' As a party we shall lose, just as we lost by the abolition of church rates and other practical grievances which did so much to alienate many from the Church which sanctioned them. When disestablishment has been obtained one of the reasons for dissent will cease to exist. The Church, free to reform itself, will put an end to abuses which are the plea of many for secession. Disinterestedly as regards their own party, which is sure to become relatively weaker, Dissenters promote disestablishment because the principles and practices of the primitive Church are opposed to political alliances by the 'kingdom' which its Divine Founder declared 'not of this world.' They consider that a return to the primitive system of freedom and self-government must benefit every Church. They therefore deprecate any State alliance for themselves. They adduce the cases of Ireland and the colonies to prove that the Episcopal Church has benefited, and not been injured, by disestablishment. In this they rejoice. They are Christians more than Dissenters, and are interested in the spiritual prosperity of the whole Church of which they are members. They also consider it would benefit the State if Parliament, composed of men of various creeds, were relieved of the burden and controversies of religious legislation ; and if there remained no cause to complain of the injustice which some must suffer by the establishment of any one religion where opinions are so divided. Not because of any gain to themselves as Dissenters, but because, as Christians and citizens, they consider both the Church and the State would be greatly benefited, they advocate the separate administration of the two.

"NEWMAN HALL.

"Christ Church, Lambeth."

I have a letter from Dean Farrar, dated Dean's Yard, January 21. In reply to my request for permission to publish it, I received the following :—

"The Deanery, Canterbury.
"July 9, 1898.

"You are quite welcome to print this letter, though it is only expressed in the very imperfect form which has to suffice for a busy man's correspondence. I really have no conception of the date at which it was written. With kind regards,

"Very sincerely yours."

As my own opinion is no secret, I have pleasure, in fairness, to publish the following defence by men of broad-hearted sympathy with Free Churches.

"I quite agree with you that there are cordial relations between the various Nonconforming bodies. I want to see the very same cordiality established between the National Church and all branches of Christian Nonconformists. Not only are unity and toleration secured for differing bodies of Churchmen within the pale of the Establishment, but added force is given to the cause of religion by their common organisation.

Many of the clergy would lose nothing whatever in income by dis-establishment and disendowment; many of them are miserably poor, and thousands of them would be wholly unable to live on what they get from the Church. But if—as I think—religion would suffer by the nation's disavowing all connexion with the creed which it has held for 1,500 years, then, in all deep matters, all matters for which good men really care, I think that the Nonconformists would suffer as heavily as we, the *nation*, would suffer. The gain would be to Romanism and to secularism ; the loss would be to the cause of Christ.

" Yours sincerely,
" F. W. FARRAR."

From the Very Rev. Dean Farrar :—

"DEAR MR. NEWMAN HALL,—Do you know Mr. Spurgeon ? I have not the pleasure of his personal acquaintance, but as I hear he has been preaching strongly against the doctrine of Eternal Hope, I should geatly value a talk with him, in which he and I alone, without anger, could calmly and quietly discuss our grounds for views which so momentously differ. Do you think that he would regard it as a liberty if I ventured to ask him to dine with me some evening in a friendly way? I do not, of course, expect that I should bring Mr. Spurgeon over to my views, or that he would convince me of his. Indeed, if the latter took place I should never have another happy hour. But it is good that Christians who are teachers should try by mutual and loving intercourse to see and understand the truth."

" January 18th, 1878.

". . . I would gladly meet Mr. Spurgeon some day quietly as a Christian brother, when he has read my book, 'Eternal Hope.' He will see that good and great saints of God, profound thinkers, wise scholars, have interpreted Scripture differently on this subject. But God will not judge anyone for the *Error in intellectu*, but only for the *Contumacia in voluntate*. However severe his language I heartily forgive him, and always honour him for his work's sake.—Yours etc.,

" W. FARRAR."

I reported to Mr. Spurgeon this courteous suggestion, but the state of his health disabled him from engaging in a dis-cussion on a subject about which both disputants were immov-ably and diametrically convinced. But it would be well if all disputants were equally willing to confer together in the hope of better understanding each other's views, and better appre-ciating each other's motives. I have just received Dr. Farrar's permission to publish these letters on my own suggestion.

Diary.—Sunday, March 24, '95.—Heard Canon Wilberforce preach this morning at St. James's, Westminster. He said :—

"Any man, however distinguished in station, fame, wealth, culture, who, to gratify selfish lust, drags down a fellow human being to the mire, instead of being flattered and courted in society, should be treated no better than if caught concealing an ace of cards up his sleeve, or refusing to pay his gambling debts ; indeed, if there be any degree of guilt in immorality, a common thief is far less guilty. Away with the idea that such crimes are not to be spoken of ; they should be unshrinkingly denounced, and the guilty man be as severely shunned as the victim—often far less guilty."

I never heard from the pulpit a more scathing denunciation of vice in high places.

The Canon said of theatres :—

"The atmosphere is flooded with this vice. The subject so pervades the theatre, that if by chance a play is acted that a young woman can attend without danger of taint, it is regarded as a marvel and a topic of general remark and surprise."

March 25.—Called at Dean's Yard. Canon Wilberforce was coming out, and cordially greeted me. I thanked him for the sermon I had heard. Told him I had met his grandfather and his father—that the "Lincoln Tower" of our church had a room dedicated to his grandfather's memory. He told me Mr. Gladstone had just lunched with him, deeply moved about Armenia. Shortly before his grandfather died Gladstone went to see him, and they two prayed together. Speaking of Home Rule and the suppression of the Liquor Traffic, he said that he did not approve of Welsh Disestablishment, but if they could not get the Veto Bill, he was prepared to accept disestablishment of the Church as a price for the disestablishment of public-houses.

January 19, 1896.—The Archbishop of York, in response to a New Year's card, enclosed a letter addressed to his clergy, saying :—

"It will not, of course, secure your consent (in every particular), but it may perhaps interest you, if only for the passage quoted from Richard Baxter, whose writings I frequently study, and rarely without profit."

To this I responded :—

" . . . I thank your Grace for the address to your clergy on the duties and privileges of the Christian priesthood, and I read it as one of those immediately appealed to. You will not be displeased at my respectful expression of solemn conviction, that every true Christian is a member of the 'holy priesthood, to offer up spiritual sacrifices acceptable to God by Jesus Christ,' of which St. Peter speaks, and which is celebrated in the heavenly choir (1 Pet. ii. 5, and Rev. i. 5, 6). I find in the New Testament two priesthoods alone—that of Christ, and that of all believers; and therefore I take to myself all those godly and faithful counsels which you urge on the special consideration of your own clergy. When you pray that your 'charge' may be blessed to the priests, I am encouraged to hope I may share in the benefit. I myself daily pray for the universal priesthood of the Church ; and in my preaching I often urge the duties and privileges of those who, by faith in Christ and renewal by the Holy Ghost, have been consecrated priests unto God. In thus writing I ask indulgence for age, being now in my eightieth year, and the sixtieth of my ministry, and rejoicing to feel increasingly that denominational differences fade away in the light of 'One Lord, one faith, one baptism, one God and Father of all,' even as they find no place among the saints in glory. Indifferently, but most heartily, I rejoice in the learning, eloquence, godliness, and usefulness of my fellow-Christians, whatever their varieties of ecclesiastical opinion or usage. Permit me to express sincere thanks for your kindness and prayers. I also in my humble sphere rejoice in the godly zeal of your Grace in your exalted position ; which may our Divine and Common Master spare you to fill during many years.

"Very faithfully and respectfully,

"Your fellow-servant,

"NEWMAN HALL."

In answer to a very kind letter from the Bishop of Ripon, I replied :—

"March 17, 1897.

"DEAR LORD BISHOP,— . . . I rejoice in your fidelity to the fundamental doctrine of your Church—of our Church—of Christ's Church —the Cross of atonement, the throne of triumph and intercession. May we all increasingly experience the 'Real Presence' of Christ in our churches and in our hearts."

Christmas, 1897.—My chief pleasure at this season was the present of the first copy of a small volume of poems by my wife, entitled "Voices in Verse." With intense interest I had watched the production, both in manuscript and then in type, but adding and altering nothing. Some were completed *currente calamo*, others after several weeks' careful revision. In railway trains I have seen the author suddenly open a sheet of paper and cover it with verses. I anticipate that this first effort will not be the last. My own small faculty of rhyming seems to have left me. The preface is racy, and has disarmed hostile criticism.

> " Upon life's stream I throw a flower,
>   Only a flower—a tiny spray.
> If it be buoyant to survive a shower
>   Of censure harsh, or unseen float away,
> I care not deeply ; I have thrown my flower,
> And gathered it may be within some friendly bower.
> A gentle voice some flowers raise,
> Speaking to us in whispered phrase ;
> To hear it fully, press them to thy heart,
> And may they, lying there, fragrance impart."

January, 1898 —I have quoted in preceding pages from " Voices" descriptions of interesting scenes. I will add another quotation, which, in very small compass, expresses a thought in useful relation to Biblical Criticism.

> Deep truths lie wrapped in human speech,
>   Which God gives in His Word ;
> And mysteries far beyond our reach
>   From children's lips are heard.
>
> Yet to all souls sincere and meek
>   Those precious truths unfold,
> And open out to those who seek
>   God in them to behold.
>
> The sheath alone by man is made,
>   By God alone the blade ;
> Confound them not, but search to find
>   Within—His heart and mind.

From many critical notices I quote this from *The Churchman* :—

"A keen observation of Nature. Poems suggestive of a thoughtful, elevated, and sympathetic life."

May 26th, 1898.—About fifty clergy of various Churches met in my study to confer with Archdeacon Sinclair on the advance of Romanist teaching and practices, which authorities, both civil and ecclesiastical, seemed unable to check. It was admitted that a certain rector near Surrey Chapel recently received consecration from a Roman bishop, and had thus conferred Roman orders on several hundred Episcopal clergy. Free Churchmen felt that their assaults on ritualism were interpreted as attacks on the Church itself, which they disclaimed. Others strongly urged that great victories of truth and freedom had always been won in the first instance by the weak against the strong; and that the feeble should all the more boldly proclaim the truth and be ready to suffer for it.

It was urged that Free Churchmen had no enmity to any Church as such, but only to those usages and doctrines which they considered contrary to our common faith. It was suggested that there should be a new series of "Tracts for the Times," issued by a joint committee—with an equal number of learned, thoughtful, godly theologians, both Anglican and Nonconformist—addressed to the people of England, and that this might be done at once. This suggestion of Dr. Oswald Dykes was warmly supported. I said that the best weapon against error was positive truth. The constant, earnest, prayerful preaching of Christ crucified, the one and only sacrificing, absolving, saving Priest was the best antidote to the false, superstitious, debasing priesthood of ritualism and Rome.

Thanks were expressed to the Archdeacon for his candid replies to various interrogations, and his cordial sympathy with all who upheld the gospel of Christ and spiritual religion. He rejoiced in the co-operation of all true Protestants, both within and without the Establishment. The conference closed with prayer by Canon Girdlestone, and the Benediction by the Archdeacon.

The only time when Mr. Gladstone worshipped in my church was on that Whit Sunday when my text was "Ye shall be witnesses of me." I had the privilege of speaking

in Hyde Park on Sunday, June 5, 1898, when 100,000 of the
people gathered to thank God for his noble and useful
career. After heartfelt tribute to his greatness I closed
thus :—

"He was throughout life a 'witness' for Christ, and as such would
condemn me if I occupied more time with praising him rather than his
Divine Master Whose kingdom it was his chief ambition to promote,
Whose teaching secures the only rational liberty, equality, and fraternity,
Whose laws bid us love our neighbour as ourselves ; the King who will
judge the people with righteousness and break in pieces the oppressor."

August, 1898.—The last portion of these reminiscences
has been chiefly written on the banks of the Clyde, where
we have occupied, during seven weeks, the manse of
Skelmorlie, and where I have preached at the United Presbyterian church. We are much indebted to the kind
neighbours for their cordial hospitalities. We revisited the
picturesque Isle of Arran, where I preached at the opening
of a small church at Corrie. In the height of the season all
dwellings are crowded; but we had the privilege of occupying
a comfortable room, seven feet wide by nine feet long, out
of the small window of which I plucked grass in common
with several hens, and a hungry young cow.

When we were at Arran previously I wrote the following description:—

SUNSET ON THE ISLE OF ARRAN.

Can we forget that July night on Arran's Isle entrancing?
We watched the fading opal light on murmuring wavelets dancing :
We oft before had watched the shore, but ne'er in years advancing
Can memory slight that July night, on Arran's Isle entrancing.

Goat-Fell rose purpling o'er the bay, alive with white sails shining,
And lovers watched the waning day, with hearts and arms entwining ;
Yes ! lovers yet—life's God-sent ray—such gift all joys enhancing,
Making so bright that July night, on Arran's Isle entrancing.

I preached two Sundays at Augustin Church, Edinburgh—of which a former pastor was Dr. Alexander, one
of my ordaining Presbyters—and spent nearly a week at
Pitlochrie, where our Alpine friends welcomed us in a
picturesque cottage of the forest of Killiecrankie. Dr.

George Adam Smith, in the intervals of excursions to the falls of the Tummell and to the heathery hills above the Lake, was busy finishing the life of his friend, Professor Drummond, and his charming wife was busy with her romping "minor prophets."

Besides grateful memories already recorded, others crowd on me, for which contracting space forbids more than names: Sir M. Peto, Sir Russell Reynolds, Joseph Tucker, Onslow, C. E. Mudie, James, Lance, Ropes, M. E. R., authoress of many juvenile tales, Sister Evangelist Anderson, Betts, Harvey, Newland, Symes, and many more whose names are affectionately remembered.

October 9th, 1898.—My last Sunday within the region of this autobiography was an illustration of Christian union. In the morning I had the privilege of hearing an eloquent sermon from my friend of the Riffel Alp, Dean Lefroy of Norwich, and of uniting with Episcopalian brethren in the Holy Communion of the Lord's Supper, at a village church across our Heath, beautiful in simplicity of structure, doctrine, and ceremonial. In the afternoon I joined the crowd convened not by Sabbath bell but by Gospel trumpet, and, being invited by the commanding officer of the Salvation Army, I stood under the colours of the clustered crosses, and told of the old, old story, how "God so loved the world," and called the miscellaneous crowd to the feast of salvation by the joyful sound "Whosoever." Then I distributed copies of "Come to Jesus" to grateful recipients. In the evening I worshipped with the Baptists, and heard from my old friend, the Rev. William Brock, the same gospel I had heard sixty years before from his father. Differences emphasised unity. The preacher of the morning wore white surplice and scarlet hood, the "rural dean" who presided in the afternoon was in military uniform, the evangelist of the evening wore his ordinary attire; but the praise of the same Saviour was sung, prayer to the same Father was offered, and the same gospel of salvation was proclaimed by faith in the "High Priest," who gave his life a ransom for many.

Would that all Christians, invoking the same Father,

through the mediation of the same Saviour, by the help of the same Spirit, would make it manifest that varieties of method do not contradict unity of belief, or break the brotherhood of all who love the Lord Jesus Christ in sincerity. The lines of Cowper, familiar to me when a child, are still more dear to me now :—

> "O, how unlike the complex work of man,
> Heaven's easy, artless, unencumbered plan !
> No meretricious graces to beguile,
> No clustering ornaments to clog the pile.
> From ostentation as from weakness free,
> It stands like the cerulean arch we see,
> Majestic in its own simplicity.
> Inscribed above the portal from afar,
> Conspicuous as the brightness of a star,
> Legible only by the light they give,
> Stand the soul-quickening words—BELIEVE AND LIVE."

Thursday, October 13th, 1898.—I have had the treat of listening to Dean Farrar deliver an eloquent discourse in Westminster Abbey on its historical associations since the time of Edward the Confessor. After referring to the recent interment of Mr. Gladstone in glowing terms, he selected for his climax Lord Shaftesbury, whose monument, near the western portal, bears two words of supreme significance— "LOVE, SERVE." I have often enjoyed Dean Farrar's sermons on Sunday afternoons, always in general sympathy without being always in special agreement. I am particularly indebted to him for a kind allusion in his preface to his volume on the Lord's Prayer.

CHAPTER XXV.

THIS book is not a Biography, which requires a full-length portraiture, but an Autobiography, which permits selection. There are scars which no one willingly exposes. Forgiveness is a human duty: forgetfulness is a divine boon. The promise that all tears shall be wiped away where none are shed may be fulfilled by the occasions of those tears being forgotten. Some readers may be disappointed that this book is not exclusively records of religious experience and ministerial work. I purposely avoided following the track of ordinary religious memoirs. No one's life is entirely spent as some writers depict that of persons known only in their public career as teachers and preachers. Such portraiture is not true to life, which has various aspects. The religious influence is not less effective when the person described is seen to be interested and active in other things, capable not only of tears but of laughter, not only of divine but of human emotions. I have felt it a great difficulty to say so much of self; but friends have urged me not to withhold what should be the chief characteristic of true autobiography. Others may think that I have occupied too much space in the opposite direction; but my heart has impelled me to depict the character of many deserving of high honour, and thus to draw away exclusive attention from myself. Though I have not made this book my confessional, I have deeply felt the faults of the years described, confessing them to God while writing for men. To Him alone I ascribe all the praise for any good He has wrought through a most unworthy instrument; and I devoutly ask Him to make these pages, as a whole, both interesting and profitable.

In closing this autobiography, it is suitable to record my matured convictions respecting my position as a minister of the Gospel, and still more my present views respecting the Gospel itself, in some aspects on which Christians are not all agreed.

The subject of " Orders " is one keenly debated. In spite of sixty years' ministry, which God has blessed, I have often been made to feel that many faithful servants of God in other sections of His Church do not consider my ministry valid, and proposals have been made to me to ignore my own ordination for theirs.   In illustration of this I record a conversation which took place when we were preparing for the opening of our new " Christ Church."

I received a kind and complimentary visit from a Church of England clergyman, who lamented that Dissent was to be introduced into the parish, and evidently hoped to induce me to accept episcopal ordination, and then to carry over with me the new building.   He said he had no official authority, but could assure me that the Archbishop would readily ordain me, and allow me at once to preach in the parish church.   I received the well-intended offer of this personal recognition, and in substance said that I was ordained as long ago as 1842, by eight presbyter-bishops, according to the usage of the Primitive Church; that I had been preaching many years while Dr. Tait was still teacher in a public school; that I honoured him for his learning, piety, and usefulness, but could not disclaim my own ordination for his, any more than I should presume or desire him to renounce his for mine; that episcopal ordination would exclude me from ministerial fraternity with the whole Church of God, and shut me up into a single Church, which, however numerous, was comparatively a small part of the whole.   While recognising all fellow-servants of Christ as brethren, whatever their ordination, I was quite satisfied with my own, and rejoiced in the liberty of fraternity with all of them.   The proposal, appreciated for its kindness, was neither reciprocated nor renewed.

I have sometimes been asked why I do not belong to the Church of England; to which I reply, "Because I include that Church within my own—with 'all who love the Lord Jesus Christ in sincerity.'"

Diary.—January 1st, 1896.—Bless the Lord for health and opportunity to preach the glorious Gospel nearly every Sunday throughout the land, and that in every place hands have been lifted in token of repentance and faith in Christ. Increasing conviction of my own need of the Atonement strengthens my assurance of its truth. I never preach without the Cross being the keynote. "O Lamb of God, that takest away the sins of the world, have mercy upon *me.*" I make no *effort* to "bring in" the Cross. This is involuntary; I could not preach without it. "Necessity is laid upon me." It is this which is "the power of God," which supplies the need, which reaches the heart of saint and sinner. I feel I ought to spend more time and heart in prayer for each service—for more of the felt presence of the Holy Spirit, more unction as "fellow-worker with God." Alas, how often too much reliance is placed on mental preparation and the power of speech and delivery! Yet I trust that in every sermon I preach from the heart, that I do strive for the holiness I urge, and myself enjoy the love of Christ and the hope of glory.

Sermon on my eightieth birthday, May 22nd, 1896.

"It may be appropriate to refer to the opinions I now hold on some controverted questions of the day. Some might praise me if I could say that my theological creed had undergone no change since at the age of eighteen I preached to Kentish hop-pickers. Others might think that such avowal was no credit either to my intellect or to my honesty. I can say there has been no change in regard to 'Repentance towards God, and faith in our Lord Jesus Christ.' The longer I live the more I feel my personal need of the Atonement, and see that in the Word of God this is revealed as the fundamental fact of Christianity, and the longer I preach the more I receive evidence that it is the power of God unto salvation; but I have long ceased to regard it as a commercial transaction. Nor could I think of the compassion of the Son as appeasing the wrath of the Father. Nor could I think of the love

of God as caused by the death of His Son, since 'God so loved the
world'—antecedently as cause—'that He gave His only begotten Son,
that whosoever believeth in Him might not perish, but have everlasting life.' Christ is revealed not as appeasing wrath, but revealing
love. Atonement is a fact, like many facts in the natural world,
beyond philosophical explanation, but declared plainly by Christ and
His apostles, 'a faithful saying,' soaring above all clouds of controversy
into the clear sky of eternity, 'worthy of acceptance by everyone.'
This I have preached with never-faltering faith and never-wearying
earnestness, and hope to do so as long as this shortening life is spared
and this stammering tongue can speak.*

"Another question of the day relates to the infinite future. The
issues are so tremendous, eternity is so immeasurable, the physical
and spiritual possibilities of God so unlimited, that we, with our
feeble intellect and restricted vision should speak humbly about
what the Almighty and all-living God can or cannot do. Myriads of
stars have existed during countless ages which have been only just
now discovered ; may there not be purposes and works of God in the
spiritual hemisphere to be revealed in some future day ? Many inquirers
after truth hesitate to affirm that the condition of souls during an
eternity as long as God's own existence can be fixed during a probation
so momentary as four-score years. Are those who in this life had no
moral chance of living otherwise than their ignorance, traditions, and
training necessitated, to suffer for ever ? Did Christ go in vain to
spirits in prison ? If there are awful threatenings of judgments to come,
are there not brighter promises of a time when Christ shall reign
supreme, when wickedness will not be rampant, cursing though crushed ?
Would unending hatred of God by countless millions be the victory
emphatically declared—'In the name of Jesus every knee shall bow,
and every tongue shall confess that Jesus Christ is Lord'?—or in
harmony with the apocalyptic vision of every created intelligence
'ascribing glory to Him that sitteth on the throne, and to the Lamb for
ever' (Rev. v. 13)? May not the threatened death mean, not unending
existence in woe, but ceasing to live, if persistent in sin ? Is it not
possible to doubt on this subject, and yet rejoice in the word of Christ,
'He that believeth in Me shall never die'? I have never felt it necessary
to demand acceptance of any theory on this subject as essential. Salvation eternally by faith in Christ is possible without believing in the
damnation eternally of those who do not believe. But I have solemnly
preached the judgment both of the righteous and the wicked—that
separation from God is a hell into which wilful sinners plunge themselves ; and I also have urged repentance by the terrors of the world to

* This question I have carefully studied, and after preaching a number of
sermons on it have condensed the argument in a small octavo volume, entitled,
"Atonement, the Fundamental Fact of Christianity." This I leave as a dying
testimony of the preaching of sixty years, and of the foundation hope of
the writer, at the age of eighty-two (September, 1898).

come and by the love of God, 'Who desireth not the death of a sinner, but rather that he may turn from his wickedness and live.'"

I have this day (September 6th, 1898), been impressed while reading in Ruskin's "Modern Painters" the following illustrative passage:—

"Our whole happiness and power of energetic action depend upon our being able to breathe and live in the cloud ; content to see it opening here and closing there ; rejoicing to catch, through the thinnest films of it, glimpses of stable and substantial things ; but yet perceiving a nobleness even in the concealment, and rejoicing that the kindly veil is spread where the untempered light might have scorched us, or the infinite clearness wearied. Every rightly constituted mind ought to rejoice, not so much in knowing anything clearly, as in feeling that there is infinitely more which it cannot know. . . . The pleasure to humble people is in knowing that the journey is endless, the treasure inexhaustible, watching the cloud still marching before them with its summitless pillar, and being sure that to the end of time, and to the length of eternity, the mysteries of its infinity will still open farther and farther, their dimness being the sign and necessary adjunct of their inexhaustibleness."

Another subject of controversy is the inspiration and authority of Scripture. This I believe, but have never advocated *verbal* inspiration. If the very words of the original writing were dictated, this cannot be claimed for the translations, nor is it consistent with various versions of the same facts and doctrines in the Book itself. We can believe that the writers were inspired without asserting a verbal dictation, which exposes the book to criticisms endangering belief. I take my stand on the authority of the Great Teacher. He quoted, expounded, sanctioned as divine, the Old Testament; the New Testament is the record of His own life and teaching. Thus believing in Christ, I accept the Book which bears His imprimatur. One of my small books expands this argument, and bears the title "The Saviour's Bible."

The great controversy of the day relates to the Roman Sacerdotalism, which claims for a human priesthood supernatural power to make sacraments chief channels of divine grace, to offer sacrifices for sins, to demand confession, to confer absolution and to obtain, by official intercession,

Y

blessings both for the living and the dead. The most effectual antidote is in upholding the sole Priesthood of Christ, as divinely ordained and solely qualified to offer sacrifice for sin by His own death, to bestow the gift of the Holy Ghost, to pronounce a real absolution, by His own Real Presence to be always with all who seek Him—"able to save to the uttermost." My own principal method of opposing the false claims of a human priesthood is to exalt the real, efficacious, and sole Priesthood of Christ—" Consider the Apostle and High Priest of our profession, Christ Jesus," for, with Him to do for us all that we need, there is no place for pretenders. Then, under Christ, all who believe in Him are themselves priests, ordained to teach, to declare forgiveness, to pray for each other, and to win the world for Christ; as St. Peter says to all Christians, " Ye are a holy priesthood"; and the anthem of heaven adores Him " Who has made us kings and priests unto God."

Other controverted questions respecting modes of Church government, sacraments, and ceremonies have their importance, but are not essential to Christian faith and holiness. I have had my own opinion, and on proper, occasions, and in due proportion to essential truths, have stated them ; but never so as to exalt them to the rank of fundamental doctrines, or so as to encourage divisions among Christians. Let us rejoice in the Unity of the Church of believers—" One Lord, one Faith, one Baptism, one God and Father of all, who is above all, and through all, and in you all," through our Lord Jesus Christ. This I have expressed in words my congregation have often sung together at the Supper of the Lord :—

> How sweet the fellowship of Christian love,
>   Communion of saints afar and near ;
> With those on earth, and those in heaven above,
>   There is a cord that binds us, close and dear.
>
> Beloved ones, passed a little on before,
>   Ye still are near us, let our anthems blend :
> To Him in Whom we're one for evermore,
>   Be honour, praise, and glory without end.

CHAPTER XXVI.

ON May 22nd, 1860, my birthday, we had a family excursion to Leith Hill. My father was so vigorous that he forgot the liabilities of eighty-four years, at which age he used to drive his pony-carriage with my mother into Regent Street. On this day, as he was getting up into the excursion van, he fell, receiving a bruise which resulted in an abscess, and terminated fatally four months afterwards. From his diary I extract his last entries:— ♦

"May 22nd.—N.'s birthday. Most lovely—nightingales. Open van —fall—mercy no bone broken. Praise the Lord."
"May 26th.—I pray the Lord to forgive my sins, and give me faith in the blood shed on Calvary for the whole world."
"June 3rd.—The large print Testament and Psalms my daily companions, praising God. Beloved wife so tender. Praise God for such a wife."
"June 25th.—Praise the Lord."

This was his last entry. I was with him very frequently; towards the end continually. I was much impressed by the combination of penitential remembrance of old sins with joyful assurance of full and free forgiveness. Present salvation should cause "joy unspeakable" although—or because?—it reminds the believer of past deliverance.

One Sunday morning, when I called to see him on my way to preach, I said, "Dear father, you seem a little sad." "Oh, Newman, I am thinking of my old sins!" "But, dear father, they were confessed, forgiven, forsaken, more than forty years ago!—as God says, ' cast into the depths of the sea'—and all this time you have been rejoicing in His love and service! You have often said you have sent your heart to heaven, and will go after it!" His eye sparkled as he said, "I sometimes

think that if, after all, I should wake up in the bad place,
I should at once call a prayer-meeting, and the devil would
say, ' Turn him out; he's making a rebellion!'" The brief
cloud was dispersed by the bright shining of the "sun of
righteousness."

September 15th.—Much weaker. 16th.—Unable to speak,
except a few words. 18th.—Looking towards his sorrowing wife,
he several times uttered her name, "Mary! Mary! Mary!" A
few hours after, with great effort and earnestness, "Jesus!
Jesus! Jesus!" Two words the dearest. During fifty years
his heart was linked with that of his wife by ties unsurpassed
in tenderness; during more than forty years the name of
Jesus was music to his soul. At the same time he was so
domestic and so godly:—

> "Type of the wise who soar but never roam,
> True to the kindred points of heaven and home."

On Wednesday, September 19th, after many hours' silence,
when we thought he was no longer able to articulate, he
suddenly began, in tones which could be heard in the other
parts of the house, to exclaim, "Jesus! Jesus! Jesus!" the
voice gradually sinking to a faint whisper. After putting his
arm once more round my mother's neck, he gradually sank
into a stupor, out of which, on Saturday morning, September
22nd, he awoke into the immediate presence of the Sinner's
Friend.

One of his most favourite hymns, which we very often
heard him repeat, closes with lines remarkably verified in his
own departure :—

> "Till then I would Thy love proclaim
> With every fleeting breath ;
> And may the music of Thy Name
> Refresh my soul in death."

In my mother's Bible is a precious MS. bearing evidence of continued use through many years. It is dated
July, 1859. It is a prayer, entirely in the words of Scripture, on behalf of her two ministerial sons, and which
formed part of her daily devotions till the close of life.

Above it is the promise, "*If ye shall ask anything in My Name, I will do it.*"

"Grace, mercy and peace, from God our Father, and Jesus Christ our Lord, to Newman and Arthur, my beloved sons. I thank Christ Jesus our Lord, who hath counted them faithful, putting them into the ministry. May the grace of our Lord be exceeding abundant towards them. May they war a good warfare, ever holding faith and a good conscience, vigilant, sober, of good behaviour, apt to teach, not given to wine, not greedy of filthy lucre, patient, not lifted up with pride, but clothed with humility. May they have a good report of them that are without.

"May they be good ministers of Jesus Christ, nourished up in the words of faith and of good doctrine. May they be examples of believers in word, in conversation, in charity, in spirit, in faith, in purity.

"Grant them the spirit of power, and of love, and of a sound mind. May they be strong in the grace that is in Christ Jesus, enduring hardness as good soldiers of Jesus Christ, studying to show themselves approved unto God, workmen that need not to be ashamed, rightly dividing the word of truth. May they follow righteousness, faith, charity, peace ; avoiding foolish and unlearned questions, knowing that they do gender strifes.

"May they be wise unto salvation, through faith which is in Christ Jesus, thoroughly furnished unto all good works, preaching the word, instant in season, out of season, reproving, rebuking, exhorting with all long-suffering. May they watch in all things, endure afflictions, do the work of evangelists, make full proof of their ministry, fight the good fight, keep the faith, and when they have finished their course give each of them that crown of righteousness which is laid up for all those who love Thy appearing. May the Lord Jesus Christ be with their spirits. Grace be with them. Amen and amen."

From a letter to my mother :—

"I had a most happy Sunday, my parents spending it with me at Surrey Chapel. They taught me to love the Saviour, and I feel as if I were now their mouthpiece to make known the Master, whose service becomes more and more delightful every day. I am just starting to open a Methodist chapel at Brixton; to-morrow at Enfield, Wednesday at Diss, Thursday at Kennington, and on Friday a great treat of music at the Crystal Palace. What a joy that preaching Christ is the best of pleasures and His Name the sweetest of music!"

"Reading some of dear father's letters. Love to Christ breathed in all he said, did, and wrote. I look at his picture and pray for some portion of the same spirit. And my dearest mother's face is before me as I write my sermons—from whom I first learned to love the blessed Book I expound; my first college tutor, and better than all the other tutors and books that I ever had, save the Bible and Christ."

I will here give an extract from my mother's diary :—

"December 31st, 1862.—For a short time I have lost the presence of friend, companion—dear, dear husband; but he has only gone a little before. For twenty years I have been in the habit of reading the Scriptures with him, and we have thus read the historical and prophetical books upwards of twenty times, the Psalms sixty, the New Testament thirty-six times. . . . Two years I have lived a widow. But God has been with me. What consolations! The love of my dear children; the joy of hearing the Gospel preached so faithfully by my beloved Newman; the return of my dear Stephen after so many years of absence, his heart overflowing with tenderness! Dear Jesus, abide with me! The shades of evening are closing round me! Leave me not!"

In a letter dated 1867, thirty years ago, at the age of above eighty, she wrote to me :—

"Stand up for Jesus. Preach Christ everywhere, in the perfection and loveliness of His human character, and in the dignity and love of His divinity. May the Lord help you, and while attempting to teach others, may the Holy Spirit fill your own soul with joy and peace, and may you delight more and more in your Master's work."

My mother kept up her habits of private prayer till old age. Her attendant tells me that after she had passed her eightieth year she rose at five o'clock, summer and winter, spending the early hours in reading the Bible and in prayer. She always lighted her own fire, saying that, if she chose to rise so early, she ought not to expect her servants to do so. After breakfast she would again retire to her chamber for prayer, and again about seven in the evening, telling her maid not to disturb her, as she liked to retire now for prayer, and not wait till she was too tired. Of late the attendant slept on a couch at the foot of her mistress's bed, and has often heard my mother, supposing the maid was asleep, praying earnestly in the night, mentioning all her children by name and invoking suitable blessings upon each. When my brother was from home, she conducted family worship, offering extempore prayer with great fervour, reverence, and beauty of expression.

She still kept up her visitation of the sick, even when the growing infirmities of age rendered it dangerous for her to go about alone. With filial watchfulness my brother and sister took care always to accompany her; but she sometimes would elude their vigilance, saying that she liked to see the sick and talk and pray with them alone. Thus she visited many of the sick poor of my brother's flock at Edmonton after she was eighty years of age.

For several years it was my habit to spend half of every Saturday with her. I used to have tea, and afterwards spend two or three hours alone with her. Oh, what swift-flying hours, with long-enduring memory! What prayers were those she offered! It mattered not to me that I had to preach two or three sermons next day. I was in no hurry to leave her. The intercourse more than made up for any lack of study. It was only a few months before her departure that she recited with great beauty of expression the whole of Thomson's hymn on "The Seasons."

September, 1868.—My dear mother became suddenly and seriously ill at my brother Arthur's house, Edmonton, where he and his wife made for her widowed years a very blessed home. We both were constantly at her bedside listening to her peaceful voice in the "land of Beulah," on her way, as we thought, to the banks of the river. I made notes of some of her utterances, and shall here recall them as if actually her "dying words," because at the very last she was speechless from paralysis. I transcribe the following:—

"Love is for immortality. It is life. It cannot die when it is interwoven with the love of Christ. Loving Jesus best is the best preservative of all other love. I am looking at the clouds and thinking how delightful it would be to see Christ coming through that opening. Delightful to believe that He will come! . . . But the Jews have to return, and the world to be converted! But if He comes He could do this at once. When Christ Who is our life shall appear! Shall we have bodies to look at each other's faces? I hope so. I want the cleaving embrace, the loving kiss. Christ had our nature, and how He desired the sympathy of His disciples!"

When I bade her "Good-night," she said, "Yes, I want the outward sign of love."

She then spoke of once visiting a poor woman who lived in a wretched hovel, but who said to her, "I have often visits here from the King of kings!"

One day she offered special prayer for my church in the following terms:—

"Bless the Pastor: at the bedside of the sick, in his study, in preaching, wherever he goes; bless the dear people of Surrey Chapel, with whom I have often worshipped, whom I love still, and bless the dear Elders and make Thy face shine upon them: O bless dear old Benn, who has so often given out hymns of praise to Thee. Bless him in his declining days. Bless the dear old place. Thou hast honoured it during many years. Still bless it and make it a blessing to multitudes."

One day, as we thought her very near death, she repeated the lines without hesitation:—

"The quiet chamber where the Christian sleeps,
    And where from year to year she prays and weeps,
    How near it is to all her faith can see,
    How short and easy may the passage be!
    One gentle sigh, one feeble struggle o'er,
    May land her safe on that eternal shore."

September 18th.—I knelt at her bedside and asked her to pray for me. She placed her hands lovingly on my head, which she frequently stroked, and said, "O I have prayed for him all his life. The Lord bless and keep him; make him mighty in words, consistent in conduct, sincere in spirit, making higher attainments in religion." Then she went on in such eloquent, loving, fervent terms that I was overwhelmed; it was as a vision of angels passing by; I remember the effect, but I cannot remember the words. Then, " Give him success in his ministry—many souls—help him to cast his cares on Thee. O how I have loved him; I think no mother ever loved son so much; but Thou hast loved us still more. Hear a mother's prayer for him! Thou didst have a human body and canst have compassion! O to meet in heaven!" Then for five minutes she went on praying with the utmost fervour, so that I began to fear the exertion would be too much for her frail body. I never heard or read such a prayer.

"If the righteousness of Christ is our only plea, what is meant by our 'offering the sacrifices of righteousness'?—is not a broken spirit the sacrifice God accepts? But that is righteous, too, being right after being wrong; Christ's own in-working."

"The way seems very long. I remember what happened when I was two years old. It will be a short and easy passage; no alarm if He is with us, and He surely will be at such a time. . . . I hope you will be permitted to hold my hand as I go down to the river. It may be fancy, but I feel I should be disappointed if you were not with me. But yet I should not be really so at such a time!"

Looking up, she said, "O Lord, Thou hast promised, if any two agree, Thou wilt give them what they ask!" Then looking at me, "We are agreed, are we not?" "O Lord, grant that whenever my dear son preaches sinners may be converted and Thy people built up in the faith. O Lord, be with him, come to him—come to him now!" Then she paused and looked at me with tender affection and said, "I cannot ask more than this—can I?"

On presenting each of her two ministerial sons with a watch-guard made of her own hair, she gave them her blessing as they knelt beside her. Her words, graven on the memory, were recorded directly afterwards, and were as follows:—

"O Lord, Thou art so great, and I know not how to speak to Thee aright. But I ask Thee to bless my dear sons. O Lord, I do thank Thee for giving them to me. O Lord, bless them both. Make them good ministers of Thy word. I believe they are. May they never trifle with Thy word. Wherever they are may they tell poor sinners of the Saviour. May they never forget they are Thy ministers, Thy appointed ministers : O make them faithful to the end ! " Then putting a hand on the head of each of us : " O God, bless them both. What can I ask for them more than this—that Thou wouldst bless them as Thy ministers and make them very useful ? O Lord, if Thou seest any sin in them, forgive it for Christ's sake. Let them never fall into any snare." Then putting her right hand on my head and pressing it fervently, she added : "O Lord, Thou knowest how I thanked Thee for this son and asked Thee to make him a minister of Thine ! and, O Lord, Thou hast done it and made him useful. O Lord, bless them both. I can do no more for them. I shall very soon have to leave them. But they will come after me. They will be clothed with Thy glory, and I shall thank Thee for them, for I shall know they are Thine, and I shall give them to Thee. Lord, I thank Thee for the comfort they have been to me. O bless them both : bless them both. Amen."

Then she kissed us both and, taking the hand of the son under whose roof she was living, said, "I did not thank God enough for all your great kindness to me and care of me. But God knows what is in my heart."

While the issue of her illness seemed in suspense I relieved my feelings by expressing them in the following sonnet :—

Forbear ! attendant angels, O forbear
To urge the saint to take her heavenly flight ;
Still let her loving smile our eyes delight ;
Still to our fond embrace such treasure spare,
And for such loss our troubled hearts prepare.
Yours are the glories of unclouded light ;
Be not too eager, from our gloomy night
To snatch a star that shines with beams so rare.
More fit for your society, we know,
But needed more by us who mourn below ;
Your social wealth congenial prize will gain ;
Our dearth without a remedy will grow :
Once gone—our arms will stretch for her in vain ;
Spare her ! once yours, you ne'er will part again.

By the goodness of God our mother recovered, and was spared to her children and friends two more years, in health

and mental capacity, enjoying as before the reading of the
Bible and religious books, and also her favourite poets and
other literature. She was constant at public worship, listening to the sermons of her dear son Arthur at his Edmonton
church, and delighting in the visits of relations and friends, as
they delighted in her varied converse, her rich Christian
experience, and her loving heart.

She went to Hastings in November, 1870, for a little
change and for giving pleasure to her children, whom she
invited by turns to be her guests on the Parade, St. Leonards.
She enjoyed her daily drive, sat out on the esplanade, and
at the window fronting the sea, dividing her attention between
the book she was reading and the ships on their long voyage
across the great ocean.

On November 23rd she repeated with perfect accuracy and
much emotion a very favourite hymn :—

> " There is a house not made with hands
>   Eternal and on high,
> And here my spirit waiting stands
>   Till God shall bid it fly.
>
> " Shortly this prison of my clay
>   Must be dissolved and fall ;
> Then, O my soul ! with joy obey
>   Thy heavenly Father's call."

While repeating the first two lines of the second verse she
pointed to her body, and then, raising her hands and eyes,
she seemed already radiant with the joy expressed in the
other couplet.

Then she exclaimed, " Come, Lord Jesus ! Come quickly
and take Thy servant home ! " A friend responded, " But do
you want to leave us ? " She answered, " I love you all, but
Jesus is more to me now, and I know my children will all
follow me, and join me in heaven, for I have prayed for
them, and I believe in prayer."

At the close of dinner she seemed to be dozing. Raising
her from her chair, we found she was helpless and her voice
inarticulate. Unable to take food, her strength gradually

declined. But she suffered no pain, and there was never a cloud across her peaceful countenance. She slept much, but, on awaking, recognised us all with a beaming smile, and responded to the pressure of her hand by a loving clasp of ours. Her face brightened with holy joy at the mention of the name of Jesus. Though withdrawn from all the world besides, her mind was responsive to the love of her children and her Lord.

As I held her hand, I reminded her that she had often expressed the wish that I should do so as she passed the river, on which, with considerable effort, she said, " I believe it is now."

On Saturday, December 2nd, 1870, thinking she was finally leaving us, I resolved to remain during the night. Early on Sunday morning she awoke, and as I knelt beside her, while during a quarter of an hour she looked at me with intense affection and tenderly caressed my hand with hers, I felt I was taking my last farewell. How sweetly she smiled at me once more! It was almost the last effort of her lips ; for she sank to sleep and fell into unconsciousness.

It cost me a struggle to return to my ministerial duties in London. As three large congregations were expecting me, I felt it was my duty to go and preach to them the Saviour who was my mother's Friend in life and death. I was sure also that she would have urged me to go had she been conscious ; for, with all her love, she never once tried to induce me to remain with her when my duties summoned me away, but, on the contrary, when I was lingering, she would urge me to hasten, lest study should be neglected or a public engagement not punctually kept. But I prayed earnestly that her life might be spared till my return. How great was my thankfulness to find, early on Monday morning, that the passage of the river was not quite completed! During two hours, my brother on one side and myself on the other, each holding a hand, together with three others of her eight children, watched the passing pilgrim till she was out of sight.

December 4th.—The clock struck twelve. It was "perfect day." The sun was streaming into the adjoining room.

The sky was without a cloud. The sea was smooth as a summer lake, and the gentle ripples were murmuring sweet music on the pebbly beach. External nature was in harmony with the spiritual world, and earth reflected heaven. It was perfect peace when she " fell asleep," aged eighty-four.

My Diary, Sunday night, December 10th.—I am sitting alone in my study after the labours of the day. I used to write *to* her at this hour thirty years ago; now I write of her departure. I bless God for sparing her to me so long. Last Sunday I was kneeling by her side as she tenderly clasped my hand during a quarter of an hour, and sweetly smiled, though unable to speak. At length, without one sigh, she fell asleep in the arms of Jesus. I felt we were compassed about with angels, and the "gates were ajar."

On the Saturday I had brushed her beautiful hair, plaited and fastened it up. Sister Mary and I now cut off some locks, and her wedding-ring was placed on my finger. It was so like the Human-Divine Jesus to grant our earnest prayer to be together at the last. Arthur and I accompanied the body home to Edmonton. On Friday morning the countenance was beautiful—all the wrinkles of age had disappeared. I saw again the mother I knew when she was at my ordination —so like the sketch taken then, which hangs before me as I write. I touched her lips with her wedding-ring on my finger, and kissed farewell on the marble lips and forehead. Brother Arthur placed on the coffin-lid some ivy leaves and two roses from her favourite tree, transplanted from her former residence, in perfect bloom. Just before starting for the cemetery her children, surrounding the coffin, sang the doxology and prayed, feeling she was joining in their worship.

The funeral was of the simplest kind. No empty carriages, plumes, scarves, or hatbands. My eldest brother with eldest sister went first—Edward and Eleanora—then my sailor-brothers, Stephen and Vine; myself and brother Warren next; Arthur, with his wife and two children; then other grandchildren; then the elders of Surrey Chapel, and several ministers, friends, and many poor who knew and loved her at Surrey

Chapel and Edmonton. Arthur and I stood at the head of
the grave. He began with the usual and touching sentences.
It was so difficult to say, "This our mother." As I looked
down into the grave, I saw my dear father's coffin, on which
my mother's was now placed—in death not divided. Thus
their bodies were buried in my parcel of ground, my cave of
Machpelah. "God is not the God of the dead, but of the
living."

The service closed with the benediction, after an address
which I reserve for my last page, as illustrating the first.

IN MEMORIAM.

"The tears we shed this day are tears of love, not anguish; of gratitude, not regret. We bless our mother's God for the best inheritance
of a holy example and a life of earnest prayer. We bless the 'God of
all consolation' for memories beautiful with earthly love, and hopes
radiant with heavenly glory. We bless the Lord of the harvest for
gathering in this shock of corn fully ripe. We bless the Lord of the
way for so peaceful a close to so long a pilgrimage. We bless Him Who
abolished death, and holds the keys of the unseen world, for so lovely
an end to so lovely a life.

"An end? Not so! End of sorrow—beginning of bliss; end of
the pilgrimage—entrance to home; end of death—dawn of life. Best
and dearest of mothers! thou livest still!—in our memories, which
will ever enshrine thee; in our hearts, which will ever embrace thee.
And will not thy spirit, though unseen, sometimes minister to us, as we
travel on after thee? Thou livest still!

"Thou art not in this cold grave! Thou hast rejoined our sainted
father, the husband who adored thee as the angel guardian of his life.
Thou hast embraced the little ones whom Jesus took from thy reluctant
bosom to train in the nursery of heaven. Thou hast been welcomed by
friends gone before, who have long been waiting for thee to rejoin them;
by many of the Lord's servants, whom it was so great a joy to thee to
receive under thy roof; by multitudes of the Lord's poor, whom it was
thy privilege and delight to succour and console; by very many rescued
from sin and led to the Saviour through thy loving counsel and fervent
prayers. Thou hast been welcomed by the glorious company of heaven,
for whose congenial society thou wast made so meet; and by thy gracious
Saviour, whom, like the Mary of Bethany, thou didst so reverentially
and ardently love. And now thou wilt be ready to welcome us, when
we also are called to cross the narrow stream.

"Yes! we will not disappoint thee! Thou shalt embrace us again, and for ever! We thy children and children's children, standing round this open grave where their ashes repose, swear by the God of our father and mother that we will walk worthy of your prayers! we will imitate your example! we will serve your Saviour! we will join you in your home! Dear mother! we will not leave thee, nor return from following after thee; for whither thou goest we will go, and where thou dwellest we will dwell. Thy people shall be our people, and thy God our God."

INDEX

z

INDEX.

Printed by CASSELL & COMPANY, LTD., La Belle Sauvage, Ludgate Hill, London, E.C.